Moonflower Murders

Moonflower Murders

A Novel

Anthony Horowitz

HARPER LARGE PRINT

An Imprint of HarperCollinsPublishers

Originally published in the United Kingdom in 2020 by Century Penguin Random House UK.

HarperCollins books may be purchased for educational, business, or sales promotional use. For information, please e-mail the Special Markets Department at SPsales@harpercollins.com or in Canada at HCOrder@harpercollins.com.

FIRST HARPER LARGE PRINT EDITION

ISBN: 978-0-06-302973-6

Library of Congress Cataloging-in-Publication Data is available upon request.

20 21 22 23 24 LSC 10 9 8 7 6 5 4 3 2 1

For Eric Hamlish and Jan Salindar – with thanks for so
many good times

Moonflower Murders

Agios Nikolaos, Crete

*T*he *Polydorus is a charming family-run hotel, located a short walk away from the lively town of Agios Nikolaos, one hour from Heraklion. Rooms cleaned daily, all with Wi-Fi and air con, some with sea views. Coffee and home-cooked meals served on our lovely terraces. Visit our website or find us on booking .com.*

You have no idea how long it took me to write that. I was worried about so many adjectives bunching up together. Was 'lively' the right word to describe Agios Nikolaos? I'd started with 'busy' but then decided it might suggest the endless traffic and noise that were very much part of the place too. We were actually fifteen minutes from the town centre. Was that a 'short walk'? Should I have mentioned Ammoudi beach next door?

The funny thing is, I spent almost all my working life as an editor and I never had any problem dealing with writers' manuscripts, but when it came to a four-line advertisement on the back of a postcard I sweated over every syllable. In the end, I handed it to Andreas, who read it in about five seconds and then just grunted and nodded, which, after all the trouble I'd taken, both pleased and infuriated me at the same time. That's something I've noticed about the Greeks. They're an incredibly emotional people. Their drama, poetry and music go straight to the heart. But when it comes to everyday business, to the little details, they prefer things to be '*siga siga*', which translates roughly as 'Who gives a damn?' It was a phrase I heard every day.

Examining what I'd written along with a cigarette and a cup of strong black coffee, two thoughts crossed my mind. We were going to put the cards in a rack beside the reception desk, but since tourists would already be in the hotel when they picked them up, what exactly was the point? And more pertinently, what the hell was I doing here? How had I allowed my life to come to this?

Just two years away from my fiftieth birthday, at a time when I had thought I would be enjoying all the comforts of life that come with a reasonable income, a small flat in London and a full social diary, I had found myself the co-owner and manager of a hotel that was actually much nicer than I'd managed to describe. The Polydorus was right on the edge of the water, with two terraces shaded from the sun by umbrellas and cypress trees. It had just twelve rooms, a young, local staff who were always cheerful even at their most haphazard, and a loyal clientele. We had simple food, Mythos lager, an in-house musician and perfect views. The sort of travellers we encouraged wouldn't dream of arriving on one of those gigantic coaches I would watch inching along roads that had never been designed to accommodate them, on their way to the six-storey monstrosities on the other side of the bay.

What we also had, unfortunately, was dodgy wiring, impossible plumbing and intermittent Wi-Fi. I don't want to slip into lazy Greek stereotyping and maybe I was just unlucky, but reliability was hardly a watchword amongst the people we employed. Panos was an excellent chef but if he argued with his wife, his children or his motorbike he would be a no-show and Andreas would have to take over in the kitchen, leaving me to host the bar and restaurant, which might be full but without any waiters or half-empty with too many of them. Somehow a happy compromise never

seemed to materialise. There was always a faint possibility that a supplier might actually arrive on time but
it would never be with the goods that we had actually
ordered. If anything broke – and everything did – we
would have hours of nervous tension waiting to see if
the mechanic or engineer would show up.

For the most part our guests seemed happy. But we
were running about like actors in one of those madcap
French farces trying to make it all look seamless and
by the time I collapsed into bed, often at one or two in
the morning, I was so exhausted that I lay there feeling almost desiccated, like a mummy in a shroud. That
was when I would be at my lowest, falling asleep with
the knowledge that the moment I opened my eyes the
whole thing would start all over again.

I'm being too negative. Of course it was wonderful too. The Aegean sunset is like nothing you will
see anywhere in the world and I would watch it every
evening, staring in wonder. No wonder the Greeks
believed in gods – Helios in his golden chariot blaz-
ing across that enormous sky, the Lasithiotika mountains transformed into strips of the thinnest gauze, first
pink, then mauve, darkening and fading at the same
time. I swam at seven o'clock every morning, washing
away in the crystal sea the traces of too much wine and
cigarette smoke. There were dinners in tiny tavernas in

Fourni and Limnes with the smell of jasmine, the stars twinkling, raucous laughter, the clink of raki glasses. I'd even started to learn Greek, working three hours a week with a girl young enough to be my daughter who managed to take the stressed syllables and verbs that weren't just irregular but downright indecent and somehow make them fun.

But this wasn't a holiday for me. I'd come to Greece after the catastrophe that was *Magpie Murders*. It was the last book I'd worked on and it had led to the death of the author, the collapse of my publishing company and the end of my career ... in that order. There had been nine Atticus Pünd novels, all of them bestsellers, and I had thought there would be many more. But that was all over now. Instead, I found myself starting a new life, and frankly too much of it was hard work.

Inevitably, this had had an effect on my relationship with Andreas. The two of us didn't quarrel – we weren't the quarrelling sort – but we'd developed a way of communicating that had become increasingly terse and wary, circling each other like two prize boxers who have no intention of starting the fight. In fact, a full-throttle punch-up might have done us both good. We had managed to drift into that awful arena, so familiar to the long-term married couple, where what was left unspoken was actually more damaging than what was said. We weren't married, by the way. Andreas had proposed to me, doing the whole diamond-ring-down-on-one-knee thing, but we had both been too busy to follow through, and anyway, my Greek wasn't good enough yet to understand the service. We had decided to wait.

Time had done us no favours. In London, Andreas had always been my best friend. Perhaps it was because we weren't living together that I had always looked forward to seeing him. We read the same books. We loved eating in ... especially when Andreas cooked. We had great sex. But Crete had trapped us in an altogether different sort of arrangement and even though it had only been a couple of years since we had left the UK, I was already thinking about a way out, even if I wasn't actively looking for one.

I didn't need to. The way out arrived early one Monday morning with a smart-looking couple, obviously English, walking arm in arm down the slope that led from the main road. I could tell at once that they were rich and that they weren't here on holiday. He was wearing a jacket and long trousers – ridiculous for the morning heat – a polo shirt and a panama hat. She had on the sort of dress that was more suited to a tennis party than the beach, a proper necklace and carried a neat little clutch bag. Both had expensive sunglasses. I guessed they were in their sixties.

The man came into the bar and uncoupled himself from his wife. I saw him examining me. 'Excuse me,' he said in a cultivated voice. 'Do you speak English?'

'Yes.'

'I don't suppose ... you wouldn't by any chance be Susan Ryeland?'

'That's me.'

'I wonder if I might have a word with you, Miss Ryeland? My name is Lawrence Treherne. This is my wife, Pauline.'

'How do you do.' Pauline Treherne smiled at me but not in a friendly way. She didn't trust me and she hadn't even met me yet.

'Can I get you a coffee?' I phrased the question carefully. I wasn't offering to buy them one. I don't want to give the impression that I'm mean, but this was something else preying on my mind. I had sold my flat in north London and ploughed most of my savings into the Polydorus, but so far I hadn't made any profit. Quite the reverse: although I'm not sure that Andreas and I were doing anything wrong, we had still managed to find ourselves almost ten thousand euros in debt. Our funds were leaking away and I sometimes felt that the distance between me and bankruptcy could be measured by the froth on a free cappuccino.

'No. We're all right, thank you.'

I steered them towards one of the tables in the bar. The terrace was already crowded, but Vangelis, who worked as a waiter when he wasn't playing his guitar, was managing fine and it was cooler out of the heat. 'So how can I help you, Mr Treherne?'

'Lawrence, please.' He took off the hat, revealing thinning silver hair and a scalp that had still managed to catch the sun. He placed the hat in front of him. 'I hope you'll forgive us for tracking you down. We have a mutual friend – Sajid Khan. He sends you his regards, by the way.'

Sajid Khan? It took me a moment to remember that he was a solicitor, living in the Suffolk town of Framlingham. He had been a friend of Alan Conway, the author of *Magpie Murders*. When Alan died, Sajid Khan was the one who had discovered the body. But I'd only met him a couple of times. I wouldn't have called him a friend, mutual or otherwise.

'Do you live in Suffolk?' I asked.

'Yes. We own a hotel near Woodbridge. Mr Khan has helped us on one or two occasions.' Lawrence hesitated, suddenly uncomfortable. 'I was speaking to him last week about a rather difficult matter and he suggested we talk to you.'

I wondered how Khan had known I was here in Crete. Someone else must have told him because I certainly hadn't. 'You came all this way to talk to me?' I asked.

'It's not really that far and we travel quite a bit anyway. We're staying at the Minos Beach.' He pointed in the direction of his hotel, which was on the other side of a tennis court, right next to mine. It confirmed my first opinion that the Trehernes were rich. The Minos Beach was a boutique hotel with private villas and a garden full of sculptures. It cost around three hundred pounds a night. 'I did think about ringing,' he went on. 'But it's not something I'd want to discuss over the phone.'

This was getting more mysterious – and, frankly, annoying – by the minute. A four-hour flight from Stansted. A one-hour drive from Heraklion. Getting here had hardly been a stroll. 'What is this about?' I asked.

'It's about a murder.'

That last word hung in the air for a moment. On the other side of the terrace, the sun was shining. A bunch of local children were laughing and shouting, splashing about in the Aegean. Families were packed together around the tables. I watched Vangelis go past with a tray laden with orange juice and iced coffee.

'What murder?' I asked.

'A man called Frank Parris. You won't have heard of him but you might know the hotel where the murder took place. It's called Branlow Hall.'

'And that's your hotel.'

'Yes. It is.' It was Pauline Treherne who answered, speaking for the first time. She sounded like a minor royal, cutting each word as if with a pair of scissors before allowing it to escape. And yet I got the feeling that she was as middle class as I was.

'He had booked in for three nights,' Lawrence said. 'He was killed on the second.'

A host of different questions were going through my mind. Who was Frank Parris? Who killed him? Why should I care? But I didn't say that. 'When did this happen?' I asked.

'About eight years ago,' Lawrence Treherne said.

Pauline Treherne set her clutch bag on the table, next to the panama hat, as if it was some agreed signal for her to take over. There was something about her – the way she used silence, her lack of emotion – that made me think she was always the one who made the important decisions. Her sunglasses were so dark that as she spoke to me I found myself almost transfixed by two images of myself listening.

'It might help if I tell you the entire story,' she said in that grating voice of hers. 'That way, you'll understand why we're here. I take it you're not too pressed for time?'

I had about fifty things I needed to be doing. 'Not at all,' I said.

'Thank you.' She collected herself. 'Frank Parris worked in advertising,' she began. 'He'd just come back to England from Australia, where he'd lived for several years. He was killed very brutally in his hotel room on the night of June the fifteenth, 2008. I'll always remember the date because it coincided with the wedding weekend of our daughter, Cecily.'

'Was he a guest?'

'No. We'd never met him. We'd taken over a dozen or so rooms for the wedding. We put up close family and friends. The hotel has thirty-two rooms in total and we'd decided, against my better judgement – my husband, I'm afraid, did not agree – to stay open to the public. Mr Parris was in Suffolk visiting relatives. He'd booked in for three nights. He was killed late on Friday night, although the body wasn't discovered until Saturday afternoon.'

'After the wedding,' Lawrence Treherne muttered.

'How was he killed?'

'He was struck several times with a hammer. His face was very badly disfigured and but for his wallet and his passport, which was found in his safe, the police would have been unable to identify him.'

'Cecily was most dreadfully upset,' Lawrence cut in. 'Well, we all were. It had been such a beautiful day. We had the wedding service in the garden and then lunch for a hundred guests. We couldn't have asked for better weather. And all the time, we were unaware that in a room actually overlooking the marquee, he'd been lying there in a pool of his own blood.'

'Cecily and Aiden had to postpone their honeymoon,' Pauline added, a tremor of indignation still there in her voice even after all these years. 'The police wouldn't allow them to leave. They said there was no question of it even though it was clear the murder had nothing to do with them.'

'Aiden is her husband?'

'Aiden MacNeil. Yes. Our son-in-law. They were meant to be leaving on the Sunday morning for Antigua, but in the end it was two weeks before they were allowed to go and by then the police had arrested the killer, so there was really no need for such a long delay.'

'So they knew who did it,' I said.

'Oh yes. It was all very straightforward,' Lawrence

explained. 'It was actually someone we employed, a Romanian by the name of Stefan Codrescu. He was working as a general maintenance man and he lived in the hotel. He actually had a criminal record – we knew that when we employed him. In fact, it was rather the point, I'm afraid to say.' His eyes flickered downwards. 'My wife and I used to run a programme at the hotel. We employed young offenders – in the kitchen, cleaning, gardening – after they were released. We're great believers in prison reform and giving young men and women a second chance. I'm sure you're aware that the reoffending rate is astronomical. That's because these people don't get a chance to integrate themselves back into society. We worked closely with the probation service and they assured us that Stefan would be suitable for our programme.' He sighed heavily. 'They were wrong.'

'Cecily believed in him,' Pauline said.

'She knew him?'

'We have two daughters and they both work with us at the hotel. Cecily was the general manager when all this happened. In fact, she was the one who interviewed Stefan and employed him.'

'She got married at the same hotel where she worked?'

'Absolutely. It's a family business. Our staff are part

of our family. She wouldn't think of having it anywhere else,' Pauline said.

'And she thought Stefan was innocent.'

'To begin with, yes. She insisted on it. That's the trouble with Cecily. She's always been far too good-natured, too trusting, the sort who believes the best in everyone. But the evidence against Stefan was over-whelming. I don't know where to begin. There were no fingerprints on the hammer . . . it had been wiped clean. But there was blood splatter on his clothes and on money – taken from the dead man – under his mattress. He was seen entering Frank Parris's room. And anyway, he confessed. When that happened, even Cecily had to admit that she was wrong and that was the end of it. She and Aiden went to Antigua. The hotel slowly returned to normal, although it took a long, long time and no one ever stayed in room twelve again. We use it for storage now. As I said, this all hap-pened years ago and we thought it was behind us. But it seems not.'

'So what happened?' I asked. I was intrigued, de-spite myself.

Lawrence took over. 'Stefan was sentenced to life in prison and he's still behind bars. Cecily wrote to him a couple of times but he never replied and I thought she'd forgotten him. She seemed perfectly happy running the hotel and also, of course, being with Aiden. She was twenty-six when they got married. Two years older than him. She'll be thirty-four next month.'

'Do they have any children?'

'Yes. A little girl. Well, she's seven now ... Roxana.'

'Our first granddaughter.' Pauline's voice faltered. 'She's a lovely child, everything we could have ever wanted.'

'Pauline and I are semi-retired,' Lawrence went on. 'We have a house near Hyères in the South of France and we spend quite a bit of time down there. Anyway, a few days ago, Cecily rang us. I took the call. This would have been around two o'clock, French time. I could tell at once that Cecily sounded very upset. More than that, I'd say she was nervous. I don't know where she was calling from, but this was a Tuesday so she was probably at the hotel. We normally have a bit of banter but she got straight to the point. She said she'd been thinking about what happened—'

'The murder.'

'Exactly. She said that she had been right all along and that Stefan Codrescu was not responsible for the crime. I asked her what she was talking about and she said she'd come across something in a book she'd been given. "It was right there – staring me in the face." Those were her exact words. Anyway, she told me she'd already sent it to me and sure enough, it turned up the very next day.'

He reached into his jacket pocket and took out a paperback. I recognised it at once – the picture on the cover, the typeface, the title – and at that moment, this entire meeting began to make sense.

The book was *Atticus Pünd Takes the Case*, number three in the series written by Alan Conway that I had edited and published. I immediately recalled that it was largely set in a hotel, but in the county of Devon, not in Suffolk, and in 1953, not the present day. I remembered the launch party at the German embassy in London. Alan had had too much to drink and had insulted the ambassador.

'Alan knew about the murder?' I asked.

'Oh yes. He came to the hotel and stayed a few nights, six weeks after it happened. We both met him. He told us that he had been a friend of the dead man, Frank Parris, and he asked us a lot of questions about the murder. He talked to our staff as well. We had absolutely no idea that he was going to turn the whole thing into an entertainment. If he'd been honest with us, we might have been more circumspect.'

Which was exactly the reason he wasn't honest with you, I thought.

'You never read the book?' I said.

'We forgot all about it,' Lawrence admitted. 'And Mr Conway certainly never sent us a copy.' He paused. 'But Cecily read it and she found something that cast new light on what had happened at Branlow Hall ... at least, that's what she believed.' He glanced at his wife as if seeking her approbation. 'Pauline and I have both read the book and we can't see any connection.'

'There are similarities,' Pauline said. 'Firstly, nearly all the characters are recognisable, clearly based on people that Mr Conway met in Woodbridge. They even have the same names ... or very similar ones. But what I don't understand is that he seems to have taken pleasure in twisting people so that they come out like horrible caricatures of themselves. The owners of the Moonflower, which is the hotel in the book, are clearly based on Lawrence and myself, for example. But they're both crooks. Why would he do that? We've never done anything dishonest in our lives.' She seemed more indignant than upset. The way she was looking at me, it was almost as if I was to blame.

'In answer to your question, we had no idea the book had been published,' she went on. 'I don't read murder mysteries myself. Neither of us does. Sajid Khan told us that Mr Conway is no longer alive. Maybe that's just as well because if he were, we might be very tempted to take legal action.'

'So let me get this straight,' I said. I had the sense of facts tumbling on top of each other, yet I knew there was something they hadn't told me. 'You believe that maybe, despite all the evidence, not to mention the confession, Stefan Codrescu did not kill Frank Parris and that Alan Conway came to the hotel and discovered – in a matter of days – who the real killer was. He then somehow identified that person in *Atticus Pünd Takes the Case*.'

'Exactly.'

'But that makes no sense at all, Pauline. If he knew the killer and there was an innocent man in prison, surely Alan would have gone straight to the police! Why would he turn it into a work of fiction?'

'That's precisely why we're here, Susan. From what Sajid Khan told us, you knew Alan Conway better than anyone. You edited the book. If there is something in there, I can't think of anyone more likely to find it.'

'Wait a minute.' Suddenly I knew what was missing. 'This all started when your daughter spotted something in *Atticus Pünd Takes the Case*. Was she the only one who read it before she sent it to you?'

'I don't know.'

'But what was it she saw? Why didn't you just call her and ask her what she meant?'

It was Lawrence Treherne who answered my question. 'Of course we called her,' he said. 'We both read the book and then we rang her several times from France. Finally we got through to Aiden and he told us what had happened.' He paused. 'It seems that our daughter has disappeared.'

Departure

I lost my temper with Andreas that evening. I really didn't mean to but the day had brought so many mishaps, one after another, that I was going to scream either at the moon or at him and he just happened to be nearer.

It had begun with that nice couple Bruce and Brenda from Macclesfield, who turned out not to be that nice after all, demanding a fifty per cent reduction in their bill or they were going to hit Trip-Advisor with a list of complaints that they'd stacked up from the day they'd arrived and which, they assured us, would put anyone off ever coming anywhere near us again. And what was their problem? An hour without Wi-Fi. The sound of guitar music at night. The sighting of a solitary cockroach. What annoyed me was they had complained every morning, always with tight little smiles, and I'd known all along that they were going to try something on. I'd developed an antenna for the tourists who arrived with extortion as part of their holiday plans. You'd be amazed how many of them there were.

Panos didn't show up. Vangelis was late. Andreas's computer had a glitch – I'd asked him to get it looked at – and it had managed to send two room requests into spam. By the time we noticed, the clients had booked elsewhere. Before we went to bed, we had a glass of Metaxa, the Greek brandy that only tastes nice in Greece, but I was still in a bad mood and it was when Andreas asked me what the matter was that I finally snapped.

'What do you think is the fucking matter, Andreas? Everything!'

I don't usually swear ... at least, not at people I like. Lying in bed, watching Andreas getting undressed, I was annoyed with myself. Part of me wanted to blame him for everything that had happened since I'd come to Crete, while another part blamed myself for letting him down. But the worst of it was the sense of help-lessness – that events had taken over and I was being steered by them rather than the other way round. Had I really chosen a life where complete strangers could humiliate me for a few euros and where my entire well-being could be decided by a lost reservation?

Right then I knew I had to go back to England and that actually I'd known it for some time, even if I'd tried to pretend otherwise.

Andreas cleaned his teeth and came out of the bathroom naked, which is how he slept, looking every inch like one of those figures – an ephebe or a satyr perhaps – that you might see on the side of an ancient vase. And it did seem to me that he had become more Greek in the past couple of years. His black hair was a little shaggier, his eyes a little darker and he had a sort of swagger that I'm sure he'd never displayed when he was teaching at Westminster School. He'd put on some weight too – or perhaps it was just that I noticed his stomach more now that he was out of a suit. He was still a handsome man. I was still attracted to him. But suddenly I needed to be away from him.

I waited until he got into bed. We slept under a single sheet with the windows open. We hardly got any mosquitoes right next to the sea and I preferred the night air to the artificial chill of the air conditioning.

'Andreas … ' I said.

'What?' He would have fallen asleep in seconds if I'd let him. His voice was already drowsy.

'I want to go back to London.'

'What?' He twisted round, propping himself up on his elbow. 'What do you mean?'

'There's something I have to do.'

'In London?'

'No. I have to go to Suffolk.' He was looking at me, his face full of concern. 'I won't be long,' I said. 'Just a couple of weeks.'

'We need you here, Susan.'

'We need money, Andreas. We're not going to be able to pay our bills if we don't get some extra finance. And I've been offered a great deal of money to do a job. Ten thousand pounds. Cash!'

*

It was true.

After the Trehernes had told me about the murder at their hotel, they had gone on to explain how their daughter had disappeared.

'It's very unlike her to wander off without telling anyone,' Lawrence had said. 'And certainly to leave her daughter behind ... '

'Who's looking after the child?' I asked.

'Aiden's there. And there's a nanny.'

'It's not "unlike" her.' Pauline gave her husband the most withering of scowls. 'She's never done anything like this in her life, and of course she wouldn't leave Roxana on her own.' She turned to me. 'We're worried sick, if you want the truth, Susan. And Lawrence may not agree, but I'm convinced it's got something to do with this book.'

'I do agree!' Lawrence muttered.

'Did anyone else know about her concerns?' I asked.

'I already told you that she telephoned us from Branlow Hall, so any one of a number of people could have overheard her.'

'I mean, had she talked about her suspicions with anyone else?'

Pauline Treherne shook her head. 'We tried several times to phone her from France and when she didn't answer we called Aiden. He hadn't rung because he didn't want to worry us, but it turned out that he had contacted the police the same day she disappeared. Unfortunately, they didn't take him very seriously ... at least, not to begin with. They suggested the two of them might be having marriage difficulties.'

'And were they?'

'Not at all,' Lawrence said. 'They've always been very happy together. The police spoke to Eloise – she's the nanny – and she said the same. She never heard any arguments.'

'Aiden's a perfect son-in-law. He's clever and he's

hard-working. I only wish Lisa could find someone like him. And he's as worried as we are!'

All the time Pauline had been speaking to me, I'd thought she was fighting something. Suddenly she pulled out a packet of cigarettes and lit one. She smoked like someone who had just taken up the habit again after a long abstinence. She inhaled, then went on.

'By the time we got back to England, the police had finally decided to take an interest. Not that they were very much help. Cecily had taken the dog for a walk. She has a shaggy golden retriever called Bear – we've always kept dogs. She left the hotel at about three o'clock in the afternoon and parked the car at Woodbridge station. She often used to take the river path. That's the River Deben. There's a circular walk that takes you along the edge and to begin with it's well populated. But then it becomes wilder and more remote until you come to a wood and on the other side there's a road that takes you back through Martlesham.'

'So if someone attacked her—'

'It's not the sort of thing that ever happens in Suffolk. But yes, there were plenty of places where she would have been on her own, out of sight.' Pauline took a breath and went on. 'Aiden got worried when she didn't come home for dinner and quite rightly called the police. Two uniformed officers came round and asked a few questions, but they didn't raise the alarm until the next morning, which was much too late of course. By that time Bear had shown up, on his own, back at the station, and after that they took everything more seriously. They had people – and their own dogs – out searching the entire area from Martlesham all the way back to Melton. But it was no good. There are fields, woods, mudflats . . . a lot of ground to cover. They didn't find anything.'

'How long is it since she went missing?' I asked.

'The last time anyone saw her was last Wednesday.'

I felt the silence fall. Five days. That was a long time, an abyss into which Cecily had fallen.

'You've come all this way to talk to me,' I said, finally. 'What exactly do you want me to do?'

Pauline glanced at her husband.

'The answer is in this book,' he explained. '*Atticus Pünd Takes the Case*. You must know it better than anyone.'

'Actually, it's been quite a few years since I read it,' I admitted.

'You worked with the author, this man, Alan Conway. You knew how his mind worked. If we were to ask you to reread it, I'm sure there are things that might occur to you that we haven't noticed. And if you actually came to Branlow Hall and read the book in situ, so to speak, maybe you might see what it was that our daughter spotted and why she felt compelled to ring us. And that in turn might tell us where she is or what's happened to her.'

His voice faltered as he spoke those last words. *What's happened to her.* There might be a simple reason why she had vanished but it was unlikely. She knew something. She was a danger to someone. The thought was better left unsaid.

'Can I have one of these?' I asked. I helped myself to one of Pauline Treherne's cigarettes. My own pack was behind the bar. The whole ritual – pulling out the cigarette, lighting it, taking the first puff – gave me time to think. 'I can't come to England,' I said eventually. 'I'm afraid I'm too busy here. But I will read the book if you don't mind leaving me your copy. I can't promise anything will come to mind. I mean, I remember the story and it doesn't correspond quite with what you've told me. But I can email you—'

'No. That won't do.' Pauline had already made up her mind. 'You need to talk to Aiden and Lisa – and Eloise, for that matter. And you should meet Derek, the night manager. He was on duty the night Frank Parris was killed and spoke to the detective in charge.

He's in Alan Conway's book too – although he's called Eric.' She leaned towards me, imploring. 'We're not asking you for a lot of your time.'

'And we'll pay you,' Lawrence added. 'We have plenty of money and we're not going to hold back if it helps find our daughter.' He paused. 'Ten thousand pounds?'

That drew a sharp look from his wife and it occurred to me that, without thinking, he had greatly increased, perhaps doubled, the amount they had intended to offer me. That was what my reluctance had done. I thought for a moment that she was going to say something, but she relaxed and nodded.

Ten thousand pounds. I thought about the replastering on the balcony. A new computer for Andreas. The ice-cream display chest that was on the blink. Panos and Vangelis, who had both been muttering about pay raises.

*

'**How could** I say no?' This was what I told Andreas now in our bedroom, late at night. 'We need the money, and anyway, maybe I can help them find their daughter.'

'You think she's still alive?'

'It's possible. But if she isn't, perhaps I can find out who killed her.'

Andreas sat up. He was wide awake now and he was worried about me. I felt bad that I had sworn at him. 'The last time you went looking for a killer, it didn't end very well,' he reminded me.

'This is different. This isn't personal. It's got nothing to do with me.'

'Which sounds to me like an argument for leaving it alone.'

'You may be right. But … '

I had made up my mind and Andreas knew it.

'I need a break anyway,' I said. 'It's been two years, Andreas, and apart from a weekend in Santorini we haven't been anywhere. I'm completely worn out, endlessly firefighting, endlessly trying to make things work. I thought you'd understand.'

'A break from the hotel or a break from me?' he asked.

I wasn't sure I had an answer to that.

'Where will you stay?' he asked.

'With Katie. It'll be nice.' I rested a hand on his arm, feeling the warm flesh and the curve of his muscle. 'You can manage perfectly well without me. I'll ask Nell to come in and look after things. And we'll talk to each other every day.'

'I don't want you to go, Susan.'

'But you're not going to stop me, Andreas.'

He paused and in that moment I could see him fighting with himself. My Andreas versus Andreas the Greek. 'No,' he said, finally. 'You must do what you have to.'

★

Two days later, he drove me to Heraklion airport. There are parts of the road from Agios Nikolaos – as you pass Neapoli and Latsida – that are actually very beautiful. The landscape is wild and empty, with the mountains stretching into the distance and the sense that nothing very much has been touched for a thousand years. Even the new motorway after Malia is surrounded by gorgeous countryside and as you draw nearer you dip down and find yourself close to a wide, white sand beach. Maybe that was what gave me a sense of sadness, an understanding of what I was leaving behind. Suddenly I wasn't thinking of all the problems and the chores of running the Polydorus. I was thinking of midnight and the waves and *pansélinos* – the full moon. Wine. Laughter. My peasant life.

When I'd been preparing to leave, I'd deliberately chosen my smallest bag. I'd thought it would be a statement to Andreas and to myself that this was just a brief business trip and that I would be home very soon. But going through my wardrobe, looking at clothes that I hadn't worn for two years, I found myself piling things up on the bed. I was going back to an English summer, which meant that it could be hot and cold, wet and dry, all in one day. I would be staying in a posh country hotel. They probably had a dress code for dinner. And I was being paid ten thousand pounds. I needed to look professional.

So by the time I arrived at Heraklion airport, I found myself dragging my old wheelie behind me, the actual wheels squeaking malevolently as they spun against the concrete floor. The two of us stood for a moment in the harsh air conditioning and the harsher electric light of the departure lounge.

He took hold of me. 'Promise me you'll look after yourself. And call me when you get there. We can FaceTime.'

'If the Wi-Fi isn't on the blink!'

'Promise me, Susan.'

'I promise.'

He held me with both hands on my arms and kissed

me. I smiled at him, then trailed my suitcase over to the stout, scowling Greek girl in her blue uniform who checked my passport and boarding card before allowing me through to security. I turned and waved.

But Andreas had already gone.

Cuttings

It was quite a shock being back in London. After so much time in Agios Nikolaos, which wasn't very much more than an overgrown fishing village, I found myself consumed by the city and I was unprepared for the intensity of it, the noise, the number of people in the streets. Everything was greyer than I remembered and it was hard to cope with the dust and petrol fumes in the air. The amount of new construction also made my head spin. Views that I had known all my working life had disappeared in the space of two years. London's various mayors, with their love of tall buildings, had allowed different architects to gouge their initials into the skyline with the result that everything was both familiar and alien at the same time. Sitting in the back of a black cab, being driven along the River Thames on the way from the airport, the cluster of new flats and offices around Battersea Power Station looked to me like a battlefield. It was as if there had been an invasion and all those cranes with their blinking red lights were monstrous birds, picking over carcasses lying unseen on the ground.

I had decided to spend the first night in a hotel, which was, frankly, weird. A lifelong Londoner, I had somehow degenerated into a tourist and I hated the hotel, a Premier Inn in Farringdon, not because there was anything wrong with it – it was perfectly clean and comfortable – but because that was where I was forced to stay. Sitting on the bed with its mauve cushions and 'sleeping moon' logo, I felt perfectly miserable. I was already missing Andreas. I had texted him from the airport but I knew that if I FaceTimed him I would probably end up crying and that would prove he was right, I should never have gone. The sooner I was in Suffolk, the better. But I wasn't ready to make the journey yet. There were one or two things I had to do.

After an intermittent sleep and a breakfast – egg, sausage, bacon, beans – that looked identical to every breakfast ever served in a cut-price hotel chain, I strolled over to King's Cross to one of the storage depots built into the arches under the railway lines. When

I moved to Crete, I had sold my flat in Crouch End and almost everything in it, but at the last moment I had decided to hang on to my car, a bright red MGB Roadster which I had bought in the moment of madness that had coincided with my fortieth birthday. I had never thought I would drive it again and storing it had been a crazy extravagance; I was paying £150 a month for the privilege. But I just couldn't bring myself to get rid of it and now, as it was wheeled out for me by two young men, it was like being reunited with an old friend. More than that. It was a part of my former life that I had back again. Just sinking into the cracked leather of the driver's seat with the wooden steering wheel and absurdly old-fashioned radio above my knees made me feel better about myself. If I did go back to Crete, I decided, I would drive there and to hell with the problems of Greek registration and left-hand drive. I turned the key and the engine started first time. I pumped the accelerator a few times, enjoying the growl of welcome that came from the engine, then drove off, heading down the Euston Road.

It was midmorning and the traffic wasn't too bad, which is to say that it was actually moving. I didn't want to go straight back to the hotel so I drove around London, taking in a few sights just for the hell of it.

Euston Station was being rebuilt. Gower Street was as shabby as ever. I don't suppose it was coincidence that brought me into Bloomsbury, the area behind the British Museum, but without really thinking about it, I found myself outside Cloverleaf Books, the independent publishing house where I had worked for eleven years. Or what was left of it. The building was an eyesore, boarded-up windows and charred bricks surrounded by scaffolding, and it occurred to me that the insurers must be refusing to pay out. Perhaps arson and attempted murder hadn't been included in the policy.

I thought of driving out to Crouch End, giving the MG a good run for its money – but that would have been too dispiriting. Anyway, I had work to do. I put the car into an NCP in Farringdon, then walked back to the hotel. I didn't need to check out until noon, which gave me an hour alone with the coffee machine, two packets of complimentary biscuits and the Internet. I opened up my laptop and began a series of searches: Branlow Hall, Stefan Codrescu, Frank Parris, murder.

These were the articles I found: a murder mystery stripped of its intrigue and told in just four indifferent chapters.

The *East Anglian Daily Times*: 18 JUNE 2008

MAN KILLED AT CELEBRITY HOTEL

Police are investigating the murder of a 53-year-old man after his body was discovered in the five-star hotel where he was staying. Branlow Hall, located close to Woodbridge in Suffolk, charges £300 a night for an executive suite and is a much sought-after venue for celebrity weddings and parties. It has also been used as a location for many television series, including ITV's *Endeavour*, *Top Gear* and *Antiques Roadshow*.

The victim has been identified as Frank Parris, a well-known figure in the advertising industry who won awards for his work on Barclays Bank and for the LGBT rights organisation Stonewall. He rose to be creative director of McCann Erickson in London before moving to Australia to set up his own agency. He was unmarried.

Detective Superintendent Richard Locke, who is heading the investigation, said: 'This was a particularly brutal murder that would seem to have been carried out by a single individual with the motive of theft. Money belonging to Mr Parris has been recovered and we expect to make an arrest shortly.'

The murder took place on the night before the wedding of Aiden MacNeil and Cecily Treherne, whose parents, Lawrence and Pauline Treherne, own the hotel. The body was discovered shortly after the ceremony, which had taken place in the hotel garden. Neither of the couples was available for comment.

The *East Anglian Daily Times*: 20 JUNE 2008
MAN HELD IN WOODBRIDGE KILLING

Police have arrested a 22-year-old man in connection with the brutal murder of a retired advertising executive at Branlow Hall, the well-known Suffolk hotel. Detective Superintendent Richard Locke, who is in charge of the investigation, said: 'This was a horrific crime, committed without any scruples. My team has worked quickly and very thoroughly and I am glad to say that we have been able to make an arrest. I have every sympathy for the young couple whose special day was ruined by these events.'

The suspect has been remanded in custody and is due to appear at Ipswich Crown Court next week.

The *Daily Mail*: 22 OCTOBER 2008
LIFE IMPRISONMENT FOR 'HAMMER HORROR'
SUFFOLK KILLER

A Romanian migrant, Stefan Codrescu, was sentenced to life imprisonment at Ipswich Crown Court, following the murder of 53-year-old Frank Parris at the £300-a-night Branlow Hall hotel near Woodbridge, Suffolk. Parris, described as 'a brilliant creative mind', had recently returned from Australia and had been planning to retire.

Codrescu, who pleaded guilty, entered the UK when he was twelve years old and quickly came to the attention of London police investigating Romanian organised crime gangs involved in cloned credit cards, stolen UK passports and false identity documents. Aged nineteen, he was arrested for aggravated burglary and assault. He was sentenced to two years in jail.

Lawrence Treherne, the owner of Branlow Hall, was in court to hear the sentence. He had employed Codrescu, who had been at the hotel for five months, as part of an outreach programme for young offenders. Mr Treherne said that he did not regret his actions. 'My wife and I were shocked by

the death of Mr Parris,' he said in a statement outside the court. 'But I still believe that it is right to
give young people a second chance and to try to
integrate them into society.'

But sentencing Codrescu to a minimum term of
twenty-five years, Judge Azra Rashid said: 'Despite
your background, you were given a unique opportunity to turn your life around. Instead, you betrayed the trust and goodwill of your employers
and committed a brutal crime for financial gain.'

The court had heard that Codrescu, now 22, had
racked up debts playing online poker and slot machines. Jonathan Clarke, defending, said that Codrescu had lost touch with reality. 'He was living in
a virtual world with debts that were spiralling out
of control. What happened that night was a sort of
madness ... a mental breakdown.'

Parris was attacked with a hammer and beaten
so badly that he was unrecognisable. Detective Superintendent Richard Locke, who made the arrest,
said that this was 'the most sickening case I have
ever encountered'.

A spokesperson for Screen Counselling, a
Norwich-based charity, has called on the gambling commission to ban online betting with credit
cards.

That was the story: the beginning, the middle and the end. But trawling through the Internet, I came across what might have been a coda to the whole affair had it not actually predated everything that had occurred.

Campaign: 12 MAY 2008

LAST CALL FOR SYDNEY-BASED SUNDOWNER

Sundowner, the Sydney-based advertising agency set up by former McCann Erickson supremo Frank Parris, has gone out of business. The Australian Securities and Investments Commission – the country's official financial watchdog – confirmed that after just three years the agency has ceased to trade.

Parris, who began his career as a copywriter, was a well-known figure in the London advertising scene for more than two decades, winning awards for his work on Barclays Bank and Domino's pizza. He created the controversial Action Fag campaign for Stonewall in 1997, promoting gay rights in the armed forces.

He was himself completely open about his sexuality and was well known for his extravagant and flamboyant parties. It has been suggested that his move to Australia was prompted by a decision to tone down his public image.

In its first month, Sundowner picked up some significant accounts, including Von Zipper sunglasses, Wagon Wheels and Kustom footwear. However, its early success took place against a subdued market that led to a significant shrinkage in consumer and advertising spending. Internet advertising and online videos are the fastest growing areas in Australia and it's clear that Sundowner, with its emphasis on traditional rather than digital media, had arrived too quickly at the last chance saloon.

So what was I to make of all this information?

Well, I suppose it was the editor in me that noticed that every single one of the reports had described the murder as brutal, as if anyone was ever murdered gently or with affection. The journalists had managed to sketch in the character of Frank Parris with what few details they had – award-winning, gay, extrovert, ultimately a failure. That hadn't stopped the *Mail* from characterising him as 'a brilliant creative mind', but then they would have been prepared to forgive him for almost anything. He had, after all, been murdered by a

Romanian. Had Stefan Codrescu really been involved in gangs trading passports and credit cards, etc.? There was no evidence of it and the fact that the police had been investigating Romanian gangs could have been entirely coincidental. He had, after all, been arrested for burglary.

As for the brilliant Frank Parris, there was something almost bizarre about his turning up in a hotel in Suffolk, particularly on the night of a wedding to which he had not been invited. Pauline Treherne had told me he was visiting relatives so why hadn't he stayed with them?

The mention of Detective Superintendent Richard Locke worried me. We had met following the death of Alan Conway and I think it's fair to say we had not got on. I remembered him – a big, angry police officer who had swept into a coffee shop on the outskirts of Ipswich, shouted at me for fifteen minutes and then left again. Alan had based a character on him and Locke had decided to blame me. It had taken him less than a week to identify Stefan as the culprit, arrest him and then charge him. Was he wrong? According to the newspaper stories and, for that matter, what the Trehernes had told me, the whole thing could hardly be more straightforward.

But eight years later, Cecily Treherne had thought otherwise. And she had disappeared.

There wasn't much more to do in London. It seemed obvious to me that I would have to talk to Stefan Codrescu, which meant visiting him in prison, but I didn't even know where he was being held and the Trehernes had been unable to help. How was I supposed to find out? I went back on the Internet but I didn't find anything there. Then I remembered an author I knew: Craig Andrews. He had come to writing late and I had published his first novel, a thriller set in the prison system. On first reading I had been impressed by the violence of his writing but also by its authenticity. He had done a lot of research.

Of course, he had another publisher now. Cloverleaf Books had rather let him down by going out of business and burning to the ground, but on the other hand the book had been a success and I had noticed a good review of his latest in the *Mail on Sunday*. I had nothing to lose so I sent him an email telling him that I was back in England and asking him if he could help me track down Stefan. I wasn't confident that he would reply.

After that, I packed up my laptop, grabbed my suitcase and rescued my MG from the car park, where it had already been charged a ridiculous sum of money for the grim, dusty corner where it had been housed. It still made me happy to see it. I got in and moments later I was roaring down the exit ramp and out onto the Farringdon Road, on my way to Suffolk.

Branlow Hall

I could have stayed with my sister while I was in
Suffolk but the Trehernes had offered me free accommodation at their hotel and I had decided to accept.
The truth was that I felt uncomfortable about spending
too much time with Katie. She was two years younger
than me and with her two adorable children, her lovely
home, her successful husband and her circle of close
friends, she could make me feel painfully inadequate,
particularly when I looked at the haphazardness of my
own life. After everything that had happened at Cloverleaf Books she had been delighted that I had flown
off to Crete for what she saw as some sort of domestic
normality and I didn't want to explain to her why I was
back. It wasn't that she would judge me. It was more
that I would feel myself being judged.

Anyway, it made more sense to base myself at the scene of the crime where so many of the witnesses would still be gathered. So I skirted Ipswich and made my way up the A12, passing the right turn that would have brought me into Woodbridge. Instead, I continued another five miles until I came to an expensive-looking sign (black paint, gold lettering) and a narrow lane that took me between hedgerows and bright red flecks of wild poppies to a stone gate and, on the other side, the ancestral home of the Branlow family, standing in a fair old slice of the Suffolk countryside.

So much of what I have to write about had either taken place or would take place here that I must describe it carefully.

It was a beautiful place, something between a country house, a castle and a French chateau, very square, surrounded by lawns dotted with ornamental trees and thicker woodland beyond. At some time in its history it might have been swivelled round because the gravel drive came in from the wrong direction, heading rather confusingly towards a side elevation with several windows but no door, while the actual entrance was round the corner, facing the other way.

It was when you stood here, in front of the house, that you appreciated its magnificence: the main door with its arched portico, the Gothic towers and crenellations, the coats of arms, and the stone chimneys that must have been connected to a multitude of fireplaces. The windows were double height with plaster heads of long-forgotten lords and ladies poking out of the corners. A number of stone birds perched high up on the very edge of the roof, with an eagle at each corner, and above the front door there was a rather fine owl with its wings outstretched. Now that I thought about it, I had seen an owl painted on the sign outside. It was the hotel logo, printed on the menus and the notepaper too.

A low wall ran all around the building with a ha-ha on the other side and this gave it a sense of imperturbability, as if it had chosen to set itself apart from the real world. On the left, which is to say on the side opposite the drive, a set of discreet, more modern doors opened from the bar onto a very flat, beautifully maintained lawn, and this was where, eight years previously, the wedding lunch had taken place. On the right, set slightly back, were two miniature versions of the main house. One was a chapel and the other a granary that had been converted into a health spa, with a conservatory and indoor swimming pool attached.

Even as I parked the MG on the gravel it occurred to me that any writers wanting to set a murder in a classic country house would find all the material they needed here. And any killers wanting to get rid of a body would have hundreds of acres in which to do it. I wondered if the police had looked for Cecily Traherne in the grounds. She had said she was going for a walk and her car had been found at Woodbridge station, but how could anyone be sure that she had been the one who had driven it?

Before I had even turned off the ignition, a young man appeared and hauled the suitcase out of the boot. He led me into the entrance hall, which was square but gave the illusion of being circular with a round table, a round carpet and a ring of marble pillars supporting a ceiling decorated with a circle of very ornate stucco. Five doors – one of them a modern lift – led in different directions but the man escorted me into a second hallway with a reception desk tucked underneath an impressive stone staircase.

The stairs curved round on themselves and I could see all the way up to the vaulted roof, three floors above. It was almost like being inside a cathedral. A huge window rose up in front of me, some of the panes made of stained glass, although there was nothing religious about it. It was more like something you might find in an old school or even a railway station. Opposite, what I might describe as a landing ran from one side to the other, partly blocked off by a wall but with a semicircular opening cut into it so that if a guest walked past, they would almost certainly be seen from below. The landing connected two corridors that ran the full length of the hotel – the crossbar, if you like, in a large letter H.

A woman in a sharply cut black dress was sitting behind the reception desk, which was made of some dark, polished wood with mirrored edges. It looked out of place. I knew that much of Branlow Hall had been constructed at the start of the eighteenth century and all the other furnishings were deliberately traditional and old-fashioned. A rocking horse stood against the opposite wall, paint peeling and eyes staring. It reminded me of the famous horror story by D. H. Lawrence. There were two small offices behind the reception desk, one on each side. Later, I would learn that Lisa Treherne occupied one and her sister, Cecily, the other. The doors were open and I could see a pair of identical desks with telephones. I wondered if Cecily had made her call to France from here.

'Ms Ryeland?' The receptionist had been expecting me. When she offered me free accommodation, Pauline Treherne had said she would tell the staff I was helping her with a certain matter but not what it was. The girl was around the same age as the man who had met me; in fact, they could have been brother and sister.

They were both fair-haired, slightly robotic, possibly Scandinavian.

'Hello!' I placed my handbag between us, ready to provide a credit card if asked.

'I hope you had a good drive from London.'

'Yes, thank you.'

'Mrs Treherne has put you in the Moonflower Wing. You'll be very comfortable there.'

Moonflower. That was the name Alan Conway had given the hotel in his book.

'It's up one flight of stairs or you can take the lift.'

'I think I can manage the stairs, thank you.'

'Lars will take the case for you and show you the room.'

Definitely Scandinavian, then. I followed Lars up the staircase to the first-floor landing. There were oil paintings on the walls – family members from across the centuries, none of them smiling. Lars turned right and we continued behind the opening that I had seen from below. Resting against the wall, I noticed a table with two glass candlesticks and, on a stand between them, a large silver brooch. This was in the shape of a circle with a silver pin and there was a typewritten card, folded in half, describing it as an eighteenth-century figeen, which pleased me as it was a word I had never come across. There was a dog basket with a tartan blanket under the table and I was reminded of Bear, Cecily Treherne's golden retriever.

'Where's the dog?' I asked.

'He went for a walk,' Lars answered vaguely, as if he was surprised I had even asked.

Everything I have described so far was antique but when we reached the corridor, I noticed that electric key-card operators had been fitted to the doors and that we were being watched by a CCTV camera mounted in a corner. It must have been added long after the murder and perhaps as a response to it – otherwise the killer would have been seen. The first door we came to was number ten. Eleven was next door. But what should have been room twelve was blank and there was no room thirteen either, presumably for reasons of superstition. Was it my imagination or had Lars quickened his pace? I could hear the floorboards creaking under his step, the wheels on my suitcase still squeaking as they bumped over the joints.

After room fourteen, we came to a fire door that opened onto a corridor which was obviously new, part of an extension that jutted out towards the rear of the building. It was as if a second, modern hotel had been added to the first and I wondered if it had been like this eight years ago, when Frank Parris had checked in ...

and out. The carpet in the new section had one of those nasty patterns that you would never find in anyone's home. The doors were made out of wood that was both lighter and newer and they were closer together, suggesting smaller rooms on the other side. The lighting was recessed. Was this the Moonflower Wing? I didn't ask Lars, who was well ahead of me, my suitcase still squeaking as it followed him.

I had been given not just a room but a suite at the very end. Lars swiped the key to let us in and I found myself in a bright, comfortable space in various shades of cream and beige with a widescreen TV mounted on the wall. The sheets on the bed were expensive. A complimentary bottle of wine and a bowl of fruit sat, waiting for me, on a table. I went over to the window and looked out at the courtyard behind the hotel and a row of what might have been converted stables on the far side. The health spa with the swimming pool was over to the right. A driveway led up to a large, modern house set back from the hotel. I saw its name, BRANLOW COTTAGE, by the gate.

Lars put my case on one of those folding luggage racks that we would never have had at the Polydorus because they took up too much space and also because they were ridiculous.

'Fridge. Air conditioning. Minibar. Coffeemaker ... '

He showed me round the room just in case I couldn't find the way myself. He was polite rather than enthusiastic. 'The Wi-Fi code is on the table and if there is anything you want, you can dial zero for the front desk.'

'Thank you, Lars,' I said.

'Is there anything else you need?'

'Actually, I'd like to go into room twelve. Could I have a key?'

He looked at me peculiarly for a moment but the Trehernes had prepared the way. 'I'll open it for you,' he said.

He went over to the door and there was that nasty moment when I wasn't sure if I should tip him and wondered whether he was expecting it or not. In Crete we had a straw hat in the bar and anyone with any euros to spare threw them in there to be shared out equally among the staff. Generally, I don't like tipping. It feels old-fashioned, a throwback to the days when waiters and hotel staff were seen as belonging to a lower class. Lars didn't agree. He scowled, turned on his heel and left.

I unpacked with a growing sense of discomfort. Transported to an expensive wardrobe in an expensive room, my clothes didn't so much hang as droop. It was a reminder that I'd bought almost nothing new in two years.

Outside, a black Range Rover drove past the stables and into the drive of Branlow Cottage, the wheels crunching on the gravel. I heard the slam of a car door and looked out of the window in time to see a young-ish man wearing a padded waistcoat and a cap get out. There was a dog with him. At the same time, the door of the house opened and a young girl with black hair ran towards him, followed by a dark, slim woman carrying a shopping bag. The man scooped the girl up in his arms. I couldn't see much of his face but I knew that he must be Aiden MacNeil. The girl was his daughter, Roxana. The woman must be Eloise, the nanny. He spoke briefly to her and then they turned round and went back into the house.

I felt guilty, as if I had been spying on them. I turned away, snatched up my handbag with money, notepad and cigarettes and left the room, heading back through the fire door to the older part of the hotel and room twelve. It seemed the obvious place to begin. Lars had propped open the door with a wastepaper basket but I didn't want to be disturbed so I removed the basket and the door swung shut behind me.

I found myself in a room that was actually half the

size of the one I had been given. There was no bed and no carpet; presumably they had both been taken away, covered in blood. I've read in so many crime books that violent acts leave a sort of echo and I've never quite believed it, but there was definitely an atmosphere in that place ... in the empty spaces where there should have been furniture, the faded paintwork on the walls showing where pictures had once hung, the curtains that would never be drawn. There were two trolleys heaped up with towels and cleaning equipment, a pile of boxes, an array of machines – toasters, coffeemakers – mops and buckets, all the junk you don't want to see when you check into a smart hotel.

This was where Frank Parris had been killed. I tried to imagine the door opening and someone creeping in. If Frank had been asleep when he was attacked, they would have needed an electronic key card, but then surely Stefan Codrescu would have had one already. I could tell where the bed must have stood from the position of the electric sockets on either side and I imagined Frank lying in the darkness. On an impulse, I opened the door again. The hinges made no sound but there would have been a buzz or a click as the electric lock disengaged. Would that have been enough to wake him? There had been few details in the newspapers and the Trehernes hadn't been able to add very much more. Somewhere there must be a police report that might tell me whether Frank had been standing up or lying down, what he was wearing, exactly when he had died. The storeroom, shabby and decrepit, told me very little.

Standing there, I was suddenly depressed. Why had I left Andreas? What the hell did I think I was doing? If it had been Atticus Pünd coming into Branlow Hall, he'd have solved the crime by now. Perhaps the position of room twelve or the dog basket might have given him a clue. What about the figeen? That was straight out of Agatha Christie, wasn't it?

But I wasn't a detective. I wasn't even an editor any more. I knew nothing.

Lisa Treherne

Pauline and Lawrence Treherne had invited me to join them for supper on the first evening of my stay but when I entered the hotel dining room, Lawrence was sitting on his own. 'I'm afraid Pauline has a headache,' he explained. I noticed that the table was still laid for three. 'Lisa said she would join us,' he added. 'But we're to start without her.'

He looked older than he had in Crete, dressed in a check shirt that hung off him and red corduroy trousers. There were more lines under his eyes and his cheeks had those dark blotches that I've always associated with illness or old age. It was obvious that the disappearance of his daughter was taking its toll and I guessed that the same was true for Pauline, that her 'headache' had been caused by exactly the same thing.

I sat down opposite him. I was wearing a long dress and wedges but I wasn't comfortable. I wanted to kick off my shoes and feel sand beneath my feet.

'It's very good of you to have come, Miss Ryeland,' he began.

'Please ... call me Susan.' I thought we had been through all that.

A waiter came over and we ordered drinks. He had a gin and tonic. I went for a glass of white wine.

'How is your room?' he asked.

'It's very nice, thank you. You have a lovely hotel.'

He sighed. 'It's not really mine any more. My daughters run it now. And it's difficult to take very much pleasure from it at the moment. It was a life's work for Pauline and me, creating the hotel and building it up, but when something like this happens, you have to ask yourself if it was worth it.'

'When did you put in the extension?'

He looked puzzled, as if I had asked something odd.

'Was the hotel like this when Frank Parris was killed?'

'Oh ... yes.' He understood. 'We did the renovation in 2005. We had two new wings added: Moonflower and Barn Owl.' He half smiled. 'The names were Cecily's idea. The moonflower blooms after the sun has gone down and of course the barn owl comes out at night.' He smiled. 'Actually, you may have noticed, we've put owls everywhere.' He picked up the menu and showed me an image stamped in gold on the cover. 'That was Cecily too. She noticed that "barn owl" is an anagram of Branlow and so she had the bright idea to make it our logo.'

I felt my heart sink. Alan Conway had also had a fondness for anagrams. In one of his books, for example, all the characters were jumbled-up versions of London Tube stations. It was a strange game he played with his readers and one that only undermined the quality of his writing.

Lawrence was still talking. 'When we were doing the rebuilding, we added a lift for disabled access,' he explained. 'And we knocked down a wall to enlarge the dining room.'

That was the room we were sitting in. I had reached it from the circular entrance hall and had noticed the new lift on my way in. The kitchen was at the far end, stretching all the way to the back of the hotel. 'Can you get upstairs from the kitchen?' I asked.

'Yes. There's a service lift and a staircase. We put those in at the same time. We also converted the stables into staff quarters and added the swimming pool and the spa.'

I took out my notepad and jotted down what he had

just said. What it meant was that whoever had killed Frank Parris could have arrived at room twelve by four separate paths: the lift at the front of the hotel, another at the back, the main staircase and a set of service stairs. If they had already been in the hotel, they could have come down from the second floor. There had been someone on the reception desk all night but it would still have been perfectly easy to get past without being noticed.

But in Crete Pauline Treherne had told me that Stefan Codrescu had been seen entering the room. Why had he been so careless?

'I don't suppose you've had any news,' I said. 'About Cecily.'

Lawrence grimaced. 'The police think she may have been caught on CCTV in Norwich, but that doesn't make a lot of sense. She doesn't know anyone there.'

'Is Detective Superintendent Locke handling the disappearance?'

'Detective Chief Superintendent, you mean. Yes. I can't say I have a lot of faith in him. He was slow getting started – which was actually when it mattered most – and he doesn't seem to be particularly efficient now.' He glanced down gloomily, then asked: 'Have you had a chance to reread the book?'

It was a good question.

You would have thought it would be the first thing I would do – go through the book from cover to cover. But I hadn't even brought it with me. Actually, I didn't have any of Alan's books in Crete: they had too many unpleasant memories. I'd looked into a bookshop while I was in London, meaning to pick up a copy, and had been surprised to find they were out of stock. I could never decide if that was a good or a bad sign when I was in publishing. Great sales or bad distribution?

The truth was that I didn't want to read it yet.

I remembered it well enough: the village of Tawleigh-on-the-Water, the death at Clarence Keep, the various clues, the identity of the killer. I still had my notes somewhere, the email 'discussions' I had with Alan during the editorial process (I've added those inverted commas because he never listened to a word I said). The story held no surprises for me. I knew the plot inside out.

But you have to remember that Alan hid things in the text: not just anagrams, but acrostics, acronyms, words within words. He did it partly to amuse himself but often to indulge the more unpleasant side of his nature. It was already clear to me that he had used many elements of Branlow Hall for *Atticus Pünd Takes the Case*, but what he hadn't done was describe what had actually happened in June 2008. There was no advertising executive, no wedding, no hammer. If Alan, during his brief visit to the hotel, had somehow discovered who had really killed Frank Parris, he could have concealed it in a single word or a name or a description of something completely irrelevant. He could have spelled out the name of the killer in the chapter headings. Something had caught Cecily Treherne's eye when she read the book, but there was very little chance that it would catch mine – not until I knew a great deal more about her and everyone else at the hotel.

'Not yet,' I said, answering Lawrence's question. 'I thought it might be sensible to meet everyone and look round first. I don't know what Alan found when he came here. The more I know about the hotel, the more chance I'll have of making a connection.'

'Yes. That's a good thought.'

'Would it be possible to see the room where Stefan Codrescu was living?'

'I'll take you there after supper. It's being used by one of our other staff members. But I'm sure they won't mind.'

The waiter came over with the drinks and at the same time Lisa Treherne arrived. At least, I assumed it was her. I had seen photographs of her sister, Cecily, in the newspaper: a pretty woman with a rather babyish face, pursed lips, round cheeks. Apart from her fair hair, cut short in an old-fashioned style, this woman looked nothing like her. She was solid, unsmiling, wearing clothes that were deliberately businesslike with cheap spectacles and sensible shoes. She had a scar on the side of her mouth and I found it hard to stop myself staring. It was a dead straight line about half an inch long: it could have been cut with a knife. If it had been me I would have softened it with a little concealer but she had allowed it to define her. She was scowling and it was as if she was unable to smile, as if the scar prevented her.

She approached the table like a boxer climbing into the ring and even before she spoke I knew we weren't going to get along. 'So you're Susan Ryeland,' she said. She sat down without any ceremony. 'I'm Lisa Treherne.'

'It's nice to meet you,' I said.

'Is it?'

'Do you want a drink, dear?' Lawrence asked, a little nervously.

'I already told the waiter.' She looked me straight in the eye. 'Was it your idea to send Alan Conway here?'

'I didn't know anything about it,' I told her. 'I knew he was writing the book but I never saw his work until it was finished and I had no idea he had come to this hotel until your father came to see me in Crete.'

I was trying to work out if Lisa was in the book. There is one character in *Atticus Pünd Takes the Case* who has a scar: a beautiful Hollywood actress called Melissa James. Yes. That would have amused Alan, to take this unattractive woman and turn her into the opposite of herself.

Lisa didn't seem to have heard what I'd said. 'Well, if something has happened to Cess because of what was in that book, I hope you'll be pleased with yourself.'

'I really don't think that's fair—' Lawrence began.

But I could stand up for myself. 'Where do you think your sister is?' I asked.

I wondered if Lisa was going to accept that she was dead, destroying any hopes that her father might still have. I could see that for a moment she was tempted, but she couldn't go that far. 'I don't know. When she first went missing, I assumed that she and Ade had had a fight.'

Cess and Ade. The pet names weren't exactly affectionate. They were more a way of saving time.

'Did they argue often?'

'Yes—'

'That's not true,' Lawrence cut in.

'Come on, Dad. I know you like to think of them as the perfect couple. Aiden as the perfect husband, perfect father! But if you ask me, he only ever married

Cess because she gave him an easy ride. Golden smile. Blue eyes. But no one ever asks what's going on behind them.'

'What exactly are you saying, Lisa?' I asked. I was surprised she should be so upfront with her feelings.

A second waiter came over with a double whisky on a silver tray. She took it without thanking him.

'I just get fed up with Ade swanning around the hotel as if he runs it. That's all. Especially when I'm the one doing all the heavy lifting.'

'Lisa does the books,' Lawrence explained.

'I do the accounts. Contracts. Insurance, HR and stock control.' She drank half the whisky in one go. 'He schmoozes with the guests.'

'Do you think he killed Frank Parris?' I asked.

Lisa stared at me. I had been deliberately provocative but actually my question was completely logical. If Cecily had been killed, then it was because she knew something about the earlier murder. It followed that whoever killed Frank Parris must have killed her.

'No,' she said, finishing the whisky.

'Why not?'

She looked at me with pity. 'Because it was Stefan! He admitted it. He's in jail.'

A few other guests had begun to drift into the room. It was a quarter to seven, still very light outside.

Lawrence picked up one of the menus that had been left on the table. 'Shall we order?' he asked.

I was hungry but I didn't want to interrupt Lisa. I waited for her to continue.

'Hiring Stefan Codrescu was a mistake and we should have fired him right at the start. I said so at the time, although nobody listened to me. He wasn't just a criminal himself. He'd grown up with criminals. We gave him an opportunity and he just sneered at us. He was only here five months, for heaven's sake, but he was ripping us off almost from the moment he walked in.'

'We don't know that,' Lawrence said.

'We do know that, Daddy. I know that.' She turned to me. 'He'd only been here for a few weeks before I started noticing anomalies. I wouldn't imagine you have any idea what it's like, running a hotel, Susan . . . '

I could have put her right on that one but I let it pass.

'It's like a machine with a thousand moving parts and the trouble is that if a few of them go missing, nobody notices. The machine doesn't stop. Wine and whisky. Champagne. Fillet steaks. Petty cash. Guests' property: jewellery, watches, designer sunglasses. Linen and towels. Antique furniture. Putting a thief in here is like giving a drug addict the keys to his local Boots.'

'When Stefan came here, he'd never been accused of theft,' Lawrence reminded her. But he didn't sound convinced.

'What are you talking about, Daddy? He had been sent to prison for burglary and assault.'

'It's not the same ... '

'You wouldn't listen to me. You never do.' Lisa dismissed him and focused her energies on me. 'I knew something was wrong. Somebody was stealing from us. But whenever I mentioned Stefan's name, everyone ganged up on me.'

'You liked him to start with. You spent lots of time with him.'

'I tried to like him because that was what you all wanted. But the only reason I stayed close to him – and I've told you this enough times – was to see what he was up to. And I was right, wasn't I! What happened in room twelve was horrible, but it showed that I'd been right all along.'

'How much money was actually stolen from Frank Parris's room?' I asked.

'A hundred and fifty pounds,' Lawrence said.

'And you really believe that Stefan would murder someone, hammer them to death, for such a small amount?'

'I'm sure Stefan didn't mean to kill anyone. He

sneaked into the room in the middle of the night, thinking he could help himself to whatever and get away with it. But the poor man woke up and challenged him and Stefan lashed out on the spur of the moment.' Lisa sniffed at me. 'It all came out in the trial.'

It didn't make any sense to me. If Stefan hadn't intended to kill Frank Parris, why had he been carrying a hammer? And why go into the room while the occupant was there? But I didn't say anything. There are some people you just never want to argue with, and Lisa was certainly one of them.

She called the waiter over and ordered another drink. I took the opportunity to order my food. Just a salad and another glass of wine. Lawrence went for a steak.

'Can you tell me what happened on the night of the murder?' I asked and even as I uttered the words I felt slightly ridiculous. They sounded so old-fashioned, so clichéd. If I'd seen them in a novel, I'd have edited them out.

Lawrence took me through it. 'We had thirty friends and relatives staying over the weekend, but as I told you, the hotel was still open to the public and we had paying guests too. Every room was full.

'Frank Parris had checked in two days before the wedding, on the Thursday. He was staying three nights.

I remember him because he was quite difficult from the start. He was tired and he was jet-lagged and he didn't like his room so he insisted that we move him.'

'Which room was he in?'

'We'd given him room sixteen. It's in the Moon-flower Wing, where you are.'

I had passed room 16 on the way to my suite. It was on the other side of the fire door, where the swirly carpet began.

'He preferred the old part of the hotel,' Lawrence went on. 'Fortunately, we were able to move things around so he got what he wanted. That's very much Aiden's job, incidentally, to keep people happy. And he's very good at it.'

'The person Frank Parris changed with didn't complain?'

'As I recall, he was a retired headmaster, travelling on his own. I don't think he ever knew.'

'Do you remember his name?'

'The headmaster? No. But I can easily find out for you if you like.'

'That would be helpful. Thank you.'

'We had the wedding on the Saturday and we did warn the guests that there would be a certain amount of disruption. For example, we closed the spa early on the Friday evening so that we could give all the staff a drink, outside beside the swimming pool. We wanted them to feel part of the celebration even if they weren't actually coming to the wedding itself. The staff drinks started at eight thirty and finished at ten o'clock.'

'Was Stefan invited?'

'Yes. He was there. So were Aiden and Cecily. Pauline and myself. Lisa ... '

Lisa's plus one, or rather his absence, hung in the air.

'It was a very warm evening. In fact, you may remember that there was quite a heatwave that summer.'

'It was a horrible, hot, sticky night,' Lisa said. 'I couldn't wait to get home.'

'Lisa doesn't live on the estate,' Lawrence said, adding, 'although she could. The grounds extend to almost three hundred acres.'

'Aiden and Cecily have my old place,' Lisa muttered, sourly.

'Branlow Cottage,' I said.

'I moved into Woodbridge, which suits me very well. I left the drinks a long time before ten o'clock. I drove home and went to bed.'

'I'm going to leave Derek to tell you the rest,' Lawrence said. 'He's the night manager and he arrived at about the same time. He wasn't at the party.'

'He wasn't invited?'

'Of course he was invited but Derek doesn't like to socialise. You'll understand when you meet him. He was actually behind reception when the murder took place.'

'When was that?'

'According to the police, Parris was killed around twelve thirty on Friday night.'

'Were you here, Lawrence?'

'No. Pauline and I bought a house in Southwold when we stopped running the hotel. We went home for the night.'

'But we were all there for the wedding the next day,' Lisa said. 'It was such a lovely day ... until, of course, there was a murder. Poor Aiden! I'm sure it wasn't what he was buying into.'

'Really, Lisa, that's too much,' Lawrence protested.

'All I'm saying is that Cess was his meal ticket. What was he doing before he met her? Nothing! He was an estate agent.'

'He was doing very well. And he was a great help to us here at the hotel, whatever you may say,' Lawrence tut-tutted. 'Anyway, I think it's hardly appropriate to talk in this way, given how worried we all are about Cecily.'

'I'm worried about her too!' Lisa exclaimed and to my surprise I saw tears start in her eyes and I knew she was telling the truth. The waiter had arrived with her second whisky and she snatched it off the tray. 'Of course I'm worried about her. She's my sister! And if something's happened to her – that's too horrible to think about.'

She gazed into her drink. The three of us sat in silence.

'What do you remember about the wedding?' I asked.

'It was a wedding like any other. We have weddings here all the time. They're our bread and butter.' She took a breath. 'The service was in the rose garden. I was the maid of honour. We had the registrar from Ipswich, then lunch in a marquee on the main lawn. I was sitting next to Aiden's mother who had come down from Glasgow.'

'Was his father there?'

'His father died when Aiden was quite young. Cancer. He has a sister but she wasn't invited. Actually, there was hardly anyone on his side of the family. Mrs MacNeil was quite sweet, a bit of an old lady, very Scottish. I was thinking how boring the whole thing was when I heard screaming coming from somewhere outside the tent and a few minutes later Helen came in, looking like she'd just seen a ghost.'

'Helen?'

'She was head of housekeeping. It turned out that one of the maids had just gone into room twelve and had found Frank Parris with his skull smashed in and bits of brain all over the sheets.' Lisa was almost gloating. Despite what she had said earlier, she couldn't help herself from being amused by the total destruction of her sister's big day. Looking at her, I wondered if she wasn't a little bit unhinged.

'The maid was called Natasha,' Lawrence cut in. 'She'd gone in to clean the room and she discovered the body.'

Lisa downed her whisky in one. 'I don't know what you hope to find, Susan. Stefan admitted to the crime and now he's got what he deserves. It'll be ten years before they even think of letting him out again and serves him right. As for Cess, she'll turn up when it suits her. She likes being the centre of attention. She's probably just playing the drama queen.'

She got unsteadily to her feet and I realised she must have been drinking before she arrived and that the two double whiskies had supplemented many others. 'I'll leave the two of you together,' she said.

'Lisa, you should eat.'

'I'm not hungry.' She leaned towards me. 'You're responsible for Cecily,' she snarled. 'You published the fucking book. You find her.'

Lawrence watched her as she wove her way across the dining room. 'I'm sorry about that,' he said. 'Lisa works very hard. She's actually responsible for the entire running of the hotel. But she can get a bit tired.'

'She doesn't seem to like her sister very much.'

'You shouldn't take any notice of that. Lisa just likes to show off.' He was trying to convince me but he didn't even sound very convinced himself. 'It started when they were very young,' he admitted. 'There was always a lot of rivalry between them.'

'How did she get that scar?'

'Ah, I thought you might ask about that.' He was reluctant to tell me. I waited. 'I'm afraid that was Cecily. It was a complete accident, but ... ' He let out a breath. 'Lisa was twelve and Cecily was ten and they had an argument. Cecily threw a kitchen knife at her. She really didn't mean it to hit her sister. It was just a stupid, childish thing to do when she lost her temper, but the blade absolutely sliced into Lisa and ... well, you've seen the result. Cecily was terribly upset.'

'What were they arguing about?'

'Does it really matter? Boys, probably. They were always jealous of each other's boyfriends. I mean, that's quite common with young girls. Cecily was always the better-looking of the two and if she met someone it would infuriate Lisa. That's why she's taken against

Aiden, incidentally. What she said about him – it's just jealousy. There's absolutely nothing wrong with him, really. He and I have always got along.'

He picked up his wine glass.

'Girls will be girls!'

He said it as a toast but I didn't join in. Girls might be girls, but not, I thought, borderline psychotics. Lisa had been disfigured by Cecily. She had a serious grudge against Aiden. And that grudge, all tied up with some sort of sexual jealousy, might have extended to Stefan Codrescu too.

Serious or murderous?

Which?

The Night Manager

I didn't eat very much dinner. I was stung by what Lisa had said to me and wondered if it was true: I had never unleashed Alan Conway on Branlow Hall but it was undoubtedly true that I had profited by what he had done. Like it or not, I was partly to blame.

After coffee, Lawrence took me out through the kitchen and I noticed the service staircase and the lift leading up to the second floor. We emerged round the back of the hotel and, looking across the courtyard, I saw the driveway that led to Branlow Cottage. There were lights on behind some of the windows. The black Range Rover was still parked outside.

'It's been absolute hell for Aiden,' Lawrence said. 'The moment he reported Cecily missing, he turned himself into the main suspect. It's always the husband in cases like this. But I can't bring myself to believe that he would do anything to hurt my daughter. I've seen them together. I know what they mean to each other.'

'They only have one child?' I said.

'Yes. I was a little sad about that. But it was a difficult birth and I think Cecily just didn't want to go through it all again. Anyway, she was so busy running the hotel.'

'You said that Roxana is seven.' I'd already done the maths. 'When is her birthday?'

Lawrence knew what I was getting at. 'Cecily was already expecting her when she got married – but that wasn't the reason for it. Young people these days don't feel under pressure... not like we did. Aiden's devoted to his daughter. Right now, she's the only thing keeping him sane.'

'Do you think he'll mind talking to me?' It was something that had been worrying me. I was here because I'd been asked to read a book which might or might not be connected to a murder that had taken place eight years before. That was one thing. Interrogating a grieving husband about his missing wife was quite another.

'I'm sure he'll be glad to talk to you. I can ask him if you like.'

'I'd be grateful. Thank you.'

As we talked, we passed the swimming pool, which was contained in an oversized conservatory that might have been modelled on Brighton Pavilion. It stood next to a handsome building, a miniature replica of the main house. This had once been a granary store but had been converted into a spa. It was closing for the night and a good-looking young man came out of the side door, dressed in a tracksuit and carrying a sports bag. He noticed us and waved.

'That's Marcus,' Lawrence told me. 'He runs the spa – but he only joined us a couple of years ago.'

'Who was running it when Frank Parris was killed?'

'An Australian. His name was Lionel Corby. But he left soon after. We actually lost quite a few staff, as you might expect.'

'Do you know where he is now?'

'He may have gone back to Australia. I've got his last phone number if that's any help.'

He had come from Australia. So had Frank Parris. It was a connection of sorts. 'Yes. That might be useful,' I said.

We reached the stable block, which had been converted into living quarters for staff: there were five small apartments, studio flats next to each other, each with a door and a single window facing the hotel. A

general maintenance room stood at the far end. Lawrence pointed. 'That was where Stefan kept his toolbox,
including the hammer that he used for the crime.'

'Can I see?'

I don't know what I expected to find. The room had
a concrete floor and several shelves piled up with card-
board boxes, cans of paint, various chemicals ... No
lock on the door. Anyone could have come in here. I
said so.

'The defence made a lot of that during the trial,'
Lawrence agreed. 'Yes, anyone could have taken the
hammer. The trouble was, that was the only thing Stefan had on his side and against all the other evidence it
was practically meaningless.'

We went to the room next door, which was the
one that Stefan had occupied: number five. Lawrence
knocked and when there was no answer he took out a
Yale key, which he turned in the lock.

'I spoke to Lars earlier,' he explained. 'He's probably at the pub with Inga. They both arrived this year.'

I remembered the smart-looking girl behind the
reception desk. 'They're Danish?' I asked.

'Yes. We got them through an agency.' He sighed.
'We don't run our Youth Offender Programme any
more.'

The door opened into a perfect shoebox of a room

with a single bed beside the door, a desk, a wardrobe and a chest of drawers. A second door led into a corner bathroom with a toilet, sink and shower. I guessed that all five rooms were exactly the same. Lars kept his frighteningly tidy. The bed looked as if it had never been slept in and in the bathroom I could see towels hanging with perfect precision on the rail. Apart from a couple of books on the desk, there was nothing personal in sight at all.

'These Scandinavians are very tidy,' Lawrence muttered, reading my thoughts. 'It certainly wasn't like this when Stefan occupied it.'

That surprised me. 'How do you know?'

'Lionel, the fitness chap I mentioned, used to spend time here. He and Stefan were quite close. You should look at the police reports.'

'That may be easier said than done.'

'I could have a word with DCS Locke.'

'No. It's all right. I know him.' I also knew that there was little chance of Locke sharing anything with me, not even the time of day. I peered into the room, not wanting to step inside. 'They found money in here that belonged to the dead man.'

'Yes. It was under his mattress.'

'Not exactly the most brilliant place to hide stolen cash.'

Lawrence nodded. 'You can think many things about Stefan Codrescu,' he said. 'But one thing is certain. He wasn't too bright.'

'Someone could have planted it.'

'I suppose that's possible, but you have to ask yourself, when? It would have been almost impossible during the day. As you can see, the door faces the hotel and there were dozens of people out here. We had wedding guests, the spa was open, there were security guards, the kitchen staff going back and forth, people looking out of windows. I don't think anyone could have slipped into the room without being seen and believe you me, the police took hundreds of witness statements.

'And it wasn't just the money. They also found traces of blood on the shower floor and on the sheets of Stefan's bed. The forensics people were able to work out that they had been there for more than twelve hours, meaning that they had definitely been there during the night. The narrative was crystal clear. On Friday night, Stefan kills Frank Parris. There's a lot of blood. He comes back and showers and goes to bed and he leaves gigantic footprints the entire way.'

'So if someone did plant the evidence on Stefan, they must have done it sometime after midnight,' I said.

'Yes. But that's not very likely either. First of all, the door self-locks – and before you ask, we did have a duplicate key in Lisa's office. But look at the position of the bed. It's right next to the door. I don't see how anyone could have got in here, messed around with the bed sheets and the shower and then left again without waking Stefan up.'

He closed the door and we walked back to the hotel together.

'Derek should be here by now,' Lawrence said. 'I asked him to come in early to talk to you.' He paused. 'Can I ask you to go easy on him? He's worked at the hotel for ten years and he's a good man. But he's quite fragile. He looks after his mother and she's not at all well. What Alan Conway did to him – to both of them – was actually appalling.'

I remembered that in the book there's a character called Eric Chandler who works as a personal chauffeur and handyman alongside his mother, Phyllis. They appear in the first chapter and it's not a sympathetic portrayal.

'Did he read *Atticus Pünd Takes the Case*?' I asked.

'Fortunately not. Derek doesn't read very much. It might be best not to mention it.'

'I won't.'

'I'll wish you a goodnight, then.'
'Goodnight. Thanks for dinner.'

★

There was absolutely no need for Lawrence Treherne's
warning. The moment I saw him, I knew that Derek
Endicott was a vulnerable man, eager to please, frightened of giving offence. It was in the blinking eyes
behind the spectacles with thick lenses, the hesitant
smile, the curly hair that fell haphazardly, without any
sense of style. He was in his forties, but his face had
a childlike quality, with plump cheeks, thick lips, the
sort of skin that suggested he never shaved. He had already taken his place behind the reception desk, tucked
away in the cave formed by the staircase that swung
diagonally over him on its way up to the first floor. I
noticed that he had some food in a plastic Tupperware
box as well as a Thermos and a puzzle magazine.

He was expecting me. Lawrence had told him why I
was there. He clumsily stood up as I approached, then
sat down before he had become fully vertical. It was
quite cool in the reception area, but I noticed a sheen of
sweat on his neck and on the sides of his face.

'Mr Endicott ... ' I began.

'Derek. Please. That's what everyone calls me.' He had a wheezy, high-pitched voice.

'You know why I'm here?'

'Yes. Mr Treherne asked me to come in early tonight.'

He waited nervously for the first question and I tried to put him at ease. 'You were here on the night Mr Parris was killed. What you saw or heard could be tremendously helpful.'

He frowned. 'I thought you were here because of Cecily.'

'Well, it's possible the two are connected.'

He thought about that for a moment. I could actually see the mental process in his eyes. 'Yes. You could be right.'

I leaned against the desk. 'I know it was a long time ago, but I wonder if you can remember what happened that night?'

'Of course I can remember! It was terrible. I didn't meet Mr Parris. I don't really see any of the guests unless they put me on the day shift and they only do that when they're short-staffed. Actually, I did see Mr Parris go upstairs. It was after dinner, but we didn't speak.' He corrected himself a second time. 'No. That's not true. We spoke on the phone. On Thursday. He called down from his room. He wanted to order a taxi first thing Friday morning. I did that for him.'

'Where did he want to go?'

'Heath House in Westleton. I wrote it down in the book. That was how I was able to remember when the police asked me, and anyway I know that house. It's very close to where I live with my mum. I hated having the police here. This is such a beautiful hotel. People come here to rest and to relax. Not for … '

He couldn't work out a way to finish the sentence and fell silent.

'To be honest with you, I wasn't feeling very well that night, the night before the wedding,' he went on, eventually. 'I was upset … '

'What had upset you?'

'No. I mean … my stomach was upset. It was something I'd eaten.'

'You didn't go to the party.'

'No. But I was invited! I was so happy for Cecily and for Mr MacNeil.' It was interesting that Cecily seemed to be the only person in the hotel he referred to by their first name. 'I thought they were a perfect match. And it was lovely to see her so happy. Do you know where she is?'

'I'm hoping to find out.'

'I hope nothing's happened to her. She's one of the

kindest people. Nothing is ever too much trouble. She's always been very good to me.'

'Can you tell me what happened on the night Mr Parris was killed?' I asked.

'Not really.' Despite his protestation, Derek had surely rehearsed all this. He drew a breath then plunged in. 'I was behind my desk – here – at ten o'clock. That was about the time the staff party finished. Everyone sounded as if they'd had a good time. They were all very happy.

'Mr Parris went up to his room about five minutes after I arrived, so that would have been about five past ten. After that, I saw quite a few of the guests go past; some of them were members of the public and some of them were here for the wedding. But anyway, at midnight I was on my own – which is fine. I like this job because I don't mind being by myself. Mother makes me a sandwich and I've got something to read and sometimes I listen to the radio. Cecily said I should watch films on the computer but I don't like to do that because I think it's my job to stay alert.'

'So did you hear or see anything that night?'

'I'm just coming to that!' He took another breath. 'A little bit after midnight, Bear suddenly cried out.'

'Bear? The dog?'

'Cecily's dog. Most of the time he sleeps in the house

but sometimes he spends the night over here on the first floor and that was where he was, in his basket.' Derek pointed up towards the circular opening, the gallery on the first floor. It was impossible to see the basket from where he was sitting, but any sound would have carried down. 'They didn't want him with them because of the wedding and everything else going on,' he continued, 'so he'd gone to bed up there.'

'And he cried out.'

'I thought someone must have stepped on his tail or something so I went up the stairs. But there was no one there. Bear was lying in his basket, absolutely fine. He must have just had a bad dream. I knelt down and gave him a stroke and it was while I was there that someone went past.'

'Went past where?'

'Along the corridor. Going from the new lift towards the Moonflower Wing.'

I've already described Branlow Hall as being built in the shape of a letter H. When Derek was crouching beside the dog, he would have been about midway along the crossbar with a corridor at each end. Whoever had travelled towards room twelve must have come from the front of the building.

'Could they have come from outside the hotel?' I asked.

'I don't know.'

'But the front door. Was it locked?'

Derek shook his head. 'We never locked the doors. Not in those days. There wasn't any need.' He grimaced and added portentously: 'We do now.'

'And you didn't see who it was.' I almost had no need to ask. The figure, flitting along the corridor, would have been in his line of vision for less than a second.

'I thought it was Stefan,' Derek admitted. The next words tumbled out quickly, in anguish. 'I didn't want to get anyone into trouble. I only told the police what I saw. He was carrying a toolbox. It was Stefan's toolbox. I'd seen it lots of times. And he was wearing a knitted hat.' He put his hands on his head to show me what he meant.

'You mean ... a beanie?'

'Yes. Stefan often wore a beanie. But the lights were on low and it was so quick. I told the police I couldn't be sure.'

'So what did you do next?' I asked. 'After you saw the man with the toolbox?'

'I went to the main corridor to see who it was – but by the time I got there it was too late. He'd gone.'

'He'd gone into one of the rooms.'

'He must have.' Derek looked miserable, as if the whole thing was somehow his fault. 'The police said he'd gone into room twelve.'

Room twelve was only five or six paces away from the point where the landing met the corridor and it was on the near side of the fire door. If Derek had walked forward straight away, the intruder must have disappeared in a matter of seconds.

'Did you hear him knock?'

'No.'

'Did anyone say anything?'

'No.'

'So what did you think?'

'I didn't think anything. I mean, I thought maybe Stefan had gone into one of the rooms to mend something – a toilet or something – although that didn't make any sense because if anyone had needed him they'd have had to call me. But everything was quiet. There wasn't any noise or anything. So after a bit I just went back to my desk and that was the end of it.'

'You didn't hear anything else?'

'No.' He shook his head.

'Derek … ' How could I put this gently? 'Frank Parris was attacked with a hammer. He must have cried out. I can't believe you didn't hear him.'

'I didn't hear anything!' His voice rose. 'I was all the way back downstairs and I was listening to music on the radio … '

'All right.' I waited for him to calm down. 'Who discovered the body?' I asked.

'That was Natasha. She was one of the maids. I think she was Russian or something.' His eyes widened as he remembered what had happened. 'She found it when she went in to clean the room. They say she screamed and screamed.'

'But that wasn't until much later ... the next day.'

'Yes.' Derek leaned forward and almost whispered, 'Someone had put a "Do Not Disturb" sign on the door of number twelve!' he told me. 'They did it on purpose. So no one would know.'

'So why did Natasha go in, then?'

'Because someone took it off again.'

'Who took it off?'

'I don't know. They never found out.'

He had nothing more to say. I could see that. He looked exhausted.

'Thank you, Derek,' I said.

'I wish it had never happened. The hotel has never been the same since then. There's always been an atmosphere ... I've said it often enough to my mum. It's as if there's something evil here. And now Cecily going missing. I knew something was wrong when she made that phone call. She was so upset. It's all part of the same thing and I don't think it's ever going to end.'

'Do you have any idea who killed Frank Parris?'

He was surprised by my question, as if nobody had ever asked him what he thought. 'It wasn't Stefan,' he said. 'Even if it was Stefan I saw going along the corridor, I'm sure it wasn't him. He seemed such a nice sort of guy. He was very quiet. I know Miss Treherne – Lisa, I mean – didn't like him very much and she said he was dishonest, but he seemed all right to me. Do you think they'll find her?'

'Cecily Treherne?'

'Yes.'

'I'm sure they will. I'm sure she'll turn up safe and sound.'

That was what I said, but in my heart I knew I was lying. I hadn't even been in the hotel for one full day but something there had reached out to me. Maybe it was the sense of evil that Derek had been talking about. But I was quite sure that Cecily was already dead.

FaceTime

Was I getting old?

I was examining myself on the computer screen as I tried to connect with Crete and although it's true that the camera on a MacBook Air never does anyone any favours, I wasn't too happy with what I saw. I looked tired. Two years of Cretan sun and cigarette smoke had not done great things for my skin. After I'd left London I'd stopped putting any colour in my hair and I wasn't sure if the result was delightfully natural or plain drab. I've never been very fashion-conscious. Kicking around alone in my flat in Crouch End, I used to go for oversized T-shirts and leggings. Of course I'd dress up for work, but with forced retirement I'd found myself liberated from the three S's – suits, stockings and stilettos – and in the Greek sunshine I'd dressed in anything that was light and loose-fitting. Andreas had always said that he loved me as I was and that there was no need to impress him, but looking at myself, I wondered if I wasn't letting myself go – a horrible phrase that brought to mind debauchery and decay.

There was a zing and my image was pushed into the corner where it belonged and in its place Andreas's face filled the screen. I had been afraid that he would be out or – worse – that he would be in and wouldn't answer. But there he was, sitting on our terrace. As he leaned back, I could see the shutters behind him and the tubs full of sage and oregano that I had planted myself. His computer was on the glass table with the crack in it, the one we had said we must replace but never would.

'*Yassou, agapiti mou!*' he said. It was a joke between us that every morning, from the first day I had arrived at the hotel, he would greet me in Greek, but I wondered now if he wasn't taunting me, reminding me that I was so far away from him.

'How are you?' I asked.

'I'm missing you.'

'How's the hotel?'

'The hotel . . . is the hotel! It's still here.'

Andreas's face lit up my screen – and I mean that in every sense. His dark skin and thick black hair emphasised the dazzling white of his teeth and I could actually see the sparkle in his eyes. He was an incredibly handsome man and looking at him in front of me, I felt a longing to climb through that rectangular window and throw myself into his arms. I hadn't left him. That was what I told myself. I had just gone away for a week. I would go back to Crete when this was all over, ten thousand pounds richer. In the end, the whole experience would bring us closer together.

'Where are you now?' Andreas asked.

'At the hotel. Branlow Hall.'

'What's it like?'

'It's barking mad. There are oil paintings on the walls and stained-glass windows. Some of the rooms have four-poster beds. You'd love it.'

'Who are you sharing yours with?'

'Stop it!'

'I miss having you in mine. It's not the same here without you. Lots of the regulars have complained.'

The mood had changed and we were serious. I realised now that I had left Crete without even thinking about the immediate consequences. There had been no discussion between us, no attempt to iron out the difficulties that had insinuated themselves into our relationship. Our last conversation had been acrimonious. *'I don't want you to go,'* he had said. But I had gone anyway. I wondered now if I had behaved badly and, worse still, if I had broken something that was precious to me.

'How are Panos and Vangelis?' I asked.

'They're fine.'

'Don't they miss me?'

'Of course they miss you.' He spread his hands so that they disappeared on either side of the screen. 'But we get by.'

I scowled. 'You mean, you can manage without me.'

'We need the money! Have you got it yet?'

In fact, Lawrence hadn't paid me anything so far. 'I'm chasing it,' I said.

'If it hadn't been for the money, I wouldn't have let you go.'

He sounded so Greek when he said that. I couldn't tell if he was joking or not.

'So tell me about the murder,' he went on. 'Do you know who did it?'

'I don't know anything yet.'

'It was the husband.'

'What?'

'The woman who disappeared. Of course he did it. It's always the husband.'

'I haven't even spoken to him yet. And it's more complicated than that. This is all about something that happened eight years ago. If someone has killed Cecily, it was because of that.'

Andreas pointed at the screen. His finger loomed towards me, out of perspective. 'Just you take care of yourself. Remember, if you get into trouble, I won't be there to help you.'

'Why don't you get on a plane?' I said, wanting him beside me.

'The Polydorus can manage without you. But it can't manage without both of us.'

I heard shouting. It was coming from underneath the terrace, I think, but it was impossible to tell who it was. Andreas listened, then shrugged his shoulders in a gesture of regret. 'I have to go,' he said.

'If it's the microwave, just turn it off and then on again.'

'That's true of everything in the hotel. In the whole country!' He leaned forward. 'I miss you, Susan. And I worry about you. Don't put yourself in any danger.'

'I won't.'

The shouting continued, louder.

'I love you.'

'I love you.'

Two thousand miles apart, we reached towards each other. Our fingers found the cursor at the same moment. We pressed. The screen went blank.

Heath House, Westleton

The next morning began with an unpleasant surprise.

I'd had breakfast in my room and was just on my way downstairs when a man in a suit appeared, walking briskly from the front of the hotel towards reception. I recognised him at once: those angry eyes, his black skin, his muscular neck and shoulders, even the way he walked – as if searching for a wall to bulldoze his way through. With or without his promotion, there could be no mistaking Detective Chief Superintendent Richard Locke, and I briefly considered turning round and going back to my room as if I had forgotten something rather than risk running into him a second time. He had been angry enough when I had involved myself in his last investigation.

But I was already committed. I couldn't avoid him. So I kept my head down and hurried forward, pretending not to notice him, as if lost in my own thoughts. We passed within inches of each other at the foot of the stairs and although he must have seen me, he didn't actually recognise me, which I couldn't help feeling showed a distinct lack of observational skills in someone who called himself a detective. To be fair, his mind must have been on other things. I heard him ask for Aiden MacNeil and realised he had come to report on the search for his wife and, presumably, his lack of progress. I was glad that Locke hadn't seen me. It was a distraction that neither of us needed.

It also gave me an excuse to postpone seeing Aiden myself, which was a meeting I was still dreading. I didn't agree with what Andreas had said. Just because Aiden was married to Cecily, it didn't make him the prime suspect in her disappearance. On the contrary, and ignoring what Lisa had said, all the evidence suggested that the two of them had been happy together. They also had a child. Surely that made it less likely that he would want to do her harm?

It was a relief to climb into my dear old MG Roadster and to feel the rush as it carried me away from the hotel. It was a beautiful day but I wanted to get on the road as quickly as possible and waited until I got to the end of the drive before stopping and folding down the roof. After that, I continued on my way, pushing against the speed limit, feeling the wind streaming over my shoulders and tangling my hair. I spun through green leaves and woodland until I reached the A12, then headed north to Westleton. Frank Parris had visited somewhere called Heath House on the day he was killed. I wondered if this was where his relatives had lived and, more to the point, if they were still there.

Westleton is a funny village in that it isn't really a village at all, more a confluence of roads. There's the Yoxford Road to Yoxford, the Dunwich Road to Dunwich and the Blythburgh Road to Blythburgh, but there doesn't seem to be a Westleton Road to Westleton. It's as if someone is trying to tell you that there's no particular reason to visit the place where you actually are. It has an old-fashioned garage, a pub that's signposted but nowhere to be seen, a second-hand bookshop and not much else. That said, it's on the edge of a superb nature reserve and you can walk to the sea. I'm sure it's a lovely place to live.

Heath House wasn't easy to find, especially in an old car without satnav. I had printed up a map at the hotel but drove in circles until I came across a farmer hosing down a tractor: he directed me to a narrow lane I hadn't noticed, mainly because it had no name. The lane led me away from the centre of the village and into the nature reserve itself, finally petering out on a stretch of grassland with a timber-frame farmhouse on the other side. This was Heath House. The name was written on an American-style mailbox beside the gate.

It was the sort of home designed to be seen on a summer morning with the lawns freshly mown, the flowers in full bloom, the hammock swaying beneath the trees and so on. It must have been a hundred years old and even without going in I knew there would be exposed beams and open fireplaces, comfy nooks and ceilings where you would have to be careful not to bang your head. It wasn't particularly beautiful: the roof had been badly repaired with tiles that changed colour halfway across, and an ugly modern conservatory had been added to one side. But it was a house that was completely comfortable with itself. It must have had five or six bedrooms, two of them tucked up in the eaves. A set of wind chimes hung from a tree, tinkling meditatively in the breeze.

I parked the car and got out. There was no need to lock it or to close the roof. As I opened the gate, I noticed a man in dark blue overalls painting a window frame. He was short and thin, quite pale, with close-cropped hair and round glasses. Did he own the house? Or did he work for the man who owned the house? It was hard to be sure.

'Hello,' he said. He didn't seem at all surprised to see me. He was smiling.

'Do you live here?' I asked.

'Yes. How can I help you?'

I hadn't been prepared for such conviviality and I wasn't sure how to introduce myself. 'I'm very sorry to bust in on you like this,' I said, 'but I wondered if I could have a word.' He waited for more. 'It's about Branlow Hall.'

At once he was interested. 'Oh yes?'

'I'm staying there.'

'Lucky you. It's a nice hotel.'

'I'm asking questions about something that happened quite a long time ago. Did you by any chance know a man called Frank Parris?'

'Yes. I knew Frank.' He noticed he was still holding the paintbrush and put it down. 'Why don't you come in and have a cup of tea?'

It baffled me that he was so amiable. He seemed not just willing but eager to talk to me. 'Thank you,' I said. I held out a hand. 'I'm Susan Ryeland.'

He examined his own hand, which was smudged

with white paint. 'Martin Williams. Forgive me if I don't shake hands. Come this way . . . '

He led me round the side and in through a sliding door. The interior of the house was exactly as I had imagined it. The kitchen was large and homely, with an Aga, an island for food preparation, pots hanging from the rafters and a pine kitchen table with eight chairs. It had modern windows looking out onto the garden and an archway leading into a hallway with red-brick walls, a round, antique table and a staircase leading up. The family did its shopping at Waitrose. There were two Bags for Life on the floor next to a row of wellington boots, a cat's litter tray, an ironing board, tennis rackets, a laundry basket and a bicycle pump. The house wasn't untidy so much as lived in. Everything was where it was meant to be. Ordnance Survey maps and birdwatching books lay spread out on the table, along with a copy of the *Guardian*. There were framed photographs everywhere – two girls from infancy to their early twenties.

'Builder's or peppermint?' Martin asked, flicking on the kettle.

But before I could answer, a woman came into the room. She was a little shorter than him, about the same age – as a couple, they were in perfect proportion. She reminded me a little of Lisa Treherne: she had that same angry quality. The difference was that she was more defensive. This was her territory and she didn't want me here.

'This is Joanne,' Martin said. He turned to her. 'And this is Susan. She's come over from Branlow Hall.'

'Branlow Hall?'

'Yes. She wants to know about Frank.'

Joanne's face changed when she heard that. She had been vaguely unwelcoming a minute or so ago but now she looked offended. She might even have been afraid.

'It's quite difficult to explain ... ' I began, trying to put her at ease.

Next to the Aga, the electric kettle began to hiss. 'I was just making Susan some tea,' Martin said. 'What will it be?'

'Builder's would be fine,' I said.

'I'll do it.' Joanne reached for mugs and tea bags.

'No, no, darling. You sit down and look after our guest.' He smiled at me. 'We don't get many visitors out this way. It's always nice to have company.'

Why did I get the impression that the two of them were playing some sort of game? They reminded me of the husband and wife in *Who's Afraid of Virginia Woolf?*, the ones who invite a young couple into their home only to rip them apart.

Joanne and I sat down at the table and I asked her about Westleton while Martin made the tea. I forget what she told me. I just remember the way she stared at me, so combative and intense. I was glad when Martin joined us. Unlike her, he was completely relaxed. He'd even brought a plate of biscuits.

'So why are you interested in Frank?' he asked.

'Were you related to him?' I asked him back.

'Yes.' Martin was completely unfazed. 'He was my brother-in-law. Joanne's his sister.'

'And he'd come to Suffolk to see you.'

'Forgive me, Susan, but you haven't answered my original question.' He smiled at me. 'Why are you asking questions about him?'

I nodded. 'I'm sure you've heard that Cecily Treherne has disappeared. Her parents own the hotel.'

'Yes. We read about that in the papers.'

'They asked me to help them because they think that her disappearance may be connected to Frank's death.'

'What are you? A clairvoyant or something?'

'No. I used to work in publishing. One of my authors wrote about what happened and they think there may be a connection.' It was too difficult to explain everything so I dived straight in. 'Did you see Frank the weekend he died?'

For a moment, I thought they might deny it. Joanne

seemed to flinch but Martin didn't even hesitate. 'Oh yes. He came round here the same day it happened. He was killed on a Friday night if I remember correctly. And he came here that same morning, just after breakfast. What time was it, darling?'

'About ten o'clock,' Joanne answered, still staring at me.

'Can you tell me why?'

'He'd just come back from Australia. He wanted to see us.'

'He didn't stay with you.'

'No. We'd have been happy to have put him up but he didn't even let us know he was in the country until he called from the hotel. That was Frank for you. He was full of surprises.'

I didn't believe a single word he was saying to me and the strange thing was, I don't think he wanted me to. Everything he said, even that playful smile of his . . . it was all a performance. He was like a magician daring me to pick a card in the certain knowledge that in two seconds' time it would have changed into a different one. It was a very strange way to behave considering I was talking about a man, a family member, who had been brutally killed.

I turned to Joanne. I thought it might be easier getting through to her. 'Look, I hate intruding,' I said. 'I know it's none of my business, but as I explained, I'm just trying to find Cecily and anything you can tell me about what happened that weekend might help.'

'I don't think we have anything to say—' Joanne began.

'You can ask anything you like,' Martin cut in. 'We've got nothing to hide.'

In Alan Conway's novels, people only said that when they most definitely did have something to hide.

I looked around me. 'How long have you been here?' I asked. I was deliberately changing the subject, coming in from a different angle.

'We moved in around ... ' Martin counted it out on his fingers. 'Well, it must have been seven years before Frank went to Australia – 1998. It was the year Joanne's mother died.'

'This was her house?'

'Yes. We were living in London before that. I was working for an insurance broker in the city. Guest Krieger ... I don't suppose you'll have heard of them. They specialise in art.'

'I don't have any art.'

'Well, fortunately there are plenty of wealthy clients who do.' He flashed that strange smile of his. It was beginning to annoy me. 'Joanne had always wanted to move out of London and as it happens, most of my work is done over the telephone. It doesn't matter where I am. Our girls were just about to start school when this house became available and so we moved in.'

'Where were your girls at school?' I asked.

'Woodbridge School.'

'My sister sent her children there,' I told them. 'My partner used to teach there.'

'It did very well for them,' Joanne said, loosening just a little. 'They're at university now.'

'They must have been pleased to see their uncle.'

'They didn't see him. They weren't at home when he visited.'

'And he didn't want to meet them? After he'd come all the way from Australia?'

'Frank was here on business,' Martin said, allowing just a little impatience to creep into his voice. He had been holding a biscuit and now he snapped it in half and laid both pieces down. 'It's very sad but he'd lost a lot of money setting up his Australian business. He came back to England with almost nothing. He had this idea of starting another agency and he wanted us to invest.' He shook his head. 'I'm afraid it was out of the question. I work for myself now and I do well enough out of it, but there was no way I was going into business with him. It wouldn't have worked.'

'Because ... ?'

'Because I didn't like him. Neither of us did.'

And there it was, suddenly out there. An admission of sorts. But where exactly did it lead?

Joanne set down her cup and saucer, the one rattling against the other. 'It wasn't really a question of liking him or disliking him,' she said. 'Frank and I had very little in common. To start with, there was the age difference. But we'd also made some very different life choices. When I was in London, I worked as a payment administrator with the NHS. I had Martin and the children. I'm not saying I disapproved, but Frank had a lifestyle that was completely alien to me.'

'In what way?'

'Well, there was his sexuality, of course. He was gay and I've got nothing against that. But why did he have to shove it in your face? There were always parties and drugs and those clothes he used to wear and so many young men—'

'Steady on!' Martin seemed amused by his wife's indignation. He tapped her gently on the arm. 'Better watch out for the PC brigade!'

'You know what I thought of him, Martin. I just thought it was disgusting, that's all.'

'Frank liked to show off,' Martin said. 'That's all.'

'So what happened when he came here?' I asked.

'He told us that he'd lost a lot of money.' Martin had

taken over again. 'He wanted us to help him. We said we'd think about it, although we'd both made up our minds that it wasn't going to happen. We called him a taxi and he went back to the hotel.'

'Did he mention the wedding?'

'As a matter of fact, he was quite pissed off about it. The place was jammed and there was a big marquee in the garden which spoiled the view. He said they should have given him a discount.'

'Did he say anything about Cecily? Or her fiancé, Aiden MacNeil?'

'He didn't mention either of them. I wish I could tell you more, Susan. But he was only here for about forty-five minutes. We had tea. We talked. And then he left.'

Joanne clearly wanted me to do the same. I had finished my tea and no second cup was being offered. I got to my feet. 'You've both been very kind,' I said. 'I may be in Suffolk for a few more days. Do you mind if I come back?'

'You're welcome any time,' Martin said. 'If you have any more questions we'll be happy to answer them, won't we, Jo?'

'Let me show you out.' Joanne had got up too. She gestured towards the archway.

If she had been just a little less formal, she might have escorted me through the sliding doors, the way I had come in. But she clearly felt a need to take me through the hallway and out through the front door, which was how I came to see the cork board half concealed behind the Aga and, as we walked past, the business card pinned in the corner.

Wesley & Khan – Solicitors
Framlingham

It was Sajid Khan who had told Lawrence and Pauline Treherne where they could find me. He had once represented Alan Conway. In what way, I wondered, was he connected to Martin and Joanne Williams?

I was about to ask Joanne how she knew him but I never got the chance. She had been tight-lipped as she led me out of the kitchen but suddenly she turned round and I saw that something extraordinary had happened. She was furious. She was staring at me as if she wanted to kill me.

'I don't want you to come here again,' she hissed, keeping her voice low so that Martin wouldn't hear.

'I'm sorry?'

'Just go away. We never wanted to see Frank and

we don't want to see you. Whatever's happened at the hotel, it's got nothing to do with us. So piss off and leave us alone.'

I don't even remember stepping out of the house. I just remember the door slamming behind me and being left with the knowledge that I had no idea what had just happened, but whatever it was, it made no sense at all.

Branlow Cottage

There was no one around when I got back to the hotel and no sign of any police car, which made me think (and hope) that Detective Chief Superintendent Locke must have left. It was just before midday, which seemed like a good time to call on Aiden MacNeil. I still had a certain dread of meeting him but knew I couldn't put it off any longer. I phoned Lawrence from the car, but it was Pauline who answered.

'Lawrence is in the garden,' she said. 'I'm sorry I couldn't see you yesterday. I wasn't feeling very well.'

'That's all right, Pauline. I'm just on my way to see Aiden.'

'Oh yes. He talked to the police this morning.'

'Is there any news?'

'Nothing.'

'I was just wondering if Lawrence spoke to him. He said he was going to mention that I might call in.'

'I don't know. Hold on a moment. I'll ask him.'

There was a click as she put the phone down and then, in the distance, her voice calling through the window: 'Daaaahling?' I waited about a minute and then she came back, slightly breathless. 'Yes. He's waiting to hear from you.'

'He doesn't mind?'

'Not at all. Anything that might help find Cecily ... '

That reassured me.

I walked through the hotel, passing Lars, who was sitting behind the reception desk reading a Danish football magazine called *Tipsbladet*. He didn't look up as I went past. I continued out the back, past the spa and swimming pool and along the gravel drive that led to Branlow Cottage.

Why were they pretending it was a cottage? What they had built was a solid, three-storey house standing in its own grounds, surrounded by a low wall and a gate. There was a swing in the garden and a partly deflated paddling pool. The Range Rover was parked in the drive. Walking past it with my feet crunching on the gravel, I had the strangest feeling of trepidation, even of fear. But I wasn't afraid of Aiden. I was thinking of Cecily, a daughter and a wife and a mother of a seven-year-old girl. She had gone for a walk in the Suffolk countryside and had never come back. Was there anything worse that could happen to anyone? When you live in the country, you spend every minute of the day surrounded by a vast emptiness. I could feel it now. But you never think for a minute that you might become part of it.

As I approached the front door it opened and Aiden came out, walking towards me. He had seen me from the window. He held out a hand. 'You must be Susan Ryeland.'

'Yes.'

'It's good timing. Roxie's out with Eloise. She's off school at the moment. Come on in.'

My first impressions of Aiden surprised me. He was a very handsome man, fair-haired, blue-eyed, in great shape. He was wearing a polo shirt, jeans and loafers. From what the Trehernes had told me, I knew he was thirty-two years old but he looked at least five years younger, with a Peter Pan quality that expressed itself even in the way he moved, light on his feet. I followed him into the kitchen and, without asking me, he flicked on the kettle. The house was very clean and orderly. There was nothing out of place on any of the surfaces.

'When did you arrive?' he asked. It was only when

he turned round that I saw the tiredness in his eyes, the worry lines. He hadn't been sleeping properly. He'd lost weight.

'Yesterday.' I didn't know how to begin. 'I'm very sorry,' I said. 'This must be awful for you.'

'Awful?' He half smiled as he considered the word. 'That doesn't even begin to describe it, if you want the truth, Susan. What's awful is that the fucking police think I had something to do with it. What's awful is that they've been here seven or eight times and they still don't have a fucking clue.'

There was a ragged quality to his voice. It was as if he was speaking with a bad sore throat.

'I know Detective Chief Superintendent Locke,' I said. 'He's a very thorough man.'

'Do you think so? If Detective Locke and his friends had been a bit more thorough to begin with, Cecily might have been home by now.'

I watched him make the tea. He did it with exactly the same taut, jerky movements that an alcoholic might use to pour himself a glass of Scotch and he talked all the while, even with his back to me.

'I called the police at eight o'clock on the evening she disappeared. That was a Wednesday. She should have been back at six to help put Roxana to bed and I rang her mobile a dozen times. No answer. I knew something was wrong but it was another hour before someone turned up – a pair of "community officers" – and even then they didn't take it seriously. Had we had an argument? Had she been depressed? It was only when the dog showed up at Woodbridge station two hours later that they began to take action. Her car was there too.'

'The Range Rover?'

'No. That's mine. She drives a Golf Estate.'

I noticed the present tense. Aiden hadn't hesitated. He thought she was still alive.

'What did Locke tell you today?' I asked.

'He told me nothing – which is exactly how much progress they've made.' He reached into the fridge and took out a carton of milk. He slammed it down on the counter, almost crumpling it. 'You have no idea what it's been like,' he said. 'They've taken her bank details, her medical records, photographs – there was one of us on our wedding day that was in all the newspapers. They had a hundred people searching around the River Deben. Nothing. And then we had reports. She'd been seen in London. She was in Norwich. She was in Amsterdam – although how she managed that when her passport was still upstairs, I don't know.'

He poured the milk.

'I'm told that the first seventy-two hours are the

ones that matter. People who were in the area are still there and they may remember things. You can still find evidence. Did you know that eighty per cent of all people who disappear are found forty kilometres from where they live?'

'I didn't know that.'

'Locke told me. He thought it would cheer me up. But they haven't found her and it's been over a week now.'

He brought the tea over and we sat facing each other, neither of us touching it. I wanted a cigarette but I knew Aiden didn't smoke. There was no smell in the house and his teeth were too white. I thought of what Andreas had said on FaceTime. *'Of course he did it. It's always the husband.'* Well, either Aiden MacNeil was the most brilliant actor I'd ever met or he was on the edge of a breakdown. I looked at him sitting hunched up opposite me. There wasn't a single part of him that was relaxed. He was a man torn apart.

'Your parents-in-law think that Cecily's disappearance may have something to do with a book she read,' I began.

He nodded. *'Atticus Pünd Takes the Case.* Yes. They told me.'

'Have you read it?'

'Yes.' There was a long pause. 'I was the one who

gave it to her. I told her to read it.' Suddenly he was angry. 'If it's true, if she's disappeared because of something in that book, then it's my fault. I wish I'd never heard of the bloody thing.'

'How did you hear of it?'

'One of the guests mentioned it to me. That's my job here, really. I talk to the guests. I keep them happy. Cecily manages everything and Lisa does the finances. I'm just PR.' He got up and went over to a sideboard, talking as he went. 'I met Alan Conway when he came here all those years ago but I had no idea that he was going to write a book about us. In fact, he told me quite specifically that he wouldn't ... the bastard. Then this guest started talking about it and said there was a hotel in the book called the Moonflower and of course we have a wing here with the same name. So I went out and got a copy and of course I saw at once that we were all in it. Lawrence and Pauline, Derek – the night manager – me ... '

He turned round and now he was holding a brand-new paperback copy. I recognised the cover with its silhouette of Atticus Pünd, the title in raised letters, 'THE *SUNDAY TIMES* BESTSELLER' printed proudly at the top. How many hours had I spent working on the look of the series? I remembered talking it through with production, telling them how we had to avoid the simple outlines and the pastel colours of a long-forgotten Enid Blyton England even if that was where these books were effectively set. There were plenty of publishers – the British Library Crime Classics, for example – who were already crowding out the front table at Waterstones with their vintage editions and we had to stand apart from them. Alan was an original, modern author, much more than an imitator of Dorothy L. Sayers or John Dickson Carr. That was the message I wanted to get across. After Alan died, when Orion Books bought the series, they'd rejacketed but they hadn't changed the design. It was still, largely, my work.

'Cecily read it. Did she say anything to you?'

'Very briefly. She said there was something strange about it and that it made her think maybe Stefan hadn't done it after all. The murder, I mean. But that's all she said to me, Susan. I would have asked her what she was going on about but we had issues at the hotel. Roxana wasn't sleeping. Lisa was being even more of a bitch than usual. There were all sorts of things happening and we just didn't have time to sit down and talk.'

We both sat staring at the tea, realising at the same time that we didn't want it. He got up and took a bottle of wine out of the fridge. He poured two glasses. 'I'm trying to hold it all together for Roxana,' he said. 'She doesn't really understand what's happening except that Mummy's gone away. How am I meant to explain this to her?' He took a gulp of wine.

I gave him a few moments for the alcohol to take its effect. Then I asked: 'Do you mind talking about the wedding? About you and Cecily?'

'Of course not. If it will help.'

'How did the two of you meet?'

'She'd come down to London because she was thinking about buying a flat. I'm actually from Glasgow myself. I was living there with my mum.'

'She came to the wedding.'

'Yes.'

'She hasn't come down now – to help?'

He shook his head. 'She has Alzheimer's. My sister, Jodie, looks after her. But I wouldn't want them here anyway. I've got Eloise. There's nothing they can do.'

'I'm sorry,' I said. 'Go on.'

'I moved south ... in about 2001, I think it was. I got a job as an estate agent and that was how I met Cecily. It was me who ended up showing her round a one-bedroom flat in Hoxton. It was great for getting to Suffolk but completely overpriced and there were problems with the roof. As it happened, it was my birthday that day and I couldn't wait to get out and go to the pub – I was meeting a bunch of friends – so I told her not to buy it and asked her to come with me instead.' He smiled at the memory. 'All my friends loved her. And they all knew we were made for each other.'

'How long after that did you get engaged?'

'Eighteen months. That was too quick for Pauline and Lawrence but we didn't want to hang around. They wanted me to come into the business and I was OK with that. What I was doing in London and what I'm doing here ... they're not so different. It's all about people.'

'So tell me about the actual day of the wedding. Everything that happened.'

The wine was helping. I don't know if Aiden was feeling more comfortable but I certainly was.

'I'll never forget it.' Aiden shook his head. 'Cecily always started the day by reading her horoscope in the newspaper. Well, on that Saturday it said prepare for ups and downs, which is the last thing you want to read on the day of your wedding and it really upset her. Of course, it turned out to be spot-on accurate. I shouldn't say this, but Lawrence and Pauline made a bloody stupid mistake keeping the hotel open. If they hadn't, everything would have been under control and at the end of the day Frank Parris wouldn't have been there and the whole thing would never have happened.'

'When did you meet him?'

'That was on Thursday afternoon, when he arrived. He'd booked a standard room and we'd put him in the Moonflower Wing. It was a perfectly nice room but he wasn't happy. He wanted something more traditional. So I managed to flip things round and put him in room twelve. That was where he was killed.'

'Describe him for me.'

Aiden considered. 'Fifty years old, curly grey hair, quite short. He was jet-lagged when he arrived and that made him a bit surly. But the next day he was friendlier.'

'You saw him twice?'

'I checked him in. And then Cecily and I met him on Friday lunchtime outside the hotel. He was just getting out of a taxi. He said that he was pleased with the new room and when he heard we were getting married, he couldn't have been nicer. He was quite camp. You could tell he was someone who liked to show off. If you'd told me he was going to be dead in just a few hours' time, I wouldn't have believed you. He was someone who was full of life.'

'Did he say what he'd been doing in Westleton?'

Aiden thought for a moment. 'No. I don't think so. He never mentioned Westleton to me, but he did say he was going to an opera in Snape Maltings that evening. It was something by Mozart. I don't know if he'd come specially for that. But people do drive for miles to come to Snape. Quite a few of them stay with us.'

'And you didn't see him again?'

'I might have. But if I did, I didn't notice him. As you can imagine, Susan, I had quite a lot on my plate.'

'There was a party on Friday night.'

'Friday evening. Yeah – that was Lawrence and Pauline. They wanted everyone to feel part of it. They're good people. The hotel's their family.' He glanced out of the window as if he had heard something. But there was still no sign of Roxana. 'The party began at about eight thirty and went on for about an hour.'

'Was Stefan there?'

'Yes. Everyone was there. Lionel, Derek, Stefan, Lisa ... No. Not Derek. But everyone else.'

'Did you talk to Stefan?'

Aiden frowned. 'Probably. I don't really remember. I don't think I spent very much time with him because he was on his way out anyway.'

'He was leaving?'

'Hasn't anyone told you? He'd been fired. Lisa didn't like him. She was convinced that he was stealing the petty cash – or something like that. Actually, she didn't need a reason to get rid of him. If Lisa doesn't like you, you're out. Everyone knows that. She doesn't like me very much if you want the truth, but that's probably because I'm married to her sister. She can't bear Cecily having something she hasn't got.'

I wondered why Lisa hadn't mentioned that she'd told Stefan to leave. What had she said over dinner? 'We should have fired him right at the start.' Maybe she was implying that she had, actually, fired him later, but it seemed to me that she had deliberately avoided mentioning it and that was strange. Apart from anything else, it made it more likely that he would have been tempted to steal from the guests, knowing that he no longer had a job. I'd have thought she would want me to know that.

'Did you see Frank Parris again?' I asked.

'No. I was with Cecily until eight thirty. Then we went to the party. Then we went to bed.'

A thought occurred to me. 'Shouldn't you have slept apart? On the night before your wedding?'

'Why would we want to do that? It was a traditional wedding in lots of ways. That was what Cecily wanted. But we didn't do a hen night or a stag night. And we certainly weren't going to sleep in separate rooms.'

I remembered something that Aiden had just told me. 'You said there were ups and downs. What exactly did you mean?'

'Well, the murder was a pretty big fucking down if you want the truth . . . '

'What were the others?'

'You really want to know? They didn't matter.'

'Everything matters. You never know what's going to be relevant.'

He sighed. 'Well, they were just little things. The sort of stuff that can happen at any wedding. First of all, the marquee was late. It didn't arrive until after lunch on the Friday and they had to work all afternoon to get it up. One of the bridesmaids got sick and had to cancel. Cecily thought that was bad luck. And then she got upset because she'd lost a pen that she was going to have with her when we got married in the rose garden.'

'A pen?'

'It belonged to her dad. He collects antique fountain pens. He never stopped going on about it on the day. He'd only just bought it from a dealer in Snape – it was brand new, unused. And it was blue.'

'I'm sorry?' I didn't get it.

'It was old but it was also new. It was borrowed and it was blue!'

'Of course.' I felt like an idiot.

'Anyway, she couldn't find it. Later on we thought Stefan might have nicked it, but there were other things too. A whole box of wine glasses got broken. The cake was wrong. Why am I even telling you this? It was a wedding just like any other.'

'Except someone got killed.'

'Yes.' That sobered him. 'It should have been the happiest day of my life,' he said. 'We got married at midday, in the garden. It wasn't a religious service; neither of us believes in God. Drinks started at about a quarter to one. And then just as we were sitting down for lunch, one of the hotel maids – a woman called Natasha Mälk – came out screaming that someone was dead and that was the end of it. That was the end of my wedding.' He emptied his glass, then pushed it away as if to indicate that he wasn't having any more. 'I loved Cecily more than you can begin to imagine. I still love her. She's smart and beautiful and she's considerate and she puts up with me. We have a wonderful daughter. And now this has happened and it's like my whole life has turned into a fucking nightmare.'

Just then, a car pulled up in the drive, a silver VW Golf Estate. I saw the nanny driving. Roxana was strapped into the back. The car stopped. The nanny got out and Bear, the golden retriever, jumped out too. This, of course, was the dog that had barked in the night. He must have been quite a puppy then. Now he was old, overweight and slow, bear-like in a meandering way.

'Do you mind if we pick this up another time?' Aiden asked.

'Of course.'

'How long are you planning to stay?'

It was a good question. I didn't really know. 'Perhaps another week,' I said.

'Thank you. Thank you for trying to help.'

So far I had done nothing.

I left Aiden MacNeil in the kitchen and showed myself out. As I opened the front door, Roxana ran past me, eager to see her father, not even noticing I was there. She was a very pretty girl with a dark complexion and deep brown eyes. He swept her into his arms.

'How's my girl?'

'Daddy!'

'Where have you been?'

'We went to the park. Has Mummy come home?'

'Not yet, baby. They're still looking ... '

Once outside, I found myself face to face with the nanny, Eloise, who was carrying a blanket and a picnic hamper. For a moment we stood there, unsure which one of us should get out of the other's way.

She was furious. In a way it was a repeat of what had happened that morning with Joanne Williams – yet this was different. The emotion coming from her was so strong, so pronounced, that I was actually quite shocked. And it was coming out of nowhere. The two of us hadn't even met. I have described Eloise as dark and slim, but she was also wraith-like, vengeful, like something out a Greek tragedy. Even on this bright summer's day, she was dressed in shades of grey. She had jet black hair with a silver-grey streak down one side; less Mary Poppins, more Cruella de Vil.

'Who are you?' she asked.

'I'm a friend of the family. I've been asked to help.'

'We don't need help. We just need to be left alone.' She had a French accent that belonged in an art-house film. Her eyes locked on to mine.

I brushed past her and walked back towards the hotel. When I was some distance away, I turned back to take a last look at the house. She was still there, standing on the doorstep, watching me, warning me not to come back.

Contacts

From: Craig Andrews <CAndrews13@aol.com>
Sent: 20 June 2016 at 14:03
To: Susan Ryeland <S.Ryeland@polydorus.co.gr>
Subject: RE: Stefan Codrescu

Hi Susan

Surprised to get your email. I see you're using a new email address. Is that in Greece? I was really sorry to hear what happened. Actually, what did happen? Everyone has got different stories. All I know is that I'm sad I don't see you any more. I used to enjoy our long sessions with Pringles and Prosecco!

Did you see my new book in the *ST* top ten?

Well, for one week only, but they can still put it on the cover. It's called *Marking Time*. (Yes – I know. Always 'Time' in the title, and it's the same character, Christopher Shaw … Hodder like to keep me in my comfort zone.)

Stefan Codrescu is being held at HMP Wayland, which is in Norfolk. If you want to meet him, you'll need to get his permission or perhaps you can talk to his brief. I checked him out on the Internet. Are you interested in the murder? I'd love to know what you're up to. Do give me a shout.

Look after yourself.

Craig

PS If you're in town and you need somewhere to stay, let me know. I'm on my own at the moment and there's plenty of room. X

★

Stefan Codrescu
HMP Wayland
Thompson Road
Griston
Thetford IP25 6RL
20 June 2016

Dear Stefan,

You and I have never met but my name is Susan Ryeland and I used to work in publishing. I was recently approached by Lawrence and Pauline Treherne who are the owners of Branlow Hall, where I understand you once worked. As you may have seen in the newspapers, their daughter, Cecily, has disappeared and they are very concerned. They think I may be able to help.

The reason they came to me is that my most famous writer was a man called Alan Conway and he wrote a book about Branlow Hall and what happened there eight years ago. Alan is now dead and I can't talk to him, but it seems there may be something in his book that is connected to Cecily Treherne. It may also be relevant to you and to your conviction.

I would very much like to meet you as soon as possible. As I understand it, I can only come to HMP Wayland if you put me on your visiting list. Would you be able to do that? If you want to reach me, you can call me on 07710 514444 or write to me at Branlow Hall.

I look forward to hearing from you.

Best wishes,

Susan Ryeland

★

From: Susan Ryeland <S.Ryeland@polydorus.co.gr>
Sent: 20 June 2016 at 14:18
To: James Taylor <JamesTaylor666!@gmail.com>
Subject: Alan Conway

Dear James

It's been a long time since we saw each other and I hope you haven't changed your email address. How are you? The last time we met was a very drunken dinner at the Crown in Framlingham and you told me you were going back to drama school. Did that ever happen? Should I have seen your name in lights by now?

You're probably wondering why I'm contacting you. It's a long story but somehow I've found myself involved with Alan Conway once again.

He wrote a book called *Atticus Pünd Takes the Case* – this was before the two of you became partners and, of course, before you turned up as Pünd's assistant! It seems that he may have based the book on a real-life story that took place in Suffolk, at a hotel called Branlow Hall. Did he ever mention that name to you? A man called Stefan Codrescu was arrested for murder but it's just possible that he wasn't the real culprit.

I know that Alan kept a lot of notes. I remember going through his study with you when I was looking for information about *Magpie Murders*. I'm assuming that you inherited all his notebooks and things when you took over Abbey Grange and although you may have put the whole lot in a skip, if you have kept anything, it might be helpful.

You can contact me on this email address or on my phone: 07710 514444. It would be good to see you anyway. I'm assuming you're in London. Right now I'm in Suffolk, but I can drop down any time.

Love,

Susan (Ryeland)

*

Fri 20 June, 14:30
Hi Lionel. I'm sending this
from Branlow Hall. Are
you still on this number?
Are you in the UK? Can we meet?
It's about Cecily Treherne.
Very important. Thanks.
Susan Ryeland.

*

From: Susan Ryeland <S.Ryeland@polydorus.co.gr>
Sent: 20 June 2016 at 14:38
To: Kate Leith <Kate@GordonLeith.com>
Subject: Alan Conway

Hi Katie

I'm back in the UK – briefly – and in Suffolk! Sorry I didn't have time to call or email. It was all very sudden. I'm afraid it's Alan Conway again. He won't leave me alone.

How are you? And Gordon, Jack, Daisy? It's been ages. You never did come to Crete!

How about dinner tonight or tomorrow (Saturday)? I can come over or you can come to me. I'm staying at Branlow Hall (free). Call or email.

Love

Susan xxx

*

Fri 20 June, 14:32
Hi Susan. Yes. I saw about
Cecily in the papers. Terrible.
Anything I can do to help.

I'm in London. Virgin Active
Barbican. Call or email:
LCorby@virginactive.co.uk
any time. All best. Lionel.

★

From: Susan Ryeland <S.Ryeland@polydorus.co.gr>
Sent: 20 June 2016 at 14:45
To: Lawrence Treherne <lawrence.treherne@
Branlow.com>
Subject: Cecily

Dear Lawrence

I hope you're OK and that Pauline is feeling better.

I met Aiden this morning and we had a good chat. I've also managed to track down Lionel Corby with the number you gave me. He's in London and I will probably go and see him tomorrow. We could talk over the phone but I think it's better to see him face to face.

While I'm away, I wonder if I could ask you a favour? Could you write everything that happened, from your perspective, on Thursday 14th, Friday 15th and Saturday 16th June? I.e. the wedding weekend. Did you talk to Frank Parris? Did you see or hear anything the night he was killed? I know this may be a lot to ask but the more people I talk to, the more complicated it all gets and it would be really helpful to have an overview.

Also, I hate to mention this, but I'd be very grateful if you could send me part or all of the payment we agreed. My partner, Andreas, is on his own in Crete and he may need to hire extra people to cover for me. I can give you his bank details if you want to send it electronically.

Thanks.

Susan

PS You said you'd let me have the name of the headmaster who moved out of room 12 when Alan Conway moved in. Did you manage to find it?

*

From: Kate Leith <Kate@GordonLeith.com>
Sent: 20 June 2016 at 15:03
To: Susan Ryeland <S.Ryeland@polydorus.co.gr>
Subject: RE: Alan Conway

Sue!
Can't believe your back and you didn't tell me. Yes. Come tonight – 7 or whenever. What are you doing

at Branlow Hall? Glad you're not paying – it's an arm and a leg.

Godron not here, I'm afraid. Working late as usual. Daisy also on her travels but Jack may grace us with an appearance.

Let me know if there's a problem. Otherwise I'll expect you around 7.

Can't wait to see you.

Katie xxxxx

*

From: Susan Ryeland <S.Ryeland@polydorus.co.gr>
Sent: 20 June 2016 at 15:20
To: Andreas Patakis <Andakis@polydorus.co.gr>
Subject: Missing you

My dearest Andreas
It feels funny to be emailing you. We never send each other emails … certainly not in the last two years (except that time when you disappeared in Athens and I was about to summon Interpol). But I'm sending out a whole raft of emails and this seems the easiest way.

First of all, I'm missing you. I really am. When I wake up in the morning, the first thing I notice is the empty bed. They've given me an absurd mountain of pillows but it's not the same. I've only been here a couple of days but it feels a long time already. I drove past Cloverleaf when I was in London (it's still in scaffolding) and I had this weird sense that I don't really belong here. I'm not sure where I am any more.

There's not much to tell you about Cecily Treherne. I met her husband, Aiden MacNeil, this morning and I liked him more than I thought I would. I'd certainly be surprised if he had anything to do with her disappearance. I wouldn't say he was in mourning exactly – but he looked quite exhausted. He's got a 7-year-old daughter and a nanny straight out of *The Omen*. And a dog who ought to be a witness as he was actually there, in his basket, on the night Frank Parris died. If only he could talk!

As far as I can see, the police have more or less given up looking for Cecily. DCS Locke is in charge of the case. He was also the detective who investigated Alan's murder and he was pretty useless then. So far we haven't spoken which is probably just as well as – you'll probably remember – we didn't get on.

As to what happened all those years ago, it feels as complicated as an Alan Conway novel but without the usual hints and tips from the author to help me solve it. And if it's true that Stefan Codrescu didn't do it, then once again it's missing the last chapter! I've found out where Stefan is in prison and I've written to him, though I don't know if he'll see me.

But I'm not writing to you about the murder.

It all happened very suddenly, the decision to come back to the UK and I know it's only supposed to be a week, but it has made me think a lot about us and the hotel and Crete. I do love you, Andreas, and I do want to be with you, but I'm beginning to worry that things aren't working between us ... not the way they used to.

We never have time to talk about anything except business and I sometimes wonder if we're running the hotel or if the hotel is running us. I've tried so hard to keep up my end of things but the two of us are working so hard that we never seem to have time for each other. And I have to be honest. I've spent my entire life in publishing. I've always loved everything about books ... manuscripts, editing, sales conferences, parties. I miss it. I just don't feel fulfilled.

God, that sounds awful. It's all about me! But it isn't. Really it's about us.

I just think we need to sit down and talk about what we're doing, why we're doing it and whether we actually want to go on doing it together. I even wonder how happy you really are at the Polydorus, especially when everything is going wrong. If we've made a mistake, we have to be brave enough to say so. The last thing we want is to end up blaming each other, but sometimes I think that's exactly where we're heading.

Anyway, I'll stop there. I'm off for dinner with Katie. Please don't be cross with me. I just wish things were as they used to be. I wish *Magpie Murders* had never happened. Bloody Alan Conway. It's all his fault.

All my love,
Susan

★

From: Susan Ryeland <S.Ryeland@polydorus.co.gr>
Sent: 20 June 2016 at 15:35
To: Michael Bealey <mbealeyt@orionbooks.com>
Subject: London/help

Michael
I know it's been a while but I'm back in London for

a few days and just wondering if there was anything doing at OB or Hachette? You may remember
you did approach me a couple of years back. We
had that nice lunch at the Wolseley and I was very
tempted ... that was before everything went awry!

Or maybe you've heard if there's anything
around? Senior editor? Commissioning editor?
Whatever.

Hope all's well. Nice to see you making money
out of Atticus Pünd – and with the original covers!

Susan X

Three Chimneys

Katie came bounding out of the house as I drove up in the MG and I guessed she must have been listening out for me. It had been two years since I had last seen her and she looked completely unchanged, happy to see me, relaxed. I got out and we embraced.

'You look wonderful. What an amazing tan. Oh my God, really, you look more Greek than English.'

I had brought her olive oil, honey, dried herbs from the village of Kritsa, up in the hills. She gathered them up and led me into the house and I had to admit that, almost for the first time since I had arrived in England, I actually felt welcome.

She had, of course, prepared a perfect meal, perfectly presented in her perfect kitchen. How did she do it? I'd emailed her at two thirty in the afternoon and this was the day she worked at the local garden centre, but even so she'd managed to conjure up a Moroccan chicken tagine with chickpeas, almonds and couscous served with a chilled rosé. I mean, come to my flat in Crouch End and you wouldn't have found even half of the ingredients. Cumin powder? Coriander leaves? Most of the jars on my spice rack had that sticky, dusty quality that comes from never being opened and you'd have had to root around in the fridge to find a vegetable that wasn't limp, bruised or withered – or all three.

Come to dinner with me and I'd have ordered takeaway, but although I'd offered to take us out to a pub or a restaurant in Woodbridge, she wouldn't hear of it.

'No. We can't talk properly in a restaurant and anyway, Jack will be home later. He'll want to see you.'

Jack was her twenty-one-year-old son, now in his first year at Bristol University. Daisy, nineteen, was on her gap year, helping refugees in northern France.

It's funny how close the two of us have always been, even though we're worlds apart. That was true even when we were children. We grew up together in a very ordinary house in north London. We went to the same school. We swapped clothes and made jokes about each other's boyfriends. But while Katie was completely happy, dreaming of the day when she would have a home and a lifestyle almost identical to the one our parents had foisted on us, I was escaping to my local library and my dreams were of a very different nature. I would join a gang at Jamaica Inn, preying on the wretched sailors who came too close. I would fall madly in love with Edward Rochester, but in my version of the story I would save him from the flames. I would travel to the lost city of Kôr and find immortality in the Pillar of Fire. We were the complete opposite of Cecily and Lisa Treherne, who had been two sisters at war, actually throwing knives. Katie and I had nothing in common except our fondness for each other and that had lasted throughout our lives.

There were times when I wished I was more like her. Katie's life was a model of comfort and orderliness: the two children now entering their twenties, the accountant husband who spent three nights a week in London but who was still devoted to her after a marriage that had lasted a quarter of a century, the part-time job, the close circle of friends, the community work … all the rest of it. I often thought of her as a smarter, more grown-up version of myself.

And yet I couldn't have lived in a house like this. I wouldn't even have bought a house that had a name. Numbers were good enough for the likes of me.

Three Chimneys was in a quiet crescent just outside Woodbridge and yes, it did have three chimneys, even if they were completely useless because all the fireplaces had been filled in with those gas-effect fires. Looking at all the polished surfaces, the sliding glass doors, the thick-pile carpets and tasteful art, I knew that if I had lived here I would have felt trapped, but Katie didn't seem to mind. She was a mother, a wife, a housewife. She liked to be defined.

Not that I would hold up my own, chaotic lifestyle as anything to be envied. My early love of books hadn't taken me to the places of my imagination. It had taken me into … books. I'd started as a junior editor at HarperCollins, then commissioning editor, then editorial director and finally Head of Fiction at a company that had, literally, gone up in flames. The publishing industry is full of idealists, people who love what they do, which is why so many of us are badly paid. I was lucky to buy a two-bedroom flat in Crouch End before prices went insane but I'd never paid off the mortgage, not until the day I sold it. I'd had plenty of relationships but they'd never lasted because I didn't want them to. At least Andreas had changed that.

So there we were. Two sisters looking at each other across a divide that had widened as we had grown older, far apart and yet close. We made judgements about each other, but perhaps those judgements told us more about ourselves.

'Do you think it's sensible, getting yourself involved in another murder enquiry?' Katie asked.

'I'll be more careful this time.'

'I hope so.'

'Anyway, I'm beginning to think the whole thing may be a waste of time.'

She was surprised. 'Why do you say that?'

'Because the more questions I ask, the more likely it seems to me that it was Stefan Codrescu who killed Frank Parris. All the evidence is stacked up against him, and as far as I can see there were only two people who had any motive, and I'm not even sure what that motive was.'

'Who are they?'

'Oh ... a couple who live in Westleton. Joanne and Martin. She was Frank's sister.'

Katie looked surprised. 'Joanne and Martin Williams?'

'Do you know them?'

'I met them once. I can't say I really liked them.' That was unusual. Katie always thought the best of everyone.

'Why was that?' I asked.

'It was nothing personal. They just weren't my type.' She saw that I wanted more and continued, reluctantly. 'She was a real ball-breaker. She dominated the table ... never let anyone get a word in edgeways. And he was a complete doormat. She walked all over him. She seemed to revel in it.'

That puzzled me. 'When did you last see them?' I asked.

'Oh ... it was ages ago. Maybe even before the murder. They were at a dinner and I only remember them because I joked about it afterwards. I didn't understand how two people like that could possibly stay married to each other!'

'And she was the one in control?'

'Absolutely.'

'It's strange because I saw them this morning and if anything, I'd say it was the other way round.' I put them out of my mind. 'It has to be Stefan,' I said. 'I mean ... blood on the pillow, blood in the shower, money under the mattress. He was even seen going into the room!'

'In that case, what happened to Cecily Treherne?'

'It could just be a coincidence. She could have fallen into the river. She could have gone for a swim and drowned. According to her sister, the marriage wasn't everything it was cracked up to be and she could have run off with somebody else.' Even as I said that, I knew it was impossible. She wouldn't have left her daughter behind.

'Will they still pay you if you don't get a result?'

That was something I hadn't considered. I reached for my cigarettes. 'Do you mind if I step outside? I want one of these.'

Katie gave me a sideways look. 'You said you were thinking of giving up.'

'I did think about it.'

'So what happened?'

'I decided not to.'

She passed me an ashtray. She'd known I was going to use it. Then she put a percolator of coffee, milk and two mugs on a tray and – unusually for her – two tumblers of whisky. 'Will you join me?' she asked.

'Just a small one. I'm driving.'

We went outside and sat at a wooden table beside the fish pond. It was a warm evening with a half-moon and a few stars. The garden looked beautiful, of course, filled with plants that Katie got at half price from her work. She had recently bought a statue of a leaping frog with water gushing out of its mouth and the sound of it only made the silence around us more profound. I noticed that one bush had died. It was very prominent, in a circular bed in the middle of the lawn. I wouldn't have been able to put a name to it – it was round and tightly cropped – but it was completely brown. For some reason, it troubled me. I would have thought Katie would have got rid of it the moment the first leaves began to droop.

I lit a cigarette and smoked peacefully, listening to the falling water.

'You are going back to Crete?' she asked.

Katie and I had no secrets from each other. We had talked about the hotel, the problems, my misgivings, while we ate.

'I don't know,' I said. 'I don't even know where I am with Andreas. Before we left England, he asked me to marry him.'

'You told me. You turned him down.'

'I said yes. But later on we both changed our minds. We didn't think marriage would suit us. I made him take the ring back. It was much more than he could afford anyway and we need every penny we can get.' I examined her over the tip of my cigarette. 'Sometimes I wish I could be more like you.'

'You know that's not true.' She looked away.

'No. I mean it. There are times when I just feel completely worn out. I don't know if I want to be with Andreas any more. I don't know what I want.'

'Listen to me, Susan. Forget this stupid murder investigation.' She had turned back and her eyes locked on to mine. 'Go back to Greece. You don't belong in England any more. Go back to Andreas.'

'Why do you say that?'

'Because he's a good man and you don't want to lose him. Honestly, I was so glad when you met him. I was the one who introduced you!'

'That's not true. It was Melissa ... '

'Well, you'd never have met him if I hadn't sent Jack and Daisy to Woodbridge School. Trust me. When you've got someone like Andreas in your life, you should count your blessings. But that's how you've always been. You're always thinking ahead, planning for the future. You never actually sit back and enjoy what you have.'

I was puzzled. I thought she was trying to tell me something quite different but she wasn't putting it into words. 'Katie, is everything all right?' I asked.

She sighed. 'Do you ever think about your age?' she asked.

'I try not to. Don't forget I'm two years older than you.'

'I know. But there are times when I can't stop myself.' She tried to make light of it. 'I hate the idea of getting old. I'm getting to the age when I look around me at this house, this garden and I think to myself ... is this it?'

'But it's everything you ever wanted, isn't it?'

'Yes. I suppose so. I've been lucky.'

A silence fell between us. For some reason it wasn't a very comfortable one.

'Did you tell Sajid Khan where to find me?' I'm not sure why I blurted the question out just then but it had been in the back of my mind ever since Lawrence and Pauline Treherne had turned up at the hotel. How had they found me? They had said that Khan had given them my address, but he didn't have it. Only Katie did.

'Sajid Khan? The solicitor?' I could see I had thrown her. 'He helped us when we had that unfair-dismissal thing at the garden centre and I see him now and then. But I don't think I said anything. Was he the one who got you into all this?'

'Apparently.'

'Well, I hope you're not blaming me. Maybe it was Gordon. He can't keep anything secret.'

Our conversation was interrupted by the sound of a motorbike pulling up. 'That's Jack,' Katie said. She sounded relieved.

A few moments later, Jack came through the garden gate, wearing a leather jacket and carrying a helmet. It was two years since I had seen him and I was a little thrown by his appearance. His hair was long and quite skanky. He hadn't shaved and the stubble didn't suit him. He came over and kissed me on both cheeks and I smelled alcohol and cigarette smoke on his breath. I was hardly in any position to judge him, but I was still surprised. He had never smoked in his teens. Looking at him, I thought a light had been switched off in his eyes. He seemed almost nervous, as if he hadn't expected to find me there.

'Hi, Susan,' he said.

'Hi, Jack. How are you?'

'I'm good. How's Crete?'

'It's OK.'

'Mum. Is there anything in the fridge?'

'There's some chicken. And you can finish the pasta if you like.'

'Thanks.' He half smiled at me. 'It's great to see you, Susan.'

And then he was gone, shuffling off towards the kitchen. I watched him leave, remembering the ten-year-old discovering *The Lord of the Rings*, the twelve-year-old shouting and laughing in the back of my new MG, the fifteen-year-old sweating over his GCSEs. Was this just part of the natural process of growing up or was I missing something?

Katie must have seen what I was thinking. 'It's all been a bit much for him, his first year at uni,' she said. 'When he comes home, all he wants is food, laundry and bed. But he'll be all right in a couple of weeks. He just needs a bit of TLC.'

'I'm surprised you let him buy a motorbike.' It was none of my business but I knew how much Katie must have hated the idea. She'd always worried – almost obsessively – about either of her children getting hurt.

She made a helpless gesture. 'He's twenty-one. He saved up for it himself. How was I going to stop him?' She put down her drink, somehow signalling that the evening was over. 'I'm sorry, Susan. I ought to go in and look after him.'

'That's OK. I'm going to London tomorrow. I've got an early start. Thanks for dinner.'

'It's been lovely to see you – but please think about what I said. Honestly, I don't think you're going to find Cecily Treherne. Maybe nobody will. And Frank Parris was killed a long time ago. You're better off out of it.'

We kissed and went our separate ways.

It was only as I drove away that I realised that the whole evening had been out of kilter, almost from the start. Katie had been trying too hard. It was as if the chicken tagine, the pink wine, the paper napkins and all the rest of it had been set out deliberately to distract me, that they were somehow fake... like the three chimneys on the roof.

I thought about the dead bush – the broom or the briar or whatever it was – sitting there untended in the middle of the lawn. And then I remembered the email she had sent me with no fewer than three typos. *Godron not here, I'm afraid.* Well, anyone can make mistakes. She had probably been in a hurry. But that wasn't Katie. She was always so precise.

Maybe I'd spent too much time playing detective, talking to people who seemed polite and pleasant on the face of it but who might turn out to be cold-blooded killers. But I couldn't help myself. I was sure Katie was hiding something. She wasn't telling me the truth.

Nightcaps

It was late when I got back to the hotel and I'd intended to go straight to bed, but coming in through the entrance hall, I noticed Aiden MacNeil, sitting on his own in the bar, and it was too good an opportunity to miss. I went in.

'Do you mind if I join you?'

I'd already sat down before he could answer but in fact he was pleased to see me. 'I'd be glad of the company,' he said.

The bar had the feel of a gentleman's club but a very empty one: we were the only guests, sitting there surrounded by leather armchairs, occasional tables, rugs and lots of wood panelling. A grandfather clock ticked in the corner, sonorously reminding us that it was twenty past ten. Aiden was wearing a cashmere jumper and jeans, moccasins but no socks. He had been cradling a tumbler of some colourless liquid that certainly wasn't water. I also noticed a paperback book, which he had turned face down. It was the copy of *Atticus Pünd Takes the Case* that he'd shown me earlier.

'What are you drinking?' I asked.

'Vodka.'

Lars was behind the bar. He and Inga seemed to be all over the hotel, like extras from *The Midwich Cuckoos*. 'I'll have a double whisky and another vodka for Mr MacNeil,' I said. I glanced at the book. 'Are you reading it?'

'Rereading it. For about the tenth time. I keep thinking that if Cecily found something in it then maybe I can find it too.'

'And?'

'Nothing. I don't usually read murder mysteries and I still think Alan Conway was a complete bastard, but I have to admit he knew how to tell a story. I like stories set in little communities where no one tells the truth. And it has some great twists – the ending has a real sucker punch ... at least it did the first time I read it. What I don't understand is why he had to be so fucking spiteful.'

'What do you mean?'

'Listen to this.' He had folded down the corner of

one of the pages. He opened it and began to read. ' "For all his faults, Algernon was well spoken. He had been educated at a small private school in West Kensington and he could be charming and witty when he wanted to be. With his fair hair cut short and his matinée-idol good looks, he was naturally attractive, particularly to older women who took him at face value and didn't make too many enquiries about his past. He still remembered buying his first suit on Savile Row. It had cost him much more than he could afford, but, like the car, it made a statement. When he walked into a room, people noticed him. When he talked, they listened." '

He put the book down.

'That's me,' he said. 'Algernon Marsh.'

'Do you think so?'

'He works as an estate agent. So did I. He looks like me. He's even got my initials. I don't know why he's got such a stupid name, though.'

He had a point. During the editing process I had urged Alan to change the name of Algernon, which I'd said sounded like something out of a Noël Coward play. 'Even Agatha Christie didn't have a character called Algernon,' I'd told him, but he hadn't listened, of course.

'Alan had a strange sense of humour,' I said. 'If it makes you feel any better, I turned up in one of his books too.'

'Really?'

'Yes. Sarah Lamb in *Gin & Cyanide*. Ryeland is a breed of sheep, apparently. She's a complete monster and she gets murdered near the end.' The drinks arrived. Aiden finished the one in front of him and went on to the next. 'Did you spend much time with Alan when he came here?'

'No.' Aiden shook his head. 'I met him twice: once when I helped sort out his new room and then again for about five minutes. I didn't terribly like him. He said he was a friend of Frank Parris and that he just wanted to know what had happened, but he was asking all these questions and right from the start I got the feeling he had another agenda. He spent more time with Lawrence and Pauline. And with Cecily. They were stupid to trust him because he went away and wrote a book about us.' He paused. 'How well did you know him?'

'I was his editor – but we were never close.'

'Are all writers like that? Stealing things from the world around them?'

'Every writer is different,' I said. 'But they don't steal, exactly. They absorb. It's such a strange profession, really, living in a sort of twilight between the world they belong to and the world they create. On the one hand, they're monstrous egotists. Self-confidence, self-examination, self-hatred even... but it's all about *self*. All those hours on their own! And yet at the same time, they're genuinely altruistic. All they want to do is please other people. I've often thought it must demand a sort of deficiency to be a writer. There's something missing in your life so you fill it with words. God knows, I couldn't do it, as much as I love reading. That's why I became an editor. I get all the rewards and the excitement of creating a new book but my job's more fun.'

I sipped my drink. Lars had given me a single malt from the Isle of Jura. I could taste the peat.

'Mind you, Alan Conway was like no writer I ever met,' I continued. 'He didn't like writing – or at least, he didn't like the books that had made him successful. He thought detective fiction was beneath him. That's one of the reasons he put you and this hotel into his novel. I think he enjoyed playing with you, turning you into Algernon, because to him the whole thing was just a game.'

'What were the other reasons?'

'I'll tell you, although I've never told anyone else. He was already running out of ideas. It was as simple as that. He actually stole the plot of his fourth book, *Night Comes Calling*, from someone he taught on a writers' course. I met them and I read their original manuscript. I think he came to Branlow Hall partly out of curiosity – he knew Frank Parris – but mainly because he was looking for inspiration for his next book.'

'But somehow he found out who the real killer was. At least, that was what Cecily believed. Isn't that what this is all about?'

I shook my head. 'I don't know, Aiden. He could have found something. But it's equally possible that he wrote it without even knowing what he was doing. When Cecily read the book, a word or a description could have stirred up a memory or triggered an association that only she knew about. I mean, if Alan had worked out that Stefan Codrescu hadn't killed Frank Parris, wouldn't he have told someone? It wouldn't have harmed his sales. It might even have helped them. What possible reason could he have had for keeping silent?'

'But in that case, what did Cecily read? And what's happened to her?'

I had no answer to that.

Behind the bar, Lars had been wiping a glass. He set it down and called out to us. 'Last orders in five minutes, Mr MacNeil.'

'That's OK, Lars. I think we're finished. You can start to close down now.'

'I haven't asked you about Cecily,' I said. This was

the conversation I was most nervous about but we seemed to be comfortable with each other and this had to be the right time. 'What happened on that last day ... '

'Wednesday.' He spoke the single word in a low voice, gazing into his drink, and I felt a distinct change in the atmosphere between us as I moved into painful territory.

'Do you mind talking about it?'

He hesitated. 'I've already gone over it, again and again, with the police. I don't see how it will help. It's got nothing to do with you.'

'That's true. And I know it's none of my business. But I'm worried about her too and if there's anything you can remember, any small detail, even if you think it's irrelevant, you never know ... '

'All right.' He called over to Lars. 'Lars – I'll have one more before you close.' He glanced at me. 'You?'

'No. I'm OK, thanks.'

He steeled himself. 'I don't really know what to tell you, Susan. It was a very ordinary day. I mean, that's the hell of it. It was just another Wednesday and I had absolutely no idea that my whole fucking life was about to be torn apart. That afternoon, Eloise took Roxie to the GP. It wasn't anything very important – just a tummy upset.'

'Tell me about Eloise.'

'What do you want to know?'

'How long has she been with you?'

'From the very start. She arrived after Roxie was born.'

'Roxana's a pretty name.'

'Yes. Cecily chose it.'

'So Eloise came to Suffolk the year after Frank Parris was killed?'

'That's right. Roxana was born in January 2009. She arrived a couple of months after that.'

'Was she in England at the time of the murder?'

'You don't think she had anything to do with it, do you? I'm sorry, but that's crazy. Eloise Radmani is from Marseille. She never knew Frank Parris. And actually how she got here is a very sad story. She was married. She met her husband in London – they were both students. But he died.'

'What of?'

'AIDS. He'd had a stomach ulcer and needed a blood transfusion. He was very unlucky. He died in France, but after that she decided to come back to England and joined a nanny agency.'

'Which agency?'

'Knightsbridge Knannies.' He spelled out the second word so that I would get the joke.

I didn't smile. I was still remembering the way Eloise had looked at me as I left the house – utterly vengeful. 'So on the day Cecily disappeared, she took Roxana to the doctor.'

'After lunch. Yes. I'd taken the dog out in the morning ... just round the grounds. It was Cecily's turn in the afternoon. She was in and out of the hotel during the day. We both were. It's not too far to go.'

'Did she talk about the book with you?'

'No.'

'Did you know that she'd sent a copy to her parents in the South of France?'

Aiden shook his head. 'The police asked me that,' he said. 'Pauline told them about the telephone call. Of course she did. I mean, was it really a coincidence that on the Tuesday she rings her parents to tell them about this stupid novel and the very next day—' He broke off and drank some of the vodka, the ice rattling against the side of the glass. 'For what it's worth, Detective Chief Superintendent Locke doesn't think there's any connection. His theory is that if Cecily was attacked, it was by someone completely random.'

'What do you think?'

'I don't know. But the answer to your question is – no, she didn't say anything about posting the book. Maybe she thought I wouldn't take her seriously. Or maybe it was because she knew I'd never had any time for Stefan Codrescu, so she didn't think I'd be interested.' He reached out and closed the book. 'It hurts me that she didn't confide in me. It makes me feel responsible.'

'When was the last time you saw her?' I asked.

'I don't know why you're asking me these questions. I don't understand what you want to know!' He stopped himself. 'I'm sorry. It's just very difficult.' He finished his drink just as Lars brought over the last one he had ordered. He took it gratefully, pouring the contents into the glass he had just emptied. 'The last time I saw her was about three o'clock in the afternoon,' he said. 'She took the VW. I went out about half an hour later in the Range Rover. I had to go over to Framlingham. I had a meeting with our solicitor, a man called Sajid Khan.'

It was funny the way Sajid Khan's name kept cropping up. He was Alan Conway's old solicitor. He had told the Trehernes where to find me. He was working for Martin and Joanne Williams. My sister, Katie, had used him. And now, on the day of Cecily's disappearance, Aiden was telling me he'd been to see him too.

'There were some papers to sign,' he went on. 'Nothing very important. And I had a few errands to run. Cecily had asked me to drop some clothes into the charity shop. She's a big supporter of EACH.'

'Each?'

'East Anglia's Children's Hospices. There isn't a branch in Woodbridge. I had to pick up a chair which we'd had reupholstered. I went to the supermarket too. I got home at fiveish. Maybe half past. I was surprised Cecily wasn't there. Inga was making Roxie her tea. She comes in and helps sometimes.'

'Where was Eloise?'

'She had the evening off.' He lifted his glass and emptied it. I did the same. 'When Cecily still hadn't got home at seven o'clock, I went looking for her in the hotel. Sometimes she'd work in the main office and lose track of the time. But she wasn't there. Nobody had seen her. I still wasn't too worried. I mean, this is Suffolk. Nothing much happens in Suffolk.'

Both Frank Parris and Alan Conway had been murdered in Suffolk, but I decided not to mention it.

'I rang a few of her friends. I tried calling Lisa but I couldn't get hold of her. I was thinking something might have happened to Bear. He's getting on a bit and sometimes he has trouble with his hips. Anyway, at eight o'clock, when I still hadn't heard from her, I made a decision and called the police.'

He fell silent. That had been when the long silence had begun.

I was trying to work out the timings. He'd left the

hotel at approximately half past three. He was back sometime after five; maybe as late as five thirty. Framlingham was about twenty minutes from Woodbridge. That felt about right for a couple of errands and a meeting.

'What time did you meet Sajid Khan?' I asked.

He gave me a peculiar look and I knew I'd asked one question too many. 'Why do you want to know?'

'I'm just trying to—'

But he didn't let me finish. 'You think I killed her, don't you?'

'No.' I denied it but I didn't sound convincing.

'Yes, you do. When did I leave? When was the last time I saw her? You think the police haven't asked me the same questions over and over again? Everyone thinks I killed her, the one woman who actually made me happy, and that's what they're going to think for the rest of my life. My daughter is going to grow up wondering if her daddy killed her mummy and I'm never going to be able to explain . . . '

He got unsteadily to his feet and I was shocked to see tears streaming down his cheeks.

'You have no right,' he continued hoarsely. 'You have no right at all. I don't mind getting it from the police. That's their job. But who are you? You're the one who caused all the trouble in the first place. You were the one who published the book – turning what happened here into some sort of entertainment. And now you come here like Sherlock Holmes or Atticus fucking Pünd asking me questions that have got nothing to do with you. If you can find something in the book, then get on with it. Do what you've been paid to do. But from now on, leave me alone!'

He left. I watched him weave his way out of the room. Behind me, Lars brought a metal shutter rattling down and crashing against the bar. Suddenly I was on my own.

Framlingham

I felt sorry for Aiden and worried that I'd gone too far. But that didn't stop me checking out his story the next day.

It was strange being back in Framlingham, the market town that Alan Conway had chosen as his home and where I had spent so much time immediately following his death. I parked on the main square opposite the Crown, where I had stayed and where I had enjoyed a remarkably drunken meal with James Taylor, Alan's partner. It reminded me that I still hadn't heard back from him and I wondered if he had received my email. I wanted to stretch my legs so I walked up the High Street, past the cemetery where Alan was buried. I thought about visiting his grave – I could see it between two yew trees – but decided against it. We'd always had a difficult, edgy relationship and if I'd gone to have a quiet chat at the gravestone there was every chance it would have turned into a quarrel.

Framlingham seemed quieter than ever. Despite its wonderful castle and surrounding countryside, it suffers from a strange midweek emptiness. It's hard to tell if the shops are open and frankly, it's hard to care. There's a country market every weekend but otherwise the main square is little more than a car park. The supermarket that Aiden had visited is right in the middle but hides away as if it knows how ugly it is and feels ashamed to be there.

The EACH charity shop was at the bottom end of the town, just along the road from an estate agent. It was quite small, occupying what must once have been a cottage, one of four identical buildings in a little terrace, but someone had imposed four large, modern windows in the front, completely divorcing it from its neighbours. I'm afraid I find charity shops quite dispiriting. There are so many of them and at the end of the day, each one is a reminder of a failed business and the general collapse of the High Street. But this one had a cheerful volunteer called Stavia, lots of books and toys and three racks of surprisingly high-end clothes. There was no one else in there apart from the two of us and

Stavia was keen to talk. In fact, once she'd started, it was hard to get her to stop.

'Aiden MacNeil? Yes, of course I remember him. I was here when he came in and afterwards I had to speak to the police. Isn't it awful, what's happened! You don't usually get that sort of thing in Suffolk, although there was that business in Earl Soham all those years ago and the death of that writer. Yes, Mr MacNeil came in that Wednesday afternoon. I saw him park his car on the other side of the road – just over there.

'He brought in four or five dresses, some jerseys, shirts. Some of them were quite old but there was a Burberry dress that had never been worn. It still had the label. We sold it almost at once for a hundred pounds, which is a lot more than we usually get for anything off the rail. The police wanted to know who bought it but I couldn't help them because they'd paid cash. They took her other clothes away – the ones we hadn't sold – and we never saw them again, which I think is a little unfair, although I suppose I can't complain, given the circumstances. Oh – and there were some men's clothes too. A jacket, some ties, an old shirt and a very nice waistcoat.'

'Did you talk to him?'

'Yes. We did have a chat. He was a very nice man,

very friendly. He told me he was going to pick up a chair. He'd had it resprung or something. He said that his wife was a big supporter of EACH and had donated quite a bit of money to our Treehouse Appeal. I can't believe he had anything to do with her disappearance. I mean, he couldn't have just stood here and chatted if he had, could he?'

'Do you remember what time he was here?'

'It was four o'clock. I know because I remember thinking that I only had half an hour until we closed and that was when he walked in. Why are you so interested in all this, by the way? Are you a journalist? I hope I'm not going to get into any trouble talking about it all ... '

I managed to reassure her and, partly out of guilt, spent five pounds on a Mexican pot with a cactus that turned out to be fake. I donated it to another charity shop on the way back to the car.

After that, I walked back up to the street with the mustard yellow building that housed Wesley & Khan Solicitors. It was two years since I had been there and I had a strange sense of déjà vu coming off the main road into what must have once been a private house. In fact, I was quite sure that it was the same bored girl sitting behind the reception desk: not only that, she might have been reading the same magazine. It was as if time had stood still. The potted plants were still half-dead. The atmosphere was as vacant as I remembered.

I had actually phoned ahead for an appointment this time and I was shown upstairs the moment I arrived, the uneven floorboards creaking under my feet. It struck me that there were two mysteries attached to the practice of Wesley & Khan. Who was Mr Wesley? Did he even exist? And how had a man like Khan, of proudly Indian ethnicity, managed to end up in a place like Framlingham? Suffolk is not racist. But it is fairly white.

Sajid Khan was exactly how I remembered him, dark and ebullient, with heavy eyebrows that almost met in the middle of his forehead, leaping up from behind his impressively large desk – fake antique – and bounding across the room to take my one proffered hand in both of his.

'My dear Ms Ryeland, what a pleasure to see you again! And staying at Branlow Hall, I understand! How very much like you to get yourself involved once again in Suffolk skulduggery.' He led me to a chair. 'Will you have some tea?'

'I'm fine, thank you.'

'I insist.' He pressed a key on his telephone. 'Tina, could you bring up tea for two?' He beamed at me. 'How is Crete?'

'It's lovely, thank you.'

'I have never been there. We normally go to Portugal for the summer. But if you're running a hotel, maybe we should give you a try.'

He sat down behind the desk. The photograph frame was still there, the one with the digital pictures sliding across the screen. I wondered if he had added new ones in the two years since I had been here. Looking at them, they seemed the same. His wife, his children, his wife and his children, him and his wife ... an endless merry-go-round of memories.

'That was an extraordinary business with Alan Conway,' he continued, more serious now. 'I never actually learned what happened, but I was led to believe that you were almost killed.' He raised an eyebrow and the other one went with it. 'Are you all right now?'

'Yes. I'm fine.'

'I haven't heard from the young man who was his partner for a while. James Taylor. He ended up with all the money, as I'm sure I don't need to remind you. The last I heard, he was in London, spending his way through his inheritance as fast as he could.' He smiled. 'So how can I help you this time round? You mentioned Cecily MacNeil on the telephone.'

It was the first time I had heard her called that. To everyone else she was Cecily Treherne, as if the marriage had never happened.

'Yes,' I said. 'Her parents came to see me in Crete. Strangely enough, Alan may be involved again. You know that he wrote a book partly based on what happened at Branlow Hall?'

'I know. I read it. And I may be completely obtuse but I never actually got the connection. It never occurred to me that he was writing about Branlow Hall. The book wasn't set in Suffolk, of course, and there wasn't any wedding or anything like that. It was somewhere in Devon.'

'Tawleigh-on-the-Water.'

'That's right. Nobody was mentioned in it by name.'

'He always changed the names. I think he was probably afraid of being sued.' It was time to get to the point. I was planning to drive to London and I wanted to be on my way. 'Lawrence and Pauline Treherne think that Cecily noticed something in the book and that it may be connected to her disappearance. Do you mind if I ask you a few questions?'

He spread his hands. 'Please fire away. I'm afraid I didn't help you very much last time. Perhaps this time I can do better.'

'OK. I want to start with Aiden. He came to see you on the day Cecily disappeared.'

'Yes. That's right.'

'Do you remember what time?'

Khan looked surprised at that, as if it wasn't something I should have asked. 'Five o'clock,' he said. 'It was a short meeting. A contract with a new supplier.' He paused. 'I hope you don't think that he had anything to do with his wife's disappearance.'

'Not exactly, no. But the day before she went missing, Cecily rang her parents. She believed she'd found new evidence about the murder of Frank Parris eight years before and she didn't tell Aiden—'

'I think I should stop you there, Ms Ryeland. First of all, Mr MacNeil is a client of this firm, and anyway, he had absolutely no reason whatsoever to murder Frank Parris, if that's what you're suggesting.'

The door opened and the young woman from the reception desk came in with two mugs of tea and a bowl of sugar on a tray. The mugs were white with the logo W&K printed on the side.

'What happened to Mr Wesley?' I asked as he passed one of them over.

'He retired.' Khan smiled at the girl. 'Thank you, Tina.'

I waited until she had gone, then continued more carefully. 'Were you here in Framlingham at the time of the murder?' I asked.

'Yes. I was. As a matter of fact, I spoke to Mr Parris. We had a brief conversation the day before he died.'

'Really?' That came as a surprise.

'Yes. I was asked to contact him on a personal matter. It was to do with an inheritance. I don't need to go into the details.'

'You were acting for Martin and Joanne Williams,' I said. I was bluffing, really. I remembered seeing his business card in their kitchen and knew he had to be referring to them. 'I went to Heath House,' I added. 'They explained it all to me.'

'How are they?'

'Very well. In fact, your ears should have been burning. They were very appreciative about what you did for them.' Now I was outright lying. Martin and Joanne hadn't told me anything very much. I just hoped that if I flattered Khan enough, I might draw some of the information out of him.

It worked. 'Well, in the end I didn't do very much for them,' he said, but in a way that suggested how pleased he was with himself. 'They told you about the house?'

'Yes.'

'The will was absolutely clear. Heath House was given fifty-fifty to the two children: Frank Parris and his sister. Just because Mr Parris had allowed them to live there, rent-free, since his mother's death, I'm afraid that did not constitute an agreement, oral or otherwise. At no point had Mr Parris relinquished his rights.'

I was trying to keep a poker face but in fact Khan had just provided me with a piece of information that might change everything. *'He had this idea of starting another agency and he wanted us to invest.'* That was what Martin had said, but he had been deliberately vague, borderline dishonest. Frank Parris had gone bust and he wanted his share of the house. That was the reason he had come to Suffolk. It might also be the reason why he was killed.

'They do love that house,' I said.

'Oh yes. Joanne grew up in it. It's a lovely place.'

Mrs Khan slid across the photograph frame, dressed in a swimming costume and holding a plastic spade.

'So you spoke to Frank Parris,' I went on.

'I called him on his mobile. This was on the Friday, just after he had visited his sister. He was planning to put the house on the market with Clarke's in Framlingham. I have to say that he was quite abrasive, but then I understand things hadn't gone well for him in Australia. I asked him to give Mr and Mrs Williams a little more time to come to terms with the move and, for that matter, to find somewhere else to live. In this, I was partially successful. He still wanted to contact Clarke's, but he agreed on a long exchange.'

'They must have been very upset.'

'Mrs Williams was not at all pleased.' He added a heaped spoonful of sugar to his tea.

I could easily imagine it. *'Piss off and leave us alone.'* I remembered her parting words. 'They can't have been too sorry when he was beaten to death,' I remarked. I'd learned what I needed to know. There was no need to mince my words.

Khan looked suitably pained. 'I'm not sure that's true. They were family and they were close. Mr and Mrs Williams had lived rent-free for ten years. They really had nothing to complain about.'

I hadn't drunk any of my tea but I didn't want it. I was wondering if Martin or Joanne had popped into Branlow Hall at the time of the murder and how I could find out. Frank Parris might have told them which room he was staying in, but if either of them had decided to kill him, they would have needed to know how to find it. I tried to imagine one or even both of them creeping round the hotel with a hammer, accidentally stepping on Bear's tail as they made their way along the corridor. Somehow, it felt unlikely. But there was nobody else with such an obvious motive.

'Thank you very much, Mr Khan,' I said. I got to my feet, ending the meeting.

He stood up too and we shook hands. 'How is your sister?' he asked.

'I saw her yesterday. She's very well, thank you.'

'I hope things have worked out with Wilcox,' he continued and then, seeing the look of surprise on my face: 'But perhaps the two of you didn't discuss it.'

'Discuss what?' I asked.

He smiled, trying to pretend that it was nothing very serious, but he had made a mistake and he knew it. He did his best to back-pedal. 'Oh, I just gave her some advice,' he said.

'Is she a client?'

The smile was still there, but faltering. 'You'd have to ask her that, Ms Ryeland. I'm sure you understand.'

If she wasn't his client, he could simply have said so.

I had known that something was wrong after the evening I'd spent with Katie. Was Jack in some sort of trouble? Did she have money problems? What was it that she hadn't told me? As I walked back to the car, Martin and Joanne Williams, Frank Parris, Branlow Court and even Cecily Treherne suddenly seemed less important.

My sister was in trouble. I needed to know why.

Martlesham Heath

I was on my way to London.

More emails had come in ... though nothing from Andreas. That didn't surprise me. He never responded very quickly at the best of times and he had a strange reticence when it came to matters that were personal or emotional. He needed time to think about things.

But James Taylor was thrilled I was back in the UK. We would be delighted to see me again and he would bring along anything he could find relating to *Atticus Pünd Takes the Case*. He suggested dinner at Le Caprice and I just hoped that he would be the one who picked up the bill. I had a meeting arranged with Lionel Corby at the gym where he now worked. And Michael Bealey had invited me for 'a quick drink' at Soho House in Greek Street.

Finally, I had called Craig Andrews. There was a possibility I might be in London for quite a few days and I wasn't too tempted by the comforts of the Premier Inn. In his original email, he had offered me a room and I remembered visiting him once in a handsome Victorian house off Ladbroke Grove. The money hadn't come from his books, incidentally, but from his former career in banking. The Christopher Shaw novels were solid, mid-list titles, nothing more, but they had given him the freedom to enjoy the money he had already made. Craig was more than pleased to put me up and it was good talking to him again on the phone, but why did I feel a pang of guilt as I hung up? It was ridiculous. All I was expecting was a spare room for a couple of nights and maybe supper and a shared bottle of wine.

I stopped off at Woodbridge before I hit the A12. I'd been just about presentable when I was at the hotel, and Katie, of course, hadn't cared what I looked like, but there was no way I was walking into Le Caprice – or, for that matter, Craig's house – in the clothes I'd brought with me. There were a couple of surprisingly good boutiques in the old square and I came away with a knee-length cocktail dress in midnight-blue velvet and a Ralph Lauren cotton jacket (25 per cent off). I'd spent much more than I'd intended, but I reminded myself of the money Lawrence owed me and just hoped it would arrive before my next credit card bill.

With the bags safely stowed away in the boot I was once again on my way south, but just a few miles outside Woodbridge I came to a roundabout and a sign for Martlesham Heath. On an impulse I hit the indicator and took the third exit. Like it or not – and the truth was, I didn't much – there was one encounter that had to take place. I couldn't put it off any longer.

The Suffolk Constabulary headquarters were based in a really ugly modern building about five minutes from the main road. It was a square block of concrete and plate glass that managed to avoid any architectural merit whatsoever. You had to ask what the people of Martlesham Heath had done to deserve this brutalism on one side of their village, along with the soaring horror that was the BT research centre spoiling the skyline on the other. I suppose, at the very least, both constructions provided them with jobs.

I went into the reception area and asked to speak with Detective Chief Superintendent Locke. No – I didn't have an appointment. What was it in connection with? The disappearance of Cecily Treherne. The uniformed officer looked doubtful but she made the call while I sat down on one of the plastic chairs provided and leafed through a copy of *Suffolk Life* that was five months out of date. I wasn't sure that Locke would see me, and the officer had given no indication that he had even answered the phone, so I was surprised when after just a few minutes he suddenly appeared, stepping out of a lift. He marched straight over to me with such determination that I wouldn't have been surprised if he had grabbed hold of me, put me under arrest and dragged me into a cell. That was his manner ... always on the edge of violence. It was as if he had caught something, some sort of virus perhaps, from the criminals he investigated. I knew he didn't like me. He'd made that clear the last time we met.

But when he spoke it was almost with amusement. 'Well, well, well. Ms Ryeland. I had a feeling it wasn't coincidence when I clocked you at the hotel. And when they told me you were here, why wasn't I surprised? All right, then. I can give you five minutes. There's an office down here where we can talk ... '

I had done him an injustice. He had noticed me when we passed in the reception area at Branlow Hall. He had just chosen not to acknowledge me. He led me into an empty, soulless room that was perfectly square, with a table and four chairs placed exactly in the middle. A window looked out onto the woodland that surrounded the building. He held the door for me, then closed it as I sat down.

'How are you?' he asked.

The question took me by surprise. 'I'm very well, thank you.'

'I heard what happened when you were here last time, investigating Alan Conway's death. You were almost killed.' He wagged his finger. 'I did warn you not to get involved.'

I couldn't remember him saying anything of the sort but I didn't argue.

'So, what are you doing back in Suffolk and at Branlow Hall? No. You don't need to tell me. I already had Aiden MacNeil on the phone complaining about you. It's funny, isn't it! I'd have said Alan Conway has already caused you enough grief, but you just can't leave him alone.'

'I'd have said he was the one who won't leave me alone, Detective Chief Superintendent.'

'He was a nasty little shit while he was alive and he's still a nasty little shit now that he's dead. Do you really believe he put something in his book? Another secret message . . . this time about Frank Parris?'

'Have you read it?' I asked.

'Yes.'

'And?'

Locke stretched out his legs and considered. It struck me that he was being unusually polite, friendly even. But then his argument had always been with Alan Conway, not with me, and with good reason. Alan had asked him for help with his research and in return had turned him into a vaguely comic character – Detective Inspector Raymond Chubb. Chubb and Locke. Get it? He had also created a grotesque parody of Locke's wife who had turned up in the second book, *No Rest for the Wicked*, although I had never met the real woman myself. Perhaps, with Alan's death, Locke had decided to forgive me for my part in all this. It might also have helped that his alter ego didn't make an appearance in *Atticus Pünd Takes the Case*.

'I thought it was the usual load of rubbish,' he said, calmly. 'You know my views on detective fiction.'

'You certainly expressed them very strongly.'

There was no need to remind me but he did. 'Who-dunnits written by the likes of Alan Conway have absolutely no bearing on real life and if the people who read them think otherwise, more fool them. There are no private detectives; not unless you want to spy on your teenage son or find out who your husband is screwing. And murders don't usually take place in thatched cottages or stately homes – or seaside villages, for that matter. *Atticus Pünd Takes the Case*! You tell me one thing in that book – one thing – that isn't complete rubbish. The Hollywood actress who buys a house in the middle of nowhere. That business with the diamond. The knife on the hall table. I mean – please! As soon as you see a knife on a table, you know it's going to end up in somebody's chest.'

'That's what Chekhov said.'

'I'm sorry?'

'The Russian playwright. He said that if you have a pistol on the wall in the first act, then it has to be fired in the second. He was explaining how every element in a story has to have a point.'

'Did he also say that the story has to be unbelievable and the ending completely ridiculous?'

'I take it you didn't guess it, then.'

'I didn't even try. I read the book because I thought it might have something to do with the disappearance of Cecily Treherne and as it turned out that was a total waste of my time.'

'It sold half a million copies worldwide.' I don't know why I was defending Alan Conway. Maybe I was just defending myself.

'Well, you know my thoughts on that, Ms Ryeland. You turn murder into a game and you ask people to join in. What's the police detective called in *Atticus Pünd*

Takes the Case? Hare. I suppose he's got that name because he's hare-brained. He's a complete idiot, isn't he? Never gets anything right.' He rapped a heavy knuckle on the table. 'You must be very proud of yourself. Half a million copies of infantile crap that trivialises crime and erodes faith in the rule of law.'

'You've made up your mind, but I think you've always been mistaken about crime fiction, Detective Chief Superintendent. Congratulations on the promotion, by the way. I don't think Alan's books ever did anyone any harm – except me. People enjoyed them and they knew perfectly well what they were getting when they read them. Not real life so much as an escape from it – and God knows we're all in need of that right now. Twenty-four-hour news. Fake news. Politicians calling each other liars when they aren't actually lying themselves. Maybe there's something a little comforting in a book that actually makes sense of the world in which it takes place and leads you to an absolute truth.'

He wasn't going to engage with me. 'Why are you here, Ms Ryeland?' he asked.

'If you mean why am I in Martlesham Heath, I was hoping you'd let me see the original police report into Stefan Codrescu. It was eight years ago so it can't be of any interest to anyone now. I'd like to see the forensic reports, the interrogations – all of it.'

He shook his head. 'That's not going to happen.'

'Why not?'

'Because it's confidential! It's police work. You really think we're going to release sensitive information to any member of the public who comes knocking at the door?'

'But suppose Stefan Codrescu didn't do it!'

That was when Locke's patience snapped and his voice took on a threatening tone.

'Listen to me,' he said. 'I was the one who led the investigation, so frankly what you just said is insulting. You weren't anywhere near when the murder happened. You just sat back and let your golden boy turn it into a fairy story. There is absolutely no doubt in my mind that Codrescu killed Frank Parris for the money that he needed to feed his gambling habit. He confessed as much in a room identical to this one just one floor above and his brief was sitting next to him all the time. There were no thumbscrews. No threats.

'Codrescu was a career criminal and it was madness having him in the hotel in the first place. If you're so interested in crime, let me tell you a story – a true story. Just one month before the murder at Branlow Hall, I was part of a team that closed down a Romanian gang operating in Ipswich. They were a charming bunch of people involved in begging, violent assaults and burglary. They were all graduates of a Romanian crime academy. I'm not kidding you. They even had their own textbooks, which taught them how to avoid electronic detection, how to hide their DNA. That sort of thing.

'Well, it turned out that their biggest earner was a brothel in the Ravenswood district and the youngest girl working there was fourteen years old. Fourteen! She'd been trafficked into the country and she was being forced to service three or four men a night. If she refused, they beat her and starved her. Now, is that something you think your readers would enjoy? The continued rape of a fourteen-year-old child? Maybe Atticus Pünd should have been sent out to investigate that one!'

'I don't understand why you're telling me this,' I said. 'Of course it's horrible, what you're describing. But was Stefan Codrescu involved?'

'No ... ' He stared at me as if I'd missed the point.

'Then what you're saying is, he must have killed Frank Parris because he was Romanian!'

Locke let out something close to a snarl and got to his feet so quickly that his chair would have toppled backwards if it hadn't been screwed to the floor. 'Just get out of here,' he said. 'And get out of Suffolk.'

'Actually, I'm driving to London.'

'That's good. Because if I get the impression that you're obstructing my investigation into the disappearance of Cecily Treherne, I will arrest you.'

I stood up. But I didn't leave yet. 'So what do you think has happened to Cecily?' I asked.

He stared at me. But then he answered. 'I don't know,' he said. 'My guess is that she's dead and that somebody may have killed her. Maybe it was her husband. Maybe they had an argument and he stuck a knife in her, although we haven't found a trace of her DNA on him or anywhere else it shouldn't be. Maybe it was that creepy guy who lives with his mother and works nights. Maybe he had a thing for her. Or maybe it was a complete stranger who just happened to be walking along the River Deben with an erection and a sick mind.

'We may never know. But I'll tell you one thing that it wasn't. It wasn't somebody who was named in a stupid detective story written eight years ago. So get that in your head and go back home. And stop asking questions. I won't warn you again.'

Lawrence Treherne

I stopped at a service station on the edge of London and picked up my emails. Still nothing from Andreas. A confirmation from James Taylor: seven thirty at Le Caprice. And a long note from Lawrence Treherne, which I read over a coffee and a croissant so stale and doughy that it bore no relation to anything you might ever buy in France. The email was very well timed. Here was a step-by-step account of what had happened at Branlow Hall, told from a single perspective. It was interesting to see how it connected with what I already knew. I could also use it as a reference when I met Lionel Corby the next morning.

This is what I read.

*

From: Lawrence Treherne <lawrence.treherne@
Branlow.com>
Sent: 21 June 2016 at 14:35
To: Susan Ryeland <S.Ryeland@polydorus.co.gr>
Subject: RE: Cecily

Dear Susan

You asked me about my memories of the wedding day. I'm writing this with assistance from my wife, although you will have to forgive the absence of any particular style, which is to say I am not much of a writer, I'm afraid. The story that Alan Conway wrote is very different from what happened at Branlow Hall in 2008 so I do wonder how any of this can be of very much use to you, but at the same time it can't hurt to have the facts set out, at least in so far as I remember them.

You might like to know how Aiden and my daughter met and I'll start there because I believe it is part of the story.

At the start of August 2005, Cecily was in London and she was thinking of leaving the hotel. As I may have already mentioned to you, and it pains me to say it, she and her sister had always had quite a difficult relationship. I don't want you to read anything into that. Two girls growing up together are always going to argue about music, clothes, boy-friends and things like that and my two were no exceptions. Lisa has always said that Cecily was our favourite but there's no truth in that. She was our first child and we loved them both equally.

At the time, the two of them were grown-up and they were working together at Branlow Hall. The idea was that they would take it off our hands eventually but the relationship wasn't working. There was a lot of tension between them and I'm not going to go into the details as it was nothing more than tittle-tattle, but the upshot was that Cecily decided to strike out on her own. She'd lived her whole life in Suffolk and she fancied having a crack at the big city. We offered to buy her a flat in London, which may sound extravagant but it was something we had been thinking about already. We liked going down to theatres and concerts and in the long run it would be more economical. So that was why she was there.

She found a place in east London that she liked the look of and Aiden was the estate agent who showed her round. They hit it off immediately. He was a couple of years younger than her but he was doing very well for himself. He'd already saved up enough money to buy himself a place on the Edg-

ware Road, near Marble Arch. Not bad for someone in their twenties, even if it was only one room.
While they were talking, Cecily discovered that it
was actually his birthday that day and she insisted
on going off with him and meeting his friends. That
was very much how Cecily behaved. She liked to
take the bull by the horns and she told me later that
she knew that the two of them were compatible
from the very start.

We met Aiden soon after and we liked him very
much. As a matter of fact, he did us a huge favour
because he was as keen to leave London as Cecily
had been to go there and he persuaded her to stay
at Branlow Hall. He didn't like the city and he didn't
think she would either, but they would keep his flat
as a useful bolt-hole if they needed to get away. But
as a matter of fact, after he arrived Cecily's relationship with Lisa got a lot better. It was two against
one, you see. Aiden gave her self-confidence.

I'm attaching a couple of photographs of Cecily,
by the way. You may have seen some of the pictures
in the newspapers but none of them did her justice.
She's a beautiful girl. She reminds me so much of
her mother at that age.

Aiden and Cecily moved into Branlow Cottage
six months before they got married. Lisa had been

living there but we persuaded her to move into a place we owned in Woodbridge. It made sense, particularly after Roxana was born. Aiden took over the PR side of the business. He did all the brochures, press releases, advertising, special events – and he did a very good job. It was about this time that Pauline and I realised that we could retire with a clear conscience. Lisa was doing a terrific job too. Despite what she said to you the other day, I don't think she disliked Aiden. I rather hoped he'd jolt her into getting married herself.

And so to the point of all this. June 15th 2008. The wedding weekend.

I've gone over every minute of it, starting on the Thursday, and all the problems that came our way. First off there was a bust-up over the phone with the contractors who were supposed to be delivering the marquee. Their lorry had broken down and they were going to be late, which is one of the poorest excuses I'd ever heard. It didn't come in until lunchtime on Friday and it was the devil's own work to get it up on time. Cecily was in a state because one of the bridesmaids had come down with bad flu and she'd managed to lose a pen which I'd lent her. It was a 1956 Montblanc 342 with a gold nib – a really lovely piece, in its original box and never been used. I was actually quite angry with her although I didn't say anything at the time. Anyway, I'd wanted her to have it because it was something old, something new, something borrowed, something blue.

Lisa was always convinced that Stefan must have taken the pen. He was in and out of the house carrying things and it was just sitting there on the table. I mentioned that to the police but it was never found. In the end, Cecily had to make do with two coins, one of Pauline's brooches and a ribbon.

What else? Cecily hadn't slept well all week. Last-minute nerves. I'd given her some diazepam. She didn't want to take it but Aiden and Pauline insisted as we didn't want her going down the aisle looking like a zombie! She needed to look her best and feel her best for the big day. At least we were lucky with the weather. Friday was absolutely glorious. The forecasters getting it right for a change. Our guests started arriving. The marquee finally went up. And we were all able to relax.

I wasn't there when Frank Parris booked in. That was on Thursday afternoon and I was at home in Southwold. I saw him very briefly early on Friday morning when I drove to the hotel. He was getting into a taxi. I caught sight of him wearing a light, fawn-coloured blazer and white trousers. He had curly silver hair, a bit like the boy in that painting by Millais, if you know what I mean. And the thing is I had an idea he was trouble even then. It's easy enough to say it after the event, but he was arguing with the driver who was a regular at the hotel, a very reliable man who was only a couple of minutes late, and I got the sense of a passing cloud. In my view, and I'm not afraid to say it, he and Alan Conway were two of a kind.

We had a party on Friday night. We wanted to thank the staff for all their hard work and of course they would be busy the next day so it seemed only fair. We had it out by the swimming pool. It was a lovely evening, perhaps a little too warm. There was sparkling wine, canapés, Pimm's. Cecily made a speech thanking everyone. It was very much appreciated.

I suppose you'll want to know who was there. Well, basically it was the entire staff, including Anton who was the chef, Lionel, Natasha, William (he looked after the grounds), Cecily, Aiden, Lisa, Pauline and myself and, of course, Stefan. I invited very few of the family, although I seem to remember that Pauline's brother was there. And Aiden's mother, who was very sweet, looked in for about ten minutes before she went to bed. This was meant to be a hotel event rather than part of the wedding. I could send you a complete list if you want it but there were about twenty-five people in all.

I need to tell you about Stefan and I might as well start by saying that despite everything that happened, I always liked him. I found him quiet, hard-working, polite and, at least as far as I could see, grateful for the opportunity we had given him. Cecily was exactly of my mind. As you know, she defended him quite passionately, at least to start with, and she was terribly disappointed when he confessed to the murder. It was only Lisa who had any doubts about him. She was convinced he was pilfering and it gives me no pleasure at all to ac-knowledge that in the end she was proved right. I wish now that we'd all listened to her sooner and got rid of Stefan but there's no point going over all that now.

In fact, Lisa and Stefan had met the day before – that was the Thursday – and she had given him his notice. So by the time he came to the pool party on Friday evening, Stefan knew that he was on his way out. We were giving him a generous pay-off – three months' wages – by the way, so he wasn't exactly going to starve, but even so it may well ex-plain what happened consequently. That evening he got quite drunk. Lionel, the spa manager, had to help him back to his room. Maybe he had already decided that he was going to make up for his loss of salary by stealing from the guests. I don't know. I don't know why Lisa had to take the action she did two days before the wedding. It could have been better timed.

One other thing about the party before I move on. Derek Endicott didn't come. He was in a strange mood that evening. I did try to talk to him but he seemed quite distracted, as if he'd had bad news. I should have mentioned this to you before but I'm only remembering it now as I write everything down. Pauline said he looked as if he'd seen a ghost!

Derek was on duty that night. Pauline and I went home at about half past ten. According to the police, Frank Parris was murdered sometime after midnight, attacked with a hammer in room 12, where he was staying. We knew nothing about that until later.

Pauline and I arrived at the hotel the following day, the day of our daughter's wedding, at ten o'clock. We had coffee and biscuits with the guests and the service took place in the rose garden, which is on the south side of the house, on the other side of the ha-ha. It took place at midday with the registrar from Suffolk County Council. Lunch was at twelve forty-five in the marquee with a hundred and ten guests arranged over eight tables. There was a fabulous menu. A Thai cashew and quinoa salad, then poached salmon and then a white peach frangipane galette. I was quite nervous because I had to make a speech and I've never been very comfortable with public speaking, but as things turned out I never said a word. Nobody did.

The moment I became aware that something was wrong was when I heard someone screaming outside the hotel. The sound was muffled by the canvas but it was still clear that something was very wrong. Then Helen came into the tent. Helen was our head of housekeeping. She was a very reliable, quiet woman and nothing would normally ruffle her feathers, but I could see at once that she was very upset. My first thought was that the hotel must be on fire because there was no earthly reason for her to come in otherwise. At first, she wouldn't tell me what was wrong. She asked me to come with her and although the first course was about to be served, I realised I had no choice.

Natasha was waiting outside and she was in a terrible state, as white as a sheet with tears running down her cheeks. She was the one who had found the body and it was an absolutely horrible sight. Frank Parris had been wearing his pyjamas. He was lying on the bed, not in it, with his head smashed in so that he was unrecognisable. There was blood everywhere as well as bits of bone and all the rest of it. Horrible. Helen had already called the police, which was exactly the right thing to do, but of course as you can imagine that signalled an immediate end to the wedding and sure enough, even as we spoke outside the marquee, I heard the first sirens heading our way from the A12.

It's almost impossible to describe what happened next. A perfect English wedding was turned, in a matter of minutes, into a total nightmare. Four police cars turned up in the end and we must have had a dozen or more officers and detectives and photographers and forensics swarming over the grounds. The first person to arrive on the scene was a detective inspector called Jane Cregan and I have to say she did a very good job taking charge. Some of the guests were coming out of the tent wondering what was going on and she made them all go inside and then went in and explained something of what had happened.

She was very sensitive to the situation, but the fact was the party was over and nobody was allowed to leave. One minute they were wedding guests, now they were either suspects or potential witnesses and the marquee had become a giant holding pen. The ones I felt most sorry for were Aiden and Cecily, of course. They had a room booked in London and a flight leaving the next day for their honeymoon in Antigua. I talked to Miss Cregan about them being allowed to go. They couldn't have had anything to do with the murder. Neither of them had even met Frank Parris. Well, briefly, the day before. But it didn't make any difference. We got the money back on our insurance in the end and they went to the Caribbean a couple of weeks later, but still, it was hardly a great start to married life.

Part of me still wishes that Natasha hadn't gone into room 12 until later in the day. Maybe Aiden and Cecily could have got away before the body was discovered. Natasha had started work at half past eight and she had gone past room 12 on her way to the Moonflower Wing. At the time, she was sure there had been a 'Do Not Disturb' notice on the door and she had decided to leave it until last. When she went back just after one o'clock, the sign wasn't there. It was actually found in a dustbin further down the corridor. It had been thrown away.

The police did wonder about that. Stefan Codrescu might have placed the sign on the door to disguise what he had done, but when you think about it, there wouldn't have been any point and why would he have taken it off again later? Later on he denied touching it, although the police found his fingerprints on it along with a tiny sample of Frank Parris's blood – so he was obviously lying.

To be honest, it's something I've often thought about and it still makes no sense. The sign was there at half past nine and at one o'clock it was in the bin. What possible explanation can there be? Did someone find the body and feel a need to hide it for three and a half hours? Did Stefan feel a need to go back into the room? In the end, the police decided that Natasha must have got it wrong. Unfortunately, you can't talk to her. She went back to Estonia and I have no idea where she is. I also heard that Helen died a couple of years ago. She had breast cancer. Perhaps DI Cregan can help.

As for Stefan, he had kept a low profile on the day of the wedding. He may have been nursing a hangover, but when I saw him he was sulky and in a bad mood. The toilet off the entrance hall had blocked and he had to deal with it, which wasn't particularly pleasant, but you might as well know that I felt duty-bound to tell the police that he

MOONFLOWER MURDERS · 205

looked as if he'd been awake half the night. His eyes were bleary with lack of sleep. He had a master key to all the rooms and so it would have been easy for him to enter room 12. And he looked exactly like someone who had just committed a horrible crime and was waiting for the axe to fall.

I hope this helps you. I'm still waiting to hear your thoughts on the book. As to your other request, if you would like to give me your partner's bank details, I would be happy to send you an advance on the sum that we agreed. Shall we say £2,500?

Best wishes

Lawrence Treherne

PS The name of the guest we moved out of room 12 was George Saunders. He had been the headmaster at Bromeswell Grove secondary school and had come to Suffolk for a reunion. LT

★

There were two photographs of Cecily attached, both taken on the day of her wedding.

Lawrence had described his daughter as beautiful and of course, as her father and on that particular day, what other word would he use? But it wasn't exactly true. She was wearing an ivory wedding dress with a locket of platinum or white gold engraved with a heart and an arrow and three stars. Her naturally blonde hair had been styled immaculately in a way that made me think of Grace Kelly and she was looking past the camera as if she had just caught sight of the perfect happiness that lay ahead and that was to be hers. And yet there was something inescapably ordinary about her. I really don't want to be cruel. She was an attractive woman. Everything about the photograph suggested to me that she was somebody I would like to have known and still hoped, faintly, to meet.

I suppose all I'm saying is that I could imagine her filling in her tax forms or doing the washing-up and the gardening, but not speeding round a series of hairpin bends in 1950s Monaco in an Aston Martin convertible.

I closed my laptop and walked back to the car. I still had to hit London and then take the North Circular Road all the way round to Ladbroke Grove. Craig Andrews had said he would be home by four to let me in and I wanted to shower and change clothes before dinner at Le Caprice.

I should have spent longer thinking about what I had read. Lawrence's email contained a great many of the answers to the puzzle. I just hadn't seen them yet.

Ladbroke Grove

W hen I was working as an editor, I liked to see
where my writers lived and worked. I wanted
to know what books they had on their shelves and the
art they had on their walls, whether their desks were
neat and orderly or a battlefield of notes and discarded
ideas. It always irritated me that my most successful
author, Alan Conway, never once invited me to the
sprawling folly that was Abbey Grange (he'd renamed
it after a Conan Doyle short story). I only saw it after
he was dead.

I'm not sure that we need to know the life story of
an author to appreciate his or her work. Take Charles
Dickens, for example. Does it add very much to our
enjoyment of *Oliver Twist* to know that he had himself
been a street urchin in London, working at a blacking

factory with a boy who happened to be called Fagin? Conversely, when we meet his female characters is it a distraction to recall how badly he treated his first wife? Literary festivals all over the country turn writers into performers and open doors into their private lives that, I often think, would be better left closed. In my view, it's more satisfying to learn about authors from the work they produce rather than the other way round.

But editing a book is a very different experience from just reading it. It's a collaboration, and I always saw it as my job to get inside my writer's head, to share something of the process of creativity. Books may be written in isolation, but their creators are to an extent defined by their surroundings and I always found that the more I knew about them, the more I could help them with what they were trying to achieve.

I'd visited Craig Andrews once when I was editing his first novel. He had a three-bedroom house on a quiet street with residential parking and lots of trees. He had converted the basement into a spacious kitchen and dining area with French windows opening onto a patio. The ground floor was given over to a study/library and a sitting room with a widescreen TV on the wall and an upright piano. The bedrooms were further up on two more floors. Craig had plenty of female friends but he had never been married so the taste was entirely his: expensive but restrained. There were books everywhere, hundreds of them on shelves that had been designed to fit into every nook and cranny, and it goes without saying that anyone who collects books can't be all bad. It might seem strange that someone whose work included graphic descriptions of gang violence and the lengths – or depths – to which women would go to smuggle drugs into jail should have a fondness for romantic poetry and French watercolours, but then it had always been the elegance of his writing – along with its authenticity – that I had admired.

I was the one who had discovered Craig. At least, I had believed the young agent who had recommended him to me and after I had read his manuscript I had snapped him up immediately with a two-book contract. His first novel came with the title *A Life Without Mirrors*, which was actually a rather marvellous quotation from Margaret Atwood: 'To live in prison is to live without mirrors. To live without mirrors is to live without the self.' It was also the first thing I changed. His book was well written but it wasn't literary fiction and Craig certainly wasn't interested in the sort of sales that, unfortunately, go with that territory. *Jail Time* may have been crasser, but it was short and sharp and looked good on the cover. As he'd told me in his email, he'd been doing time ever since.

He greeted me at the door, dressed in his trademark T-shirt and jeans with, I noticed, bare feet. I suppose anyone who has spent twenty years in banking has earned the right to go without a tie or socks. He was forty-four, I remembered from his biography. He looked younger. He belonged to a local gym and he used it. He had the sort of cover photograph that helped sell books.

'Susan! How great to see you.' A kiss on both cheeks. 'Let me help you with that bag. Come on in.'

He showed me up to a comfortable room on the top floor. It was built into the eaves with windows over-looking communal gardens at the back; certainly a step up from the Premier Inn. There was an en-suite bathroom with one of those showers that squirt water in every direction, and Craig suggested I might like to use it and change while he put on the kettle. We would both be out that evening. He was going to the theatre. I had dinner with James Taylor.

'I'll give you a spare set of keys and show you where the fridge is and after that you're on your own.'

It was good to see him again, a reminder of the life I had managed to mislay in the course of my involve-ment with Alan Conway. I unzipped my wheelie and pulled out my clothes, along with the purchases I'd made in Woodbridge. I'd transferred them to the case when I got out of the car; there was no way I was going to turn up on his doorstep looking as if I'd just been to the sales.

Even so, I was a little uncomfortable as I laid everything out on the bed. Part of it was a feeling I often get when I stay in other people's houses: a sense of crossing a line, of intrusion. It was one of the reasons I had decided against asking Katie to put me up. Had I really come here to save the cost of a couple of nights in a cheap hotel? No. That wasn't fair. Craig had invited me and I hadn't seen any reason not to accept. It would be more pleasant than being on my own.

But I had definitely felt a pang of guilt when I'd called him and now, glancing at my laptop, which was also on the bed, I knew why. I was engaged to Andreas. We might have postponed the wedding but we hadn't completely called it off. The diamond ring was back in the shop, but there were other diamond rings. So what was I doing in the home of a man I barely knew – moreover, a man who was wealthy, single and about my age? I hadn't mentioned any of this to Andreas. What would I have said if he had gone sneaking off to some Athenian lovely? How would I have felt?

Of course, I reminded myself, nothing was going to happen. Craig had never shown any interest in me, or the other way round. But it probably didn't help that even as these thoughts went through my head I was standing in his shower, enjoying, incidentally, the sort of water pressure that we had never been able to achieve in Crete. I felt exposed in every way. I wondered if I should FaceTime Andreas and tell him where I was. At least it would remove any hint of betrayal. I was on business. I was earning ten thousand pounds, which would all go into the hotel. With the time difference, it would be eight o'clock in Crete, dinner time for the guests even though the locals preferred to eat much later. Andreas might be helping out in the kitchen. He might be looking after the bar. He must have read my email by now! Why hadn't he FaceTimed me?

The laptop was still sitting there accusingly when I came out. I decided to give it another day before I emailed him again. Craig was waiting for me downstairs and it would be rude to keep him waiting too long. And maybe I didn't want to talk to Andreas. He was the one who needed to talk to me.

I put on the new cocktail dress and a pair of simple silver earrings I'd bought myself in Crete. A final dash of perfume on each wrist and I went downstairs.

'You look great.' Craig flicked off the kettle as I came into the kitchen and poured boiling water into a glass teapot with big, authentic-looking leaves. He had also changed, into a long-sleeved shirt. And he had socks on as well as shoes. 'It's white tea from Sri Lanka,' he continued. 'I was at the Galle festival last February.'

'How was it?'

'Wonderful. Except that any writers who upset them, they tend to throw in jail. I shouldn't have gone.' He brought two cups and saucers over to the table. 'And on the subject of jail, did you write to Stefan Codrescu?'

'I'm still waiting to hear from him.'

'So what's that about?'

I told him about the book that Alan had written, about Lawrence and Pauline Treherne and their visit to Crete, about Cecily's disappearance. I did my best to make it sound less like an adventure with me as the plucky heroine on the trail of a killer. Maybe I was thinking of what Richard Locke had said to me in Martlesham Heath. Cecily Treherne, a mother with a young child, could have been murdered while she was out walking her dog. There was no doubt that Frank Parris had been beaten to death eight years before. It was all too easy to trivialise these two events, to make them sound merely entertaining. That wasn't why I was here. I wasn't Atticus Pünd. My job, I explained, was to read the book and to see if I could find in it anything that might help.

'How well did you know Alan Conway?' Craig asked.

'Well, I published his first novel, the same as yours,' I said. 'You were a lot nicer, though.'

Craig smiled. 'Thanks.'

'I mean it. In the end I worked on nine of his novels and I loved them ... at least until I got to the end.'

'Are you going to tell me what happened?'

I had no choice. After all, I had accepted his hospitality. I told him everything, aware of the passing of time only from the fact that at some stage we moved on from white tea to white wine.

'That's an extraordinary story,' he said, when I had finally finished. 'Do you mind if I ask you something?'

'Go ahead.'

'You nearly got yourself killed while you were investigating. And now you're doing it a second time? You're suggesting that someone may have murdered Cecily because of what she knew. Couldn't the same thing happen to you?'

Katie had said exactly the same thing and I gave him the same reply. 'I'm being careful.'

But was it true? I'd had meetings with Aiden Mac-Neil, with Derek Endicott, with Lisa Treherne and with Martin and Joanne Williams. I'd been on my own with them and any one of them could have been lying to me. Any one of them could have beaten a man to death with a hammer. The nanny was creepy and even the detective was vaguely threatening. These certainly weren't the sort of people I should be mixing with, but how could I get anything out of them without trusting them, at least to some extent? Maybe I was putting myself in danger after all.

'Have you reread the book?' Craig asked.

'*Atticus Pünd Takes the Case?* Not yet. I thought I'd start it on Monday.'

'Here – you can have my copy if you like.' He went over to a bookshelf and returned with the new edition in his hand. 'Someone bought it for me, but I've still got the old edition upstairs. Unless you've already got one ... ?'

'No. I was going to buy it.'

'Then that'll save you.' He looked at his watch. 'I have to go,' he said. 'I may not see you later. The play doesn't finish until half ten.'

'Why don't you let me buy you dinner tomorrow night? I haven't asked you anything about your writing or your new publishers and all the rest of it. I take it you're not married or anything?'

'Good God, no!'

'Then let's go somewhere local. If you don't mind me staying a second night.'

'Not at all. I'd like that.'

He left ahead of me and it was only after he had gone that I realised what should have been obvious from the start. With his neat beard, his dark skin and his brown eyes, Craig reminded me very much of Andreas, several years younger and wealthier – in every respect in better shape. The thought was an unworthy one but it was true. I've always been attracted to a certain type of man and it occurred to me that if Andreas was the reality, Craig was the ideal.

But I was with Andreas.

I took an Uber into town. There would have been nowhere to park my MG so I'd left it in a car park near Ladbroke Grove station. It took me half an hour to get to Le Caprice.

And all the way I thought of Craig.

Le Caprice, London

The last time I'd had dinner with James Taylor, the two of us had got very drunk together and I was determined it wasn't going to happen again – certainly not at the sorts of prices you pay at Le Caprice. I'd only ever been there once – Charles Clover, my boss, took me for my birthday and that wasn't a relationship that had ended well. The food was great, but what I remember was everyone staring at me as I crossed the room. It's impossible to reach your table without being seen, which may be the point for half the people who eat there but it doesn't work for me. I prefer places that are more anonymous, where I don't feel I have to be on my best behaviour. I wondered why James had chosen it. It was certainly a step up from the Crown in Framlingham.

He was ten minutes late and I was beginning to think he was going to stand me up when he came bounding in, shown to our table by a waiter who seemed to know him well. It was two years since I had seen him and as he crossed the room I thought he looked exactly the same. The long hair, the baby face with its contradictory stubble, the eyes full of enjoyment and enthusiasm, though with just a hint of something sly around the corner ... I had taken an immediate liking to him when we'd first met at Abbey Grange and hoped I would feel the same now.

But as he sat down, apologising about the traffic, I saw that something wasn't quite right, that he looked tired, strained. He had been partying too late, drinking too much and possibly taking too many drugs – he had the classic looks of a sybarite, and if there was something Byronesque about him, I had to remind myself that Lord Byron was dead, killed by sepsis, at just thirty-six. He was dressed in the same black leather jacket and T-shirt that he had always favoured, although the brands were more expensive. As he raised a hand to order champagne, I noticed a gold bracelet and two rings that hadn't been there before.

'Susan, it was such a surprise to hear from you! Dinner's on me and I won't hear of any argument. How are you? I heard you got hurt when you were trying to find out who killed Alan. That's awful! It's hard to believe that he was actually murdered. I wonder what he would have thought of that! It probably helped sell the books.'

I relaxed. His appearance might have changed but James was still very much his old self. 'I don't think he'd have been too impressed,' I said. 'He didn't much like murder stories.'

'He'd have liked being in the newspapers. We often used to talk about how many inches he'd get. In his obituary, I mean!' He hooted with laughter, then grabbed the menu. 'I'm going to have scallops and steak and chips. I love the food here. And I want to hear everything that happened. Why was Alan killed, exactly? Who had he upset? And how did you get involved?'

'I'll tell you everything,' I said, thinking that I'd already gone through it all with Craig and was beginning to feel fed up with the whole thing. 'But first I want to hear about you and how you've been getting on. Are you acting in anything? The last time we met, you said you were going back to drama school.'

'I did apply to RADA and Central but they weren't interested in me. I'm probably too old and debauched. Anyway, my heart isn't really in it and I've got so much money now I don't need to work. Did you know that we sold Abbey Grange for two million quid? I don't know who'd pay that much to sit in a field in the middle of sodding Suffolk, but I'm not complaining. Alan's books are still selling and they keep sending me royalty cheques. It's like winning the lottery except it happens every six months.'

Alan Conway had been married. He'd had a child with his wife, Melissa, but six months after the publication of *Atticus Pünd Takes the Case*, he had come out as gay, the two of them had divorced and eventually she'd moved to Bradford-on-Avon in Wiltshire. For at least one year during their relationship, Alan had taken to using rent boys. He'd picked them up in London in the early days of the Internet, when cards in telephone boxes were slowly being phased out. My dinner companion had been one of them.

James had spared no details telling me about their time together – the sex, the surreptitious travel to France and the USA. I'd actually found his shamelessness quite endearing. Alan had employed James as his 'researcher' and I'm sure all the money he was paying – effectively for sex – he had claimed as a tax-deductible expense. After the divorce, James had moved in with him, although the twenty-year age gap hadn't made things easy for either of them. James Fraser, who turned up in the fourth novel as Pünd's sidekick, was based on him; a slightly kinder portrait than the one

Conway had inflicted on me. He had appeared in every book until the end.

We ordered our food. The champagne arrived and James told me about his new life in London. He had bought himself a flat in Kensington, which was where he had been living before. He travelled a lot. He'd had a series of affairs but now he was in a serious relationship with an older man, a jewellery designer. 'He's a bit like Alan, really. It's funny how you always end up going back for more of the same.' His partner, Ian, was encouraging him to settle down, to do something with his life, but he couldn't decide what.

'Did you know they're making the TV series of the first Atticus Pünd?' he told me.

'When do they start shooting?'

'They already have. They've got Sir Kenneth Branagh playing Atticus Pünd and I'm an executive producer!' He beamed with pleasure. 'I'm not in the first book, but if they make all of them, someone will end up playing me. I've suggested Ben Whishaw. What do you think?'

After the first course – and the food was delicious – I reluctantly steered the conversation back to Alan Conway. It was, after all, the whole point of the meeting. That meant giving him a quick rundown of everything that had happened since Crete. He had read about Cecily Treherne's disappearance in the papers but it hadn't made much of an impression on him. He was much more interested in Alan's involvement in the original murder and when I told him the name of the victim, he took me completely by surprise.

'I knew Frank Parris,' he said.

'How?'

'How do you think, darling? He fucked me ... quite a few times, as I recall.'

The tables at Le Caprice are quite close together and I noticed the couple eating next to us turn their heads.

'Where?'

'In London! He had a flat in Shepherd Market – not far from here, actually. I never liked having clients in my own space. I usually went to hotels. Nice and anonymous. But Frank wasn't in the closet. Far from it! He'd take you to restaurants and clubs and show you off to his friends before he took you home.'

'Why did he use rent boys?'

'Because he could! Frank had a taste for young boys and he could afford to pay for them. He wasn't into marriage and partners and all that ... or maybe he was but he never admitted it. Anyway, he was quite kinky. It might not have been easy to find a partner who wanted to do the sort of things he liked.'

'What sort of things?'

The words had slipped out before I could stop them but James wasn't embarrassed. 'Humiliation, mainly. Dressing up. A bit of bondage. I met quite a few men like that. Out to give you a bad time ... '

The people at the next table were listening with interest.

'How did Alan meet him?' I asked, deliberately lowering my voice and hoping he would do the same.

'I don't know exactly but it wouldn't have been difficult. There were plenty of bars in London, or it could have been in one of those Chariots places. You know – a bathhouse. We actually had a foursome once – me and Alan and Frank and Leo. I'm talking about dinner, by the way! Not what you think! I got the impression that Frank was Alan's spirit guide, if you like. Alan was still very unsure of himself, his sexuality, and Frank encouraged him along the way.'

'Who was Leo?'

'Another rent boy. Like me.' James still hadn't lowered his voice and I was aware of a certain hush at the other tables around us. I'm sure this wasn't the usual sort of conversation you'd hear at Le Caprice. 'A lot of us knew each other,' he went on. 'We didn't exactly socialise, but it helped to know if there were any weirdos out there ... pretty policemen, that sort of thing.'

'Were you living with Alan at the time Frank was murdered?'

'No. Not yet. Although we were seeing quite a bit of each other and Alan was already talking about us moving in together. We were actually away when it happened. We heard the news on the radio.' He thought back. 'I have to say, I was quite shocked. I mean, if Frank had been hammered to death in his London flat or in a backstreet in Soho, you wouldn't have blinked. It would have just gone with the territory – particularly with his predilections. But in a posh hotel in the middle of the country ... !'

'Was Alan upset?'

That was more difficult to answer. 'I wouldn't say he was upset. No. But he was intrigued. He was on a book tour in Europe. You probably remember. Alan hated touring. That was the funny thing about him. He hated the people who loved his books. We were in France and Holland and Germany, and after it was all over he rented a villa in Tuscany for three weeks, up in the hills. It was a beautiful place.'

'So when did he hear about the death?'

'I heard about it on the radio and I told him. Anyway, he went round to the hotel almost as soon as we got back – not because he gave a toss about Frank Parris, but because he thought he might be able to use it in his next book.'

The second course came. Steak for James, Dover sole for me. As I watched the waiter expertly slicing away with two knives, it occurred to me that in a way he and I were doing exactly the same thing: separating the flesh to find the bones underneath. The only difference was that he would discard them. I needed them to make sense of what had happened.

'The thing is that Alan was stuck,' James went on. 'He was in a foul mood in Tuscany. The first two books had done brilliantly. He was already well known and the money was pouring in. Well, of course, you'd know that, wouldn't you. It was mainly thanks to you. But the third book wouldn't come.'

'Not until he visited Branlow Hall.'

'That's right. He actually took a room and stayed there a couple of nights, although there was hardly any need as he only lived twenty minutes away and he was quite nervous he was going to run into Melissa.'

'Why?' I was puzzled. 'I thought she'd moved to Bradford-on-Avon.'

'No. That was later. After they split up and sold their house in Orford, she wanted to stay close for a while. I don't know why. Maybe she just needed time to work things out. So she rented a house that was actually right next to the hotel. In fact, there was a gate at the bottom of her garden and it led into the grounds.'

So Melissa had been on the scene too! I filed the information away for later.

'That never happened, thank goodness,' James went on. 'You have to remember that she knew he was gay but nobody else did. He hadn't come out yet and he hadn't told anyone about me! Did you know about him?'

'No! I only found out when I read about it in the newspapers.'

'Well, that was Alan for you. Anyway, he spent three or four days there and I knew he'd got the story for his book because when he came back he was in a great mood and he said he'd spoken to loads of people and knew what he was going to write.'

My ears pricked up at that. 'Do you know who he spoke to?'

'Everyone!' When James had come in, he had been carrying a plastic shopping bag that he had dumped on the floor, under the table. Now he picked it up and showed it to me. 'I've brought everything I could find. There are photographs, notes, memory sticks ... some of them with recordings. There may be more stuff at the house. If I find anything else, I'll let you know.'

'That's fantastic, James. Thank you.' I was actually very surprised. 'I didn't think you'd have kept his old papers.'

James nodded. 'I wasn't going to,' he said. 'When I sold the house I was going to chuck it all out. You have no idea how much of it there was. For a start there were hundreds of books. Nine titles in thirty languages!'

'Thirty-four,' I corrected him.

'What was I going to do with Atticus Pünd in Japanese? And then there were the manuscripts, the proof copies, the notepads, all the different drafts. I actually had someone coming in a van from Ipswich to take it all to the local dump. But then two things happened. First of all, I got a call from some university in America. They said they were very sorry to hear of Alan's death and that they were interested in acquiring his archive. Note the word "acquiring"! They didn't say they would pay, at least not in so many words, but they did make it clear that all his old manuscripts and all the rest of it had a value.

'And then – this was before probate came through and I was very short of cash – I decided to sell some of Alan's books. I chose some of his Agatha Christies. He had the whole lot, you know. So I took a handful into a second-hand bookshop in Felixstowe and I was very lucky that the owner was honest because he told me that they were all first editions and they were worth a small fortune! The one about Roger Ackroyd was worth two thousand on its own. And there was me expecting to get enough money for fish and chips … and I'm not talking about the sort of fish and chips you get here!'

'So you've still got everything,' I said.

'I've told the university to make an offer. I'm still waiting. But I kept everything else – the whole lot of it! I was meaning to go through it all and work out what was what, but I'm a lazy bastard and I still haven't got round to it. Anyway, after you rang, I pulled out everything I could find relating to *Atticus Pünd Takes the Case*. That was the right book, wasn't it?'

'Yes.'

'You're lucky that everything is labelled. Alan was like that. If anyone wrote anything about him in the newspapers, he cut it out and stuck it in a book. He was quite an expert on himself.' He laughed gleefully. 'I'd like to have it all back, if you don't mind. You might be looking at my old age pension.'

It was hard to imagine James Taylor ever being old.

'Did he talk to you about the murder?'

'Alan never talked to me about his books, even when he put me in them. But, like I say, he was in a much better mood when he came home and I'll tell you one thing he did say: "*They've got the wrong man.*" He was quite smug about it.'

'He was talking about Stefan Codrescu.'

'I don't know who that is.'

'He was the man who was arrested.'

'Well, I think that's exactly what Alan meant. He actually knew the detective in charge of the investigation and he was quite convinced he'd ballsed it all up.'

'But he didn't tell you who the killer was.'

'No. I'm sorry.'

'You'd have thought if he really knew who murdered Frank Parris, he'd have said. Especially since Frank was his friend.'

James grimaced. 'That's not necessarily true. I was fond of Alan, but he could be a complete tosser. He was one of the most selfish men I've ever met. I don't think he gave a damn about Frank Parris or whoever killed him.' He prodded his fork in my direction. 'Anyway, it's quite possible he didn't know. Do you?'

'No,' I admitted.

'But you'll find out.' He smiled. 'I must say, Susan, it is funny the two of us here, together again. And the ghost of Alan still hovering over us. I wonder if he'll ever leave us alone?' He picked up his glass. 'To Alan!'

We clinked glasses.

But I didn't drink.

Cecily Treherne

It was late when I got back to Ladbroke Grove but there was no way I was going to sleep. I upended the plastic bag that James had given me and allowed the contents to spill out onto the bed. There was a full typescript of *Atticus Pünd Takes the Case* with annotations in the margins, the whole thing bound in a plastic cover, several notebooks, half a dozen photographs, some drawings, newspaper clippings about the murder at Branlow Hall, including the pieces from the *East Anglian Daily Times* I had already read, various computer printouts and three memory sticks. Looking at this collection, I was quite certain that the answers I was looking for must be in front of me. Who had killed Frank Parris and where was Cecily Treherne? This was evidence that even the police hadn't seen. But where was I to begin?

The manuscript was, as far as I could see, a second draft and it might have been of interest to a keen-eyed archivist. For example, the first sentence of the book originally read: *Tawleigh-on-the-Water was a tiny village that consisted of little more than a harbour and two narrow streets surrounded by no fewer than four different stretches of water.* Alan had circled three words, *tiny*, *little* and *narrow*, and I would have done the same. There are just too many descriptions relating to smallness in one sentence. He then crossed out the whole paragraph and used it later on in the first chapter, opening it instead in the kitchen of Clarence Keep, or Clarence Court, as it was originally called.

And so on. There was nothing here that would have been of any interest to the world at large and it certainly had no relevance to the murder.

The notebooks were similarly academic. I recognised Alan's neat, cramped handwriting, the pale blue ink that he favoured. There were dozens of pages filled with questions, ideas, crossings-out, arrows.

Algernon knows about will.
Blackmails him?
Jason had one-night stand with Nancy.
£60
Knickers stolen from drawer.

Some of the names would change but most of these ideas would turn up in one form or another. He had drawn detailed floor plans of Branlow Hall, which he had used as the basis of the Moonflower Hotel in his book, simply lifting it up brick by brick and depositing it in Devon. As with all of his books, the village where the crime takes place does not really exist, but looking at the maps, he seemed to have imagined it somewhere just down the coast from Appledore.

The computer printouts mainly came from the writer's best friend, Wikipedia, and included articles about famous diamonds, cinema in the UK, the growth of St-Tropez, the Homicide Act of 21 March 1957, and other plot strands that I recognised from the novel.

One of the memory sticks contained images of the people he had met. I recognised Lawrence and Pauline Treherne, Lisa and Cecily, Aiden MacNeil and Derek. Another picture showed a short, stocky woman with cropped hair and narrow eyes wearing a black dress and a white apron. I assumed this must be Natasha Mälk, the Estonian maid who had found the body. Another man – possibly Lionel Corby – had been snapped posing outside the spa. There were also pictures of the building: room 12, the stable block, the bar, the lawn

where the wedding had taken place. It gave me an uneasy feeling to recognise that, from the very start, I had
been following in his footsteps.

James had added one old-fashioned photograph, actually printed on paper, and it caught my eye at once
because Alan was in it. He was sitting between two
people in what looked like an expensive restaurant,
possibly in London. A very much younger James was
on one side. A man with curly grey hair and a deep sun-
tan, dressed in a velvet jacket, was on the other. This
had to be Frank Parris. Had James been with Frank or
with Alan that night? It was hard to be sure. The three
of them were close together, smiling.

I had assumed that the picture must have been taken
by a waiter, but looking at it more closely, I realised
that the camera was too low and too close. The table
was laid for four and it was being held by the fourth
member of the group. Could this have been Leo, the
rent boy James had mentioned? Two men and two
boys. It seemed quite possible.

Downstairs, I heard the front door open and close.
Craig had got back from the theatre. I had only put on
one bedside lamp and had drawn the curtains before I
sat down, and it was when I found myself staying quite
still and holding my breath that I realised I had done

all this quite deliberately, so that no light would escape and there was no chance that I would be disturbed. I waited as Craig climbed the stairs. I heard a second door open and close. I let out a breath.

I turned my attention to the other memory sticks. I plugged the second one into my laptop. It contained interviews with Lawrence, with Pauline and with Lisa. Those weren't the ones I was interested in, not right now. I took the last one and plugged it in. And there it was – exactly what I had hoped for.

Cecily Treherne.

I'd brought headphones and, feeling quite nervous, I plugged them in. I didn't know if Cecily was dead or alive, but she was the reason I was here and I had felt her ghost hovering over me from the moment I had arrived in Suffolk. Did I actually want to hear her voice? There was something quite macabre in the thought that this might be all that remained of her. For that matter, it had been quite a few years since I had heard Alan Conway and I certainly had no desire to commune with him beyond the grave. But this was the interview I most needed to hear. There was no way I was going to wait until the morning.

I moved the cursor and hit PLAY.

There was a brief pause and then I heard them. It

was a shame that video cameras wouldn't be introduced into smart phones for another few years because
I would have loved to have seen them too. What was
Cecily wearing? What did she look like, even, when
she moved? And where were they? Somewhere inside
the hotel from the sounds of it, but it was impossible to
be sure.

Alan was on his best behaviour. I almost smiled,
recognising the slightly smarmy quality to his voice.
He could be ingratiating when he wanted to be, as I
knew from experience, although in my case it had always been followed by a series of complaints or an un-
reasonable demand. It didn't bother me that I couldn't
see him. Nearly all of my conversations with him had
been over the telephone and this was how I knew him.
With Cecily it was different. For the first time, she had
half come to life – though only half. She had a similar
voice to her sister, Lisa. She sounded like a nice person,
warm and relaxed.

It was hard to believe that the conversation had taken
place eight years ago. The voices were perfectly pre-
served and it suddenly struck me that when my parents
died, the first memory that I'd lost had been what they
sounded like. That would never happen again. Modern
technology has changed the nature of death.

ALAN: Hello, Mrs MacNeil. Thank you for talking to me.

CECILY: I'm still not used to being called that. Please, call me Cecily.

ALAN: Ah yes. Of course. How was the honeymoon?

CECILY: Well, obviously it was quite difficult, at first, after what happened. It was two weeks late. But we stayed at a lovely hotel. Have you ever been to Antigua?

ALAN: No.

CECILY: Nelson's Bay. We both needed a holiday, that's for sure.

ALAN: Well, you've managed to get a fantastic tan.

CECILY: Thank you.

ALAN: I don't want to take up too much of your time.

CECILY: That's OK. Everything's very quiet today. How's your room?

ALAN: It's very nice. This is a lovely hotel.

CECILY: Yes.

ALAN: By the way, did you know that my ex-wife is renting a property from you?

CECILY: Which property?

ALAN: Oaklands.

CECILY: Melissa! I didn't know the two of you ...

ALAN: We separated last year.

CECILY: Oh. I'm sorry. We've chatted once or twice. I sometimes see her in the spa.

ALAN: Don't worry. It was all very amicable and I'm just glad that she's happy here. I hope it doesn't upset you, talking about what happened.

CECILY: No. It's been more than a month now and we've had room twelve cleaned out. A lot of bad things happen in hotels ... it's like in that film, *The Shining*. I don't know if you ever saw it? I hardly met Frank Parris and fortunately I didn't see into the room, so it doesn't bother me too much. I'm sorry. I don't mean to be dismissive. I know he was your friend.

ALAN: I hadn't seen him for a while. We met in London.

CECILY: And you live in Framlingham now?

ALAN: Yes.

CECILY: Aiden tells me you're a writer.

ALAN: Yes. I've had two books published. *Atticus Pünd Investigates* and *No Rest for the Wicked*.

CECILY: I'm afraid I haven't read them. I never have time to read very much.

ALAN: They've done quite well.

CECILY: Are you going to write about us?

ALAN: That's not my plan. As I explained to your

parents, I just want to know what happened.
Frank was very kind to me when I was trying to
work things out and I feel I owe it to him.

CECILY: I'd just feel very uncomfortable being in a
book.

ALAN: I never put people in my books and certainly
not without their permission. And I don't write
true crime.

CECILY: Well, I suppose that's all right, then.

ALAN: Anyway, I understand the police have made
an arrest.

CECILY: Stefan. Yes.

ALAN: Can you tell me about him?

CECILY: What do you want to know?

ALAN: Were you surprised when they arrested him?

CECILY: Yes, I was. Very. In fact, I was shocked.
You know my parents have always employed
young offenders at the hotel and I think it's a
wonderful idea. We have to help these people. I
know Stefan had been in trouble but that wasn't
his fault. He never really had a chance when you
think about the world he grew up in. But once he
came to the hotel, he was always very grateful,
he worked hard and I think he was kind-hearted.
I know my sister didn't like him, but that was
because he wouldn't do what she wanted.

ALAN: And what was that?

CECILY: I mean, he didn't work hard enough.
That's what she said. She also thought he was
stealing, but that could have been anyone. It could
have been Lionel or Natasha or anyone. She only
picked on him because she knew I liked him and
I thought it was wrong to fire him. I wouldn't tell
you this if I hadn't said exactly the same to her.
She didn't have any proof. I think it was unfair.

ALAN: The police think he may have broken into
Frank's room because he had been fired . . .
because he knew he was leaving the hotel.

CECILY: That's what they said, but I'm not sure it's
true.

ALAN: You don't think he did it?

CECILY: I don't know, Mr Conway. I didn't think
so to begin with. I talked about it with Aiden and
even he agreed with me, even though he'd never
been one of Stefan's greatest fans. Stefan was one
of the gentlest people I'd ever met. He was always
very proper in his dealings with me. And like I
said, he knew my parents had given him a real
opportunity having him here and he would never
have let them down. When I heard he'd confessed,
I couldn't believe it. And now the police are
saying that they've got more than enough

evidence to prosecute, although they won't tell me what it is. I don't know. They seem to think it's an open-and-shut case. They say they found money in his room ... I'm sorry. Can you excuse me a moment? It's just that it's all so horrible and upsetting ... someone getting killed.

The recording is turned off, then turned on again.

CECILY: I'm sorry.

ALAN: No. I can understand. It was your wedding day. The whole thing must have been awful for you.

CECILY: It was.

ALAN: We can do this later, if you like.

CECILY: No. Let's do it now.

ALAN: Well, I was wondering if you could tell me more about Frank Parris.

CECILY: I didn't see very much of him. I told you.

ALAN: Did you see him on the Thursday he arrived?

CECILY: No. I heard he didn't like his room – but Aiden dealt with that. Aiden's brilliant with the guests. Everyone seems to like him and if there's ever any problems, he always finds a way round them.

ALAN: He moved Frank into room twelve.

CECILY: He swapped him with another guest. A teacher or something. He hadn't arrived yet so he wouldn't know.

ALAN: And then on Friday he went in a taxi to Westleton.

CECILY: Derek arranged that for him. Have you spoken to Derek?

ALAN: Your night manager? I'm seeing him this evening.

CECILY: I saw Mr Parris around lunchtime when he got back. I was having to deal with the people about the marquee. They'd actually let us down quite badly – we won't use them again – by arriving late. It was all right in the end but I was out on the east lawn when he came back in another taxi and Aiden came out at that moment and I saw the two of them chatting.

ALAN: Do you know what they were talking about?

CECILY: Oh – just the hotel, the room, that sort of thing. I wanted to see Aiden so I went over and joined them. He introduced me.

ALAN: What did you make of Frank Parris?

CECILY: Can I be honest? I know he was your friend and I don't want to offend you.

ALAN: Please. You can say what you like.

CECILY: Well, I didn't really take to him. It's difficult to explain and part of it may be that I had my mind on other things. But I found him quite ... I didn't believe him. I thought he was being just too friendly and pleasant – he was all over Aiden for changing his room – but all the time I got the feeling that he was just pretending. When he said he loved the hotel I got the feeling that he didn't really like it at all. And when he congratulated Aiden and me because we were getting married, it was almost as if he was sneering at us.

ALAN: Frank could be a little bit ... supercilious.

CECILY: I'm not even sure I know what that means.

ALAN: Condescending.

CECILY: It was more than that. He was lying. And actually, I can give you an example. Aiden said that we were having a party that night to celebrate the wedding and he hoped the noise wouldn't disturb him. And Frank said it didn't matter because he was out that evening. He was going to Snape Maltings to see a performance of *The Marriage of Figaro*. I don't know anything about opera, but I remember that he was absolutely specific about the name. He went on and on about how it was his favourite opera and he'd always enjoyed it and that he couldn't wait to see it.

ALAN: What makes you think he was lying?

CECILY: I know he was lying because I happened to go to Snape Maltings a couple of days later – they had a market – and I saw a list of all the events and *The Marriage of Figaro* wasn't on it. They had a youth orchestra playing Benjamin Britten that Friday night.

ALAN: Why do you think he would make up something like that?

CECILY: Because of what I just told you. He was sneering at us.

ALAN: It still seems quite a strange thing to do.

CECILY: I don't think there was any reason for it. I just think he enjoyed being superior. Maybe it was because he was gay and we were straight. Is that a bad thing to say? He'd lived in London and we were stuck out in the country. He was the guest and we were just the staff. I don't know. When he said goodbye to us, he had this weird handshake. He sort of took Aiden's hand in both of his like he was the president or something and didn't want to let him go. And then he gave me a kiss, which I didn't think was at all appropriate, and at the same time he had his hand very low on my back. I don't know why I'm telling you all this. All I'm saying is, he was playing with us. I only met him for a few minutes and you knew him a lot better than me, but I didn't think he was a nice man. I'm sorry, but that's the truth.

ALAN: Did you see him again?

CECILY: No. I had the party on Friday night and I didn't even think about him. The hotel was full anyway, so there were plenty of other guests to worry about. I went to bed early with a sleeping pill and of course the next day was my wedding.

ALAN: Did you see Stefan Codrescu at the party?

CECILY: Yes. He was there.

ALAN: How was he?

CECILY: Well, obviously Lisa had just fired him so he wasn't very happy. In fact, he hardly said anything. Aiden said he'd had too much to drink. He left quite early. I think Lionel took him back to his room.

ALAN: But a few hours later he was up again. According to the police that's when he went back into the hotel, into room twelve.

CECILY: That's what they said.

ALAN: Derek saw him.

CECILY: He might have been wrong.

ALAN: You think so?

CECILY: I don't know. I can't talk to you about all that. Actually, if you haven't got any other questions, I think I've told you everything I know.

ALAN: You've been very helpful, Cecily. And that is a great tan. How are you enjoying married life?

CECILY: (*Laughs.*) Well, it's early days. But we had a wonderful time in Antigua and now I'm glad to be back. We're very happy in Branlow Cottage and I just want to put everything behind us and get on with it.

ALAN: Thank you very much.

CECILY: Thank you.

The recording ended and there was something quite oppressive about the silence that followed. It reminded me that she was still missing after ten days and I wondered if anyone would ever hear her voice again.

There was another interview on the memory stick. Aiden had told me that he had met Alan briefly. I had to play it a couple of times before I realised that this must have happened before Alan spoke to Cecily. The two men were introduced by Pauline Treherne and Alan was already recording.

PAULINE: I'm sorry. I don't really want to be recorded.

ALAN: It's just for my private use. Easier than taking notes.

PAULINE: Even so, I don't feel comfortable about what happened. You're sure you're not going to write about it?

ALAN: No, no. My new book doesn't even take place in Suffolk.

PAULINE: Do you have a title for it?

ALAN: Not yet.

Aiden arrives.

PAULINE: This is Aiden MacNeil. My son-in-law.

ALAN: We've already met, I think.

AIDEN: Yes. I was in reception when you arrived. I helped you change rooms. I hope you're more comfortable now.

ALAN: It's fine, thank you very much.

AIDEN: Excuse me, are you recording this?

ALAN: Yes, I am. Do you mind?

AIDEN: As a matter of fact, I do.

PAULINE: Mr Conway is asking questions about the murder.

AIDEN: Well, I'd prefer not to talk about it.

ALAN: I'm sorry ... ?

AIDEN: Forgive me, Mr Conway. My whole job here is to look after the interests of the hotel. This business with Stefan Codrescu has been nothing but trouble for us and I really don't think we need any more publicity.

ALAN: I'm not going to share these tapes with anyone.

AIDEN: Even so. We told the police everything that happened that day. We didn't hide anything. And if you're going to suggest that the hotel was in some way responsible ...

ALAN: That isn't my intention.

AIDEN: We can't be sure of that.

PAULINE: Aiden ... !

AIDEN: I'm sorry, Pauline. I already told Lawrence that I think this is a bad idea. I'm sure Mr Conway is a very respected writer—

ALAN: Please, call me Alan ...

AIDEN: I'm not playing this game. I'm sorry. Do you mind turning that off?

ALAN: If you insist.

AIDEN: I do.

And that was the end of it.

It was obvious that Aiden had disliked Alan Conway

from the moment they met – and I could understand that. Should I read something into the fact that he had refused to be interviewed? No. As Aiden had clearly said, he was only doing his job.

It was after midnight and I had an early start, but the last thing I did before I went to bed was go to Apple Music and download *The Marriage of Figaro*. I would listen to it the next day.

Lionel Corby (Breakfast)

I was tired the next morning. I hadn't slept well and I left the house at first light, before Craig had even got up. I had to cross the whole of London for my 7 a.m. meeting with Lionel Corby, the spa manager who had been working at Branlow Hall at the time of the murder, and I sat bleary-eyed on the Tube for what felt like an eternity, glancing through a free newspaper that only had enough material for two or three stops.

My first impression of Lionel Corby wasn't a very favourable one. He came weaving through the traffic on one of those very expensive bikes with ultra-thin wheels, wearing Lycra that stopped halfway down his thigh and which had clearly been designed to show off his perfect musculature and, for that matter, his well-formed genitalia. I like to think the best of people, a trait not entirely helpful when investigating a murder perhaps, but there was something about him that instantly struck me as ... well, cocky. Yes, he worked in a gym. He had to advertise his physique, but did he have to do it so loudly? As we shook hands, his eyes travelled over me and I felt positively dowdy. By contrast, he crooned over the bicycle as he chained it to the rack.

'So, Susan, are you going to have some breakfast?' He had one of those exaggerated, sing-song Australian accents. 'They've got a decent café and I get a discount.'

We went inside. Virgin Active occupied a concrete bunker on a busy main road. Curiously, Atticus Pünd had lived in a flat just round the corner ... which is to say, Alan Conway had used the building as his inspiration. The café had only just opened and there was no one else there. The air conditioning had already turned it into a refrigerator. Lionel ordered himself a power drink of some sort: any number of health-giving fruits and vegetables compounded into an unappealing green slime. I noticed that he had pulled on a knitted beanie as he sat down. He had luxurious hair but it was thinning on top and he was probably self-conscious. I was longing for scrambled eggs, but the nearest they had was poached eggs on smashed avocado with sourdough toast, none of which had the slightest appeal. I settled for a cappuccino.

We took a table by the window.

'I'm afraid I've only got half an hour,' Lionel said.

'It's very kind of you to see me.'

'Not at all, Sue. It's so awful about Cess.' He sounded almost too genuine to be genuine. 'Is there any news?'

'I'm afraid not.'

'That's terrible. And how are you involved in all this? Are you a friend of the family?'

'Not exactly. Lawrence Treherne asked me to help.' I didn't want to go into all that again and Lionel had already said we only had half an hour so I moved on swiftly, explaining how Cecily's disappearance might be connected to Frank Parris's murder eight years be-fore.

'Frank Parris!' He let out a low whistle. 'When I got your text, I wondered how I could help. I haven't been back to Branlow Hall since I left. I'll be straight up with you, Sue. I couldn't stand the place! I was glad to get out.'

'But you were there for quite a while, Lionel. Four years.'

He smiled at that. 'You've done your homework. Actually, it was three years and nine months. I took over the new spa once it was finished and that was cool. State-of-the-art equipment, everything brand new, great pool. I had some decent clients, too ... especially the ones from outside. But the pay was lousy and although I was doing personal training the Trehernes only paid me twenty-five per cent of the fee. They were shit employers. And let me tell you, sometimes the whole place was more like a madhouse than a smart hotel. Stefan was OK. And I got on with some of the kitchen staff. But I couldn't stand the rest of them.'

'I don't suppose you had a client called Melissa Conway?' I don't know why I asked about her. It had come as a surprise to me when James had mentioned she was living in Woodbridge and on the memory stick Cecily had said that she used the spa.

'Melissa? Yes, there was a lady called Melissa – she was in all the time. But her name was Melissa Johnson, I think. She rented a house on the estate.'

That was her, but she had gone back to her maiden name.

'Why do you want to know about her?' Lionel asked.

'She was married to Alan Conway,' I said.

'Oh! I get it. Well, since you mention it, she actually

came in on the Wednesday or the Thursday evening before it happened. I remember because she was in a foul mood. No fun at all.'

'Do you know what had upset her?'

He shrugged. 'No idea.'

'So how did you end up at Branlow Hall?' I asked. 'How did you get the job?'

'Yeah, well, I didn't know what I was walking into. I came to London from Perth about eleven years ago. That's Perth, Australia, of course. My mother was English. I rented a room in Earls Court and got a job as a personal trainer. I was only twenty but I'd done a CEC course at a uni in Perth and I was lucky. I landed on my feet. I had a few private clients and they recommended me to others. Even so, London's an expensive place and I had a devil of a job keeping my head above water. You have no idea of the sort of stuff I got up to! Then I was training this guy and he mentioned he'd just got back from Branlow Hall and they were looking for someone to run their spa. It seemed a good way to earn some cash, so I went for an interview and I got it.'

'Who was the client who recommended you?' I asked.

'I don't remember.'

'Were all your clients men?'

'No. They split about fifty-fifty. Why do you ask?'

'No reason. Go on. Why were the Trehernes such bad employers – apart from the pay?'

'Well, the pay was the main thing, but they really made you put in the hours. Ten hours a day, six days a week. I'm not even sure that's legal, is it? And there were no perks. Everything you ate in the hotel you had to pay for and although the food was cheap, they gave you zero discount in the bar. You weren't even allowed to go in if there were any guests there.

'And that thing they were doing with crims! The Youth Offender Programme, they called it, but that wasn't what it was about. It was the pits. They were paying Stefan way under the minimum wage and he was on call literally twenty-four hours a day. He was meant to be general maintenance but they had him doing all the shit jobs, including the toilets, the gutters on the roof, the trash ... you name it. He got really sick once and they didn't even want to give him the day off. They had him over a barrel, you see. If he complained, they could throw him out. He was Romanian. He had a prison record. He wasn't going to get another job – and certainly not without a reference from them. They knew that. They were bastards.

'And then there was Lisa Treherne.' He shook his

head in admiration. 'The older daughter. She was a real piece of work.'

'She accused him of stealing.'

'She knew he wasn't a thief. That was Natasha.'

'The maid?'

'Yes. Everyone knew that. She was shameless! Shake hands and check you're still wearing your watch. But Lisa was playing the same power game as her dad. She wanted Stefan.'

'Wanted him . . . how?'

'How do you think?' Lionel looked at me disdainfully. 'Lisa had the hots for him. A nice hunk of twenty-two-year-old Eastern European flesh. She couldn't keep her eyes off him.'

Could I trust what Lionel was telling me? According to him, Melissa was angry, Lawrence was crooked, Stefan was exploited and Lisa was rapacious. He didn't have a good word to say about anyone. And yet I thought back to the meeting I'd had with Lisa in the dining room at Branlow Hall. She'd been fairly vengeful herself. *'Hiring Stefan Codrescu was a mistake from the very start. I said so at the time, although nobody listened to me.'* And what was it her father had said? *'You liked him to start with. You spent lots of time with him.'* I'd made a note of the contradiction. Perhaps Lionel had just explained it.

'For what it's worth, Lisa tried it on with me as well,' he continued. 'She was always in and out of the spa, and I'm telling you, mate, the sort of workout she wanted didn't involve anything I'd been taught in Perth.'

'Did she have a relationship with Stefan?' Even as I asked the question, I thought it was unlikely. Surely, if they had been sleeping together, it would have come out at the trial.

Lionel shook his head. 'I wouldn't call it a relationship. Stefan didn't fancy her any more than I did.' He pointed at his mouth. 'You know, she had that scar, and even without it she wasn't exactly Miranda Kerr. But they were having sex, if that's what you mean. The poor bugger couldn't say no to her! After all, she was more or less running the hotel. She had complete power over him.'

'Did he talk to you about it?'

'No. He never talked about that sort of stuff. But he was always miserable when she was around and one time I actually saw them together.'

Another couple of people had come into the café. Lionel leaned forward conspiratorially.

'It happened about two or three weeks before the murder,' he said. 'I'd finished at the spa and I was doing a quick run around the grounds. It was a warm night.

Beautiful. There was a full moon. So I ran and did some stretches and then I decided to do some chin-ups. There was a tree I liked to use. It had a branch at the perfect height. It was in this wood – near to Oaklands, the cottage where Melissa lived, as a matter of fact. So there I was, making my way along, when suddenly I heard noises and the next thing I knew, there they were the two of them, him on top of her, both of them stark naked in the grass.'

'Are you sure it was Lisa and Stefan?'

'That's a fair question, Sue. It was night and there was a distance between us, and at first I got the idea it was Aiden having it away with his future sister-in-law, which would have been quite a laugh. But I'd worked out with Aiden and he's got this big tattoo on his shoulder. He always called it his cosmic snake, but to me it just looked like a giant tadpole!' He laughed. 'Whoever the guy was out there, it wasn't Aiden. He had bare skin – I'd have easily seen a tattoo in the moonlight.

'Anyway, I didn't want to hang around like some kind of perv, whoever it was out there, so I started to move away. And of course you're going to guess what happened. I only stepped on a branch and the bloody thing went off like a gunshot. Well, that stopped them.

The guy looked round and I saw his face as clearly as I'm seeing you now. It was definitely Stefan.'

'Did he see you?'

'I don't think so.'

'You never talked to him about it?'

'Are you kidding?'

I thought it through. 'But I don't understand,' I said. 'Lisa fired him a couple of weeks later. If they were having sex, why would she do that?'

'I wondered about that. But my guess is that he'd told her to get lost. What she was doing was exploitation, no more, no less. Maybe he threatened to put in a complaint.'

I still hadn't heard from Stefan Codrescu and I wondered how long it would take for my letter to reach him in jail. There was still the question of whether he would agree to see me, but it was critical that the two of us should meet. I needed to know everything that had happened between him and Lisa Treherne. She wasn't going to say anything. Only he could tell me the truth.

'You were with him on the Friday night,' I said. 'He got drunk at the party.'

'That's right.' Lionel glanced at the clock on the wall. We had been talking for twenty minutes of our allotted half-hour. He drained his protein shake, leaving a green half-moon on his upper lip. 'That wasn't like Stefan. He could usually hold his liquor. But of course he'd just been fired, so maybe he was drowning his sorrows.'

'You took him back to his room.'

'That would have been about ten o'clock. We walked over to the stable block, which is where they put us up. I had the room next to his. I said goodnight and we both went to bed. I was pretty knackered myself, actually.'

'What time did you get to sleep?'

'I guess about ten or fifteen minutes later – but before you ask, I didn't hear anything. I'm a heavy sleeper. If Stefan got up and went into the hotel, I'm afraid I can't help you. All I can tell you is that he was lying on his bed when I left.'

'Did you see him the next day?'

'No. I was in the spa. He was helping with the wedding.'

'Do you believe he killed Frank Parris?'

He had to think about that. Eventually, he nodded. 'Yeah. Probably. I mean, the police found plenty of evidence and I know he was broke. He did a lot of online gambling. All these Romanians do. He often asked me to bail him out before he got paid at the end of the month.'

He looked at the clock again and got to his feet. Our time was up.

'I hope you can help him, Sue,' he said. 'Because actually, I quite liked him and I think what happened to him was pretty crook. And I hope you find Cecily. Do they have any idea what happened to her?'

'Not yet.' There was one last thing I wanted to ask. 'You said that, at first, you thought it might be Aiden with Lisa in the wood. Was that because he was usually promiscuous?'

'Promiscuous! That's a funny word to use. You mean did he fool around?' Lionel gave me a crooked smile. 'I don't know anything about his marriage, and when I saw those two people out there I don't know why it popped into my head that it might be him. Maybe he and Cecily were happy together and maybe they weren't – but I'll tell you one thing. I don't think Aiden would've dared go behind her back. I mean, she was the one who'd found him and brought him up from London, and in her own way Cecily was as tough as her sister. If she'd found out he was cheating on her, she'd have had his balls for breakfast.'

We shook hands. Another trainer had come into the café, also in Lycra, and I watched the two of them give each other a man hug, bumping chests and rubbing each other's back.

I still wasn't sure that I liked Lionel Corby. Could I believe the version of events that he had presented to me? I wasn't sure about that either.

Michael Bealey (Lunch)

Michael J. Bealey was a busy man.

His PA had rung to say that drinks at Soho House would no longer work but could I meet him for lunch at twelve thirty? Lunch turned out to be a sandwich and a cup of coffee at a Prêt just around the corner from his flat on the King's Road, but that was fine by me. I wasn't sure if Michael would have had enough conversation for a two-course meal. He had always been a man of few words, despite having published millions of them. The "J." on his business card was important to him, by the way. It was said that he had known both Arthur C. Clarke and Philip K. Dick and had adapted his own name as a sort of tribute to them both. He was well known as an expert on their work and had written long articles that had been published in *Constellations* (which he had also edited at Gollancz) and *Strange Horizons*.

He was already there when I arrived, scrolling through a typescript on his iPad. There was something mole-like about the way he worked, hunched forward as if he was trying to burrow his way into the screen. I had to remind myself that he was about the same age as me. His grey hair, glasses and old-fashioned suit added an extra ten years, which he seemed to embrace. There are some men who are never really young, who don't even want to be.

'Oh, hello, Susan!' He didn't get up. He wasn't the kissing sort, not even a peck on the cheek. But he did at least fold the cover over his iPad and smile at me, blinking in the sun. He already had a coffee and a Bakewell tart, which was sitting on the paper bag it had come in. 'What can I get you?' he asked.

'Actually, I'm all right, thank you.' I had glanced at the rather depressing muffins and pastries on offer and hadn't been tempted. Anyway, I wanted to get this over with.

'Well, do help yourself to a piece of this.' He pushed the tart towards me. 'It's quite good.'

That clipped speech. I remembered it so well. He

was like an actor in one of those plays from between the wars where everyone talks for a long time but very little happens.

'How are you?' he asked.

'I'm very well, thank you.'

'And in Greece, I understand!'

'Crete, actually.'

'I've never been to Crete.'

'You should. It's beautiful.'

Even on a Sunday, the traffic trundled past on the King's Road, and I could smell dust and petrol in the air.

'So how are things?' I asked, snatching at the question to fill the silence.

He sighed and blinked several times. 'Well, you know, it's been one of those years.' It always was, where Michael was concerned. He'd turned gloom into an art form.

'I was pleased to see you picked up the Atticus Pünd series.' I was determined to be positive. 'And you kept my old covers. Somebody gave me a copy the other day. I thought it looked great.'

'It seemed both pointless and uneconomical to re-jacket them.'

'Are they selling well?'

'They were.'

I waited for him to explain what he meant but he just sat there, sipping whatever was in his paper cup. 'So what happened?' I asked eventually.

'Well, it was that business with David Boyd.'

I vaguely knew the name but couldn't place it. 'Who is David Boyd?'

'The writer.'

There was another silence. Then, hesitantly, Michael continued. 'I actually brought him into the company so in a way I suppose it was my fault. I bought his first book at Frankfurt. A three-way auction, but we were lucky. One publisher dropped out and the second wasn't overenthusiastic, so we got it at a good price. We published the first book eighteen months ago and the second last January.'

'Science fiction?'

'Not exactly. Cybercrime. Very well researched. Quite well written. It's actually quite terrifying stuff. Big business, fraud, politics, the Chinese. Disappointing sales, though. I don't know what went wrong, but the first book underperformed and the second book was actually much weaker. At the same time, he had an aggressive agent – Ross Simmons at Curtis Brown – trying to tie us down to a new deal, so we took a decision and let him go. Sad, but there you are. These things happen.'

Was that the end of the story? 'What *did* happen?' I asked.

'Well, he took umbrage. Not the agent. The writer. He felt we'd let him down, gone back on our word. It was all very unpleasant, but the worst of it was that he – actually, you're not going to believe this – but it seems that he hacked into the Hely Hutchinson Centre to get his revenge.'

A whole series of terrifying possibilities opened up before my eyes. I had read about Hely Hutchinson in the *Bookseller*: a brand-new, state-of-the-art distribution centre near Didcot in Oxfordshire. Two hundred and fifty thousand square feet. Robot technology. Sixty million books shipped every year.

It had been a nightmare, Michael explained. 'It was absolute chaos. We had the wrong titles being sent to the wrong bookstores. Orders got ignored. We had one customer who received thirty copies of the same Harlan Coben ... one a day for a whole month. Other books just disappeared. If you tried to find them it was as if they had never been written. That included the reissues of *Atticus Pünd*.' He realised that he had managed several sentences in one go and stopped himself. 'Very annoying.'

'How long did this go on for?' I asked.

'It's still going on. We've got people in there now,

sorting it out. The last two months were the worst. God knows what it's going to do to our sales and operating profit for this quarter!'

'I'm very sorry,' I said. 'Have you gone to the police?'

'The police are involved, yes. I really can't say any more than that. We've managed to keep it out of the press. I shouldn't really even be talking to you about it.'

Why was he talking to me about it? I guessed. 'I suppose this isn't a very good time to be approaching you,' I said. 'I mean, for a job.'

'I'd love to help you, Susan. I think you did a very good job with the Pünd novels – and I understand Alan Conway wasn't an easy man to work with.'

'You don't know the half of it.'

'What actually happened? At Cloverleaf Books?'

'It wasn't my fault, Michael.'

'I'm sure it wasn't.' He broke off a piece of Bakewell tart. 'But, of course, there were rumours.'

'The rumours weren't true.'

'Rumours very rarely are.' He popped the fragment into his mouth and waited until it had melted. He didn't chew or swallow. 'Look, I'm firefighting at the moment and I really can't help you. But I can put the word out and see. What are you looking for? Publisher? Editorial director?'

'I'll take anything.'

'How about freelance? Project by project?'

'Yes. That might work.'

'There might be something.'

Or there might not. That was it.

'Are you sure you won't have a coffee?' he asked.

'No. Thank you, Michael.'

He didn't dismiss me quite yet. To have done so would have been a humiliation. We talked for another ten minutes about the business, about the collapse of Cloverleaf, about Crete. He finished his coffee and his pastry and then we parted company without shaking hands because he had icing sugar on his fingers. So much for the Ralph Lauren jacket! The meeting had been a complete waste of time.

Craig Andrews (Dinner)

It was my third meal of the day and I still hadn't eaten.

This time, however, I was going to make up for it. Craig had taken me to an old-fashioned trattoria in Notting Hill, one of those places where the waiters wear black and white and the pepper grinders are about six inches too long. The pasta was home-made, the wine rough and reasonably priced and the tables a little too close together. It was exactly the sort of restaurant I liked.

'So what do you think?' he asked as we tucked into very good bruschetta with ripe tomatoes and thick leaves of fresh basil.

'The food? The restaurant?'

'The crime! Do you think they'll find Cecily Treherne?'

I shook my head. 'If she was going to turn up, I think she'd have done so by now.'

'So she's dead.'

'Yes.' I thought for a moment. I hated writing her off like that. 'Probably.'

'Do you have any idea who killed her?'

'It's complicated, Craig.' I tried to collect my thoughts. 'Let's start with the call that Cecily made to her parents. And let's assume that someone overheard her talking. I thought at first that she had telephoned from Branlow Cottage, in which case it could only have been Aiden or Eloise, the nanny. But actually she made the call from her office in the hotel and that widens the field.'

'How do you know?'

'Because Derek, the night manager, was there and he told me. *"I knew something was wrong when she made that phone call. She was so upset."* That was what he said.'

'So he overheard her.'

'Yes. But Lisa Treherne had the office next door and she might have too. It could have been one of the guests. It could have been someone walking past the window outside.' I sighed. 'Here's the problem. If you accept that Cecily had to be silenced because she knew something about the death of Frank Parris, then it follows that whoever killed her killed him. But as far as I can tell, none of the people I've mentioned had ever met Frank before. Not Derek, not Aiden, not Lisa. None of them had any motive.'

'Could they have killed Cecily to protect someone else?'

'I suppose so. But who? Frank Parris had been in Australia. He turned up by chance on the weekend of the wedding and he had no connection whatsoever with Branlow Hall except that he had booked himself in for three days.' I drank some of the wine, which had rather pleasingly arrived at the table tucked into a straw basket. 'Funnily enough, I have found two people who had a proper motive for killing him. And they've lied to me! But the trouble is, they live outside the hotel and I can't see any way that they could have overheard Cecily making her telephone call.' I thought about it. 'Unless they happened to be there for a drink . . . '

'Who are they?'

'Joanne and Martin Williams. Sister and brother-in-law of the deceased. They live in Westleton and Frank had a half-share in their house. That was the reason he was in Suffolk. He was going to force them to sell it.'

'How do you know they lied?'

'It was a small thing, really.'

It was Aiden who had first mentioned it. The marquee for the wedding had arrived late. It hadn't come to the hotel until Friday lunchtime. When Martin Williams was talking about his brother-in-law, he had said that Frank had complained about the wedding and in particular about the marquee, which spoiled the view of the garden. But he had also told me that Frank had come to the house early, after breakfast. So, putting two and two together, Frank couldn't possibly have seen the marquee.

On the other hand, Martin most certainly had. He must have gone to Branlow House sometime after Friday afternoon. Why? It was just possible that he wanted to find out which room Frank was in because he'd decided to kill him. Which would also explain Joanne's last words to me: *'Piss off and leave us alone.'* She knew what had happened and she was scared.

I told Craig all this and he smiled. 'That's very clever, Susan. Do you think this guy, Martin Williams, had it in him to kill his brother-in-law?'

'Well, as I say, he was the only one with any motive. Unless … ' I hadn't meant to put my thoughts into words, but Craig was fascinated by the whole story and I knew I had to go on. 'Well, it's a crazy idea, but it has occurred to me that Frank might not have been the target.'

'Meaning?'

'First of all, he changed rooms. He was originally in room sixteen but apparently it was too modern for him. So they put him in room twelve.'

'Who went into room sixteen?'

'A retired headmaster called George Saunders. He taught at a local school. Bromeswell Grove. But suppose someone didn't know that. They knock on the door of room twelve in the middle of the night and he opens it and in the half-light they whack him on the head with a hammer and kill him before they know what they've done.'

'Would he have opened the door in the middle of the night?'

'That's a good point. But I've had another thought. Suppose this wasn't about Frank Parris or George Saunders or any of the guests. It could have been all about Stefan Codrescu. It seems that he was having an affair with Lisa Treherne and there was all sorts of sexual jealousy and anger bubbling away at Branlow Hall. Suppose someone wanted to frame him?'

'For murder?'

'Why not?'

'And just killed a guest at random?' He didn't need to inject so much scepticism into his voice. I wasn't sure I believed it myself. 'I can see why you need to talk to Stefan,' he said.

'If he ever gets back to me.'

'It may take a while. The prison system makes things as difficult as possible for everyone involved – inside and out. That's what it looks like, anyway.'

The main course came. We talked for a while about prisons.

When I'd first met Craig, four years earlier, he'd had the nervousness of all new writers; the sense that he needed to apologise for what he was doing. He had just turned forty, quite old to be starting out as a writer, although quite a bit younger than Alexander McCall Smith had been when he published his first major hit, *The No. 1 Ladies' Detective Agency*, and maybe that was partly in my mind when I took him on. He was also wealthy. He didn't show off, but his clothes, his car, the house in Ladbroke Grove, all told their own story. He had just left Goldman Sachs, where he'd headed up their UK Shares division. This information never appeared in his blurb.

I had assured him that *Jail Time* (as it eventually became) didn't need any apology and I had enjoyed working with him. His main character, Christopher Shaw, was a plain-clothes policeman, sent into maximum-security jails to get information from high-profile inmates, and this was a formula that had worked well for the first three books in the series.

'What got you interested in prisons?' I asked him now. We were getting to the end of the main course. We'd worked our way through the bottle of wine.

'Didn't I ever tell you?' I saw him hesitate. The lights from the candles were reflecting in his eyes. 'My brother was in prison.'

'I'm sorry ... ' I was surprised he had never told me before. The more cynical part of me could have used it as publicity.

'John was the chief executive of one of the high-street banks. He was trying to raise investment from Qatar – this was in 2008, just after the financial crisis. He was paying them sweeteners, which of course he didn't declare. The Serious Fraud Office went after him. And ... ' he waved a hand ' ... he got three years.'

'I shouldn't have asked.'

'No. It's OK. John was scared and stupid rather than greedy, and what happened to him made me re-think my whole career. It could just as easily have been me. And prison! I'm not saying he shouldn't have been punished, but prison is such a bloody waste of time. I'm convinced that one day people will look back on the twenty-first century and wonder how we could perpetuate such an absurd, Victorian idea. Do you want a dessert?'

'No.'

'Then let's have coffee at home.'

It was another warm night and we decided to walk back. I wondered if I had spoiled the evening by asking about his personal life, but it had actually brought us closer.

'Were you ever married?' he asked.

'No.' The question took me by surprise.

'Me neither. I came close a couple of times but it didn't work out, and now I suppose it's too late.'

'What are you talking about?' I said. 'You're not even fifty.'

'That's not what I mean. Who in their right mind would want to marry a writer?'

'I know lots of writers who are very happily married.'

'I was seeing someone last year. She was divorced, about my age. We shared a lot of interests. I really liked her. But I never allowed her anywhere near me ... not when I was working. And the trouble was, I was working all the time. In the end she got fed up with it and I can't blame her. When you're writing a book, the book is all that matters and some people can't accept that.'

We had reached his front door. He opened it and we went inside.

'Are you with anyone, Susan?' he asked.

That was the moment when everything changed. God knows, I've read enough romantic novels to recognise when subtext comes galloping over the horizon and I knew exactly what Craig was asking – or rather, I saw the invitation behind the question he had just put to me. It should have been obvious the moment I'd entered his swish bachelor's home or accepted dinner at that quaint local restaurant with its candles and its wine bottles in straw baskets.

The worst of it was that I didn't know how to answer.

I wasn't in Crete. I wasn't with Andreas. I was tempted. Why not? Craig represented a metropolitan lifestyle, parties, bestselling books ... everything, in fact, that I had left behind. He was also handsome, good company, civilised and rich. And if one little voice whispered in my ear that this was what I had been afraid of from the moment I had invited myself into his home, another reminded me that it was what I'd actually wanted and advised me to grab it with both hands.

'No. I was with someone but we broke up.'

That was what I wanted to say. That was what I could have said. It would have been so easy. But right then it wasn't true. Not yet. And maybe I didn't want it to be.

'Are you with anyone, Susan?' he asked

'Yes. Didn't I tell you? I'm engaged.'

I watched as he took that in. 'Congratulations,' he said. 'Who's the lucky man?'

'His name is Andreas. He's the co-owner of the hotel in Crete.'

'I have to say, it's the last thing I'd have expected you to get up to but that's wonderful. So – shall we have a coffee?'

'No, thanks. It's been a lovely evening, but I've got an early start if I'm going to get back to Suffolk.'

'Of course.'

'Thanks for dinner, Craig.'

'My pleasure.'

We were like two actors in a play, reciting lines that had been written by someone else. He gave me a peck on the cheek and then – *exit stage right* – I went upstairs on my own.

Page One

Alarge gin and tonic. A club sandwich held together by a cocktail stick flying a miniature Stars and Stripes. A packet of cigarettes. And the book.

I was ready.

I had driven back to Suffolk in time for lunch and after unpacking and taking a quick shower in my room, I had deposited myself at one of the wooden tables in the area outside the bar. I was right next to the stretch of grass – the east lawn – where Aiden and Cecily's wedding marquee had been pitched. The main entrance to the hotel was round the corner and I thought of Helen, the house manager (I imagined her as elderly and serious in a well-cut uniform), running breathlessly across the gravel to find Lawrence and tell him what Natasha had just found in room 12. How horrible it must have been for all of them that day! All the guests in their smart clothes, Aiden and Cecily married barely an hour, and then suddenly police cars and photographers and questions from the unlovely Detective Superintendent Locke and finally the body brought out on a stretcher . . .

The sun was shining but I shuddered. I'd have been more comfortable indoors, but I'm afraid reading and smoking have always gone together for me and even though it was a disgusting habit (the smoking, obviously) I needed to concentrate. The book was *Atticus Pünd Takes the Case*. It was the copy that Craig had given me in London. The time had finally come to confront not just the text but my memories of its creation. It felt strange. I was about to read one murder mystery while sitting inside another.

I had put off reading it for reasons that I have already explained. I was perfectly well aware of the identity of the killer in the novel and I remembered all the clues. I think it would be fair to say that a whodunnit is one of the very few forms of literature that rarely merit a second read.

But by now I had a good idea of what had happened at Branlow Hall on the 14th and 15th of June. I had met most of the characters involved. Alan Conway had come to the hotel. Perhaps he had even sat where I was sitting now. And he had seen something. '*They've got the wrong man.*' That was what he had said to James Taylor. He had come here in search of inspiration but he had left with much more. And yet he hadn't gone to the police. He had hidden the answer in his book. It was the only way to make sense of Cecily's disappearance and I was going to find it.

The paperback was in front of me. I ran my finger across the raised letters of the title, feeling them as if they were in Braille. It was extraordinary how much damage Alan Conway had managed to do in his career. *Magpie Murders* had almost killed me. Had this prequel killed Cecily Treherne?

I lit a cigarette. I turned to the first page.

I began to read.

Alan Conway

Atticus Pünd Takes The Case

HOTEL

HOTEL

ABOUT THE AUTHOR

Alan Conway had not written anything before his first published novel, *Atticus Pünd Investigates*, which became an overnight sensation and won the Gold Dagger award given by the Crime Writers' Association for the best crime novel of the year. It was to be the first in a series of nine books, all featuring the German detective, which only ended following the sudden death of the author at his home in Framlingham, Suffolk, in 2014. Formerly married, with one son, he came out as gay six months after *Atticus Pünd Takes the Case* was published, by which time he had become an internationally recognised bestseller. In his obituary in *The Times*, Conway was compared to Agatha Christie for the ingenuity of his plotting, and he has been frequently mentioned as a late arrival to the 'Golden Age' of detective writing. More than twenty million copies of his books have now been sold and the BBC 1 adaptation of *Atticus Pünd Investigates*, starring Sir Kenneth Branagh, will soon be aired.

The Atticus Pünd Series

Praise for
Atticus Pünd Takes the Case

'Lock the door, curl up in front of the fire and get into the latest Alan Conway. It won't disappoint.'
—*Good Housekeeping*

'I love a whodunnit with a real sucker punch and, boy, this absolutely delivers. I can't wait for the next one!'
—Peter James

'Once again, Conway serves up a vision of a gentler, long-forgotten England. And he does it murderously well.'
—*New Statesman*

'Number three in the series and Atticus Pünd is still going strong. A terrific, twisty story that will leave you guessing all the way.'
—*Observer*

'A new *Atticus Pünd* has almost become an annual event. Will you guess the ending? I didn't!'

—*Publishers Weekly*

'Atticus Pünd has become even more famous than Angela Merkel. And he's more entertaining too.'

—*Der Tagesspiegel*

'A famous actress is strangled and who's the suspect? Everyone! The latest Atticus Pünd is a real blast.'

—Lee Child

'Murder and skulduggery beside the English sea. *Atticus Pünd Takes the Case* could be my favorite so far.'

—*New Yorker*

ATTICUS PÜND
TAKES
THE CASE

Alan Conway

ORION BOOKS

An Orion paperback

First published in Great Britain in 2009
by Cloverleaf Books
This paperback edition published in 2016
by Orion Fiction,
an imprint of The Orion Publishing Group Ltd,
Carmelite House, 50 Victoria Embankment,
London EC4Y 0DZ

An Hachette UK Company

5 7 9 12 8 6 4

A CIP catalogue record for this book is
available from the British Library.

ISBN (Mass Market Paperback) 771 0 5144 4566 6

Typeset by Arkline Wales

Printed and bound in Great Britain by Anus & Sons, Appledore

www.orionbooks.co.uk

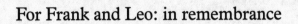
For Frank and Leo: in remembrance

CONTENTS

CHARACTERS

Melissa James	A Hollywood actress living in Tawleigh
Francis Pendleton	Melissa's husband
Phyllis Chandler	Cook/housekeeper at Melissa's home
Eric Chandler	Chauffeur/handyman – Phyllis's son
Lance Gardner	Manager of the Moonflower Hotel
Maureen Gardner	Lance's wife, also running the hotel
Algernon Marsh	A property developer and businessman
Samantha Collins	Algernon's sister, Leonard's wife

Dr Leonard Collins	The local GP, married to Samantha
Joyce Campion	Algernon and Samantha's aunt
Harlan Goodis	An American millionaire, married to Joyce
Nancy Mitchell	Receptionist at the Moonflower Hotel
Brenda Mitchell	Her mother
Bill Mitchell	Her father
Simon Cox	(aka Sīmanis Čaks), a film producer
Charles Pargeter	Owner of the Ludendorff Diamond
Elaine Pargeter	His wife
Detective Inspector Gilbert	Investigating the Ludendorff Diamond
Detective Sergeant Dickinson	Working with Gilbert
Atticus Pünd	World-famous detective
Madeline Cain	His secretary
DCI Edward Hare	Investigating the Moonflower murders

ONE
CLARENCE KEEP

'Are you just going to sit there, Eric? Or are you going to give me a hand with the washing-up?'

Eric Chandler looked up from the racing pages of the *Cornish & Devon Post*, biting back the answer that had been on the tip of his tongue. He had spent the last two hours cleaning and polishing the Bentley, a complete waste of time as once again the weather was on the turn. This had been a horrible April so far, with squalls of rain driving in across the sea. When Eric had finally come into the kitchen he had been cold and damp and definitely in no mood to help his mother with the dishes or anything else.

Phyllis Chandler had been bending over the oven, but now as she straightened up she was holding a tray of freshly baked florentines, each one a perfect golden brown disc. She took them over to the counter and, reaching for a spatula, began to transfer them onto a plate. Sometimes Eric wondered how she did it, especially with eggs and sugar still rationed almost eight years after the end of the war, but somehow she never let such things get in her way. The first time white bread had reappeared it had been in two shopping bags she had carried up from the village, and she had always managed to stretch her one-and-eightpence meat ration much further than it had any right to go.

Eric's mother reminded him of a hedgehog as she busied herself around the kitchen. What was that story she had read him as a child? *Mrs Tiggy-Winkle*. That was the one. The so-called adventures of a hedgehog washerwoman living in the Lake District ... not that anything very much ever happened. His mother certainly looked the part: small and round, even wearing the same clothes, a printed gown with a white apron across her ample stomach. And prickly. That was definitely the right word to describe her.

He glanced at the sink. His mother had been busy for the last few days, preparing for the weekend. Devilled eggs, split-pea soup, chicken à la King ... Melissa James was expecting guests and had, as always, been very precise about what they were going to eat. It was definitely the weather for soups and casseroles, although there were also a pair of capons and a leg of lamb in the larder. Kippers and porridge for breakfast. Tom Collins cocktails at six. He felt his stomach rumbling, which reminded him that he hadn't put anything in it since lunch. His mother had turned back to the oven and he reached out and helped himself to one of the florentines. It was still hot. He had to transfer it quickly from hand to hand.

'I saw that!' his mother exclaimed.

How was that even possible? She'd had her back to him, her bottom in the air. 'You've got plenty to spare,' he said. The smell of dried fruit and golden syrup rose into his nostrils. Why did she have to be such a good cook?

'Those aren't for you! They're for Miss James's guests.'

'Miss James's guests won't notice one missing.'

It often seemed to Eric that he was trapped and that he had been from the moment of his birth. He couldn't remember a time when he hadn't been attached to his mother, not as part of her family but as a sort of appendage, tied to her apron strings. His father had been a captain in the army and he had actually been excited when the Great War kicked off, dreaming of medals and glory and putting one over on the Boche. In fact, all he'd got was a bullet in the head in some faraway place that Eric couldn't even spell. He had been seven years old when the telegram came and he still remembered his feelings ... or lack of them. He had been unable to mourn a man he hardly knew.

He and his mother were already living in Tawleigh-on-the-Water, in a cottage so small they were always having to step aside to allow one another to pass. Eric hadn't done well at school and did odd jobs in the village, working at the pub, the butcher's shop, the harbour ... but never for long. Although he was the right age for conscription when the Second World War began, there was never any chance of that. He had been born with a club foot. When he was growing up, the boys had called him Lumpy and the girls had ignored him, sniggering when they saw him limping up the street. He had joined the Local Defence Volunteers, but even they had been reluctant to have him in their company.

The war had ended. Melissa James had come to Tawleigh and Phyllis had gone into service. Given no real choice in the matter, Eric had gone with her. She was the housekeeper and cook. He was the butler, the chauffeur, the gardener, the general handyman. But not the washer-up. That had never been part of the deal.

He was forty-three years old now and he was beginning to see that this was his life. These were the cards that he had been dealt. He would clean the car and polish the silver and 'Yes, Miss James' and 'No, Miss James,' and even in the best suit that she had bought him and which she insisted he must wear when he drove her into town, he was still Lumpy. He always would be.

He took a bite out of the florentine, which had cooled a little, and tasted the butter as it oozed over his tongue. That was also part of the trap. She cooked. He got fat.

'If you're hungry, there are coconut biscuits in the tin,' Phyllis said, adopting a kinder tone of voice.

'They're stale.'

'I can put them in the oven for a few minutes and they'll be fine.'

Even when she was being nice to him, she managed to humiliate him. Was he supposed to be grateful to her because she was offering him the leftovers that Melissa James and her friends didn't want? Sitting at the table, Eric felt the anger rise up inside him. He had noticed that recently it had become darker and much more difficult to control; not just the anger but other emotions too. He wondered if he should talk to Dr Collins, who had treated him on several occasions for minor infections and calluses. Dr Collins always seemed friendly enough.

But he knew he couldn't do it. He couldn't tell anyone what he was feeling because at the end of the day it wasn't his fault and there was nothing he could do about it. It was better kept locked up inside him, his secret.

Unless Phyllis knew. Sometimes, the way she looked at him, he wondered.

There was a movement at the door. Melissa James appeared, walking into the kitchen wearing high-waisted trousers, a silk shirt and a page-boy jacket with gold-coloured buttons. Eric got quickly to his feet, leaving the half-eaten florentine on the table. Phyllis turned round, wiping her hands on her apron as if to signal how busy she had been.

'No need to get up, Eric,' Melissa said. She had been born in England but had spent so long working in Hollywood that some of her words had a distinct American twang. 'I'm just going into Tawleigh … '

'Can I drive you, Miss James?'

'No. I'll take the Bentley.'

'I've just finished cleaning it.'

'Thank you. That's great!'

'What time would you like dinner this evening?' Phyllis asked.

'That's what I came in to say. Francis is going into Barnstaple tonight. I've got a slight headache so I'm going to take an early night.'

There it was again, Eric thought. An Englishwoman would have 'had' an early night, not 'taken' it. Melissa wore her Americanisms like cheap jewellery.

'I can warm up some soup if you like.' Phyllis sounded concerned. To her way of thinking, soup was the equivalent of medicine, only more effective.

'Actually, I thought you might like to see your sister. Eric can drive you over in the Bentley.'

'That's very thoughtful of you, Miss James.'

Phyllis's sister – Eric's aunt – lived in Bude, further down the coast. She hadn't been well recently and it was possible she might have to have an operation.

'I'll be back by six. Once I'm in, you two head off and have a nice evening.'

Eric had fallen silent. It was always the same when Melissa James came into the room. He couldn't take his eyes off her. It wasn't just that she was a remarkably attractive woman. She was also a film star. There was hardly anyone in England who wouldn't recognise her blonde hair with its almost boyish cut, her brilliant blue eyes, the smile made somehow more appealing by the faintest scar at the corner of her mouth. Even after all these years working for her, Eric couldn't quite believe that she was actually in the room with him. When he looked at her, it was as if he was in the cinema and she was five times bigger than him, on the screen.

'I'll see you later then.' Melissa turned on her heel and walked out of the room.

'You'd better take an umbrella, miss! It looks like rain,' Phyllis called after her.

Melissa answered with a single raised hand. And then she had gone.

Phyllis waited a few seconds before she turned on Eric. 'What do you think you were doing?' she demanded, angrily.

'What do you mean?' Eric braced himself.

'You were staring at her.'

'I was doing no such thing!'

'Eyes like saucers!' Phyllis rested her hands on her hips in true Mrs Tiggy-Winkle mode. 'You're going to get us both thrown out of here if you behave like that.'

'Mum ... ' Eric felt the violence, rising in waves.

'Sometimes I don't know what's wrong with you, Eric. Sitting here all the time, on your own. It's not healthy.'

Eric closed his eyes. Here it comes again, he thought.

'You should have found yourself a young lady by now, someone to walk out with. I know you're not much to look at and you've got that foot of yours – but even so! There's that girl at the Moonflower. Nancy. I know her mother. They're a perfectly nice family. Why don't you invite her over to tea?'

He allowed her to prattle on, her voice fading into the distance. One day, he knew, he would have had enough. He wouldn't be able to control himself any more. And what then?

He had no idea.

*

Melissa James came out of the kitchen and crossed the hall on her way to the front door. The floor was uncarpeted and almost automatically, not thinking what she was doing, she walked as quietly as possible, her feet making no sound on the wooden floor. It would be so nice to leave the house without another confrontation. Didn't she have enough on her mind already?

Phyllis had been right. It did look as if more rain was on its way – it had barely stopped all week – but she had no intention of taking an umbrella. Melissa had always thought of umbrellas as ridiculous inventions. Either the rain swept in underneath them or the wind tried to tug them out of your hand. She would only use one if someone else was holding it for her, when she was on set or when she got out of a car at a movie premiere. But that was different. That was what was expected of her. Right now, she reached out for the raincoat on the hatstand by the door and draped it over her shoulders.

She had bought Clarence Keep in a moment of madness – at a time when she could buy almost anything without giving the cost any thought. It was an odd name for a house. A keep was the strongest part of a castle, a last resort. But that wasn't at all what she had intended it to be. And although she had fallen in love with it the moment she saw it, it looked nothing like a castle.

Clarence Keep was a Regency folly built by a military

commander, Sir James Clarence, who had fought in the American War of Independence and who had gone on to become governor of Jamaica. Perhaps that was where he had found his inspiration as the house he had built was largely made of wood, painted a dazzling white, with elegant windows looking out onto wide, empty lawns that dropped down towards the sea. A wide veranda ran either side of the front door and there was a balcony coming off the main bedroom, which was directly above. The lawns were perfectly flat and an intense, almost tropical green. Only the palm trees were missing. The house could have belonged on a plantation.

It was said that Queen Victoria had once stayed there. It had briefly belonged to William Railton, the architect who had designed Nelson's Column in Trafalgar Square. When Melissa had found it, Clarence Keep had long been abandoned and she had taken it on in the full knowledge that it would cost a lot of money to restore it to its Regency prime. Just how much money, though, had come as an unpleasant surprise. She had no sooner dealt with the dry rot than the damp presented itself as the next challenge. Flood damage, foundation failure, subsidence and a dozen other problems had queued up for her autograph, in each case on the front of a cheque. Had it finally been worth it? The house was beautiful. She loved living there, waking up with the sea views and the sound of the breaking waves, strolling in the garden (when the weather allowed), hosting weekend parties. But sometimes she thought that the fight had exhausted her in more ways than one.

Financially, certainly.

How had she allowed things to get so out of hand? It had been five years since she had made a film in Hollywood, three years since she had done any acting work at all. She had completely thrown herself into life in Tawleigh-on-the-Water, finishing the house, extending her business interests, playing tennis and bridge, horse riding, making friends ... getting married. It was as if she had decided to turn her life into the greatest part she had ever played. Of course, her bank manager had warned her. Her accountants had written to her. She still remembered her agents screaming down the phone at her from New York. But Melissa had been enjoying herself too much to listen to them. She had made a string of successful films in England and in America. Her face had been on the front covers of *Woman's Weekly*, *Life* and even (after she had played opposite James Cagney) *True Detective*. She would work when she needed to work. She was Melissa James. When she chose to make her comeback, she would be even bigger than she had been before.

It had to be soon. Somehow, she had allowed the bills

to mount up to such an extent that they almost took her breath away. She was paying five salaries. She was supporting a boat and two horses. The business she had bought – the Moonflower Hotel – was full for at least half the year and should have been making her a handsome profit. Instead, it was running at a loss. She had been assured that her investments were doing well but so far they hadn't actually returned any profit. Worse still, as both her British and her American agents had explained, there might not be quite as many film parts for her as she had expected. It seemed that, having turned forty, she had moved into a new marketplace. There were younger actresses – Jayne Mansfield, Natalie Wood, Elizabeth Taylor – who had inherited her mantle. Suddenly she was being asked to play their mother! And the worst of it was that being the mother didn't pay.

Still, Melissa refused to worry. When she had started out years ago, as a bit-part actress in the cheap 'quota quickies' that British producers had made simply because they were forced to, she had dreamed of the day when she would be an international star. She had known with absolute certainty that it would happen. She was the sort of person who always got what she wanted. And that was exactly how she felt now. Only that morning she had received a wonderful script, a thriller in which she would play the lead part, a woman whose husband tried to murder her and who then framed her when the attempt went wrong. It was going to be directed by Alfred Hitchcock, which meant that it would certainly be a box-office hit. It was true that the part hadn't actually been offered to her. She was going to have to meet Mr Hitchcock in London when he arrived in a couple of weeks. But Melissa was confident. The part could have been written for her and, she reflected, as soon as she got into a room with the screenwriters, she would make sure that it was.

All these thoughts had gone through her mind as she walked to the door, but before she could open it she heard footsteps behind her and knew at once that it was Francis Pendleton, her husband, coming down the stairs. For a brief moment she thought about continuing on her way, leaving the house as if she hadn't heard him. But that would never work. Better not to make a thing of it.

She turned and smiled. 'I'm just going out,' she said.

'Where?'

'The hotel. I want to talk to the Gardners.'

'Do you want me to come with you?'

'No! No need! I'll only be half an hour.'

It was funny how much more difficult it was to act when you weren't facing cameras, lights and a crowd of about fifty people, when the lines hadn't been written for you, when you had effectively to be yourself. Melissa was trying to look relaxed, to pretend that everything was all right. But her co-performer wasn't playing the game. In fact he was looking at her with deep suspicion.

She had met Francis on the set of the last film she had made in England, the reason she had come back to her country of birth. *Hostage to Fortune* had been a disappointing thriller based on a novel by John Buchan in which Melissa had played a young mother searching for her kidnapped daughter. Some of the scenes had been shot in Devon, on Saunton Sands, and Francis had been assigned to her as a personal assistant. Although he was ten years younger than her, there had been an immediate chemistry between them that had warned her exactly where things might lead. Not that a romance during filming was anything new. In fact, Melissa couldn't remember a film she had made where she hadn't found herself romantically involved with either another actor or a member of the crew. But this time it had been different. Somehow, when the final scene had wrapped and everyone had gone their separate ways, Francis had still been there and she had realised that he had come to the conclusion that their relationship should be a permanent one.

And why not? Francis was good-looking, with his curly hair, his tanned skin and his excellent physique, the latter two gained on their sailing boat, the *Sundowner*. He was intelligent and, most important of all, utterly devoted to her. Nor was the match as unbalanced as it might seem. His parents were wealthy, his father a viscount with a twenty-thousand-acre estate in Cornwall. He was actually the Honourable Francis Pendleton and although he would inherit neither the land nor the title and had chosen never to use the honorific, he was still highly eligible. When the engagement had been announced, they had appeared in every single gossip column in the London newspapers and it had occurred to Melissa that when she did finally return to Hollywood and walked into the Polo Lounge or the Chateau Marmont with an extremely handsome, sophisticated British aristocrat on her arm, she would be sending exactly the right message about herself.

Francis had been the only person to support Melissa in the purchase of Clarence Keep. More than that, he had encouraged her and now she understood why. First of all, it was close to his home territory. The family estate was in the next county and although his parents no longer spoke to him – they had been unimpressed by what they had read in the gossip columns – this was exactly the lifestyle he had always wanted. He didn't help with the hotel or the horses or anything, really. He didn't even get out of bed before ten. He had become the lord of his own manor with his *tropaeum uxor*, or trophy wife.

She looked at him now, standing at the foot of the stairs wearing a blue blazer and white trousers, as if he was about to go out sailing on the yacht they could no longer afford, clenching and unclenching his fists as he struggled to find the right words to say. It seemed to her that he had become more and more ineffectual. Sometimes, quite often in fact, she blamed him for the decisions she had made as if it had always been his plan to fold her into his world.

'I think we need to talk,' he said.

'Not now, Francis. The ghastly Gardners are waiting for me.'

'Well, when you get back, then ...'

'I thought you were going out tonight.'

He frowned. 'We both are.'

'No.' She pouted. 'I'm sorry, darling. I've got a headache. You will forgive me, won't you? I'm going to take an early night.'

'Well, if you're not coming, I won't go either.'

Melissa sighed. This was the last thing she wanted. She'd already worked out what she was going to do with an evening on her own. 'Don't be silly,' she said. 'You've been looking forward to the opera for weeks and you know you enjoy it more on your own. You always say I fall asleep in the second act.'

'That's because you do.'

'I don't like it. I don't understand the stories. They never make any sense.' This wasn't going to work if it became a confrontation. She went over to him and laid a hand on his arm. 'You enjoy yourself, Francis. I've got a lot on my mind at the moment with the hotel and the new script and everything else. We can talk tomorrow or the day after.' She tried to make light of it. 'I'm not going anywhere!'

But Francis took her last words quite seriously. Before she could move her hand he took hold of it, pressing it tightly against his arm. 'You are going to stay with me, Melissa. You know I still love you. I'd do anything for you.'

'I know. You don't need to tell me that.'

'I'd die if you left me. I couldn't live without you.'

'Stop being silly, Francis.' She tried to break free but he was still holding her. 'I can't talk now,' she insisted. 'Anyway . . . ' she lowered her voice ' . . . Eric and his mother are in the kitchen.'

'They can't hear us.'

'They might come out.'

That did the trick, as she had known it would. He let her go and at once she stepped back, out of his reach.

'Don't wait for me,' she said. 'You might get stuck be-hind a tractor and you don't want to miss the first act.'

'I thought you said you were only going to be half an hour.'

'I don't know how long I'm going to be. I've got to talk to the Gardners about the accounts. Actually, I've got an idea that might just put them on the spot.'

'What do you mean?'

'I'll tell you after I've seen them. We can talk tomorrow.'

She really was about to leave. But then there came a huffing and a scratching of claws against the wooden floor and a little dog appeared, running across the hall towards its mistress. The dog was a chow, a solid block of reddish fur with a squat face, pointed, triangular ears and a dark purple tongue. Melissa couldn't help herself. She squealed with pleasure and knelt down, running her fingers through the dog's fur where it was thickest, around its neck.

'Little Kimba!' she crooned. 'How's my baby?' She was holding her face close to the dog's and didn't pull back when he licked her nose and lips. 'How's my beautiful boy? Mummy's just going into town. But I'll be back soon. Are you going to be on the bed? Are you going to be waiting for me?'

Francis pulled a face. He didn't like having the dog on the bed, but he said nothing.

'Go on then! Good boy! Mummy will see you soon.'

Melissa straightened up. She glanced at Francis. 'Enjoy the opera. I'll see you tomorrow,' she said. And then she really was gone, hurrying outside, closing the front door behind her, leaving Francis with the bleak awareness that she had been much more affectionate to the chow than she had been to him.

TWO
ALGERNON MARSH

Melissa loved her Bentley in much the same way as she loved her pet chow. It was a beautiful car. It was an indulgence. And it belonged, entirely, to her. It was the belonging that mattered most, the sense of empowerment. Sitting on the silvery leather upholstery, listening to the low growl of the engine, knowing that the car would be recognised a mile away, she felt the unease that had resulted from her meeting with Francis slipping away in the jet stream behind her. The car was pale blue, a Mark VI with a power-operated hood, which, unfortunately, would have to stay up as the rain had indeed returned, this time falling as a miserable, grey drizzle. Why did the weather have to be so cold and miserable at the end of April? According to her agent, Alfred Hitchcock was planning to shoot his new film at the Warner Brothers

Studios in Burbank, California, and that couldn't have suited her more. It would be nice to be back in the sun.

Clarence Keep was less than half a mile outside Tawleigh-on-the-Water, a seaside village whose name hardly did it justice. Tawleigh was surrounded by no fewer than four different stretches of water: the Bristol Channel to the right, the Irish Sea to the left and the estuaries of two rivers, the Taw and the Torridge, swelling up behind. Sometimes it seemed as if the little harbour was battling for its very existence, particularly when the wind blew and the waves came crashing down in relentless grey spumes. Then the fishing boats would tear at their moorings and the lighthouse would blink helplessly, illuminating only the swirling clouds that engulfed it.

The village population numbered about three hundred. Most of the houses were contained on Marine Parade, which stretched along the front, with a second, narrower road behind it called Rectory Lane. The other buildings that made up Tawleigh-on-the-Water consisted of a church – St Daniel's – a butcher's, a baker's, a garage and a chandlery that also sold various household goods. For years there had been just one pub, the Red Lion, in the village. But then Melissa had bought the nineteenth-century customs house and converted it into a hotel that she had called the Moonflower after one of her films. It had twelve bedrooms, a restaurant and a comfortable bar.

There was no police station in Tawleigh-on-the-Water but nor was there any need for one as, apart from a few teenagers getting drunk and causing mischief on the beach, there had been no trouble in the village for as long as anyone could remember. Nor was there a post office, a bank, a library or a cinema. For any of those you would have to make your way to Bideford, which was about twenty minutes away on the steam train that ploughed up and down the single line from Instow, or about a quarter of an hour by car, on the other side of Bideford Long Bridge. Visitors were sometimes surprised that there was no fish shop either. The fishermen sold their catch directly from their boats.

The Moonflower had been built for the growing number of families from London and elsewhere who dreamed of escaping to the coast during the summer months and Melissa had made sure that it was attractive to children and adults alike. The more expensive rooms had bathrooms *en suite*. Although dinner was served strictly at seven o'clock, there was a high tea for younger guests at half past five. Every weekend there were concerts, tea parties and croquet or French cricket on the lawn. Nannies and personal valets were accommodated in a separate building at the bottom of the garden, discreetly out of sight.

Melissa drew up in front of the main door. The rain

was coming down harder now and although there were only a few steps across the gravel, her hair and the shoulders of her coat were still splattered with water by the time she arrived in the entrance hall. Lance Gardner, the manager, had seen her arrive, standing there unctuously as if it had never occurred to him to come out with an umbrella and help her into the building. Was this the way he greeted the guests?

'Good evening, Miss James,' he said, completely unaware that he had already put her in a bad mood.

'Hello, Mr Gardner.'

The two of them had never been on first-name terms. It simply wasn't appropriate. Lance and Maureen Gardner were Melissa's employees, not her friends. When she had found them, they had been the landlord and chief barmaid at the Red Lion and she had been rather pleased that she had been able to poach them to run her new hotel. After all, they knew the area. They had friends on the council and in the police. If there were any problems with licences or local suppliers, they would find ways around them. It had seemed like a good idea at the time and it was only now, three and a half years after the Moonflower had opened, that she wondered if it had been right to trust the couple so completely. She knew almost nothing about them. The pub had been making a profit when they worked there – that much she had managed to find out – but they had been tied to a major brewery chain with only minimal control.

They certainly hadn't made any profit running the Moonflower. Something had to be wrong. The hotel was popular. All the newspapers had written positively about it, obviously attracted by the idea that it was owned by a bona fide Hollywood star. In the beginning, she had known that a number of her clients had only come in the hope of seeing her and would be disappointed if they didn't go home with at least an autograph. But as the hotel had bedded in and she had turned up less often, it had been accepted for what it was: an elegant, comfortable retreat in an attractive seaside village with a great beach and lovely views. It was successful – full for most of the summer and busy even in the wetter months.

But it was devouring money. Her money. Whose fault was it? Melissa had already taken steps to find out, but she had called this meeting to test a theory, one that had been forming in her mind for some time.

'How are things?' she asked quite casually as she followed Lance Gardner through the empty reception area and into his office.

'We can't complain, Miss James. Not really. Nine rooms occupied. I'm afraid this bad weather really isn't on our side. But I've been looking at the reports from the

Meteorological Office and they say that May is going to be lovely.'

They had passed through the doorway into a large, square room with two desks, filing cabinets and an old-fashioned safe prominent in one corner. There was a complicated switchboard along one wall, connecting all the rooms, and Melissa remembered authorising it even though it had cost a small fortune. Maureen Gardner was sitting at her desk, going through paperwork, but stood up as Melissa came in.

'Good evening, Miss James.'

'Would you like a cup of tea?' Gardner asked. 'Or perhaps something stronger?' he added with a hint of conspiracy. The bar wouldn't open until half past six.

'No, thank you.'

'These came for you, Miss James ... ' Maureen Gardner had produced a packet of three envelopes, already opened, and handed them across as Melissa sat down. The first of them was lilac-coloured. She had expected the scent of lavender and already smelled it. She knew who it came from.

She received far fewer letters than she had at the height of her career but she still had fan clubs in America and Britain, and of course her address at the Moon-flower had been well publicised. Every month there were two or three of them, imploring her to make another film, telling her how much she was missed. The woman who wrote on lilac paper and who signed herself only as 'Your number-one fan' had strong, neat handwriting with every comma and full stop in place. Melissa wondered if she was single or married, happy or sad. It was something she had never understood, the neediness of some of the people who had followed her career – and sometimes it worried her. Glancing at the page now, she read: '*How can you do it to us, dear Miss James? The screen is diminished without you. A light has gone out of our lives.*' Wouldn't you have to be a little disturbed to write something like that? And this must be the ninth or tenth message that Miss Lilac had sent her over the years.

'Thank you,' she said, sliding the letter back into its envelope. She wouldn't reply. She never did any more. 'I've been looking at the accounts up until February,' she went on, wanting to get back to the subject in hand.

'We did very well over Christmas,' Mrs Gardner said.

'Well, we lost less in December than we had in the month before, if that's what you mean.'

'I think we need to raise our prices, Miss James,' Lance Gardner exclaimed. 'The room rates and the restaurant—'

'But we're already one of the most expensive hotels in Devonshire.'

'We run a very tight ship. We've cut back on staff. Obviously, we have to keep an eye on the quality of our service ... '

There were times when Lance Gardner looked and sounded like nothing more than a spiv. It wasn't just the double-breasted jacket, the slicked-back hair, the pencil moustache. It was in his entire manner, the way he never quite met your eyes. His wife was the same. She was larger than him, with a louder voice. She wore too much make-up. Melissa remembered the first time she had seen her behind the bar at the Red Lion and that was exactly where she belonged. The two of them were about fifty years old. They had been married for a long time but had no children. In a way, they were reflections of each other, but in fairground mirrors that twisted and distorted the images almost beyond recognition.

She decided to spring her trap. 'I've been thinking about calling in a team of accountants,' she said.

'I'm sorry?' Lance Gardner looked at her with undisguised dismay.

'I want someone from London to go over the books for the last two years: the income, all the outlays, the redecoration ...' she waved a hand '... the new switchboard. What I want is a complete audit.'

'I hope you're not suggesting that Maureen and myself—'

'I'm not suggesting anything, Mr Gardner. I'm sure the two of you have done a terrific job. I'm only doing what's sensible. We're losing money and we don't see how. If we're going to make a profit, we need to find out.'

'We do things our own way down here in Tawleigh, Miss James.' Lance Gardner had fallen silent, so his wife took over. 'For example, we always pay the fishermen in cash. That's what they want and there are no receipts. And the last time Mr Hocking came in, we gave him dinner and a bottle of Scotch. He didn't take a penny.' Melissa vaguely remembered. Mr Hocking was a local electrician. 'All I'm saying is,' she went on, 'I'm not sure a London firm would be able to help.'

'Well, we'll see.' Melissa had known they would argue. She had been watching them carefully, waiting for it. 'My mind is made up. I want you to start preparing for when they arrive.'

'And when will that be?' Lance asked. 'Have you written to them yet?'

'I'm going to write to them tomorrow. I imagine they'll be here in a week or two. I'll let you know as soon as I've heard.'

She got to her feet. She had said everything she wanted to say.

Lance and Maureen Gardner stayed where they were.

'Thank you very much.' She had almost forgotten the

letters. She snatched them up and took them with her as she left the room.

There was a long silence. It was as if the Gardners were waiting to be sure that they were on their own.

'What are we going to do?' Maureen asked. She looked nervous.

'We don't have anything to worry about. You heard what she said.' Lance took a packet of cigarettes out of the desk drawer and lit one. 'We're doing a great job.'

'These accountants of hers may not agree.'

'These accountants may never appear. She hasn't sent the letter yet and maybe she never will.'

'What do you mean?' Maureen looked at her husband with horror in her eyes. 'What are you going to do?'

'I'll talk to her. I'll persuade her that hiring a bunch of city slickers is just throwing good money after bad. I'll recommend someone local. Someone cheaper. I'm sure I can make her see sense.'

'And what if she doesn't listen to you?'

Lance Gardner blew out smoke. It hung in the air around him. 'Then I'll think of something else ... '

*

While Melissa had been driving towards the Moonflower, another car had been heading down the Braunton Road that skirted around Barnstaple, but going considerably faster. The car was French, a cream-coloured Peugeot, not a model that one would see very often on British roads, but it had been chosen carefully by its owner. It was more than a means of transport. It was a calling card.

The man behind the wheel was relaxed, smoking a cigarette, even as the needle of his speedometer crept towards fifty. There were trees on either side of the road and they swept past, forming a green tunnel that he found strangely hypnotic. It was still raining and the windscreen wipers added to the sense of hypnotism, swinging left and right, left and right, like a pocket watch.

He hadn't realised how late it was. A long lunch at the golf club had turned into a marathon drinking session, the alcohol sneaked in through the back door of the private members' room. He would have to stop and buy some peppermints before he got back to the house. His sister wouldn't approve if she smelled whisky on his breath. And even though he was only staying there until the weekend, her husband, the jumped-up little doctor, was only waiting for an opportunity to ask him to leave.

Algernon Marsh sighed. Things had been going so well until they had started going badly and then everything had turned upside down at once. He was in trouble and he knew it.

But was any of it really his own fault?

His parents had died in the first week of the Blitz. He had been just sixteen years old and although he had been nowhere near London at the time, he often felt that he had been a victim of the same bomb. After all, it had wiped out his home, the room where he slept, all his possessions, all his childhood memories. He and Samantha had moved in with their spinster aunt Joyce, and although she and Samantha had got on – well, it really had been like a house on fire, hadn't it? – she and Algernon had never seen eye to eye.

And so it had continued into adult life. Samantha had gone on to marry the doctor and had built a new life for herself with the house in Tawleigh, two children, nice neighbours, a seat on the local council. But after an undistinguished war, Algernon had been lost in a great vacuum, on his own, with nothing to define him. Briefly he had flirted with some of the south London gangs – the Elephant Boys, the Brixton mob – but if he suspected he wasn't cut out for serious crime, a three-month sentence for affray following a fight at the well-known Nut House in Piccadilly had confirmed it. After his release, he had become a shop assistant, a bookmaker, a door-to-door salesman and finally an estate agent, and it was in this last occupation that he had found his calling.

For all his faults, Algernon was well spoken. He had

been educated at a small private school in West Kensington and he could be charming and witty when he wanted to be. With his fair hair cut short and his matinée-idol good looks, he was naturally attractive, particularly to older women who took him at face value and didn't make too many enquiries about his past. He still remembered buying his first suit on Savile Row. It had cost him much more than he could afford, but, like the car, it made a statement. When he walked into a room, people noticed him. When he talked, they listened.

He had moved into property development. More than a hundred thousand buildings in London had been destroyed during the war and that translated into a major opportunity for construction and reconstruction. The trouble was, it was a crowded market and Algernon was only a small player.

He had managed to buy himself a flat in Mayfair. He had one or two nice projects on the go. And then he had discovered the South of France and a place he had never heard of called St-Tropez. That was where the serious money was going. The whole coast was being turned into a pleasure ground for the rich, with five-star hotels, new apartment blocks, restaurants, marinas and casinos, and it would be perfect for the idea he had in mind; near enough for his clients to feel comfortable, but not too near for them to know what was actually going on. It had taken Algernon less than a minute to come up with the name of his new company: Sun Trap Holdings. He had travelled to France and come back with a smattering of French and a car that, fortunately, had the steering wheel on the right side. He was ready to begin.

It had gone better than he had ever expected. So far, thirty clients had invested in Sun Trap Holdings, some of them more than once. He had promised them that the profits would be as much as five or even ten times the original investment. All they had to do was wait. And although he'd had to pay out dividends to a few of them, the rest were always satisfied with extra shares in the company, which would add up to even greater rewards further down the line.

Algernon had started coming down to Devon to visit his sister not because the two of them were particularly close but because she had a large house that provided him with the occasional refuge from London when he needed it. There were business partners he had fallen out with, old associates that he preferred to avoid, and when it became necessary he would jump in his car and head south-west. He didn't much like Tawleigh-on-the-Water. He thought it was dull. He would never have expected to find his biggest investor in such a backwater, but that was exactly what had happened.

He had been introduced to Melissa James just after

she bought the Moonflower. At first, he had been over-awed meeting such a famous actress, but he had quickly reminded himself that she was just another wealthy woman almost begging to be separated from her money and he had achieved this more quickly than he could have believed. The two of them had become business associates, then friends, then something rather more than friends. It had been easy to persuade her that Sun Trap Holdings would eventually pay her far more than the films she had decided to give up.

She was the reason for this trip. The telephone call had come just a few days ago, when Algernon had been at his Mayfair flat.

'Is that you, darling?'

'Melissa, darling. What a lovely surprise! How are you?'

'I want to see you. Can you come down?'

'Of course. You know you don't have to ask me twice.' Algernon paused. 'Is there something wrong?'

'I want to talk to you about my investment—'

'It's doing fantastically well.'

'I know. You've been brilliant. And that's exactly why I've decided that now would be the best time to sell my shares.'

Algernon sat bolt upright in bed. 'You're not serious!'

'Yes, I am.'

'But another six months and the value will have doubled. We have the new hotel opening. And as soon as the villas in Cap Ferrat are completed—'

'I know, I know. But I'm happy with the money I've made. So come down and bring the paperwork. It'll be lovely to see you anyway.'

'Of course, darling. Whatever you say.'

Whatever you say! Unless he could persuade her otherwise, Algernon would have to find a sum close to a hundred thousand pounds to pay Melissa back for profits that existed only in her imagination. He pressed his foot down on the accelerator and saw a great sloosh of water spray to one side as he drove through a puddle. He was meeting Melissa tomorrow. Hopefully, it would be just the two of them. It would all be a lot easier with her husband out of the way.

What time was it? Algernon glanced down at the clock on the dashboard and scowled. Twenty past five. Had he really spent the whole afternoon drinking at the Saunton Golf Club?

He looked up just in time to see the man filling the windscreen.

Too late, he realised that somehow, in the few seconds he had taken his eyes off the road, he had allowed the car to drift over to one side. He actually felt the front tyre mount the grassy verge that separated the road from the hedgerow. That was where the man had been walking. He saw a face, staring eyes, a mouth drawing back in what must have been a cry of horror. Desperately, he scrabbled with the steering wheel, trying to veer away. But it was hopeless. He had been travelling at over fifty miles per hour.

The roar of the engine drowned out any sound the man might have made, but the impact of the car hitting him was the most horrible thing Algernon had ever heard. It seemed impossibly loud. He stamped his foot on the brake, noticing that the man had disappeared as if by magic. He had simply gone. As the car squealed to a halt, Algernon tried to persuade himself that he had imagined the whole thing, that it hadn't been a man but a rabbit or maybe a deer. But he knew what he had seen. He felt sick, the alcohol churning in his stomach.

The car had come to a halt, slanting diagonally into the road. Now he heard the windscreen wipers grinding against the glass and reached down for the switch that turned them off. What next? He grabbed the gear stick and reversed, pulling in next to the hedge. He could feel tears welling up in his eyes, but they weren't tears for the man he had just injured – or possibly killed. He was thinking of himself, of the fact that he had been drinking and that, following an incident with a police car at

Hyde Park Corner, he had been disqualified for driving for one year and shouldn't have been behind the wheel at all. What would happen to him? If he had killed the man, he might go to jail!

He turned off the engine and opened the car door. The rain swept gleefully towards him, driving into his face. He was still holding the cigarette but suddenly he didn't want it and threw it into the grass. Where was he? Where was the man he had just hit, and anyway, what had he been doing out on his own, walking along a major road in the middle of nowhere? Another car rushed past.

He had to get this over with. He stepped out of his car and walked a short distance further down the road. He came to the man almost at once. He was wearing a raincoat and lying face down in the grass. He looked completely broken, his legs and arms pointing in different directions as if some monster had grabbed hold of him and tried to pull him apart. He didn't seem to be breathing and Algernon was quite sure he was dead. Nobody could have survived a collision like that. It was murder, then. In the two seconds that he had looked down at the clock on the dashboard he had killed someone, at the same time destroying his own life.

One car had passed him. It hadn't stopped.

With the rain coming down so hard, the driver

couldn't have seen him. He certainly wouldn't have seen the man who'd been hit. Suddenly, Algernon regretted having a French car in England. It was probably the only one in the whole county. He looked behind him. The road was empty. He was on his own.

He made the decision instantly. He turned and hurried back to the car, noticing that there was now a dent in the radiator grille and a smear of bright red blood on the silver Peugeot badge. With a shudder, Algernon took out a handkerchief and wiped it clean. He wanted to throw the handkerchief away but thought better of it. Then he remembered the cigarette. What madness had made him discard it like that? It was too late. It would have been carried away by the wind. He wasn't going to crawl on his hands and knees looking for it. All that mattered was to get as far from here as possible.

He got back into the car, closed the door and turned the key. The engine coughed but refused to start. He was soaking wet. Water was dripping down his forehead. He slammed his hands against the steering wheel, then tried again. This time the engine fired.

He punched the car into gear and drove away. He didn't look back. He didn't stop until he had reached Tawleigh, but he didn't dare go into his sister's house, not looking like this, soaking wet and with trembling hands. Instead, he pulled into a quiet lane and sat there for the next twenty minutes, his head in his hands, wondering what he was going to do.

*

While Algernon Marsh was sitting miserably in his car, watching the rain still streaking down the windscreen, his sister was also in something close to a state of shock, staring at a letter that lay on the table in front of her.

'I don't understand,' she said. 'What does it mean?'

'I think it's fairly clear, my dearest,' her husband said. 'Your aunt—'

'Aunt Joyce.'

'Joyce Campion has made you her sole beneficiary. And sadly, she has recently passed away. The solicitors want to get in touch with you to discuss the inheritance, and it might be considerable. My love, this could be good news – for both of us! I could be married to a multimillionaire!'

'Oh Len, don't say that!'

'Well, it's possible.'

The letter had arrived in the morning post but they had both been so busy that Samantha had only just opened it. It had come from a firm of solicitors in London – Parker & Bentley – and even the letterhead, with an address in Lincoln's Inn in raised black letters, had somehow seemed threatening. Samantha had always been nervous of the law. She was nervous of anything she didn't completely understand.

She had read the single page with its three typed paragraphs. She had read them again. Then she had called for Leonard and asked him to read them too.

Leonard and Samantha Collins were sitting in the kitchen of the five-bedroom house that also contained the doctor's surgery. It was a handsome, old building in need of a fresh coat of paint. The salt-water spray from the sea had done its worst and the wind had taken a few tiles off the roof. The garden, too, had been damaged by bad weather and marauding children. But it was still a solid family home with a vegetable patch that delivered pounds of raspberries in the summer, an orchard and a tree house. It was situated in Rectory Lane, right next to St Daniel's, and this was one of the reasons Samantha had chosen it. A committed churchgoer, she never missed a Sunday service and helped the vicar with the flowers, all the major festivals, the various fund-raising efforts, tea for the old age pensioners on Thursdays and even with the allocation of plots in the cemetery (available to anyone who lived in the parish on receipt of a moderate fee).

Samantha divided her time equally between the

church and her family, which included two children, Mark and Agnes, aged seven and five. She also looked after her husband's medical practice, keeping a close eye on his accounts, his patient records, the daily running of his surgery. There were some who found her a rather severe woman, the sort who was never without a scarf and handbag and who always seemed to be in a hurry. And yet she was always polite. She smiled at everyone, even if she preferred not to stop and chat.

Nobody knew more about the people who lived in Tawleigh-on-the-Water than her. From her conversations with the vicar, who considered her his closest confidante, she had learned about their spiritual needs, their concerns, even their sins. From her husband she had got a snapshot – an X-ray, perhaps – of their physical condition and what had caused it. Mr Doyle, the butcher, drank too much and had cirrhosis of the liver. Nancy Mitchell, who worked at the Moonflower and who was not married, was three months pregnant. And even Melissa James, for all her fame, had been prescribed pills for stress and sleeplessness.

It never occurred to Samantha that she might, in fact, be in possession of too much knowledge – for her own good and everyone else's. Anyway, she was much too sensible to indulge in the sort of gossip that sometimes made the village seem impossibly small. It might be said that she believed in the silence of the confessional and patients were welcomed into the surgery with the same formality with which they were greeted at church on Sundays. Even Mrs Mitchell, Nancy's mother, who came to the house three times a week and who helped with the children, knew nothing about her daughter's condition. That had been difficult for both Leonard and Samantha, but, it went without saying, they were bound by the Hippocratic oath.

They had now been married for eight years. Dr Leonard Collins had been a consultant at the King Edward VII Hospital in Slough. Samantha had been doing volunteer work when they met and they had got engaged soon after. He was lithe and elegant, a darkly handsome man with a well-trimmed beard and a fondness for tweed suits. Everyone in the village agreed that they were ideally matched, living and working together and always in perfect agreement apart from two things. Dr Collins was not a particularly religious man. He accompanied his wife to church out of respect rather than any personal belief. And, much to her displeasure, he smoked a pipe, a Stanwell Royal Briar that he had owned since his teens. She had been unable to persuade him to give it up, but, as a compromise, he never smoked it when the children were in the room.

'But I hadn't seen Aunt Joyce for years and years,' she

said now. 'We didn't really contact each other – apart from Christmas and birthday cards.'

'She obviously hadn't forgotten you,' Leonard remarked. He picked up his pipe, thought for a moment, then set it down again.

'She was a wonderful person and I'm very sad to hear she's dead.' Samantha had the sort of face – square and serious – that was better equipped to express sorrow than pleasure. 'I will ask the vicar to say a special prayer for her this Sunday.'

'I'm sure she would have appreciated that.'

'I feel bad. I really should have made more effort to stay in touch.'

Samantha sat in silence, thinking about Joyce Campion, who had stepped in after her parents died. It was actually Aunt Joyce who had first encouraged her to go to church. Her brother Algernon, of course, had refused to come. Aunt Joyce had also paid for her to go to secretarial school, where she had learned shorthand and typing, and later on she had used her contacts to get her niece a position in the typing pool of Horlicks, the malted-milk company in Slough. Samantha had always thought of her aunt as the quintessential spinster so it had come as a complete surprise when she had suddenly announced her engagement to Harlan Goodis, a multi-millionaire with an advertising agency in New York. That had happened at around the same time that Samantha had met and married Leonard, moving with him first to a house he had inherited near Torrington and later to Tawleigh. It was perhaps inevitable that the two women should have lost touch.

'Her husband died two years ago,' Samantha said. 'They didn't have any children. As far as I know, they didn't have any family at all.'

'From what the solicitors are saying, it looks as if everything is going to you.'

'Do you really think it could be … a lot?'

'It's hard to say. I mean, he was doing pretty well for himself. I suppose it all depends how much of his money she spent before she died. Would you like to ring them or shall I?'

'I think I'd prefer it if you did, Len. I'd be too nervous.' Samantha glanced down at the letter for perhaps the twentieth time. From the way she was looking at it, she might have been happier if it had never arrived.

'Maybe we shouldn't set our expectations too high,' she said. 'It doesn't even say anything about money. She could have left us something we don't need. A few paintings or some old jewellery.'

'A few Picassos or a diamond tiara.'

'Stop it! You're just imagining things.'

'If it wasn't a lot of money, why would they want to see you?'

'I don't know. Because—'

She was about to continue when the door opened and a small boy came in, dressed in pyjamas, fresh from the bath. This was Mark, her seven-year-old son. 'Mummy, are you going to come up and read to me?' he asked.

Samantha was tired. She hadn't even served the children their tea yet and there was still dinner to be made. But she smiled and got to her feet. 'Of course, darling. Mummy's coming up right now.'

The two of them had just started reading C. S. Lewis. Mark loved the books. Only the night before, Samantha had found him in the back of his wardrobe, trying to find his way into Narnia. He ran out of the room and she was about to follow when a thought occurred to her. She turned back to her husband. 'The letter doesn't mention Algernon,' she said.

'Yes. I noticed that.' Leonard scowled. 'It says quite specifically that you are the sole beneficiary.'

'Aunt Joyce was horrified when Algie was sent to prison,' Samantha said. 'You remember – that business in Piccadilly.'

'That was before I met you.'

'I told you about it.' Samantha was standing at the

doorway, aware that Mark was waiting for her upstairs. 'She always said that he was untrustworthy,' she went on. 'Falling in with the wrong crowd – and all those business ideas of his. Do you think she's cut him out?'

'It rather looks like it.'

'Well, I'll have to share it with him. I can't take it all for myself. I mean, if it is …' she paused as if unwilling to consider the possibility ' … lots!'

'I suppose so. Yes.' Leonard lowered his voice, as if he was afraid that the children were listening. 'Would you mind if I said something, my dear?'

'You know I always listen to you, Leonard.' It was true. He had always been the first person she came to for advice. Even if she didn't always take it.

'Well, if I were you, I wouldn't say anything to your brother.'

'What? Don't tell him?'

'Not yet. I mean – you're right. We don't have any idea how much money we're talking about and we won't know until we go up to London and talk to these solicitors. It would be a shame to make a fuss about nothing.'

'But just now you were saying—'

'I know what I was saying, but listen to me.' Leonard chose his words carefully. Samantha and Algernon didn't see a lot of each other, but he knew that they were close. After what had happened during the war, the sudden death of their parents and the loss of everything they had, how could it have been otherwise? 'I'm not sure we should have this conversation now, not while Algernon is staying in the house, but it does worry me a bit.'

'What do you mean?'

'I don't want to alarm you, my dear, but there is a side to him that we don't really know about. And it's just possible that he might be ... '

'What?'

'Dangerous. You know how he is with his schemes and dreams. Let's not say anything about it for the time being. Let's at least find out how much we're talking about before we come to any decisions.' Leonard smiled and at that moment he was as handsome as the day they had met and Samantha was reminded of why she had married him. 'You deserve a break,' he said. 'I'm afraid I've never been able to look after you properly. Not on my salary. This could be a new beginning for you.'

'Don't be ridiculous. I've got nothing to complain about. I've been perfectly happy.'

'So have I. I'm a very lucky man.'

Samantha hurried over to the table and kissed her husband lightly on the cheek. Then she went off to read about Narnia.

THREE
THE QUEEN'S RANSOM

Melissa had planned to leave the Moonflower as soon as she had spoken to the Gardners. But when she came out of the manager's office, she noticed Nancy Mitchell behind the reception desk and of course she had to stop for a quick chat. Nancy had worked for the hotel from the very start. She was a good, reliable girl, the daughter of the lighthouse keeper, and it was always Melissa's policy to be friendly with the staff. She knew how easy it would be to get a reputation for being standoffish.

'How are you, Nancy?' she asked with a smile.

'I'm very well, thank you, Miss James.'

But she didn't look well. Nancy always had a slightly nervous quality, as if she was terrified of causing offence, but today she seemed to be completely exhausted. Her eyes were red from either tiredness or tears and her long fair hair was tangled, in need of a brush. It must be boyfriend trouble – but did Nancy even have a boy-friend? She was in her early twenties and though not unattractive, her features didn't quite marry, like one of those paintings where the artist is trying to be too clever. That was Melissa's first thought. The second was that she couldn't have guests coming in and out of the hotel past a weeping receptionist. It really wouldn't do.

'Is everything all right?' she enquired.

'Yes, Miss James.' Now Nancy seemed fearful.

'How are your parents?' Melissa was trying to be pleasant, unthreatening.

'They're very well, thank you, Miss James.'

'I'm glad to hear it.' She looked around her. The two of them were alone. 'Look,' she said. 'If there's something worrying you, you can tell me. I'd like to think we've known each other long enough to consider ourselves friends.'

To her surprise, the girl was looking at her with some-thing close to horror. 'No!' she exclaimed, then more quietly: 'I mean…you're very kind, Miss James. But the thing is … I've just been having a few problems at home. Dad's been worried about his knee, going up and down all those stairs.'

Only a moment ago Nancy had said that her par-ents were both fine. As an actress herself, Melissa knew immediately when someone wasn't telling her the truth. She was actually getting quite irritated with the girl. 'Well, it's just that you are the public face of the Moonflower,' she warned. 'To be honest with you, Nancy, you can't sit here looking like that. If you don't feel well, you should go home.'

'I'm sorry, Miss James.' Nancy did her best to pull herself together, forcing a smile onto her face. 'I'll just go to the ladies' room and powder my nose and then I'll be fine.'

'That's right. You look after yourself.'

Melissa gave her a brief smile and continued on her way. There was something about the encounter that worried her. It was her suggestion that the two of them were friends. Anyone else would have been flattered, but Nancy had seemed shocked. Had the Gardners said something to her? Did she know something about the hotel's financial difficulties?

She decided to put the girl out of her mind, but her troubles were far from over. As she reached the car, there was a man standing there and Melissa knew, with a sinking feeling in her stomach, that he was deliberately waiting for her. The man was small and thickset, dressed in a dark suit that had got crumpled after being in the rain. His hair, what little he had of it, was also damp. Although he had shaved, there were dark shadows over his chin and upper lip. He looked completely out of place in a seaside village, like a small-time gangster who had just been released from jail. Even before he spoke, with an accent that betrayed his Eastern European origins, it was obvious that he had come from abroad.

'Good evening, Melissa,' he began.

'Simon! This is a surprise. Why didn't you tell me you were coming?'

'Because if I had told you I was coming, I think I would not have found you here.' He beamed at her as he said this, as if he was making a joke. But they both knew that he was serious and that what he had said was true.

'You know I always love seeing you,' she replied, gaily. 'But I wish you'd told me because I'm afraid I can't talk to you right now ...'

'Five minutes, Melissa.'

'I have to get home, Simon. Francis and I are going to the opera.'

'No. I have driven for five hours from London to see you. Five minutes is not so very much to ask.'

She couldn't have an argument with him. Not here, in front of the hotel. There were guests who might come in or out. Anyway, perhaps it was best to get this over with. She raised both hands in a gesture of surrender and smiled. 'Of course. Let's go into the bar. Are you staying at the Moonflower?'

'Yes.'

'I'm afraid I can't offer you a drink. These stupid licensing laws. But I can get someone to put on the kettle ...'

They walked back in together.

Simon Cox wasn't his real name, of course. He would have anglicised it when he arrived in the country. He was probably Simeon or Semjén or something equally unwieldy. Her agent had introduced him to her in London, explaining that he was a successful businessman who had made a fortune in insurance and banking and was now wanting to move into film. Melissa had met plenty of those, but to be fair, Simon had gone further; he had actually gone out and bought the rights to a book and then commissioned a screenplay. He wanted Melissa to play the lead part.

The film was called *The Queen's Ransom* and it was a historical romance, set in the twelfth century. Melissa would be playing Eleanor of Aquitaine, who had become queen of England after her marriage to the duke of Normandy – later Henry II – in 1152. The screenplay focused on her relationship with her favourite son, Richard, and her time as queen dowager, fighting to raise the enormous ransom that had been demanded for him when he was captured after the Third Crusade. Shooting was due to start in two months' time and all the terms had been agreed, but Melissa's contract was still sitting, unsigned, on her desk.

She had decided that she didn't want to do it.

She had been impressed to begin with. The screenplay was strong, written by a former history teacher who had worked with Roy Boulting and Anthony Asquith as a technical adviser before he had started writing himself. The character of Eleanor was absolutely central to the action. In fact, she would barely be off the screen ... the sort of performance that would demand attention once the awards season came around. It had been years since she had made a film in England and her agent had assured her that, despite the relatively low budget, her fans would be thrilled. He had sold it to her as the perfect vehicle for a comeback.

Unfortunately, it now turned out that the dates clashed with the film she hoped to make with Alfred Hitchcock. *Dial M for Murder* (she wasn't sure about the title) would be bigger, glossier, more international and better paid. It would be shot in America, in the sunshine – not in the drab backwaters of Shepperton Studios. Looking at Simon Cox as he perched himself on one of the leather banquettes in the hotel bar, she felt a stab of annoyance – with herself as much as with him. What had possessed her to lend her name to a producer with no experience and no credits to his name? And how dare he come here and approach her in this way? He should have called her agents in London or New York. If he had something to say, he should say it to them.

Well, she would get this over with as quickly as possible. It was unlikely, she reminded herself, that they would ever meet again.

'Melissa—' he began.

'I'm sorry, Simon,' she cut in. 'I don't think we should be having this conversation. Not here. Not now.'

He gazed at her in surprise. 'What do you mean?'

'This isn't the right way to do things. If you had more experience of the film industry, you'd understand. You don't talk to the talent! You have to talk to the agent.'

'I did talk to your agent and he told me he sent you everything, but I don't hear from you. Nothing! And filming is now only three months – ten weeks – away. We have everything in place, except you. Where is your contract? Why do you not come for meeting the director, for costume fittings, for script!'

Melissa couldn't take any more of this. 'I'm sorry,' she said. 'Things have changed and I've decided I'm not interested in *The Queen's Ransom*.'

'What?' He looked as if he had been punched in the face.

'I'm not doing it.'

'Melissa … !'

'It's a good script. There are lots of great things in it. But I don't think it's right for me.'

'But it was written for you! Your agent said it is perfect for you!'

'There are plenty of other actresses who could do it.' She wanted to stand up and walk away but he was staring at her. 'I haven't signed my contract because the truth is that I've had a better offer and I've decided this project isn't right for me. Even so, I wish you lots of success—'

'You'll ruin me!' The words caught in his throat. He had difficulty getting them out. 'All the money I have borrowed, it is because of your name. The director, the designer, the studios, the scripts, the cast. Already we have built the palace, the tower, the walls of Jerusalem ... This is all happening because of you. If you say now that you do not do it, I am finish!' His English was deteriorating the angrier he got.

'That's exactly what I'm telling you. If you knew the first thing about film production, you'd know this sort of thing happens all the time. People change their minds. I've changed my mind!' She tried to find some hint of sympathy. 'My agent represents some very big names. Maybe I can talk to him—'

'I don't want big names. I want you. That is what we agreed.'

'We never agreed anything. That's what I'm trying to tell you. Honestly, Simon, this is all wrong. You shouldn't have come down here. You can't put pressure on me.'

The man looked as if he was going to have a heart attack. Melissa had had enough. She broke free of him and got to her feet.

'I suggest you go back to London and find someone quickly,' she said. 'Please don't try and speak to me again.'

She left.

Simon Cox stayed where he was. He seemed to have shrunk into his chair. His hand was stretched out on the table but slowly his fingers curled into a fist. Outside, he heard the slam of a car door and the quiet cough of an engine starting. Still he didn't move.

Someone else had come into the bar. It was the girl from the reception desk, Nancy. She was looking at him with concern. 'Is there anything I can get you, sir?' she asked.

'No. No, thank you.'

He got up and brushed past her, walking out of the hotel. Another couple, coming in, stepped out of his way, alarmed.

Later on, they would say he had been a man with murder in his eyes.

*

Nancy Mitchell had heard much of the conversation between Melissa James and the producer from her place behind the reception desk. It wasn't her fault. She hadn't meant to eavesdrop but the door had been open and with nobody around, sound carried easily in the Moonflower. She saw Miss James emerge from the bar and disappear through the main door of the hotel and then, when she went in to see him, the little man who had signed in as Mr Cox did exactly the same. Out of curiosity, Nancy followed him outside, just in time to see him climb into a stubby black car and drive off. She could tell that he was heading out of Tawleigh in the direction of Clarence Keep. Was he going after her?

It was none of her business. She watched until the car had disappeared from sight, noticing that the rain had stopped once again, although water was still dripping off the trees and the driveway was full of puddles. She glanced at her watch and went back to the reception desk. There were only fifteen minutes left until six o'clock and the end of her shift. Mrs Gardner took over in the evening until ten o'clock, when the night manager arrived.

She took out a hand mirror and examined herself, remembering what Miss James had said. Her hair was still a bit of a mess but nobody would have known she had been crying. She wished that Miss James – of all people – hadn't been the one to notice it. And the very idea that the two of them could be friends! Nancy had heard things about the rich and famous Melissa James that nobody else in Tawleigh would ever have suspected. She pretended to be nice. But she wasn't.

Even so, she needed a friend, now more than ever. The very thought of it brought tears to her eyes. How could she have let it happen? How could she have been so stupid?

It was two weeks since she had seen Dr Collins. Nancy hadn't even told her parents that she had an appointment. Her father was the sort of man who had never had a day's illness in his life and expected the same of everyone else. She hadn't thought it was anything serious and she had been completely stunned when Dr Collins had come up with his diagnosis.

'I'm not sure you're going to be happy about this, Nancy. But you're pregnant.'

It was a word that Nancy had never even heard, certainly not spoken to her by a man – even if he was a doctor. It opened up a world that she only partly understood. It changed everything in ways that she couldn't even begin to consider. 'It's impossible!' she whispered.

'Why do you say that? Are you telling me that you've never...been with a man?'

She couldn't answer. She could feel her cheeks burning.

'If there's someone you've been seeing, you're going to have to tell him. Whatever you decide, he's going to be part of it.'

What could she do? What would happen when her father found out? All sorts of questions had rushed into her head. But there were no answers. Unless, of course, it wasn't true. It could still be a mistake.

'It was only once,' she said, on the edge of tears. She was looking down at the floor, unable to meet his eye.

'I'm afraid once is enough.'

'Are you sure, Dr Collins?'

'A hundred per cent. Would you perhaps like to talk to my wife? You might find it easier, woman to woman.'

'No! I don't want anyone else to know.'

'Well, they're going to find out soon enough. You're already beginning to show and another month ... '

Show! She cradled her stomach with her hands.

'We'll have to make further tests and I'm going to want you to go into the hospital in Barnstaple. You're young and you're in very good health, so there are no worries there ... '

There were only worries. She could think of nothing else.

'Do you want to tell me something about the father of your baby?'

'No!' She couldn't tell anyone – not until she had told him. But could she even tell him?

'It might help if the two of you came in and met me together.' Dr Collins could see how distressed she had become. He gave her a kindly smile. 'What's his name?' he asked.

'John.' She blurted it out. 'He's a local boy. I met him in Bideford. We ... ' She bit her lip. 'It was only once, Doctor. I never thought ... '

'Would you like a cup of tea?'

She shook her head. Tears were streaming down her cheeks.

Dr Collins came over to her and laid a hand on her shoulder. 'You mustn't upset yourself,' he said. 'Having a child is a wonderful thing. My wife would say it's a miracle, creating a new life. And you're not the only young woman to have made a mistake. You have to be strong ... for the baby's sake.'

'No one can know!'

'Well, obviously you must tell your parents. They ought to be the first to know. And they'll send you to stay with relatives. Everything can be arranged for you, Nancy. The baby will be put up for adoption and when you come back it will be as if it never happened.'

The very next day, Nancy had gone to the library in Bideford and looked at the medical books, but they hadn't told her what she wanted to know. She had to stop the baby being born. Somewhere she had heard that drinking a lot of gin would do it. Wasn't that why it was called 'mother's ruin'? And there was a girl at the Red Lion who had once said that you had to have a very hot bath. So the following Saturday evening, while her parents were at the pictures, she had done both. She had drunk half a bottle of Old Tom and sat in the bath, fully dressed, with the steaming water up to her neck. Later that night she had been thoroughly sick and she thought that maybe it had done the trick, but, going back to Dr Collins, she had discovered her condition hadn't changed.

And so she had written to the man she had called John, to the father of her child. She had made it clear that he was the father, that there had never been anyone else, and she had tried to be conciliatory. She would keep his secret, she had told him. But she was frightened and she was on her own and she needed his help.

The answer had come the following morning, a thick white envelope that had surprised her by the weight of its contents, with her name in typed letters on the front. He must have written her a very long letter, she thought, but when she opened it her eyes had fallen on twelve five-pound notes and a single sheet of paper with a name and an address: a doctor in Baker Street, London.

Could it have been any crueller? The note was un-signed and the typewriter concealed his handwriting so that it could never be traced back to him. There was no attempt at sympathy or understanding. Nor was there to be any discussion. Get rid of it. That was the simple message. And there was something uniquely horrible about the payment, the amount – sixty pounds – worked out precisely and paid in used five-pound notes. Nancy knew that he must have made enquiries. If he had dis-covered that an illegal abortion would cost sixty pounds and two shillings, he would have thrown in a handful of coins.

The letter had changed everything.

Previously, Nancy had been ashamed of herself. She had thought it was all her fault. Now she thought other-wise. She knew she couldn't name the father. It would be a scandal that would rebound entirely on her, forcing her to leave Tawleigh for good. But she wasn't completely powerless. She could still make him pay for what he had done – and it would cost him a lot more than sixty pounds.

Sitting there, watching the minute hand on the clock in the corridor move slowly towards the hour, Nancy Mitchell made her decision. The father of her child had thought he could buy her off. She was going to prove him wrong.

FOUR
SECRETS AND SHADOWS

At Clarence Keep, Phyllis Chandler was applying one last coat of lipstick as she prepared to leave. She was standing in her bedroom, which was part of the servants' quarters she shared with her son. The entire east wing was their domain, separated from the rest of the house by thick walls and solid doors. A service staircase led up from behind the kitchen to an area with two bedrooms, a shared bathroom, a living room with a sofa and a television set and a second, small kitchen. It was separated from the main house by an archway with a heavy velvet curtain drawn across when Miss James was in residence. Her bedroom was immediately on the left, allowing Phyllis easy access when it was time to change the linen or to clean. In fact, the whole arrangement was perfectly satisfactory. The Chandlers had plenty of space and comfort. But they were tucked away out of sound, out of sight.

She was worried that she was going to be late. She had told her sister, Betty, that she would be with her at seven o'clock but it was almost six now and of course they couldn't leave until Miss James got back. They needed the car. Eric was in the living room, where he had been watching *The Appleyards* on television. It was a programme for children, really, but of course it was his favourite. Outside, she heard the sound of a car slowing down. That might be her! Phyllis made sure her hat was in place and went out to see.

A narrow corridor ran all the way from the back of the house to the front with a window at each end. It was lined with pictures, photographs of Tawleigh: the lighthouse, the beach, the hotel. Phyllis was heading for the front window, which gave a good view of the drive, but even as she came out of the bedroom, something caught her eye. She had noticed it before. She had always prided herself on a strict attention to detail, whether it was the crimps in a pie crust or the way a towel hung on a rail.

Something was wrong.

Frowning, puzzled, she edged towards it, unaware that the living-room door was open and, on the other side, Eric was watching her every move.

*

Francis Pendleton had also heard the car. He looked out of the window for the eleventh or twelfth time but saw nothing. Where was Melissa? She had said she would only be thirty minutes with the Gardners, but surely she had left more than an hour ago? She should have been back by now. He glanced at his watch, a Rolex Oyster Elegante that she had bought him on their first anniversary. It was five fifty-five. If he waited too much longer, he might be late for the performance of *The Marriage of Figaro* in Barnstaple. But that didn't bother him. He wasn't in the mood for opera. He needed to see Melissa.

He went into the living room and took a cigarette out of a silver box that had been given to her by the studio executives at MGM. The studio's logo was engraved on the lid, along with its famous motto: *Ars Gratia Artis.* Clarence Keep was littered with movie memorabilia, awards and gifts. Even the cigarette lighter that he now flicked open had been used by Humphrey Bogart in *Casablanca.*

As Francis smoked, his eyes were drawn to the cluster of framed black-and-white photographs on the piano. Melissa in Los Angeles. Melissa with Walt Disney. Melissa on the set of *Hostage to Fortune.* This last picture reminded him of the first time they had met. She had been the star. He had taken the job as her assistant, not because he needed the money but because he thought it would be fun to see how a film was made.

When Melissa had walked into the room, he had been transfixed. He knew her face, of course, like everyone in the country, but he was utterly unprepared for the beauty and serenity that she radiated in real life. It wasn't just the perfect skin, the dazzling blue eyes, the playful smile. It wasn't even the self-confidence that came from being admired across the world. She was, quite simply, adorable and he had known immediately that despite the inequality of their respective positions and the ten-year age gap between them, he would not rest until he had made her his own.

He had quickly learned what she did and did not like. Floris orange blossom soap in the bathroom, roses but never carnations, du Maurier cigarettes, no unauthorised photographers, an umbrella to be held for her when it was raining. Rationing had still been in full force in 1946, but with help from her American agents and from the studio, he had been able to find anything she wanted. All she had to do was mention it. And Melissa had quickly learned that she could ring him at any time of the day or night. He would always be there for her.

Their relationship had changed when Melissa had

realised that her enthusiastic young assistant was much more than she had suspected. He was actually a member of the British aristocracy, the second son in a family that could trace its roots back to the Middle Ages. Francis hadn't told her this himself but he had made sure that she found out. He remembered coming with her to Clarence Keep after she had seen it advertised. The two of them had been shown around together and all the time he had dreamed that it would be a home not just for her but for both of them.

Francis tapped his cigarette against a crystal ashtray that had been a birthday gift from the director of *The Moonflower*. Not his birthday, of course. It was remarkable how little there was in the house that belonged to him. Looking around the room at the piano she had bought for a fortune but which she only occasionally played, the books she read but never finished, the photographs in which only she appeared, he could almost have been a stranger here. By marrying her, he had got everything he wanted. But it had come at a price. He had become, to all intents and purposes, invisible.

It didn't trouble him. Francis Pendleton understood that if you choose to stand too close to the sun you can't complain when you become nothing more than a silhouette. Even his surname had been taken from him. She was always Melissa James and his family had given up on him. 'You're marrying an actress!' It should have been impossible to put so much scorn into four simple words but his father, Lord Pendleton, had easily managed it. He hadn't been surprised by that either. His father was a self-opinionated snob who had never gone to the cinema and who wouldn't have dreamed of letting a television set into the ancestral pile he called home. Faded, leather-bound copies of Dickens and Smollett were more his style. Culture, not entertainment. The words could have been part of the family crest. He had made it very clear that Francis would never inherit anything from him. His future was entirely in Melissa's hands.

And then, over the last year, everything had gone wrong. The financial worries had crept in like a flood tide in the full moon, silent and relentless. The cost of restoring Clarence Keep had been close to ruinous. The hotel was losing money. Melissa spent much too much time with her so-called financial adviser, Algernon Marsh, and none of his investment schemes had so far returned a penny. Worse than all this, her own market value seemed to have shrunk. Nobody wanted to cast her. She wasn't meeting Alfred Hitchcock. He was auditioning her. There was a distinct difference and it would never have happened five years ago.

Francis ground out the cigarette. On an impulse he got up and went over to a bureau that stood against the far wall. He opened the bottom drawer, which was filled with old bills and invoices that Melissa never looked at – which was why he had hidden the letter there. He took it out now, a single sheet of paper that had been crumpled into a ball and then smoothed out. It was written in the navy blue ink that Melissa always used, her handwriting immediately recognisable. Francis had read it so many times that he knew every word by heart, but still he forced himself to read it again.

13th February
My darling darling,
I can't go on living this lie any more. I simply can't. We have to be brave and tell the world our destiny and what we mean to each other, even though we recognise the hurt it will cause to those who are closest to us. Francis knows that it's over between him and me. I want to go back to America, back to my career and it's a journey that I want to make with you. I know how you feel but

She had crossed out the last sentence, her nib leaving a series of blots as it scratched across the paper, and then she had decided to stop altogether, crumpling up the page and throwing it into the bedroom waste-paper basket, which was where Francis had found it. Why hadn't she torn it up? Perhaps it had always been her hope, sub-conscious or otherwise, that he would read it and dis-cover the truth. Melissa often behaved as if she were living in one of those cheap dramas she had made when she was starting her career. Even the language of the letter, the mention of destiny and that repeated 'darling' had the flavour of melodrama.

Holding the letter, Francis found himself almost struggling to breathe. He still hadn't told her he had found it. There were so many moments when he had been tempted, but he was afraid of the consequences. He wanted to know who she had written it to, but at the same time it seemed completely unimportant. It was the thought of losing her that consumed him, the emptiness of a life without her.

He knew, though, that he couldn't put it off any lon-ger. He had to confront her. Even now, he thought it might not be too late. He would do anything to keep hold of her.

Anything.

*

Seven thirty in the evening.

Detective Chief Inspector Edward Hare glanced up at the clock mounted on the wall opposite his desk just as the minute hand hit the half-hour with a sonorous click that seemed to announce it no longer had the strength to climb back up to the twelve.

He was working late, sitting in his office in Waterbeer Street, in the building that had housed Exeter's police force for seventy years. The rain was pattering down the window, throwing dark shadows, like tears, on the wall opposite. He liked this room, with its dark, cosy feel, the books on the shelves, a sense of everything in its right place. He was going to miss it.

Although it hadn't yet been announced, the entire department was being moved to the east of the city, to the more modern surroundings of Heavitree. It seemed to Hare that the pace of change had become ever faster since the end of the war and although he had tried to attune himself to it, he was still a little sad. The police station in Waterbeer Street was unique. It reminded him of a Bavarian railway station or perhaps a folk-story palace, with its grey bricks, narrow windows and circular towers. His own office was in a corner underneath a roof shaped like a wizard's hat with views all the way down to Walton's Food Hall, which had opened soon after he'd started. He'd seen designs for the new building: as drearily modern and utilitarian as he might have expected. Of course, it would be better equipped. The electric lighting might not leave you with eye strain. But he was glad he wouldn't be going there.

After thirty years in the job, aged fifty-five, he was retiring. He should have been able to look back on a career that had taken him from police constable to detective chief inspector with some degree of satisfaction. And yet he couldn't avoid a sense of failure. He knew that his superiors considered him reliable, hard-working, a safe pair of hands, but what did all these epithets add up to? Simply, that he had never shown the promise of his early years. He would have a leaving party. There would be a few glasses of wine, cheese on sticks, a speech and the presentation of a clock. And then it would all be over. He would be gone.

With a sigh, he put his glasses back on and returned to the papers he had been studying. He was preparing for a court case that was about to take place in the same building – the police station and the court were neighbours – and as this would be his last appearance he wanted to be fluent, in command of the facts.

The telephone rang.

His first reaction was one of surprise. Who would be calling him at this late hour? He assumed that it must be Margaret, his long-suffering wife, wondering where he was, and he snatched up the receiver to explain. The voice at the other end quickly put him right. It was the assistant chief constable.

'Good to catch you, Hare. You're working late.'

'Yes, sir.'

'Well, I'm afraid I'm going to have to cut into your evening. There's been a murder, in the village of Tawleigh-on-the-Water. Do you know it?'

Hare knew the name vaguely. It was more than forty miles away, over on the west coast of Devon. He guessed that the victim had to be someone important. The assistant chief wouldn't be contacting him otherwise.

'I can't say I've ever been there, sir,' he said, although it occurred to him that perhaps he had, once, with his wife and the girls, on a beach holiday. Or had that been Instow?

'There's an actress. Name of Melissa James. She's been found strangled in her home.'

'Was there a break-in?'

'I don't have the details yet. The local police called it in and I'm passing it over to you. I want you to get on to it with immediate effect. Melissa James was very well known and the press are going to be all over it.'

'Sir, you are aware that I'm leaving the force next month?'

'Yes – and I'm sorry to hear it. We'll just have to hope

it'll focus your mind. I need a result, Hare, the sooner the better. I don't go to the cinema much myself but apparently Miss James was quite a star. We can't have high-profile residents being bumped off. It gives the county a bad name. I want you to report directly to me.'

'Whatever you say, sir.'

'I do say! This might be just what you need, Hare. Things have been a bit quiet at your end for quite a while. It might allow you to bow out in style. Good luck!'

The phone went dead.

As he set down the receiver, Hare reflected on what his superior officer had just said. He was probably right in every respect. He had actually seen several of Melissa James's films, including the one she had made locally. What was it called? *Hostage to Fortune*. He had taken his wife and although he had found the plot rather contrived, there had certainly been something special about her performance. Given her profile, it would certainly reflect badly on the force if her assailant was not quickly brought to justice.

It might also be exactly what he needed: something to make his children proud of him. It would be nice to see his name in the headlines for once. The press nearly always ignored him, being more interested in the criminals he had arrested.

He leaned forward, picked up the phone and dialled.

He'd get someone in the car pool to drive him over to Tawleigh, but first he needed to call his wife and tell her to put the supper back in the oven. There would be no time for dinner. He would be staying overnight in Tawleigh and he needed to pack.

FIVE
THE LUDENDORFF DIAMOND

Atticus Pünd adjusted his bow tie, at the same time taking the opportunity to examine himself in the bathroom mirror. He was not by nature a vain man but he had to admit that he was pleased by what he saw. He was, all in all, in remarkably good shape. He was slight but he was healthy, not showing his age, which was all the more remarkable considering the experiences he had been through. He had survived the war and much worse, and although there had been times when he thought he would never again see the light of day, he had come out of it unharmed and more successful than he could have imagined.

He could not help smiling and, as if in agreement, his reflection smiled back. It helped perhaps that he had lost his hair when he was quite young. There were no telltale wisps of grey to give his sixty-two years away. He owed his Mediterranean complexion to the Greek blood that ran in his veins, even though he had been born and lived most of his life in Germany. It was strange, really. He had been a foreigner from the day of his birth and here he was, living in London, still an outsider. But that also suited him. He was an investigator, a detective. He owed his living to communities of people he had never met before and would never meet again, always working from the outside in. It was both a profession and a way of life.

Were there fresh lines at the corners of his eyes? He reached out for his wire-frame spectacles and put them on. He had not slept well the night before and he was beginning to think that he had made a mistake in the choice of his new bed and its 'Airfoam' mattress. '*You fall asleep on a foamy cloud of tiny air cells*', the advertisement had promised, but he should not have trusted it. He had slept alone since his wife had died and it was at night that he missed her most, lying there surrounded by so much space. What he needed was something smaller and simpler, a bed like the one he had slept on at school. Yes. The thought appealed to him. He would mention it to Miss Cain the next day.

He glanced at his watch. It was ten past six. He had plenty of time to walk over to Gresham Street; he wasn't expected until seven o'clock. Very unusually, Pünd had agreed to give a speech. Writing about his work was one thing, but talking about it, perhaps giving away confidences, was quite another. That was the trouble. In his experience, people were never interested in the abstract theory of detective work – which was the subject of his still unfinished book, *The Landscape of Criminal Investigation*. They wanted the sensational details: the bloody fingerprint, the smoking gun, the killer going about his work. Pünd had never seen murder as a game, not even as a puzzle to be solved. His work was an examination of humanity at its darkest and most desperate. You could not solve crime unless you understood its genesis.

He had allowed two considerations to change his mind. First of all, his hosts were serious people. A City guild, the Worshipful Company of Goldsmiths no less, had invited him to be the guest speaker at their annual dinner and they had made it clear that the subject could be of his own choosing, though obviously related to his work. And in return for thirty minutes of his time, he would be rewarded with an excellent dinner, first-class wine and a sizeable payment to the Metropolitan and City Police Orphans Fund, one of his favourite charities.

He splashed a little cologne on his cheeks, then turned off the light and went into the bedroom, where his dinner jacket was waiting for him on the back of a chair. Miss Cain had prepared his speech for him. It was lying on the bed, twelve pristine white pages held together with a paperclip. The title – CRIME AND PUNISHMENT – was in capital letters at the top. Pünd slipped on his jacket, carefully folded the pages, placed them inside his pocket and went into the next room.

He had only recently moved into the flat on the seventh floor of Tanner Court, the elegant mansion block in Farringdon, and he wasn't quite used to it. The furniture was antique and German. He had brought much of it with him when he moved to England after the war. But everything else was still foreign to him. The rooms with their double-height ceilings seemed much larger than they had any right to be. The carpets and curtains were brand new and he remembered choosing them, aghast at both how expensive they were and how easily he could now afford them. The kitchen was so sparkling clean that he felt nervous about using it – not that he ever cooked for himself. For lunch he would have a salad. In the evening he usually ate out.

He glanced at what had once been his father's pendulum box clock, hanging in the corner. Made by Erhard Junghans in the nineteenth century and so almost a hundred years old, it had never lost a minute's time. He didn't need to leave yet. He poured himself a small sherry and took a black Sobranie cigarette out of an ebony box that had been given to him by a grateful client. In fact, the entire apartment had only come his way thanks to a recent case. He lit the cigarette and sat down, trying to relax in his surroundings and remembering the strange affair of the Ludendorff Diamond, which had been, in many respects, his greatest success yet.

On the face of it, the theft had been impossible, a magic trick that had baffled the police, the British public and, most significantly, the frustrated owner, who had lost not just the diamond but several other pieces of jewellery plus cash and certified share certificates to the value of almost a hundred thousand pounds.

His name was Charles Pargeter, a multimillionaire with homes in New York and Knightsbridge who had made his fortune in the oil industry. His wife, Elaine, was a well-known society hostess, a patron of the arts, a member of several boards, a woman of great beauty. The robbery had taken place just before Christmas the year before.

In fact, the Pargeters had been on their way back from a party when they found that their house had been broken into. It was clearly the work of professionals. The alarm system had been disconnected and a window on the ground floor forced. The house had not been completely empty. It was a Saturday and two of the servants – the cook and the maid – had been given the weekend off.

The butler had stayed behind but he was almost seventy years old and had slept through the entire business. The Pargeters had returned home with John Berkeley, a business associate and friend, and he had noticed the broken window before they even got in.

To begin with, Charles Pargeter had not been worried. He was a careful man and had installed a safe on the second floor of the house. It was not just any safe. It was the best that money could buy: a solid steel, fireproof box that weighed over two hundred pounds, manufactured by Sentry in America and bolted into the floor. Inside the combination lock, which had been strengthened to prevent any possibility of its being forced, there were no fewer than seven wheels, requiring, therefore, a seven-part sequence to get it open. Only three people knew the combination: Pargeter, his wife, and Henry Chase, their lawyer. There was a second lock, key-operated, and only one key had ever been manufactured. Charles Pargeter kept it close to him all the time. The safe stood against the far wall of a narrow, dark walk-in closet. The thieves would have had to have inside information even to know that it was there.

The three of them – Charles Pargeter, Elaine Pargeter and John Berkeley – had entered the darkened house together and at first they believed that they had arrived in time and that nothing had been disturbed. But when

Charles turned the lights on in the bedroom, the terrible truth hit him full in the face. The safe door was wide open. All the contents had been removed.

Elaine Pargeter had called the police while Berkeley led his friend downstairs and poured him a large whisky. They were careful not to touch anything. The police – in the persons of Detective Inspector Gilbert, accompanied by Detective Sergeant Dickinson – arrived very soon after, asked various questions and examined the empty safe. Both the safe and the broken window were searched for fingerprints but none were found.

Pünd remembered reading about the theft in the newspapers. The whole country had been gripped by what had happened – for two reasons. The first was that the safe really was impregnable. The American manufacturers had flown to England immediately and after a careful examination they had announced that their product could not be to blame. The lock could not be forced and had not been forced: whoever opened it must have known the combination, even though this narrowed the crime down to just two suspects: Charles Pargeter and his wife. Their lawyer, Henry Chase, the only other person trusted with the combination, had been abroad on the night in question. Of course, he could have passed on the combination to an accomplice but that still left the problem of the key. Pargeter kept it on his main key ring and it was never out of his sight. He had had it with him at the party and he had handed it to DI Gilbert, who had confirmed that it was the right key and definitely fitted the lock. Could someone have taken it and made a copy? Again, the manufacturers insisted this was impossible. The key was like no other, with a unique, patented design. They had given a press conference in which they had come perilously close to accusing Pargeter and his wife of insurance fraud. But that, too, was highly unlikely. Pargeter had no money troubles. On the contrary, his business was booming. He was one of the richest people in the world.

But it was the Ludendorff Diamond that had really captured the public's imagination. There are many precious jewels that seem to exist in a world of fantasy and folklore and this one was no exception. A flawless 'pear double rose-cut diamond', it had 33 carats and 140 facets. It had been found in Golconda, the same region of India that had produced the Koh-i-Noor. It had belonged to a Russian aristocrat, Prince Andrei Ludendorff, who had been killed in a duel, but not by his opponent. His gun had jammed and exploded in his hand, sending a fragment of metal into his eye. It was said that the diamond had been buried with him, but that his not entirely mournful widow had sent a pair of grave robbers to retrieve it. Pargeter had bought it privately in New York for an undisclosed price, although the figure of two million American dollars had been mentioned. It might well have been more.

And now it was gone. Pargeter had also lost cash and shares. His wife had kept several pearl and diamond necklaces, rings and a tiara in the safe. Even their passports and birth certificates had been taken. But all this seemed inconsequential compared to the Ludendorff Diamond. There was, Pünd noticed, a certain amount of sympathy for the criminals who had pulled off this spectacular coup without violence. At the same time, there was very little sympathy for Pargeter, who was seen almost as the instigator of the crime rather than its victim, as if his extreme wealth had made it only reasonable that he should be targeted.

Pargeter was not, in fact, an unpleasant man. When he had arrived at Pünd's office in the Old Marylebone Road, he had come across as quiet and self-effacing. He had the look of a Harvard professor, with thick, silver hair and glasses and immaculately dressed in a double-breasted suit and tie. Pünd remembered every word of what he had said.

'Mr Pünd,' he had begun, standing with his hands behind his back, 'my people tell me that you are the best detective in the world, and having looked into your history, I believe you are the only man who can return the

Ludendorff Diamond to me.' He spoke with an American accent, carefully judging his words before he allowed them to pass his lips. 'I want to explain to you
why I have come here today. First, as I'm sure you are
aware, the police have been unable to come up with any
possible explanation for what appears, on the face of it,
to be an impossible crime. I have repeatedly told them –
and I will assure you of the same thing – that only three
people knew the combination to that lock and I would
trust the other two with my life.'

'You have never told it to anyone else?' Pünd interrupted.

'No.'

'And it was never written down? Perhaps as an aide-
memoire?'

'No.'

'But I understand that there were seven separate numerals.'

'I have an excellent memory.'

'Then I will ask you this. Were the numbers selected
by you? Did they perhaps have some reference to events
in your life? Your date of birth, for example, or that of
your wife?'

'Absolutely not. The safe arrived with the combination integrated. And before you ask, Sentry have their
own security protocols. Nobody in the company knew

which safe had been sold to me or where it was going to be installed. It had come all the way from America on a container ship. I had workmen pick it up in Southampton and bring it to my London home. The combination was sent to me by post a few days later.'

'Thank you. Please continue.'

Charles Pargeter took a breath. He was not the sort of man who was used to asking favours. In his business, he would issue instructions and expect them to be followed to the letter. Pünd got the impression that he had rehearsed what he was about to say.

'I bought the Ludendorff Diamond for many reasons,' he said. 'It is an object of great beauty which could be more than a billion years old. Think of that! It is unique. It is also, strangely enough, a wise investment. And if I'm going to be honest with you, Mr Pünd, there may have been an element of vanity in my decision. When you have been fortunate enough to amass a great deal of wealth, there is always the temptation to make a statement, not to the general public but to yourself. To remind yourself of your own success.

'So when I tell you that I have been hurt by the theft, I mean it in every sense. Whoever took the diamond has made a fool out of me. I have always been fond of the British and frankly, following this incident, I've been surprised how quickly they seem to have taken against me. There was even a cartoon of me in *Punch* magazine. You may have seen it.'

Pünd made a gesture to suggest that he hadn't, although in fact he remembered it well. It had shown the multimillionaire sitting at the breakfast table in his pyjamas, eating a boiled egg with the diamond concealed inside the shell. The caption underneath read: *'Now, why didn't I look there?'*

'It's even been suggested that I myself was involved in the robbery,' Pargeter continued. 'An accusation that's as absurd as it's damaging. In short, I'm being humiliated all over the country, and frankly, I find this almost as hard to bear as the loss of the jewel itself. So let me get to the point. I will pay you any money you demand to investigate what actually happened. Who did it and how it was done. If you are able to return my property to me, I will pay you a bonus of fifty thousand pounds. Forgive me for being so direct, Mr Pünd. I'm sure you're a busy man, so let me know what you think and I won't waste any more of your time.'

In fact, Pünd had made his decision the moment Pargeter walked into the room. He was intrigued. This was one of those very rare examples of a crime committed without violence that could, perhaps, be approached purely as an intellectual challenge. The timing, also, was fortuitous. The lease on his flat and office was about to expire. He had been looking for somewhere new to live and had found a flat in Farringdon that seemed ideal except that it was well out of his price range. Pünd did not believe in fate or destiny. But Charles Pargeter might have been sent in answer to his prayers.

He went round to Knightsbridge the next day, driven by Pargeter's chauffeur, who had picked him up in a silver Rolls-Royce. The house was in one of the quiet streets behind Harrods department store. It was unusual in that it stood alone, surrounded by a low brick wall with a gravel drive and flower beds. Pünd began with the broken window, which was round the side of the house. Already, that puzzled him. It did not fit in with what he had read in the papers and what he had been told. He was shown in through the front door to find Charles Pargeter and his wife waiting for him. She was an extremely elegant woman, taller than her husband, dressed simply in a cashmere jersey and slacks. She had no jewellery. The house itself was quite ordinary. As far as Pünd could see, there were no masterpieces on the walls, no priceless silver on display. Perhaps the Pargeters' home in New York was more ostentatious.

'Would you like some coffee, Mr Pünd?' Elaine Pargeter asked. 'We can go into the drawing room ...'

'I would prefer to begin upstairs, if you don't mind, Mrs Pargeter. To start with, I would like to see this safe that was, according to its makers ... impregnable. Is that the word?'

'I'll take you there,' Charles Pargeter said.

As they climbed the stairs, Pünd raised the question that had occurred to him outside. 'I am puzzled,' he said. 'You arrived, quite late, from the party on the night that the robbery took place.'

'Yes. It was about one o'clock.'

'There were three of you.'

'Yes. John Berkeley is an old friend of mine. He's a vice president with Shell Transport and Trading. We were actually at college together. He happened to be in London for a few days and he usually stays with us. Saves paying out for a hotel.'

'Which one of you saw that the window had been broken? It seems to me that walking from the car to the front door, you would not have had a view of the side of the house.'

'Actually, that was me,' Elaine Pargeter explained. 'John saw fragments of glass on the drive. They were reflecting the moon. I went round to investigate and that was when I saw the window was broken.'

'Did you go straight upstairs?'

'I wanted Elaine to stay in the car,' Pargeter said. 'I was afraid there might be intruders in the house and I didn't want to put her in harm's way—'

'I wasn't having any of that!' Elaine exclaimed.

'That's right. So the three of us went in together. I saw that the alarms were off and that told me something was wrong. We have a butler, Harris, and he'd have been asleep in the servants' wing, but even so the alarms should have been on in the main house. We went straight to the master bedroom. I knew that everything that was valuable to me, and that includes the diamond, of course, was in the safe. I remember putting my hand in my pocket and feeling my key. It never occurred to me that the safe could have been opened.'

They had reached the top of the stairs and crossed the corridor, entering a room decorated in a vaguely Chinese style with dark red wallpaper and views over the back garden. As with the rest of the house, the most impressive thing about the bedroom was its size. The bed was huge, the curtains theatrical, the dressing table antique. One door led into a bathroom. The other opened into a narrow corridor with wardrobes on either side. After about ten feet, the wardrobes stopped and there was a small alcove with a domed ceiling. It could have been purpose-built for the safe that stood there with its back against the far wall.

If the millionaire and his wife had expected Pünd to move forward and examine the safe, they were disappointed. He stood where he was, half frowning, as if he was trying to sense the atmosphere. Finally, he spoke. 'Did you turn the lights on when you came into the room?' he asked.

'In the bedroom. Yes. But not in the walk-in closet.'

'And why was that?'

'We didn't want to leave footmarks or fingerprints. But I can tell you, there was enough light for us to see everything. The safe door was open and the inside was clearly empty. I have to say that I was very glad to have John Berkeley with me right then. I'm not an emotional man. I guess I'm used to keeping things damped down. But I felt sick. I thought I was going to faint. I stand by what I said to you yesterday, Mr Pünd, but right then I was thinking about how much had been taken from me. I had lost millions and millions of dollars and at the same time it was impossible. I was holding the only key to the safe, goddamn it! I had it right in my hand.'

'So what did you do then?'

'Obviously, I couldn't go into the room. It was a crime scene. I didn't want to disturb any possible evidence.'

'That is very sensible.'

'John took control of the situation. He got Elaine to call the police while he took me downstairs and gave me a large Scotch. He also got Harris out of bed and asked him if he'd heard anything, but there was no joy there. The truth is, Harris is much too old for the job, but he's been with me so long I don't have the heart to get rid of him. I just keep hoping he'll retire.'

'And you trust him?'

'He's been with us for thirty years, Mr Pünd. When he does finally go, we'll look after him. He knows that. And what's a man of his age going to do with a diamond like that? It's inconceivable he had anything to do with it.'

Pünd nodded. 'You will permit me … ?'

He walked into the corridor between the wardrobes and crouched down beside the safe, resting a hand on the steel surface. Given that it weighed more than two hundred pounds, the safe was smaller than he had imagined. It had the proportions of a deck of cards, taller than it was deep, completely bare but for a handle, a combination lock and, next to it, a keyhole. The name of the manufacturer was written across the top. The door fitted absolutely flush with the outer shell, making it impossible to slip even a sheet of paper inside, let alone the tip of a crowbar. The safe was grey in colour. Its setting was almost theatrical, with dark red wallpaper on three sides, again picking up the Chinese theme from the bedroom. Pünd did not try to move it. He could tell at once that it was utterly solid, bolted into place.

'Would it be possible for you to open the safe?' Pünd asked.

'Of course. But it is empty now.'

'The police examined it?'

'Yes. They were meticulous. No fingerprints. No forced entry. Nothing.'

Pargeter leaned forward and began to spin the combination dial. Sixteen to the left, five to the right, back to twenty-two on the left ... there were seven separate movements before the wheel flies aligned. He turned the key in the lock, then pulled the handle. There was a click and the door opened. Looking past him, Pünd saw that there was indeed nothing inside.

Pünd swung the safe door open and shut again, feeling the weight of it, its solidity, in his hand. There was nothing more to be seen. He straightened up and turned his attention to the surrounding walls, tapping them with his knuckles as if searching for a secret passage. Elaine Pargeter was watching him from the bedroom and did not look impressed. Pünd ran a finger over a small tear in the wallpaper, then rubbed his thumb against it, deep in thought. The safe was locked again. The three of them went back downstairs.

They went into the drawing room and Pünd accepted a second offer of coffee, which was brought in by the maid, who had been away on the night of the crime and seemed unaware that anything untoward had taken place. The Pargeters were sitting opposite him on a sofa. He was perched, slightly above them, on a high-backed antique chair that might have come out of a church.

'It might be helpful to speak to your friend, Mr Berkeley,' he said.

'I'm not sure what he can tell you,' Pargeter replied. 'He gave the police a full statement and now he's back in New York. But I can put a call into Shell for you, if you like.'

'The police ... ' Pünd took a sip of his coffee, carefully lowering the cup onto its saucer, which he had balanced on his knee. He turned to Elaine. 'It was you, Mrs Pargeter, who telephoned them?'

'Yes. Detective Inspector Gilbert arrived about thirty minutes later. He had a sergeant with him, a pleasant young man. It was two o'clock in the morning by that time; the two of them were on night duty. They interviewed us in the room where we're sitting now and asked a great many questions. They went upstairs and they also looked round the side of the house, where the window had been broken. They told us not to go into the closet – John had been right about that. The next morning we had a whole crowd of people from Scotland Yard: forensics, photographers, the lot!'

'I would be interested to know if, at any stage, the

police suggested that you yourself might be involved in the disappearance of the diamond.'

'No. Quite the opposite,' Pargeter said. 'They were scrupulously polite. They were interested in the safe and the way it operated. They examined the key – they had obviously never seen anything quite like it.' He paused. 'They did, however, want to know who else had been given the combination.'

'You told them the same as you have told me.'

'Exactly. There are only three people in the world who have it. My wife, myself and my lawyer.'

'But that is not true, Mr Pargeter.'

'What?' The businessman glanced angrily at Pünd, unhappy at being contradicted.

'Nobody else knows the combination,' his wife insisted.

Pünd closed his eyes. 'Sixteen left, five right, twenty-two left, thirty right, twenty-five left, eleven right, thirty-nine left.' He opened them again. 'That is correct, is it not?'

Pargeter flushed. 'You were watching me when I opened it!'

'That is exactly what I did.'

'Well, that's a cute trick, Mr Pünd, but I'm not quite sure what point you are trying to make. Nobody else ever came into that room with me apart from my wife, and for what it's worth, I saw you looking over my shoulder. You've got a good memory, but you might as well forget those numbers. They don't matter any more. That horse has bolted, as the saying goes. I'll be getting rid of the safe and buying a new one.'

'Ah, yes! You do not close the door after the horse has bolted. That is the saying to which you refer.' Pünd smiled. 'And for me, you open it!'

'I'm sorry?'

Pünd got to his feet. 'I need to make a few enquiries,' he said. 'But it is clear to me how the Ludendorff Diamond and all the other contents were removed from the safe and by whom. You will be in England for a few more days?'

'I'll stay as long as it takes.'

'Not long, Mr Pargeter. Then all will be revealed!'

The arrests had taken place four days later and in the end the diamond, all of Mrs Pargeter's jewellery and most of the money had been recovered. And Pargeter had been true to his word. Sitting in his brand-new living room with his sherry and his cigarette, Pünd thought about the cheque that had arrived with a brief note of thanks, more money than he had earned in several years. He had put down a deposit on Tanner Court the same day. He had bought new furniture, including a handsome Biedermeier desk. He had hired a secretary to assist him with his administrative work. That reminded him. He must tell Miss Cain to get rid of the bed. That had definitely been a mistake.

And the culprits?

It hadn't taken him long to discover that John Berkeley, Pargeter's old school friend, had serious money problems. Pargeter had more or less told him that himself. He had stayed in the house because he couldn't afford a hotel. A little further digging had revealed that it was no coincidence that Detective Inspector Gilbert (who was getting divorced) and Detective Sergeant Dickinson (who had a fondness for racing) had been in the Knightsbridge police station at half past one in the morning. They had actually volunteered for the night shift, knowing they would be called out. It had taken three of them to get past the security of the world's most impregnable safe, and although Pünd couldn't be certain of all the details, there was only one way it could have worked.

Berkeley had been the key. He had left with the Pargeters, knowing that the house was empty apart from an elderly butler who would sleep through the whole thing. While they were away, Dickinson had broken in, smashing a window and silencing the alarms. He would have had plenty of time to prepare the scene for the robbery.

First, he had placed a simple flat – a piece of theatrical scenery covered in dark red Chinese wallpaper – in front of the locked safe. Then he had brought in a second safe, a perfect replica of the Sentry model, but made out of much lighter material – painted wood – with the door open and the interior obviously empty.

When the Pargeters had got back from the party, Berkeley had 'spotted' the broken pieces of glass on the drive. It was actually important that Pargeter and his wife should realise that they had been burgled before they went into the house; it would influence how they behaved. Of course, they went straight to the safe and once again it was Berkeley who had taken control of the situation. Those were the exact words that Pargeter had used. He had stopped them from turning on the light in the alcove. He had told them not to go in. From a distance of ten feet, and even with the reflected light, the illusion would have been perfect. The fake wall blended in with the real one. The real safe was concealed behind it. The wooden safe was open and empty.

The Pargeters believed that they had been robbed even though they had no idea how it had happened. Berkeley had led his friend downstairs, supposedly to look after him but in reality to prevent him investigating too closely himself. Of course, at this stage, if the

Pargeters had worked out they were being tricked, there would have been no danger to Berkeley or to his co-conspirators. The whole thing would have been put down as some sort of bizarre hoax. Nobody would ever find out what had been planned.

Things changed with the arrival of Gilbert and Dickinson. Pünd could imagine exactly how it had worked. *'And what exactly is the combination of the safe, sir?'* Charles Pargeter would have volunteered the numbers without a second thought. After all, these were the police. And the horse had bolted. *'I wonder if I might take a look at this key of yours, sir?'* Again, Pargeter would have handed it over. He believed he had already been robbed, but in fact the robbery took place while he was sitting in the downstairs living room being interviewed. One of them – probably Dickinson again – had hurried back upstairs and opened the real safe, removing the contents. Then he had taken them outside, using the back door, along with the fake safe and the theatrical flat, leaving things exactly as they had appeared when the Pargeters got home.

He had made just one small mistake. Moving the flat, which had been wedged into place across the alcove, he had very slightly torn the wallpaper. Pünd had found that tear and everything else had fallen into place.

He looked at the clock. Half past six. It was time to go. He finished his sherry, stubbed out his cigarette and finally picked up the rosewood walking stick that he carried as an affectation and not because it was needed. He glanced at himself one last time in the mirror, patted the speech nestling in his inside pocket, and left.

SIX

CRIME AND PUNISHMENT

There were three hundred people in Goldsmiths' Hall, the women in long gowns, the men in black tie. They were sitting at four long tables in a room whose magnificence was beyond anything Pünd had ever experienced: soaring columns, massive chandeliers and more than enough gold ornamentation to remind those present of the industry to which it owed its existence. Perhaps it was because he was a foreigner that he felt a particular admiration for this ancient British tradition. The guild had been formed in the Middle Ages and now, six hundred years later, it still existed to provide education and support for its fellow citizens. The meal had been excellent, the conversation lively. He was glad that he had come.

His speech had also been well received. He had been

talking for half an hour and had covered his experiences as a police officer in the Ordnungspolizei in Germany and what had happened when it had been brought under Nazi control. But as he approached the last few pages, he changed direction. He had, after all, been given free rein when he was invited to speak and there was a point he wanted to make.

'You will be aware,' he said, 'that the Royal Commission on Capital Punishment set up by the last prime minister will be reporting in the next few months and it is my hope and belief that even if we do not see the end of capital punishment altogether, the law will soon be changed. It is not just the possible mistakes that were made in the cases of Timothy Evans and Derek Bentley earlier this year. No, surely, if our experience of Nazism and the war has taught us anything it is that we must believe in the sanctity of life, even the life of a criminal.

'Is it right that all murderers should die? Is the man who loses control for one terrible moment, who perhaps lashes out and kills his wife or best friend in an argument, to be treated no differently from the man who has planned and cold-bloodedly executed a murder for his personal gain? Is it not time to consider different types of murder and to apply appropriate sentences?

'Judges no longer have any appetite for the death penalty, ladies and gentlemen. You should be aware that almost half of all murderers are reprieved. In the first half of this century, five hundred and thirty-three death sentences out of one thousand, two hundred and ten were commuted, and that figure is rising. I have met many murderers. I have abhorred what they have done, but often I have found some sympathy for the terrible circumstances that have led them to commit their crimes. At the end of the day, they are human too.

'To kill the killer is to descend to his or her level. I await the result of the Royal Commission with interest. I believe it will lead us to a new age.'

Pünd had feared that his comments might not connect with this audience but the applause as he sat down was warm and sustained. It was only later, as the port and cigars were being passed round, that the treasurer, a slightly hard-edged man who was sitting next to him, suddenly remarked: 'I don't suppose you saw that story about Melissa James?'

'The actress who was killed in Devonshire a few days ago?'

'Yes. Forgive me, Mr Pünd, but I really wonder if what you said just now would apply to what happened to her.'

'The police have yet to identify her killer, I believe.'

'Well, it all points to the husband from what I understand. He was the last person to see her alive. Strangling someone is a very personal way of killing them, I would say, and all the circumstances would seem to suggest what the Americans call a "crime of passion". Now, here's a beautiful and talented young woman, loved all over the world. She made some superb films. My wife and I were definitely fans. Would you really be so willing to forgive her assassin?'

'Clemency and forgiveness are not the same thing.'

'Are you so sure of that? I would say it sends out a message. Lose your temper. Kill your wife. The law understands!'

Pünd did not agree but he kept his thoughts to himself. He had made his speech, which is what he had been asked to do, and that was the end of it. Even so, he was still thinking about the treasurer's words the following morning as he finished his breakfast and went into his office. His secretary had arrived promptly at nine o'clock and was waiting for him, sorting through his mail.

'How did your speech go, Mr Pünd?' she asked.

'It went extremely well, I think, Miss Cain.' He had brought home a cheque and he handed it to her. 'Could you send this, please, to the Police Orphans Fund.'

Miss Cain picked up the slip of paper and glanced at the amount. Her eyebrows rose. 'That was very generous of them,' she said.

'It is certainly a considerable donation,' Pünd agreed.

'And very good of you to give up your time, Mr Pünd.'

Atticus Pünd smiled. He had, he thought, found the perfect secretary in Madeline Cain, who had come to him through a highly respected agency. He had actually interviewed three women and she had seemed the most formidable, answering his questions with the brisk efficiency that she now brought to her work. She was forty-five years old, a graduate of Cheltenham Ladies' College, unmarried, with a flat in Shepherd's Bush. She had worked as the private secretary to a small number of senior businessmen, all of whom had given her excellent references. With her jet black hair, her dress sense – which was definitely on the austere side – and her horn-rimmed spectacles, she might seem daunting on first appearance. But she could be warm-hearted too. She had only been with Pünd for three months but she was already devoted to him.

'May I ask you a question, Miss Cain?'

'Of course, Mr Pünd.'

'What was your opinion of what I said last night?'

'The speech?'

'Yes.'

'Well, I'm not sure it's my place to say.' Miss Cain frowned. She had, of course, typed the speech and was familiar with its contents. 'I thought your description of Germany in the forties was very interesting.'

'And my remarks on capital punishment?'

'I don't really know. It's not something I've ever really thought about. I think it's right to show mercy in certain cases, but you don't want to encourage people to believe that evil will go unpunished.' She changed the subject. 'You have a Mrs Allingham coming in at eleven o'clock. She wants to talk to you about her husband.'

'And what is it that her husband has done?'

'He's disappeared with his secretary. Would you like me to be present?'

'It would most certainly be a good idea.'

Miss Cain had already opened the mail and had been glancing through the various letters as she spoke. Now she stopped with one of them in her hand. 'Someone's written to you from New York,' she said.

'Is it perhaps Herr Pargeter?'

'No, no. It's an agency.' She slid the letter in front of him.

Pünd picked it up, noticing that it had been typed on high-quality paper. According to the letterhead, it had been sent from the William Morris Agency, 1740 Broadway, New York. It read:

> *Dear Mr Pünd,*
> *My name is Edgar Schultz and I am a senior part-*
> *ner at the William Morris Agency in New York. It*
> *was my privilege to represent Miss Melissa James, a*

major motion-picture talent and a wonderful human being. I am sure you will understand how shocked we all are by the news of her passing.

As I write this, there have been no answers as to what took place at her home in Devonshire one week ago. Without wishing to disparage the work of the British police, my partners and I would like to engage you to investigate the crime.

If you would like to call my office on Judson 6–5100, I would be most glad to speak with you.

Yours sincerely,
Edgar Schultz

Pünd read the letter carefully, then laid it down. 'It is most curious,' he said. 'I was speaking of this matter only yesterday.'

'Everyone's talking about Melissa James,' Miss Cain agreed.

'That is indeed so. It is a story of great public interest and this invitation is as timely as it is unexpected. And yet, on reflection, it seems to me that Devonshire is a great distance from here and the facts of the case, insofar as I am aware, are quite straightforward. I am surprised that the police have not yet come up with a solution.'

'Maybe they need your help.'

'That is often the case. But to travel such a distance ...'

'Whatever you say, Mr Pünd.' She thought for a moment. 'But Miss James was a very good actress and you don't really have anything on your desk at the moment.'

'What of Mrs Allingham?'

'I thought it sounded rather sordid. I'm sure this would be much more up your street.'

Pünd smiled. 'Yes, you may perhaps be right.' He made up his mind. 'Let us see. If you would be so kind as to book a transatlantic call for this afternoon, we will hear what this man, Herr Schultz, has to say.'

'Certainly, Mr Pünd. I'll see to that for you.'

The call was arranged for three o'clock, which would be midmorning in New York. Miss Cain made the connection and was put through to Schultz's office. Only then did she hand the receiver to Pünd. As he held it against his ear, he heard a low hissing and then, surprisingly clear, a voice with a strong Brooklyn accent.

'Hello? Is that Mr Pünd? Can you hear me?'

'Yes, yes. I can hear you. Is this Mr Schultz?'

'Thank you for calling us, sir. I want you to know, you have a great many admirers here in New York.'

'You are too kind.'

'Not at all. If you ever decided to write a book about

your exploits, I hope you would allow this agency to represent you.'

That was, Pünd reflected, exactly what he would have expected from a New York agent. Even as he was discussing the death of one of his clients, he was attempting to secure another. He said nothing, ignoring the invitation – and perhaps the man at the end of the line realised he had stepped out of line.

'We're all heartbroken by the death of Miss James,' he continued earnestly. 'As you may know, she hadn't acted for some time, but she was about to make a comeback and all I can say is, it's a great loss to the movie industry. I'm sorry I can't be in London to speak with you personally but I very much hope you'll help us out here. We want to know who did this. We want to know what happened. We feel we owe it to her.'

'And if I do find the truth,' Pünd said, 'what then?'

'Well, obviously, that will be a matter for the British police. But our feeling is we can't just sit on our butts and do nothing. We wanted to get involved and then some bright spark in the office suggested you and we got in touch straight away. We were lucky that one of our associates was in London this week and he carried my letter with him on the flight. I'm sure you'll agree with me that we can't waste any time. We don't want to let the trail go cold.'

'It is certainly true that an investigation is at its most effective in the days immediately following the crime,' Pünd agreed.

'We'll pay your usual fee, Mr Pünd. You can ask your assistant to get in touch with our finance department. I can't tell you how much it would mean to us if you came on board. There are a lot of sharks in this business – male and female – but Melissa was one of the kindest and most considerate people I had the privilege to meet. She never let success go to her head and she never forgot her fans.'

'When did you last speak with her, Mr Schultz?'

'I'm sorry? I can't hear you.'

'When did you last speak with her?'

'About two weeks ago. We were discussing a contract for a new film. She was going to earn a lot of money – and it strikes me that may have had something to do with what happened.'

'It is, I suppose, possible.' Pünd sounded unsure.

'Well, I'll leave the thinking to you. Can I tell my partners that we have an agreement?'

'You can tell them, certainly, that I will consider the matter.'

'Thank you, sir. I am truly appreciative. I'll look forward to hearing from you.'

He rang off. Pünd sat in silence.

'What did he say?' Miss Cain asked. She had been sitting opposite him throughout the conversation but she had only heard one side of what was discussed.

'It is interesting,' Pünd said. 'If I decide to take this assignment, it will be the first time I have been engaged by a long-distance telephone call!'

'You would have thought they could have flown over,' Miss Cain sniffed.

'That is true.'

'Are you going to do it?'

Pünd turned the letter round and tapped his fingers gently against the paper as if there was something hidden inside the words and he was trying to dislodge it. Finally, he nodded. 'Yes,' he said. 'Only last night this case was mentioned to me and now this has occurred. There is something about the approach from her agents that persuades me that, as you suggested, this could be a case of great interest. Please can I ask you to book two first-class rail tickets to . . . I believe Tawleigh-on-the-Water is the name of the village? We will also need accommodation in a comfortable hotel.'

Miss Cain stood up. 'I'll get on to it straight away.'

'As a courtesy, we will need to contact the local police and inform them of our arrival, and you can also call back Herr Schultz and inform him that I have decided to take the case.'

'Yes. I'll also organise the contract and the payment.'

'That too. I take it you have no issues that would prevent you from accompanying me?'

'None at all, Mr Pünd. I'll pack the moment I get home.'

'Thank you, Miss Cain. And if you will be so kind as to pick up the train tickets, the two of us will leave tomorrow.'

SEVEN
A QUESTION OF TIME

It took them six hours to reach Tawleigh-on-the-Water, starting from Paddington at midday and changing trains twice, at Exeter and at Barnstaple. Miss Cain had made all the arrangements with the efficiency that Pünd had come to admire. She knew the different platform numbers and porters met them at each stop, ensuring that the journey was as smooth as possible. Pünd passed the time absorbed in a study that he had received from the highly respected American Academy of Forensic Sciences: an examination of the so-called Nutshell Studies of Frances Glessner Lee, who had constructed intricate models of complicated crime scenes in order to analyse them. His secretary, meanwhile, had brought a library book, *A Daughter's a Daughter,* the new Mary Westmacott.

There was a taxi waiting for them at Bideford and it drove them across the Bideford Bridge to Tawleigh just as the sun was beginning to set. The rain had finally cleared and their first view of the village could have been taken from one of the picture postcards on sale inside the chandlery. They drove past a brightly painted lighthouse at the far end of a harbour, a line of fishing boats, the Red Lion pub, then a long crescent of sand and shingle. It was true that there were no children and no sandcastles, no donkeys or ice cream, but they could be easily imagined. A carpet of brilliant red lay shimmering on the water and the waves broke with a soft, gentle rhythm as the moon took its place in the sky and the darkness gathered.

'You wouldn't have thought a murder could happen in a place like this,' Miss Cain muttered as she looked out of the window.

'It is the nature of murder that it will take place anywhere,' Pünd responded.

They were staying at the Moonflower Hotel. The taxi drew up but nobody came out to help them with their luggage. Miss Cain rolled her eyes, but Pünd was more forgiving. The hotel was in the middle of a police investigation. It was unlikely that things would be running smoothly.

At least the young girl behind the reception desk was

friendlier. 'Welcome to the Moonflower.' She smiled. 'I see you've reserved for two nights.'

'It may be longer,' Miss Cain warned her.

'Just let me know.' She turned to Pünd. 'You're in the Captain's Room, Mr Pünd. I'm sure you'll be very comfortable there. And I've put your assistant on the floor above. If you'd like to leave your luggage here, I'll have it brought up for you ...'

The Captain's Room had originally been an office when the building had functioned as a customs house. It was very square with a bed where the desk might have been and two windows looking out over the Marine Parade and the beach on the other side. It still had a strong nautical feel: there was a sea chest at the end of the bed, a captain's swivel chair in the corner and even a globe between the windows. Pünd was intrigued by the ship's cabinet in the bathroom with its dozens of tiny drawers to keep things in place if there was a swell. Meanwhile, Miss Cain had been shown to a smaller room in the eaves. They were both tired after their long journey and so went to bed early, having had supper brought to their rooms on trays.

Pünd opened his eyes to blue skies and the sound of seagulls. It was half past seven when he came down to breakfast and the girl who had greeted them the evening before had not yet started work. Her place had been taken by a man with a moustache and slicked-back hair, dressed in a blazer and cravat. He had been laboriously typing a letter, using just one finger on each hand, but he looked up as Pünd appeared.

'Good morning,' he muttered. 'You came down from London yesterday. Is that right?'

Pünd told him that it was.

'Do you like your room?'

'It is most comfortable, thank you.'

'I'm Lance Gardner, the general manager. Let me know if there's anything you need. I suppose you'll be wanting your breakfast now.'

'That was my intention.'

'We don't usually serve until eight. I'll see if the chef has got in yet.' But Gardner didn't move. 'Are you here about the murder?'

'I am here to assist the police. Yes.'

'I'm glad you're not a journalist. We've had them crawling around the place all week – all on expenses, of course, drinking the bar dry. As for the police, if you ask me, they need all the assistance they can get. It's been over a week now and they haven't got anywhere, keeping us all here with their damn fool questions. It's like living in Russia!'

'You knew Miss James?' Pünd asked, reflecting that

actually Tawleigh-on-the-Water had very little in common with the Soviet Union.

'Of course I knew her. She owned the hotel. I ran it for her – not that she ever gave me much thanks for it.'

'You would not say that she was an easy person with whom to work?'

'I'll tell you the truth, Mr ...'

'My name is Atticus Pünd.'

'German? I'll make no comment. I didn't fight in the war. Rickets.' He rubbed his neck as he considered what Pünd had asked. 'Was she easy to work with? Well, I liked her. We had a good relationship. But the truth is, she didn't know very much about the hotel business, certainly not the way we do things round here. Nothing's cut and dried. When you're working with farmers and fishermen who've been in Tawleigh for generations, you have to learn how to adapt. She wasn't from this part of the world and she never quite worked it out. And that's the truth of it.'

Lance Gardner had used the word 'truth' three times in almost the same sentence. From Pünd's experience, people who were so insistent on the truth were very rarely telling it.

'It must be very frustrating for you,' Pünd suggested. 'Awaiting the end of the investigation.'

'I certainly won't be sorry to see it over.'

'Do you have any theory as to who might have killed her?'

Lance Gardner leaned forward, pleased to have been asked. 'They're all saying it was her husband. But then it's always the husband, isn't it? God knows, if my wife drove herself off Beachy Head, they'd say I was the one behind the wheel. They'd be quite wrong. I'd be pushing it from behind!' He let out a bark of laughter. 'Take it from me, Francis Pendleton doesn't have it in him. He's not a killer.'

'Who then?'

'If you ask me, it wasn't anyone from around here. Melissa James was a star. She had all sorts of loopy followers and fans. They used to send her letters here at the hotel. They knew where she lived. It wouldn't surprise me if one of them had come down here with some sort of lunatic scheme in his head and killed her simply because he didn't like her last film or she hadn't sent him an autograph or he just wanted to be famous like her. The police are blundering about asking questions, but I think they're just wasting their time. And ours!'

'It is an interesting theory, Mr Gardner. Where is the breakfast served?'

'In the dining room.' Gardner pointed. 'Through those doors. I'll see if the chef is around.'

*

Breakfast was surprisingly good. Pünd had purchased a copy of *The Times*, which had come down on the night train, and he read it as he ate scrambled eggs and bacon, toast and marmalade and a cup of strong tea from Ceylon. Miss Cain did not join him and he was not surprised. She was the sort of woman who was very sensitive to all the niceties and she would have considered it overfamiliar to have eaten breakfast even in the same room as her employer.

In fact, she appeared at nine o'clock, the same time that she began work in London, and the two of them repaired to the main living room. They were sitting there when, ten minutes later, Detective Chief Inspector Hare appeared. He saw them at once and joined them.

'Mr Pünd?' The detective chief inspector stood in front of him as Pünd got to his feet and the two men shook hands. Hare's first impression was of a lean, smartly presented foreigner who seemed to carry a world of experience about him and who was already measuring him up with eyes that would miss nothing. He was right about that. Pünd was seeing a police officer who was being beaten down by a case that refused to unlock itself for him and who was approaching the edges of failure and disappointment. And yet at once there was a warmth between them, as if their coming together might finally open up new possibilities.

'Detective Chief Inspector Hare, I believe.'

'It's a very great pleasure to meet you, sir. It goes without saying that your reputation precedes you.'

In fact, Hare had consulted his files in Exeter the moment he had heard that Pünd was on his way. He had read the details of several of his investigations, including the arrest of Luce Julien, an internationally renowned artist living in Highgate who had killed her husband with a palette knife on their fortieth wedding anniversary – a case that had brought him to fame just after the war. More recently, of course, the return of the Ludendorff Diamond had been the talk of the whole country.

'May I introduce you to my secretary, Miss Cain?'

Pünd gestured and Hare shook hands with her too. 'A pleasure to meet you.'

'And can I offer you some tea?'

'No, thank you, sir. I've just had breakfast.'

'I hope you do not consider my presence here to be an intrusion,' Pünd began as the two men sat down again.

'Not at all, Mr Pünd. Quite frankly, I couldn't be happier to see you.' The detective drew a hand across his brow. 'I've been a serving police officer for thirty years. For what it's worth, I wanted to join the army when the war started but they wouldn't let me. They said they needed me here. The fact of the matter is, though, that I'm not used to murder. In my entire time with the Devon and Cornwall Police, I've investigated barely a dozen cases and in the first three of them, the perpetrators turned themselves in the next day. Any help you can give me will be more than appreciated.'

Pünd was pleased. He had known straight away that he was going to get on with Hare and what he had just heard confirmed it. 'You are fortunate, Detective Chief Inspector, to be living in a part of the country where violent crime is a rarity.'

'You're right there, Mr Pünd. In the war years, we had looting, racketeering, desertion. There was a lot of upheaval when everyone came home again and as you might expect, there were guns all over the place. But Devonshire folk don't tend to do each other in. That's been my experience – until now.' He paused. 'May I ask why you have taken an interest in this case, sir?'

'Miss James's agents in New York asked me to look into it on their behalf.'

'Meaning, I suppose, that they have no faith in me.'

'Whether that is true or not, Detective Chief Inspector, I can assure you it is not my opinion. I would like to think that we can work on this together.'

Hare's eyes brightened. 'I see absolutely no reason why not.'

'You are already several days ahead of me. Perhaps you could share with me what you have found so far.'

'Certainly.'

'Would you mind if I took notes, Detective Chief Inspector?' Miss Cain asked, drawing a pen and a shorthand pad out of her handbag.

'Please go ahead.' Hare had produced his own notebook. He cleared his throat. 'The trouble with this investigation is that it should be fairly cut and dried. This is a small community. Miss James was an extremely well-known figure. And there's a time period of just seventeen minutes in which the crime must have taken place. I don't know why the answer isn't more obvious.'

'It is my experience that the more obvious the answer, the more difficult it can be to find,' Pünd remarked.

'You may be right, sir.' Hare opened his own notepad and referred to what he had written. For the next few minutes, he spoke uninterrupted.

'The last person to see Miss James alive was her husband, Francis Pendleton. You may wonder why I don't refer to her as Mrs Pendleton, incidentally, but she was known to the whole world by the name with which she appeared in her films and that's the name she used here. Mr Pendleton is ten years younger than his wife and comes from a wealthy family. His father is Lord Pendleton, a Conservative peer, and I'm afraid he didn't approve of the marriage, so his son was subsequently cut off without a penny, as they like to say.

'There is a suggestion that there was a certain amount of friction between Francis Pendleton and his wife. Of course, there's a lot of gossip in a place like Tawleigh-on-the-Water and it only makes my job more difficult, trying to separate truth from speculation. Anyway, they have a cook and a butler who live in the house – a nineteenth-century folly by the name of Clarence Keep, about half a mile outside the village. The two halves of Clarence Keep – that is, the part for Miss James and Francis Pendleton and the part for the servants – are carefully separated and sound doesn't travel easily from one to the other, but even so they have told me there were occasions when they heard the two of them arguing. The Gardners, who run this hotel, have also confirmed that things between them were not going well.

'Miss James was in a meeting, here at the Moon-flower, which finished at 5.40 p.m. She went home, arriving just after 6 p.m. That time is confirmed by the cook and the butler, who saw her very distinctive car, a Bentley, draw in. According to Mr Pendleton, he and his wife had a brief and friendly conversation before Mr Pendleton left in his other car, an Austin, to attend the performance of an opera, *The Marriage of Figaro*, which started at 7 p.m. in Barnstaple. He left at 6.15 p.m., he says, although we only have his word for it as nobody saw or heard him go. His car was parked around the side of the house, out of sight of the servants' quarters. Miss James was meant to be going with him, incidentally, but had decided that she wanted an early night.

'So, if the evidence is to be believed, at 6.15 p.m. there were just three people in the house. Miss James was upstairs in her bedroom. Phyllis and Eric Chandler, the cook and the butler, were downstairs in the kitchen.'

'They are husband and wife?'

'No, sir. Mother and son.'

'That is unusual.'

'I'd say "unusual" is a good word to describe them.' Hare coughed. 'At about 6.18 p.m., a few minutes after Francis says he left, a stranger arrived at the house. We have no idea who he was. We only know of his existence because the Chandlers heard the dog barking. Melissa James had a pet chow by the name of Kimba. The dog always barked when strangers came to the door. If it was Melissa James or her husband or their servants or their friends, it remained silent. But at 6.18, it began to bark frantically. And a minute or two later, both the Chandlers heard the front door open and close.'

'Neither of them left the kitchen to see who it was?'

'No, Mr Pünd. They were off duty, meaning they were also out of uniform, so it wouldn't have been appropriate.

It's a crying shame because if they'd only looked through the door the whole mystery might have been solved.

'As it is, we have to ask ourselves this question. Did Melissa James open the door at 6.20 p.m. and allow a stranger into the house and was that person her killer? It would seem to be the natural conclusion. At 6.25 p.m., Phyllis and Eric Chandler did finally leave the house, taking Miss James's Bentley. She had said they could drive over to Bude to visit Mrs Chandler's sister, who was unwell. Eric noticed that the Austin was no longer there, by the way. And before you ask, there is absolutely no question that the Chandlers did actually leave Clarence Keep. I've spoken to a couple of witnesses who saw them drive past – you tend to notice a car like that – and the sister in Bude corroborates their story.

'If I'm correct, Miss James was now alone in the house with someone who was a stranger to her. She became very upset and at 6.28 p.m. she made a call to Dr Leonard Collins, who was her GP and also a close friend, so it's obvious that at that time she was still alive. Dr Collins was at his home in Tawleigh with his wife. I should perhaps mention that the call was logged at the local exchange and there can be no doubt that it took place. According to Dr Collins, Miss James was terrified. She said she needed help and asked him to come to the house. Samantha Collins, Dr Collins's wife, was in the room when he took the call and was able to hear at least part of it. She saw him leave and happened to notice the time of his departure, which was 6.35 p.m.

'Dr Collins arrived at Clarence Keep at 6.45 p.m. and was surprised to find the front door open. He went in. There was no sign that anything was wrong, but having heard what he had heard on the telephone call, he was concerned. He called out for Melissa but got no answer. Nothing seemed to have been disturbed but he still continued upstairs.

'He found Miss James in her bedroom. She had been strangled with the cord from the telephone that stood on a cabinet by the bed. In the course of what must have been a violent struggle, the wire had been torn out of the wall. She had also struck her head on an ornamental table beside the bed. We found a contusion under her hair and there was a bloodstain on the wooden surface – AB positive, which was her blood type.

'Dr Collins did everything he could to revive Miss James with chest compressions and mouth-to-mouth resuscitation. According to his testimony, she was still warm when he arrived and he might have succeeded. Sadly, he didn't. He called for the police and an ambulance at 6.56 p.m. – that call, of course, was also logged. A team was sent out from Barnstaple and arrived about thirty minutes later.

'And that, Mr Pünd, is about the shape of it. I said that the murder could have taken place only within an interval of seventeen minutes and by that I mean between 6.28 p.m., when Miss James called the doctor, and 6.45 p.m., when he arrived. There are other details, other testimonies of which you need to be made aware, but actually they only complicate matters. What I've given you is the basic timeline. I'm fairly sure it's accurate, but actually, that's part of the problem. When you have everything down to the minute like this, it's very hard to see how the killer could have seized his opportunity.'

'You have assembled the facts and the timings with great precision, Detective Chief Inspector,' Pünd remarked. 'I am grateful to you. It will make our work a great deal easier at the end of the day.'

Hare smiled, perhaps acknowledging the word 'our' that Pünd had used.

'Is there anything more you can tell me about the crime scene itself?' Pünd asked.

'Not a great deal. Melissa James had clearly been extremely upset in the moments before her death. We know that already from the call she made to Dr Collins, but we also found two balls of tissue paper on the floor of the bedroom and another in the sitting room. They were impregnated with lacrimal fluid.'

'Tears,' Pünd said.

'She was crying when she spoke to Dr Collins. I hate to say this, Mr Pünd, but it seems highly likely that her attacker was actually in the house when she called her GP.'

'That may well be the case, Detective Chief Inspector. Although it would beg the question as to why he allowed her to make the call if he was intending to kill her.'

'That's true.' Hare flicked a page in his notebook. 'She must have put up quite a struggle. The bed was in disarray, a lamp had been knocked over and there were several ligature marks around her neck, suggesting that she at least tried to escape from the telephone cord that was used to strangle her.'

He sighed.

'I have various witness statements which I can share with you, but I expect you'd rather speak to the people concerned yourself. They're all still here in Tawleigh, although one or two of them aren't too happy about it. There are two points which I should bring to your attention straight away, however.

'The first relates to a businessman by the name of Simon Cox. He had strong words with Miss James in the hotel bar shortly after half past five. We know this because they were overheard by Nancy Mitchell, who works behind the bar. She's a nice, respectable girl, by the way. Her father looks after the lighthouse. But I have a suspicion that she may have got herself into trouble, got herself in the family way.'

'What causes you to believe this, Detective Chief Inspector?'

Hare smiled. 'I have a daughter. Happily married and doing very well for herself. I'm due to be a grandfather for the first time in September and all I can say is you get to know the symptoms.'

'You have my congratulations.'

'Thank you, Mr Pünd. I haven't spoken to Nancy about it because it may not be relevant and I don't want to upset her unnecessarily.' He glanced back at his notes. 'Anyway, Simon Cox followed Miss James out of the hotel when he left and is unable to account for his movements between that time and a quarter to seven, when he came down for dinner. He says he went for a walk but I've heard that one before!'

'Have you threatened him with arrest?'

'For obstruction, you mean? Or on suspicion of murder? It could be either of them, I suppose. I was intending to speak to him again today. Perhaps we might do that together.'

'Indeed. And what was the second point?'

'A chap called Algernon Marsh, staying here with his

sister, who's married to Dr Collins. A good-looking young man, presents himself very well. Drives a rather natty French car. But I've had a word with Scotland Yard and they've been looking into his business dealings. By all accounts he's a nasty piece of work, although that didn't stop him having a close relationship with Miss James.'

'How close?'

'He refuses to say.'

'Could they have been romantically involved?'

Hare shook his head. 'Francis Pendleton insists that everything was lovey-dovey between himself and his wife, although he would want us to believe that, wouldn't he. He's still the number-one suspect in her murder.'

'And yet according to Dr Collins, Melissa James called him *after* her husband had left for the opera in Barnstaple.'

'Well, yes. I suppose he could have left the house and come back again.'

'Then why did she not say as much when she spoke to Dr Collins?'

Hare sighed. 'These are all good questions. And they absolutely sum up my problem. The whole thing should be easy when actually it makes no sense at all.'

Pünd considered what he had been told. 'With your permission, Detective Chief Inspector, I would like to begin at the home of Melissa James. Clarence Keep, I believe you said. It would be very useful for me to meet Francis Pendleton and to make a judgement for myself.'

'Absolutely. I can drive you over now.'

'I wonder if this might help?' Miss Cain had not spoken for some time, but now she turned her notepad around and handed it to Pünd. On a single page, she had set out in neat columns:

5.40 p.m.: Miss James leaves the Moonflower.

6.05 p.m.: Miss James arrives home.

6.15 p.m.: Francis Pendleton leaves Clarence Keep for the opera.

6.18 p.m.: Dog heard barking. Stranger arrives at Clarence Keep?

6.20 p.m.: Front door heard opening and closing at Clarence Keep.

6.25 p.m.: The Chandlers leave. The Austin has gone.

6.28 p.m.: Melissa James calls Dr Collins.

6.35 p.m.: Dr Collins leaves his home.

6.45 p.m.: Dr Collins arrives at Clarence Keep. Melissa James dead.

6.56 p.m.: Dr Collins calls police & ambulance.

Pünd examined the paper. He had already committed the details to his memory, but even so, he appreciated having them laid out for him in this way. It was as if the different moments of time had become signposts on the road to the truth.

'Thank you, Miss Cain,' he said. 'It would be good if you could arrange for this to be typed.'

'I'm sure I can organise that for you, Mr Pünd.'

'I would like a copy for myself and one for Detective Chief Inspector Hare. It is quite clear to me that the answer to this problem is concealed somewhere in the ten moments in time that you have listed. All we have to do is look carefully and it will be found.'

EIGHT
TAKEN BY THE TIDE

They were about to leave when a short, dark man came storming into the room, making straight for Detective Chief Inspector Hare. It was Simon Cox. The businessman and would-be film producer was in the same suit he had been wearing on the day he'd met Melissa and he was in a furious mood.

'Detective Inspector!' he began. 'They told me you were here and I want to make it completely clear that I have had enough of this absurd imprisonment. I have telephoned my lawyers and they assure me that it is outrageous and that you do not have the authority to keep me here. The death of Melissa James had nothing to do with me. I already told you. I met her in the bar. We talked for about ten minutes and then she left. I absolutely insist that you allow me to do the same.'

Pünd examined the new arrival, the thick black hair and the heavy features, which, along with his accent, suggested Russian or Slavonic origins. Anger didn't really suit him. He was too small, too unimpressive. He managed to sound only truculent.

'You haven't met my associate, Mr Atticus Pünd,' the detective chief inspector replied, casually batting aside the outrage that had just been directed at him.

'I've not had this pleasure. No.'

'I think perhaps you should talk to him, Mr Cox. I'm sure he has quite a few questions for you.'

'My God! Are you deaf? Did you not hear what I just said?'

'About keeping you here? Well, I suppose I could put you under arrest, if you like. Maybe that would satisfy your lawyers.'

'Arrest me? For what?'

'For lying to a police officer. For obstructing a police officer in the execution of his duty—'

'I have not lied to you!' Cox stood his ground but now there was a hint of uncertainty in his voice.

'Why do you not sit down?' Pünd suggested in his most avuncular tone, gesturing at an empty chair. 'This is, I am sure, all a misunderstanding. A few more minutes of your time, Mr Cox, and maybe we can put this matter to rest and you can be on your way.'

The businessman glanced at Pünd and, given a choice between a quiet chat and imprisonment, nodded his agreement. He took his place on the sofa between Pünd and Hare. Madeline Cain had retrieved her notebook and was waiting, her pen poised.

'You came to England before the war?' Pünd asked. He sounded genuinely interested.

Cox nodded. 'In 1938. From Latvia.'

'Cox is not then your family name.'

'It is not dissimilar. It is in fact Sīmanis Čaks. I have nothing to hide, Mr Pünd. But you must understand that it is not easy to do business in this country if you are a foreigner. At least, you must not appear to be *too* foreign . . . !'

'I understand completely. For me, too, this is not the country of my birth.' He smiled as if the two of them had arrived at a common purpose. 'You travelled down to this village with the intention of meeting with Miss James,' he went on.

'Yes.'

'It must, then, have been important business. I myself made the journey only yesterday and it was an undertaking of a great many hours. Three trains. And the British Rail sandwiches! They were not good.'

'Well, in fact, I drove down. But you're right. I told the detective inspector. We were talking about making a film together.'

'And what film was that?'

'It's a historical drama. The title is *The Queen's Ransom*. Melissa was interested in playing the lead part – Eleanor of Aquitaine.'

'The wife of King Henry II!' In his youth, Pünd had studied history at the University of Salzburg. 'You say she was interested. Had you agreed terms?'

'That was what the meeting was about. Production begins in a little over two months and I wanted to be sure that she was still on board.'

'And was she?'

Cox was about to answer but before he could begin, Pünd held up a single finger in a gesture of warning.

'I must advise you, Mr Cox, that a hotel is a very public place and its bar particularly so. You should be aware that your conversation will have been overheard by many people. It would be foolish of you to – how would you say it? – bend the truth, particularly in the context of a murder investigation.'

Cox fell silent. He was clearly considering his options. But he could see that there was only one way forward. 'Well, if you must know,' he began, 'Melissa James had changed her mind. It seems she had accepted a better offer. It is, of course, unprofessional behaviour, but that is what you must expect, working with an actress. I was angry. She had lied to me and she had wasted my time.

But it was not a matter of great importance to me. There were many other actresses I could approach. After all, she had not made anything for five years. She was not quite the star that she believed herself to be.'

He had been speaking rapidly and it took Miss Cain a few moments to catch up. Pünd heard the scratch of her nib on the page as she underlined his last words.

'You then followed her out of the hotel,' Hare muttered. He had already interviewed Cox and he was quite put out that, under Pünd's questioning, he had come up with a quite different version of events.

'I left shortly after she did. I did not follow her out.'

'So where did you go?'

'I told you.' The glint was back in Simon Cox's eye. 'I had been in the car for many hours. I'd come straight to my room in the hotel. I needed a walk and to see something of the area, and fortunately the rain had stopped.'

'You went over to Appledore,' Hare said.

'This I also told you.'

'You said you walked along the beach.'

'I walked for about an hour, yes. The beach was called Gray Sands.'

'And you didn't meet anybody. Nobody saw you.'

Cox turned to Pünd as if he expected him to take his side. 'I have already explained to the detective inspector. It was late in the afternoon, a quarter to six. It was a grey sky and it was damp after the rain. I was alone! In the distance I saw a man with a dog but he was too far away and he will not have been able to recognise me. In fact, I wanted to be alone! I had to consider what I would do next and it was helpful to me to find myself with nobody else nearby.'

Hare shook his head doubtfully. 'You do see, sir, that it makes it very difficult for us to confirm your story.'

'That is your problem, Detective Inspector. It is not mine.'

There was a long silence and Hare thought that the interview must be over when suddenly Miss Cain spoke. She had contributed so little to either meeting that it came as a surprise to hear her voice. 'Excuse me, Mr Pünd. I wonder if I might say something?'

'Of course, Miss Cain.'

'Well, I'm sure it's wrong of me to intrude, but the fact is that I was brought up in Appledore. I actually lived there until I was fifteen and my parents moved to London. But the thing is, I know the coast around here like the back of my hand, and with all respect to the gentleman, it would have been impossible to walk along Gray Sands, not after five o'clock, not at the end of April.'

'And why is that?'

'Because of the spring tide. At four o'clock every afternoon it comes right up to the cliff and for the next four or five hours there's no beach at all. You can walk along the cliff edge but even that is quite dangerous. There are warning signs everywhere. We actually had a couple of people drown once. They got caught halfway.'

There was another silence. Detective Chief Inspector Hare turned accusingly to Simon Cox. 'What do you have to say to that, sir?'

'I … I … ' Cox couldn't find the right words.

'You didn't walk on Gray Sands?'

'I walked on a beach. Maybe … maybe I got the name wrong.'

'Then can you describe which beach you actually visited?'

'No! I don't remember. You're confusing me.' He buried his face in his hands.

'I'm afraid I'm going to have to ask you to come into Exeter with me, Mr Cox. We're going to continue this interview under caution and with another officer present. You can consider yourself under arrest.'

'Wait!' All the colour had drained out of Simon Cox's face. His mouth was opening and closing as he fought for breath. None of them would have been surprised if he had succumbed to a serious heart attack. 'I'd like a glass of water,' he gasped.

'I'll get it for you,' Miss Cain said cheerfully. She got up and left the room, returning a few moments later with a glass and a jug.

Cox drank greedily. Miss Cain picked up her note-book. Pünd and the detective chief inspector waited for him to speak. 'All right!' he said at last. 'I lied to you. But I had no choice. This whole business has been a nightmare.'

'It was a nightmare for Melissa James,' Hare said, showing no sympathy. 'And for everyone who knew her. Her killer could still be out there. He could strike again. Has that never occurred to you? Or did you kill her? Did you follow her home? Is that what happened?'

'I did go after her.' Cox refilled his glass and drank more water. 'You have no idea how bad it was for me, her decision. It will ruin me! I owe thousands of pounds. *The Queen's Ransom*! Ha! That is exactly what it is!'

'So you went to her house,' Pünd said.

'I went to her house. If I had told you this, of course you would think that I murdered her and maybe you would be right. I could have. There was so much anger in my heart. She had broken her promises. She had lied to me. And she had dismissed me without a single thought because I am a nobody, because in her eyes I am a Lat-vian peasant and I had only my good faith and my entire heart to give to her. Yes, I could well have strangled her. I admit it. But I didn't. I did not speak to her again.'

'So what happened?'

'I found Clarence Keep. It is less than a mile from the hotel and it took me only a few minutes to drive there. I thought that Melissa would have arrived ahead of me so I was surprised that I could not see the Bentley outside. I had certainly not overtaken her so I assumed that she must have gone another way and that she would arrive very soon.'

'Where were you parked?'

'I was on the edge of the road, close to some trees that concealed me. I did not want to be seen by her when she returned. I thought she would only drive away again.'

'When did she arrive?'

'A little after six o'clock.'

'So where had she been for the past twenty minutes?'

Hare had addressed the question to himself as much as to anyone else, but Cox answered anyway. 'I have no idea. She drove past me without seeing me and entered the driveway. I saw her get out of the car and enter the house.'

'What happened next?'

'I waited a few minutes, trying to think what I would say to her. I was beginning to regret coming there. I knew that she had made up her mind and that there was nothing I could do. Even so, I got out of the car and walked up the drive. I got to the front door, but before I could ring the bell I heard a voice coming from a window that was open a little bit, on the side. It was a woman – not Melissa. She was older and she was angry with someone. She said they were disgusting. She was accusing them.'

'Phyllis Chandler and her son,' Hare said. 'They must have been in the kitchen.'

'I don't know who it was. I couldn't see them.'

'Did you hear what she said?'

'Some of it ... yes. But not the exact words. She said something about the Moonflower being crooked and that she'd seen through it.' He took a breath. 'And then she said that if Melissa found the truth, they would have to kill her.'

There was a long silence. Hare was staring at the producer. 'They threatened to kill her. She's been strangled. And you chose not to tell us?'

Cox looked completely wretched. 'I already explained to you, Detective Inspector. I couldn't see who was in the room and who she was talking to. And I still don't know what I heard. Not exactly ...'

'But you heard her say they'd kill her!'

'I think so.' Cox took out a handkerchief and wiped his face. There was a sheen of sweat on his upper lip. 'They didn't want Melissa to find the truth.'

'What did you do next?' Pünd asked, a little more gently.

'I left the house. I had decided it was a mistake to have driven there in the first place. It was useless. Melissa wouldn't see me. Why should I humiliate myself again?'

'What time did you arrive back at the hotel?' Hare asked.

'It was a short while later. I cannot tell you the time exactly and nobody saw me arrive – I'm sorry. The young lady was no longer behind the reception. I went up to my room to have a shower and to change before supper. I came down again at a quarter to seven, when I met Mrs Gardner, the wife of the manager.'

'Did you really have to make up such an elaborate story?' Hare demanded. 'A long walk on Gray Sands! From what you've just told us, you were only away from the hotel for about half an hour. If you were going to lie to me, you could have just told me you'd stayed in your room.'

'I was seen leaving,' Cox said, miserably. 'It is possible that someone saw me on the way to Clarence Keep. It was stupid of me, yes. But the facts are still the facts,

Detective Inspector. I had a very good reason to kill Melissa James. We argued before she died and I followed her to her home. It was obvious to me that when all this came out I would be your number-one suspect. I did not think you would even believe me about what I had heard. You would think I had made it up.'

Pünd glanced at Detective Chief Inspector Hare as if asking his permission and, on receiving a quick nod, said: 'You should return to London, Mr Cox. It was most foolish of you to lie to the police and you could have done great harm by delaying the investigation. But now that you have told us the truth, there is no need to detain you. We will, however, contact you again if there are any further questions.'

Cox looked up. 'Thank you, Mr Pünd. I really am very sorry, Detective Inspector.'

'Detective *Chief* Inspector,' Hare corrected him. He was finally unable to resist it.

'I'm sorry. Yes . . .'

Simon Cox got up and left the room.

'So *do* we believe him, then?' Hare asked, once he had gone. 'And if we do, perhaps we should be arresting Phyllis Chandler and her son!'

'We must certainly question them,' Pünd agreed. 'But we must also remember that Mr Cox is not in full command of the English language, and moreover, he heard the conversation through a window while he was in an agitated state of mind.'

'I understand the Moonflower is losing money,' Hare muttered. 'And it's clear that Miss James suspected some sort of embezzlement ... '

'I am sure that Mr Pendleton will be able to give us more information on that matter.' Pünd turned to his assistant. 'But before we leave, there is something I must ask you, Miss Cain. I do not remember you mentioning that you had lived in Devonshire when we were discussing your resumé.'

Now it was the secretary's turn to blush. 'Actually, Mr Pünd, I've never been here in my life.'

'Wait a minute!' Hare couldn't believe what he had just heard. 'Are you telling me all that stuff about Gray Sands ... ?'

'I hope you'll forgive me, sir. But I'm afraid I made it up.' She blinked several times, then continued hurriedly. 'It was obvious that the gentleman was lying to you and it suddenly occurred to me that I might be able to call his bluff, so to speak. I gambled on the fact that he was down here for the first time, so I decided to tell him that the beach he had walked on didn't exist – at least, not at the time he was there.' She turned to Pünd. 'I hope you're not angry with me, Mr Pünd.'

Detective Chief Inspector Hare burst out laughing.

'Angry with you? You deserve a medal, Miss Cain. It was brilliantly done.'

'It was indeed very helpful,' Pünd said.

'The two of you make a perfect team.'

'Yes,' Pünd agreed. 'We do.'

NINE
SCENE OF THE CRIME

It took Detective Chief Inspector Hare less than five minutes to drive Atticus Pünd and his assistant from the Moonflower Hotel to Clarence Keep. On the night of the murder, it had taken Melissa James more than twenty, meaning that she had at least fifteen minutes that were unaccounted for. What could she have got up to in that time? There might be an innocent explanation. She could have walked to the postbox. She could have met someone in the street and stopped for a chat. But the fact remained that she had then gone home to her death and everything she had done that evening had a significance that might be critical. As Pünd had written in the preface to *The Landscape of Criminal Investigation*: 'In some respects, the roles of the detective and the scientist are closely related. The events that lead up to a murder are as closely bound together as the atoms that make up a molecule. It is all too easy to disregard or overlook a single atom, but if you do so, the sugar that you were expecting may turn out to be salt.'

In other words, the choices that Melissa had made might well have contributed to her murder. Pünd wanted to know everything she had done.

They drove through the gates of Clarence Keep and pulled up at the front door. The house was immediately impressive, with its veranda and ornate balcony, sitting on an immaculate lawn rising up from the coastal road. Looking back, Pünd took in the entire sweep of the coast, the lighthouse and Tawleigh-on-the-Water just beyond, half a mile to the east. The Bentley was parked on the gravel, now bereft of its owner and somehow, despite its elegance, a little sad. There was a second car, a rather beaten-about Morris Minor, next to it and a bright green Austin-Healey in a bay around the side of the house.

'The Austin belongs to Francis Pendleton,' Hare muttered. 'The Bentley, of course, was hers. Not sure about the Morris.'

Pünd examined the front of the house. Francis Pendleton claimed that he had left Clarence Keep at 6.15 p.m. It was one of Miss Cain's ten moments in time. Now, Pünd saw that, given the horseshoe shape of the driveway with its twin gates, it would have been quite possible for him to have left the house through the set of French windows that opened onto the bay where the Austin was parked. He could have driven down to the main road, disappearing down the slope, and could have been on his way without anyone noticing. They only had his word for the time he had actually left.

Meanwhile, Miss Cain had climbed out of Hare's car and was gazing at the house with what was, for her, unusual enthusiasm. 'What a lovely house!' she exclaimed.

'I thought the same,' the detective chief inspector said. 'You can understand why Miss James would want to live here.'

'It's gorgeous.'

'Must have cost an arm and a leg to run it, though. She was having financial difficulties, by the way.' These last words were addressed to Pünd. 'I've spoken to her bank manager. She was thinking about putting the Moonflower back on the market to raise funds and she was looking at her other assets too. She definitely needed a new film.'

They were about to ring the bell when the front door opened and a man in a tweed suit came out, carrying a bulky medicine bag. It would have been obvious who he was even if Hare hadn't already described him when discussing the investigation. Now he introduced him to

Pünd. 'This is Dr Collins. You'll recall that he was the one who found Miss James's body.'

Atticus Pünd did not need reminding. He smiled and shook hands with the doctor.

'Pünd?' It took Collins a moment to connect the name. 'You're the chap who sorted out that business with the Ludendorff Diamond! What on earth brings you to this neck of the woods?'

'Mr Pünd has kindly agreed to help me with my enquiries,' Hare explained, slipping into the official language that he had been using for the past thirty years.

'Yes. Of course. How stupid of me. Why else would you be here?'

'You have been treating Mr Pendleton,' Pünd said.

'That's right.' Collins grimaced. 'I hope you haven't come out here to talk to him.'

'He is too ill to speak?'

'Well, he's barely slept since his wife died and I'd say he's a nervous wreck. I popped in on my rounds this morning, took one look at him and told him that if he didn't get some proper sleep soon, I'd have no alternative but to admit him to hospital. He didn't want that so I've given him a fairly hefty dose of reserpine.'

'It is a tranquilliser?'

'Yes. An alkaloid extracted from a plant that grows in India. *Rauwolfia serpentia*. I prescribed a lot of it during the war and it certainly does the job. He downed it in front of me and although it may be a while before it kicks in, I don't think you're going to find him completely compos mentis.'

'I am sure you did what you had to, Dr Collins.'

'Are you on your way home, sir?' Hare asked.

'I've just got to look in on Mrs Green at Leavenworth Cottage and young Nancy at the lighthouse and then I'll be back in plenty of time for lunch. Why? Do you want to talk to me?'

'We might want to have a word, sir. If you don't mind.'

'I thought I'd already told you everything I know, but I'm happy to go over it again. I'll ask Samantha to put the kettle on.'

He walked past them and, stooping low, climbed into his car. It took three attempts to get the engine to fire but then he was off down the driveway and out onto the road.

'I hope I didn't jump ahead of you there, Mr Pünd,' Hare said. 'I assumed you might want to talk to him next.'

'You are quite correct. He is most certainly another atom to be considered,' Pünd replied, cryptically.

They rang the doorbell and at once there was a fierce, high-pitched barking from inside. The door opened and a little dog ran out, a ball of red-coloured fur with short legs and a bushy tail curling up over its hindquarters. At the same time, a voice called out, 'Kimba, come back in here,' and as the dog obeyed, Pünd found himself facing a rather dishevelled man dressed in a dark suit.

'This is Eric Chandler,' Hare said, introducing him.

Pünd examined the servant with interest, wondering if he was looking at a man who, at the very least, had been prepared to commit murder. He thought not. Eric was aged in his forties and somehow childlike, although not in a good way. He was going bald, but he had allowed what hair remained to grow so that it touched his collar. He had a way of standing that was lopsided, giving the illusion that one arm was longer than the other.

'Good morning, Detective Chief Inspector,' Eric said.

'Good morning, Eric. Can we come in?'

'Of course, sir. I'm sorry about the dog. He always gets excited when there are strangers.'

The three of them were shown into the hall with oak floorboards and scattered rugs. A staircase with wooden bannisters led up to the first floor.

'You can certainly tell whose house this was,' Miss Cain said quietly.

It was true. The hall, which ran from the living room on one side to the kitchen on the other, was very spacious, a room in itself, and it had been decorated throughout with souvenirs of Melissa James's career, starting with a glass-fronted cabinet that housed a dozen awards, including two Golden Globes. Displayed on twin tables were a strange assembly of objects that included a wicked-looking Turkish dagger studded with coloured stones. Pünd picked it up and was surprised to find that the blade was both real and serviceable. He did not often go to the cinema himself, but Hare had seen and had quite enjoyed *Harem Nights*, a comedy set in Istanbul. It reminded him now that Melissa, playing an English tourist, had been threatened with that very same knife in the final scene.

Meanwhile, Madeline Cain was examining the various pictures that decorated the walls. They were all film posters, including one from *The Moonflower* and another from *The Wizard of Oz* signed '*To my brightest star, with love, Bert Lahr*'.

'I can't remember her appearing in that one,' she said, almost to herself.

Eric overheard her. 'Mr Lahr appeared with Miss James in *She's My Angel* and the two of them became good friends,' he explained. '*The Wizard of Oz* was one of her favourite films.' He swallowed hard. 'It's a terrible thing what's happened. We're all going to miss her more than I can say.'

The dog had finally decided that the new arrivals were to be trusted after all and had disappeared in the direction of the kitchen.

'We'd like to see Mr Pendleton,' Hare announced.

'Yes, sir. I'll take you upstairs.' Eric Chandler moved towards the stairs, his gait uneven, his shoulders swaying slightly. 'Mr Pendleton is in the spare room,' he confided. 'He hasn't been able to enter the master bedroom since this awful thing happened. You do know that the doctor has been with him?'

'That's why we want to see him straight away. We'll talk to him. Then Mr Pünd will want to take a look around the house. And I expect he'll want to talk to you.'

'I'll be with Mother in the kitchen.'

'How is your mother, Eric?'

'Still much the same, sir. She's taken this all very badly.' Eric shook his head. 'I don't know what will happen to us now. It doesn't bear thinking about.'

He led them upstairs to a corridor that ran from one side of the house to the other, with an archway at the far end. A velvet curtain had been drawn back to reveal a second hallway beyond. He pointed at a doorway beside the staircase. 'That was Miss James's room,' he said. 'The servants' quarters are on the other side of the arch. Mr Pendleton is this way ... '

He turned left and took them to a door about halfway

down. He knocked, at first quietly, then again with more force. 'Come in.' The voice coming from the other side was almost inaudible.

Eric stepped aside and Pünd, followed by Detective Chief Inspector Hare and Miss Cain, entered the darkened room. Although it was half past ten in the morning, the curtains had been drawn together and what little sunlight there was on another cloudy day had found itself unable to break in. Francis Pendleton looked the very image of an invalid, lying on the bed, propped up with pillows, wearing a dressing gown and pyjamas, his face colourless and emaciated, his arms stretched out helplessly at his sides. He turned his head as they entered and Pünd saw the emptiness in his eyes, the result of both grief and the drug he had been given to fight it. Of course, grief and remorse were close cousins. It was quite possible that Pendleton might have ended up in exactly this state if he had, in fact, killed his wife.

'Mr Pendleton—' Pünd began.

'I'm sorry. I don't think I know you.'

'This is Mr Atticus Pünd,' Hare explained, taking a seat beside the bed. 'If it's all right with you, sir, he wants to ask you a few questions.'

'I'm so very tired.'

'Of course, sir. You've been through a lot. We'll try not to take up too much of your time.'

Madeline Cain had perched herself on a chair in the corner of the room, doing her best to keep out of sight. Pünd was the only one standing.

'I can understand that this must have come as a great shock to you, Mr Pendleton,' he said.

'I loved her. You have no idea. She was everything to me.' The words were almost disembodied. Pendleton wasn't speaking to Pünd. He might not even have been aware that there was anyone with him in the room. 'I met her on the set of her film. I was her assistant. It was just meant to be a laugh. I had no interest in cinema and I thought it was a stupid film – a girl being kidnapped, gangs and conspiracy. I knew it would be rubbish. But when Melissa came into the room, everything changed. It was like all the lights came on. I knew that I wanted to marry her. There was never anyone else.'

'You had been married for how long, Mr Pendleton?'

'Four years. I'm very tired. I'm sorry. Could we maybe talk later?'

'Please, Mr Pendleton.' Pünd took a step forward. 'I must ask you about the day that it happened.'

Hare thought it was useless, that Pendleton was too drugged to remember anything. But the question seemed to rouse him. He sat up in the bed and gazed at Pünd with fear in his eyes. 'The day that it happened! I'll never forget it ... '

'Your wife returned to the house from the Moon-flower.'

'It's losing money. It's those bloody managers of hers. I warned her against them but she didn't listen to me. That was the thing about Melissa. She believed the best of everyone.'

'But you think there was something crooked going on.' Hare used the word deliberately. He was remembering what Simon Cox had said.

'Crooked. Yes ... '

'She had gone in to see Mr and Mrs Gardner?' Pünd asked.

'That's right. She was going to have to sell the hotel. She didn't want to but she had no option. Not if we were going to hang on to this place. But before she could sell it, she had to find out where the money was going ... '

'She believed that her managers were stealing from her?'

'I believed it. And she believed me.'

'You saw her when she came home?'

'I waited for her. I was supposed to be going to Barnstaple. We had tickets for the opera ... *The Marriage of Figaro*. But she had a headache and she didn't want to go. That's what she said, but I think she just wanted to be on her own. She had all these troubles. I wanted to help her. I tried.'

'So you went to the opera without her.'

'Yes. *The Marriage of Figaro*. Did I tell you that?'

'Before you left, the two of you talked for ... ten minutes?'

'Maybe a little longer.'

'Did you argue?

'No! You didn't argue with Melissa.' Pendleton smiled weakly. 'You did what she wanted. I always did what she wanted. It was easier that way.' He yawned. 'We talked about the Gardners. She said she saw Nancy. And that producer. What's his name? Cox! That was a nasty surprise. He'd followed her down here and he was waiting for her at the hotel.' He settled back, resting his head in the pillows. It was clear that he would soon be asleep.

But Pünd still hadn't finished. 'Was it possible she was meeting somebody after she left the hotel?' he asked.

'I don't know. She'd have told me ... '

'You were happy together.'

'I have never been so happy since I met Melissa. How can you understand? She was rich. She was famous. She was beautiful. But it was more than all that. She was unique. I can't live without her. I won't ... '

Finally, the tranquilliser took effect. Francis Pendleton closed his eyes. A moment later he was sound asleep.

The three of them quietly left the room.

'I'm afraid that wasn't very much help to you,' Hare said.

'You have already interviewed him, Detective Chief Inspector, and if you will be so kind as to make your notes available to me ...'

'I'll have the transcripts sent over to you, Mr Pünd.'

'I am sure they will tell me everything I need to know. But I will tell you straight away that the young man was not lying when he spoke to us of his love for Melissa James. The drug that he had taken may have confused his mind but not his heart.' Pünd looked around him. 'We will speak with him again, but for now it would be useful, I think, to visit the bedroom where the crime took place.'

'It's just along here.'

They went back down the corridor. Pünd continued through the archway and glanced briefly at the corridor with four photographs on the wall and a window at the end. Then he returned to the door that Eric had indicated. It opened into a large, bright room at the front of the house with three windows looking out over the lawn and the sea just beyond. A second door opened onto the balcony that he had seen when he arrived and Pünd could imagine the view in the summer months with the sun shining and the water sparkling. It would be a lovely place to wake up.

The room itself was decorated with silk wallpaper that was Chinese in style, incorporating birds and lotus leaves. It immediately reminded Pünd of somewhere he had been recently, but it took him a few moments to connect it with the room in Knightsbridge where the Pargeters had slept. He wondered why it should have entered his mind. Melissa's taste was more feminine. She had added muslin curtains, dried flowers, a silk canopy hanging over an antique four-poster bed. The carpet was ivory-coloured and the furniture looked French, hand-painted: a Breton bonnetière, a chest of drawers and a writing bureau with two neat piles of letters. A pair of ormolu tables and two lamps stood on either side of the bed. One of the lamps had a crack clearly visible in its glass shade. Pünd noticed a telephone socket in the wall and guessed that the telephone itself must have stood on the table furthest away from the door. The police would have removed it because it was, after all, a murder weapon. An open door led into a large bathroom with a shower, a bath, a toilet and – unusually – a bidet.

'I'm afraid the room's been cleaned and tidied up,' Hare explained. 'We left it how it was for four or five days and we've got plenty of photographs which I can show you. But Mr Pendleton was very unhappy, leaving it like that. It was a constant reminder of what had happened and in the end, given his mental condition, I gave way and let them rearrange it. Of course, I didn't know you would be coming down. I'm sorry.'

'Not at all, Detective Chief Inspector. You did exactly the right thing. But it would be helpful to me if you could describe the room as it was when you found it.'

'Certainly.' Hare looked around him, taking his time before he began. 'Melissa James was on the bed. It was a horrible sight. I don't know if you've ever seen a strangulation victim, but it's a dreadful way to die. She was lying with her head bent and one arm twisted behind her neck. Her eyes were staring and bloodshot. She had swollen lips. Are you all right with this, Miss Cain?'

Madeline Cain had been standing beside the writing bureau, but on hearing the lurid details she had become faint. She reached behind her as if to steady herself, then staggered and almost fell, sending one pile of letters tumbling to the floor. For a moment, she looked as if she was about to follow them.

Pünd hurried over to her. 'Miss Cain?'

'Forgive me, Mr Pünd.' Her eyes were staring out from behind her horn-rimmed spectacles. With difficulty, she knelt down and collected the letters. 'So clumsy of me ... I'm sorry.'

'There is absolutely no need to apologise,' he said. 'I am a fool to have been so inconsiderate. You must go downstairs.'

'Thank you, Mr Pünd.' He helped her to her feet and she handed the letters over to him. 'I'm afraid this has really been too much for me.'

'Would you like me to accompany you?'

'No. I'll be absolutely fine. I'm sorry.' She tried to force a smile. 'I never had any of this sort of thing at United Biscuits.'

She hurried out of the room.

'Do you want me to take notes for you?' Hare asked. He was clearly concerned by what he had just witnessed.

'I am sure I will be able to remember all the details.' Pünd closed the door again. 'It was wrong of me to bring Miss Cain to the scene of the crime,' he added. He returned the letters to the bureau. 'But I have not had a secretary before and I have not yet established the correct procedure.'

'Shall I go on?'

'Indeed so, Detective Chief Inspector.'

'Well, there were two sets of abrasions around the neck and traces of blood coming from the ear canals. I'm afraid she hadn't put up much of a fight. The bedclothes were crumpled and she had lost one of her shoes, but there was nothing under her nails. I think she must have been attacked from behind. That would explain why she was unable to reach the man who was killing her.'

'You are certain it was a man?'

'You can correct me, Mr Pünd, but somehow I find it difficult to think of a woman strangling another woman.'

'It would be unusual, certainly.'

'It was, of course, Dr Collins who discovered the body. He is a sensible chap and although he tried to revive Miss James, he didn't touch anything else.'

'What of the murder weapon?'

'She was strangled with the cord from the phone, which was next to the bed. That suggests to me that the murder hadn't been planned. If someone had come here with the intention of killing her, you'd think they'd have brought their own murder weapon. There were no fingerprints on the phone, by the way. We checked it and there was nothing. Either the killer wiped it clean or he was wearing gloves.'

Pünd absorbed this without making any further comment. 'You mentioned to me that there were two tissues that had been discarded.'

'Actually, there were three. One of them was downstairs.' Hare walked over to the make-up table. 'There was a box of tissues here,' he said. 'Right now it's in Exeter, along with the other evidence.' He paused. 'Before she was attacked, Melissa James was obviously distraught. We found both of the tissues here, one in the waste-paper basket, one on the floor. We have those too. She had cried a lot, Mr Pünd.'

'Do you have any idea what had upset her?'

'Well, you heard what Pendleton said. It might have been the meetings she had in the hotel – first with the Gardners and then with Simon Cox. On the other hand, they all agree that she was absolutely fine when she left.'

'They may not be reliable witnesses.'

'That's true. But she also chatted to Nancy Mitchell, the girl behind the reception desk, and she agreed – there didn't seem to be anything wrong.'

'So it is clear that something must have greatly upset her *after* she left the Moonflower.'

'Exactly. It could, of course, have happened in the missing twenty minutes, when Melissa managed to disappear. But my guess is that it's more likely to have been the meeting she had with her husband. Let's not forget, he was the last person who saw her alive. They talked for about ten minutes before he left for the opera … which he says was about 6.15 p.m. She was certainly crying when she called Dr Collins twelve or thirteen minutes later.'

'You have not told me what she said to him.'

'It might be better if you heard it from the doctor.' Hare shook his head and sighed. 'It doesn't make a lot of sense.'

'Very well. And now I would like to see the room where the third tissue was found.'

They left the bedroom and went downstairs into the living room, which occupied the front corner of the house with two windows facing the sea and two more at the side. A pair of glass doors opened onto the bay where Francis Pendleton's Austin had been parked. Pünd noted the many other references to Melissa James's life as a film star: the framed photographs, the silver cigarette box from MGM, more posters, a clapperboard from one of her films.

'We found the other ball of tissue over there ... ' Hare pointed in the direction of a pedestal desk made of aluminium that stood against the far door. It seemed to be there for decorative purposes. There was a large vase of dried flowers in the centre and, next to it, a heavy-looking Bakelite telephone. 'It was on the floor, under the desk.'

'Are there other telephones in the house?' Pünd asked.

Hare thought for a moment. 'I think there's one in the kitchen. But that's about it.'

'It is interesting ... ' Pünd was speaking almost to himself. 'You are correct in your observation that Miss James shed many tears. She wept in her bedroom, and it would seem from the evidence that she also wept in here. But this is the question for you, Detective Chief

Inspector. What was it that upset her and why did it propel her to two quite separate parts of the house?'

'I'm not sure I can answer that,' Hare replied.

'Forgive me, my friend, but I think that you must. We know that she was killed in the bedroom. And yet it is equally possible that she made the telephone call to Dr Collins downstairs, in this very room. How could that have happened?'

'That's easy. She doesn't make the phone call here for the simple reason that the killer is with her. She knows that he's a danger to her and she becomes upset. She cries. She makes some excuse and goes upstairs to the bedroom. She calls Dr Collins from there. But the killer has followed her and strangles her with the cord.'

'There were two balls of tissue in the bedroom and only one down here. Does that not suggest to you that she spent more time upstairs than down?'

'I'm sorry, Mr Pünd. I really don't see what you're getting at.'

'I am only trying to understand what happened here, Detective Chief Inspector. And at the moment it makes no sense to me.'

'I'm with you there. Nothing in this case makes any sense at all.'

'Then let us talk to the Chandlers. They were in the house almost until the moment of the crime. And I am sure you are keen to know exactly what it was they discussed while they were together in the kitchen.'

They left the living room and crossed the hallway to the kitchen, where they found Phyllis Chandler and her son sitting at an empty table. For once there were no cakes, no florentines, no signs of any cooking. The Aga was cold; the weekend parties had been cancelled. Francis Pendleton had barely eaten anything since his wife had died. There was nothing to occupy either of the two servants.

'I never thought it would end like this,' Phyllis said once they were all sitting around the table. 'I'll be sixty-five next year and I was looking forward to my retirement. I don't know what we're going to do with ourselves if we lose our positions here. We've got nowhere else to go.'

'You do not think it possible that Mr Pendleton will ask you to stay?' Pünd asked. He was sitting opposite her with the detective chief inspector next to him.

'I'm not even sure that he'll stay himself now that she's gone. I've never met two people who were so inseparable and that's a fact.'

'And yet I have heard it suggested that there was at times a certain friction between them?' Pünd was only repeating what Hare had told him and he, of course, had learned it from the housekeeper. He looked at Phyllis almost apologetically.

She blushed. 'Well, it's true they had their run-ins from time to time. That's true of any married couple. Miss James had a lot on her mind with the hotel and her new film. But Mr Pendleton was devoted to her. He went against the wishes of his family when he married her and none of them ever came here, but that didn't matter to him. Look at him now! She was his whole world.'

'Do you know a man by the name of Algernon Marsh?'

'Yes. I've met him.' Now she was uncomfortable. Pünd waited for her to continue. 'He often stays with his sister in the village. She's married to the doctor.' She fell silent again, then, realising that he wanted more, she added: 'He came to the house quite a few times and Miss James seemed to have a liking for him. I don't know why. I don't want to speak out of turn, but I think she may have been too generous in her feelings for him and you can make of that what you will.'

That was all she was going to say – and it could have meant many things. On the other side of the table, Eric Chandler shifted uncomfortably, avoiding his mother's gaze.

'Can you tell me, please, what occurred on the evening when Miss James was attacked? I know that you have already told the detective chief inspector, but I would like to hear it directly from you.'

'Certainly, sir, although there's not a lot to tell. Eric and I had the evening off. We were going to visit my sister in Bude. Miss James had kindly said we could take the Bentley, so we were waiting until she got back from the village.'

'Did she tell you the purpose of her visit?'

'No. But she said she had a slight headache and wanted an early night. I got changed upstairs ... that would have been a little before six. Eric and I have our living accommodation there. After that I came down here to the kitchen and the two of us waited for her to return.'

'We heard a car, but it wasn't her,' Eric added.

'And when was that?'

He shrugged. 'About six.'

What Eric had just said corresponded with what Pünd had already heard from Simon Cox. The producer had pulled up outside the house at that time but he had stayed in his car.

'Miss James arrived a few minutes later,' Phyllis continued. 'She went into the house and continued straight upstairs, I think. It's hard to be sure because my hearing isn't too good and anyway, the walls in this house are very thick. My son, Eric, can tell you about that.'

Eric looked up briefly from the table but said nothing.

'What time did you leave the house?' Pünd asked.

'It was actually later than I liked. We were visiting my sister, Betty, and we were expected at seven but we didn't leave until twenty-five past six.'

'Had you seen Mr Pendleton leave?'

'No, sir. But he kept his car in the bay on the other side of the house. He would have gone out through the French windows in the living room.'

'But you informed the police that somebody came to the house after he had gone.'

'That's right, sir. The doorbell didn't ring but we heard Kimba barking, which was a sure sign that there was a stranger here. And then about a minute later the door opened and closed, which proved it.'

'But you did not go out to see who it was.'

'We were off duty. We weren't properly dressed to receive visitors.'

'It is quite possible, then, that when you left the house, Miss James was alone with this stranger – whoever it was – who had come to the door.'

Mrs Chandler's cheeks reddened. 'I don't know what you're suggesting, sir. We had no reason to believe that any harm would come to her. Tawleigh is a very quiet place. We don't even lock the house up at night. Nothing like this has ever happened before.' She pointed at a door. 'Eric and I went out the back way. We got into the Bentley and we drove off.'

'And you heard nothing more before you left? No sound of a struggle? The breaking of a lamp?'

'We didn't hear anything, sir. The house was completely quiet.'

The interview seemed to be over. Pünd got to his feet. 'There is one last thing I must ask you,' he said. 'You were arguing with your son just before you left.' He spoke the words as if they were an afterthought, with no great relevance.

Phyllis Chandler was offended. 'I don't believe that's the case, sir.'

'You were not discussing the Moonflower Hotel? You do not believe that there is something there that might be described as crooked?'

Eric looked puzzled, but his mother cut in quickly. 'We may have mentioned the hotel,' she said. 'Everyone knows it's been losing money, and since you ask, Miss James did have her concerns about the way it was being managed.'

'You're referring to the Gardners, I believe?'

'I couldn't say, sir. It had nothing to do with Eric or with me.'

'And yet you were angry with your son.'

'I'm disappointed in my son. If you'd ever known his father, you'd understand why.'

'Ma! You can't talk about me like that.' Eric stood up for himself for the first time.

'I will talk like that!' Phyllis glared at him. 'Every day of your life I've been disappointed in you. Your father was a war hero. But what have you done with yourself?' She folded her arms. 'I've nothing more to say.'

'I have one last question.' Pünd examined her closely. 'Were you afraid of Miss James discovering a truth that you have not revealed to us? Was that what you were discussing in the kitchen that evening?'

Pünd had not repeated the entire accusation that Cox had made. He had claimed that the Chandlers would kill Melissa James if she found out.

Phyllis Chandler rounded on him. 'It's wicked how people are always spying on each other. Yes. Eric and I did have a few words, but it was nothing important. It takes it out of you running a house like this, and do you think we get any pleasure in working together? Maybe we argued. But everyone argues. And if someone was eavesdropping, they should come here and confront us themselves rather than acting like a coward and going behind our backs.'

'I am sorry, Mrs Chandler. But it is my job to understand every last detail.'

'Well, it's completely irrelevant.' She drew a breath. 'Eric hasn't been pulling his weight. That's all. I felt it necessary to have a few words and so I did.'

'Very well, Mrs Chandler. We will say no more.'

Atticus Pünd smiled as if to reassure the woman that there was nothing to worry about, then he and the detective chief inspector left the kitchen and went back into the hall.

Miss Cain was waiting for them, sitting in a chair. 'I'm so sorry, Mr Pünd,' she exclaimed.

'I hope you have recovered, Miss Cain.'

'Yes, sir. I just took a turn around the garden.' She tried to smile but it was clear she was still shaken.

'Do you wish to return to the hotel?'

'No, sir. I'd like to stay with you.' There was a pinch of anger in her cheeks. 'It was such a wicked thing to do. I want to find out who was responsible.'

'I hope I will not disappoint you,' Pünd said.

'What did you make of those two?' Hare asked, glancing in the direction of the kitchen.

'They are unhappy,' Pünd replied. 'And they have something to hide. That much is clear. But we must remember, Detective Chief Inspector, that Melissa James telephoned Dr Collins *after* they had both left.'

'That's what they say.'

'Perhaps Dr Collins will be able to tell us more.'

*

Phyllis Chandler watched them leave from the kitchen window. Eric got up from the kitchen table and walked over to her.

'He knows,' Phyllis said, without turning round. 'And if he doesn't know yet, he'll find out.'

'What are we going to do?' Eric's voice came out as a whine. He felt like a small child all over again, watching his father leave for the army, coming home from school, waiting to hear what his mother had planned for him.

But this time she wasn't having any part of it. 'You mean, what are you going to do?'

She turned and walked away, leaving Eric alone with his dark thoughts.

TEN
COME, SWEET DEATH

'Good morning. Welcome to Bedside Manor.'

Dr Collins had met them at the door of his home. He had taken off his jacket but still wore the shirt, tie and waistcoat they had seen him in earlier. There was a pipe in his hand.

'It's not actually called that,' he went on. 'The house has a rather dull name. Church Lodge. I wanted to change it but Samantha wouldn't hear of it. She rather likes being lodged next to a church. But all my patients call it Bedside Manor and so do I. Come on in and have that cup of tea I promised you.'

With Pünd leading the way, they entered the cosy family home that the doctor and his wife had made for themselves in Rectory Lane. Everything – from the carpets to the curtains to the wallpaper – was a little the worse for wear but that was part of its charm. With coats of every size and colour bundled together in the hall, wellington boots lined up in a row, a wireless playing somewhere upstairs and the smell of freshly baked bread coming from the kitchen, it immediately felt lived in, in a way that Clarence Keep had not.

'That's my surgery over there,' Dr Collins said, pointing at a door with the stem of his pipe. 'Come into the living room.'

He showed them into a simple, square room with two bulging sofas, lots of shelves jammed with books, an upright piano that even before it was played managed to look completely out of tune, and some fading Victorian portraits. There was a cross, a crucifix, on top of the piano and a page of sheet music: 'Come, Sweet Death' by J. S. Bach.

'Do you play the piano?' Pünd asked.

'Samantha does.' Collins noticed the music. 'She likes Bach, but I suppose that's not completely appropriate at the moment.' He turned it round so that the title was hidden. 'Please take a seat. Samantha saw you arrive and she'll be with you in a tick.'

'Is your brother-in-law here, sir?' Hare asked.

'Algernon? Yes. He's upstairs. Don't tell me you want to see him too.'

'It might be a good idea, sir. Before we leave.'

'I hope you don't think he had anything to do with it, Detective Chief Inspector. Algie is a bit of a loose cannon, but I don't think he'd go that far!'

It was unclear to what extent Dr Collins was joking. A certain steel had come into his eyes as soon as Algernon's name had been mentioned.

A few moments later, Samantha Collins arrived with the tea. It would, Pünd thought, have been hard to imagine her without a tray in her hands – or perhaps a basket of washing or a vacuum cleaner. There was, he remembered, an English word he might use to describe her. A busybody? No – that was not quite what he meant, although she had that sort of body, an attitude that suggested she was always busy. She had brownish hair that had begun to lose much of its colour, tied back with a ribbon. She wore no make-up. It struck Pünd that she did not seem to care very much how she looked, or perhaps it was simply that with her twin roles in the church and the surgery, she never had the time to do anything about it.

'Good morning, Mr Pünd,' she said. According to the clock, it was exactly 10 a.m.

'Mrs Collins.' He began to get to his feet.

'Do sit down, please! I hope you don't mind tea bags. It was either that or Earl Grey. It's good to see you again, Detective Chief Inspector. And you must be Miss Cain.'

'How do you do.' Madeline Cain nodded but did not get up.

'My husband told me that he'd met you at Clarence Keep and that you were coming here. You chose a good time. The children are with Mrs Mitchell at the light-house because we're going out this afternoon, so it's nice and quiet in the house. Do you take milk?'

'A little, please.'

'I'll have mine with a slice of lemon if that's possible,' Miss Cain said.

'Len – I left a saucer with some lemon slices in the kitchen. Do you mind?'

'Right-ho!' The doctor got up and left the room.

'This has been the most terribly upsetting business,' Samantha continued as she poured the tea. 'A murder is such a horrible thing, and somehow strangling someone makes it worse. The last thing Melissa saw was the person who was killing her. The last thing she felt was his hands around her throat. We prayed for her last Sunday in the church. We had a reading of Psalm 23. "The Lord is my shepherd; I shall not want. He maketh me to lie down in green pastures ... "'

'*Pastures Green!*' Miss Cain had been making notes but now she looked up.

'That's right. That was the title of one of her films,

so we thought it was an appropriate choice. The vicar delivered a wonderful homily about her.'

'Were you close to her?' Pünd asked.

Samantha thought before answering. 'I can't say that I was particularly close, Mr Pünd. Of course, everyone knew who she was and maybe that was part of the trouble. It's not very easy to become friends with someone who's famous.'

'Here you are!' Dr Collins had come back in with the lemon.

'But you were acquainted with her,' Pünd continued his line of questioning.

'Oh yes. She came to this house quite a few times.'

'She was not well?'

'She was a bit run-down with all the problems she'd been having,' Dr Collins said. 'But actually it wasn't me she came to see.'

'My brother, Algernon, worked as her financial adviser,' Samantha explained. 'They spent a lot of time together.'

'And I understand that your brother was staying with you on the day the crime took place.'

'Yes, he was. He was out all afternoon with some friends and got in about seven o'clock.'

No alibi at time of death. Pünd noticed Miss Cain scribbling the words down on her pad.

'Did you speak to him?' Pünd asked.

'No. He went straight to his room.' Samantha looked perplexed. 'Why are you asking all these questions about Algie? He would never hurt anyone.'

'I am trying only to establish the facts,' Pünd reassured her. He turned to Dr Collins. 'It would help me if you could tell me exactly what occurred at the time of Miss James's death, starting with the telephone call you received.'

Dr Collins nodded. 'You know, I tried to save her,' he said. 'If I'd got there just a few minutes earlier, I might have.'

'I am sure you did everything you could.'

'I thought at first that I'd arrived in time. She was lying on the bed and I could see there'd been a struggle, but she looked – well, she might have been alive. The first thing I did was to feel for a pulse and there wasn't one.'

'Please. Begin at the beginning.'

Dr Collins drew a breath. 'I was in the surgery with Samantha. What time was it, dear?'

'Just before half past six.'

'That's right. The surgery had been fairly quiet that evening. Just Mr Highsmith with his rheumatism. And Mrs Leigh came in with the twins – both of them with whooping cough, although fortunately we caught it early.

I was just packing up when the phone rang and it was Melissa.'

'What did she say?'

'She didn't make a great deal of sense, Mr Pünd. She was clearly very upset. She said there was somebody in the house with her and could I come over straight away.'

'She did not tell you the person's name?'

'I'm not sure she actually knew it. "*He's here!*" – that was what she said. "*I don't know what he wants. I'm frightened.*" She was crying. I told her to calm down and said I'd be right round.' Once again he turned to his wife. 'How long was I on the phone?'

'Only a minute. Maybe not even as much as that.'

'And did you hear any of the conversation, Mrs Collins?'

Samantha considered. 'I could hear her voice. It was definitely Miss James. And I could see Len was alarmed so I came over to him. I heard her calling out for help.'

'I got off the phone as quickly as I could,' Dr Collins said. 'I knew I had to get round there straight away. I grabbed my medicine bag and I went.'

'And it took you how long to reach Clarence Keep?'

'Well, obviously it's the other side of the village from here and it took me a few goes to get the car started. We're going to have to buy a new one. The Morris is on its last legs – or wheels! Anyway, I went round as quickly as I could.'

'And what happened when you arrived?'

'I rang the doorbell but there was no answer. So I opened the door – it was unlocked – and went in. That little dog of hers came rushing out, barking at me, but apart from that the place was as quiet as – well, the grave. I called Melissa's name but there was no answer. I went into the kitchen to see if I could find Eric or Phyllis but they were out. I remembered then that there had been no cars parked in the drive. I tried the living room and the dining room but they were both empty and there was no sign of any disturbance. Even so, I have to say, I was quite worried. I went upstairs, with the dog following me, and I headed straight for the main bedroom. You may be wondering how I knew my way around, but of course I'd visited the house on several occasions when Melissa was unwell.

'My first thought was that she might be in bed, but as I turned the corner, I saw at once what had happened. The door was open and she was lying on her back with the telephone cord wrapped around her neck. One of the tables had been knocked over. She had kicked off one of her shoes. I rushed straight in, tried to find a sign of life and then gave her CPR. But without success.'

'You were not concerned for your own safety, Dr Collins? Her attacker might still have been there.'

'Do you know – that never really occurred to me! My only thoughts were for Melissa. When I realised there was nothing I could do, I went back downstairs as I obviously couldn't call the police from the bedroom. The cord had been torn out of the wall. I went into the living room and made the call there.'

'And what of the dog?'

'What a very strange question, Mr Pünd. What do you mean?'

'Did it follow you?'

'Yes, it did. The poor chap seemed quite distressed. Not that I had any time for him. I went back outside and sat in my car and waited for the police to arrive.'

There was a brief pause while Pünd took all this in. Miss Cain had been writing rapidly but she finally caught up with what had been said and stopped.

'Can you describe your relationship with Miss James?' Pünd asked. 'I notice that you refer to her as Melissa and, as you say, you were intimate with the layout of her house. I ask only because it puzzles me why she should have called you first.'

'As opposed to … ?'

'Well, the police.'

Dr Collins nodded. 'There's a simple answer to that. I was much nearer. The police would have had to come all the way from Bideford. As to our relationship, Melissa was something of a hypochondriac so we saw quite a lot of each other. To be honest, there wasn't very much I could do for her medically speaking, but she liked having someone to talk to and I would say we ended up as good friends. I think she found me reassuring.'

'You became her confidant.'

'You could say that.'

'Did she speak to you of her relationship with her husband? The possibility that she was perhaps seeing somebody else?'

'I'm not sure I should answer that.' Dr Collins frowned. 'I have to think of doctor–patient confidentiality. But actually, she didn't say anything about Francis. She was an actress. She liked to talk about herself, particularly her work. She was going to do a film with Alfred Hitchcock. She was excited about that.'

'We ought to be leaving,' Samantha Collins said, glancing at the clock. 'We have a train to catch.'

'Where are you going?' Hare asked.

'Up to London,' Dr Collins replied. 'But only for one day. We'll be back tomorrow.'

'Business or pleasure?'

'Private business, Detective Chief Inspector.'

'With respect, sir, nothing is private when you're in the middle of a murder investigation.'

'I'm sorry. Of course, you're right.' Dr Collins reached out and took hold of Samantha's hand. 'We're seeing a solicitor about a sum of money that my wife may have inherited from her aunt. I can assure you that it has absolutely nothing to do with the death of Melissa James.'

Hare nodded. 'Is there anything more you need to know, Mr Pünd?'

'Just one thing.' Pünd turned to Dr Collins. 'When she spoke to you on the telephone, I do not suppose that Miss James suggested where she had been before she returned to the house?'

'I'm sorry?'

'She left the hotel at 5.40 p.m. but she didn't get home until a little after 6 p.m.,' Hare explained. 'We're trying to work out what happened in the missing twenty minutes.'

'I can tell you that,' Samantha Collins replied. She paused, seeing that she had taken everyone by surprise. 'She was in the church.'

'St Daniel's?'

'That's right, Detective Chief Inspector. I went upstairs briefly to read to my son and I glanced out of the window and saw her car parked beside the gate. You get a good view of the church from Mark's room. She got out and stood there for a moment. Then she went inside.'

Pünd thought for a moment. 'I understand that you are very active with the local church, Mrs Collins.'

'Yes. I try to help where I can.'

'Did you often see Miss James there?'

'She didn't attend many services, although she was quite good about doing a reading at Christmas and Harvest Festival, and as you may know she asked to be buried in the churchyard, although so far the police haven't released the body.' Samantha looked accusingly at Hare.

'That will happen very soon,' Hare assured her.

'But since you ask, I did see her going in and out quite a few times.'

Pünd frowned. 'Is that not a little strange? She does not strike me as having been a very religious person.'

'You don't have to be religious to enjoy the peace and comfort that you find in a church,' Samantha said.

'Was she alone, on that last day?'

'Yes.'

'Did you see her leave?'

'No, I didn't. I came back down to the surgery and after that I forgot all about her.'

Dr Collins stood up. 'Time we were on our way,' he said. 'You mentioned you wanted to see my brother-in-law.'

'It would be helpful, yes,' Pünd said.

'I'll call him down.' He went over to the door, then hesitated, suddenly uncomfortable. 'This may sound a bit strange, but I'd appreciate it if you didn't mention what I told you – about where we're going. As I said, it's something that Samantha and I are trying to keep private.'

'Of course.'

'Algie and Aunt Joyce didn't get on very well,' Samantha explained after her husband had left the room.

They heard him calling up from the hallway.

'I'm surprised you have to leave your children with Mrs Mitchell,' Hare remarked. 'Wouldn't they be better off staying here with their uncle?'

'I'm afraid he's not very good with children. Anyway, they love being with Brenda. They know her because she comes here and helps me with the housekeeping. And it's a real treat for them, sleeping in a lighthouse.'

Dr Collins walked into the room, followed by a nervously smiling, fair-haired man with a gold signet ring on one finger and an expensive watch. He was wearing a white shirt and cavalry twill trousers.

'I hope you'll forgive us, leaving you like this,' Dr Collins said as he came in. 'We have to be on our way.'

Samantha got up and put on her gloves. 'We'll see you tomorrow, Algernon. There's dinner in the fridge. And the number of the hotel is on my desk in the surgery if you need to reach us.'

'Enjoy the play.'

So they had told him they were going to the theatre. Pünd made a mental note. That was most certainly of interest.

Algernon Marsh stood where he was until Leonard and Samantha Collins had left. Only then did he say: 'Len said you wanted to speak to me. What exactly is this about?'

'What do you think it's about, Mr Marsh?' Hare replied. 'We're still investigating the death of Miss Melissa James.'

'Well, of course. Yes.' He had seemed very tense but now he relaxed a little. 'I've already spoken to you, Chief Inspector. I've answered all your questions. So I'm a little surprised you want to talk to me again.'

'It is I who am responsible, Mr Marsh,' Pünd explained, apologetically. 'But I am led to believe that you were very close to Miss James.'

'I wouldn't say that. I was advising her on some of her investments.'

'But you were also a good friend to her.'

'I'd like to think I'm a good friend to all my clients.'

'How often did you see her?' The question sounded innocent but arrived like the twist of a knife.

'We met socially in London now and then.' Algernon had sensed that the private detective with his round glasses and rosewood walking stick might actually be a danger to him. He did his best to sound non-committal.

'And you also came down here to visit her.'

'No. I came to see my sister. It was actually Sam who introduced me to Melissa in the first place.'

'And what investments were you advising her on?' Hare asked.

'It was a very wide portfolio, Detective Chief Inspector. But I can assure you that Melissa was completely happy with my advice.'

'I'm certain that was the case, sir,' Hare muttered. There was more than a hint of sarcasm in his voice.

Algernon Marsh didn't notice. He seemed to be in complete control of the situation, as if a weight had been lifted from his shoulders. 'Is there anything else I can help you with?'

'You could perhaps tell us where you were between six o'clock and seven o'clock on the evening that the murder took place.'

'I was here. I was sound asleep upstairs.' Algernon smiled. 'A little bit too much to drink at lunchtime. I was sleeping it off.'

So he must have been driving under the influence of alcohol, Hare thought. This wasn't the right time to go into it, but he wouldn't forget about it either. Instead he said: 'Your sister informed us that you didn't get home until seven.'

'Then she was wrong. It was about a quarter past six. I came in and went straight upstairs.' He shrugged. 'I'm afraid nobody actually saw me, which is a bit of a shame. If you want me to supply you with an alibi, I haven't got one.'

'How much longer do you plan to stay in Tawleigh, Mr Marsh?' Pünd asked.

'A few more days. With Melissa gone, there's not really much point in my hanging around.'

'But just a moment ago, you remarked that you were here for your sister.'

'I was here for both of them, Mr Pünd. Can I show you to the door?'

Moments later, the three of them found themselves walking away from the house as the front door slammed shut behind them.

'Now that's one man I wouldn't trust an inch!' Miss Cain muttered.

'A nasty piece of work,' Hare agreed. They passed the Peugeot, parked in the driveway, and Pünd glanced briefly at the silver badge and the dent in the radiator grille. 'What now?' the detective chief inspector asked.

'I think we have done enough for today. I would like

to read the transcripts of your interviews and to reflect on what we have seen. You will return to Exeter?'

'No, Mr Pünd. I thought I'd stay on in Tawleigh now that you're here. Margaret – my wife – won't mind seeing the back of me for a few more days and the truth of it is, I want to spend as much time as I can with you. I have a feeling I might learn a thing or two. That said, I couldn't afford the Moonflower, I'm afraid. I've taken a room at the Red Lion.'

'You are too kind, Detective Chief Inspector. Maybe you would like to meet with me for dinner tonight.'

'There's nothing I'd like more.'

'Then it is agreed.'

The three of them climbed into the police officer's car and drove away, past the cemetery of St Daniel's, past the freshly dug grave where Melissa James would soon lie.

ELEVEN
DARKNESS FALLS

I

The moon had risen over Tawleigh-on-the-Water but somehow the soft wash of the light only made the little harbour town seem all the darker. The streets were empty, the steeple of St Daniel's a stark silhouette against the sky. The beam from the lighthouse flashed over a sea that went on for ever, and the fishing boats, bobbing up and down together, seemed almost afraid, lost in the void. It was impossible to tell where the shingle ended and the water began.

Detective Chief Inspector Hare walked the short distance from the Red Lion, his feet rapping against the pavement. It was funny how much sharper sound became once the sun had set. Although he had accepted the dinner invitation immediately, he was beginning to have second thoughts. He couldn't ignore the obvious fact that just eight years ago England and Germany had been at war. Hare knew nothing about Pünd's activities at the time and wondered if he should in some way consider him the enemy. The same thought applied to the case. Pünd had presented himself as an equal. He had suggested that they work together to find the killer. But was it actually true? Or was he destined to sit back and contribute nothing, simply watching as his last opportunity to prove himself was snatched away?

He had just spoken to his wife on the telephone and she had tried to put his mind at ease. She had always been proud of him. His career might be coming to an end, but no matter what happened in Tawleigh, he had nothing to be ashamed of. Anyway, wasn't he getting his priorities wrong? Catching the killer was all that mattered, making sure he couldn't ever do it again. It didn't matter who took the credit.

She was right, of course. She always was.

Atticus Pünd was waiting for him in the reception area when he reached the Moonflower. Hare was surprised to see that he was alone.

'Miss Cain isn't joining us?' he asked.

'She has retired early to her room.'

In fact, the secretary had tactfully declined Pünd's

invitation, once again deciding it improper to eat with her employer. She was upstairs, perfectly happy to be on her own with a book, a hot-water bottle and an early night.

The dining room was attractive, formal without being fussy, and nearly all the tables were taken, mainly by families with children. Pünd had asked for privacy and the two men were shown to a table tucked away in an alcove next to a bay window. There was a menu with just two choices for each course. The detective chief inspector blinked when he saw the prices.

Pünd noticed. 'You are, of course, my guest this evening,' he said. 'It is one of the benefits of being a private detective that, within reason, one is entitled to expenses.'

'I wish it was the same in the police force,' Hare said. 'But the chief constable wouldn't sanction so much as an iced bun in the station canteen. At least, he might – but it would take three committee meetings and a mountain of paperwork.'

'How is the Red Lion?'

'It's surprisingly comfortable, thank you very much. No sea view, though. In fact, my room looks out over the butcher's yard, which I suppose might be appropriate one way or another.'

The waitress came over and they both ordered prawn cocktails and Dover sole. Dessert was a choice of mar-

malade sponge or fruit salad. 'You will have some wine?'
Pünd asked.

'I'm not sure I should drink while I'm on duty.'

'It is after seven o'clock, Detective Chief Inspector.
And since I do not wish to drink alone, I must insist. A
half-bottle of the Chablis I think.'

These last words were spoken to the waitress, who
went to fetch it.

'Well, if I'm off duty and having dinner on you, I think
you should call me by my first name, Mr Pünd.'

'And what is that?'

'Edward.'

'And I, as you know, am Atticus.'

'Is that a Turkish name?'

'Greek, in fact, although my parents moved to Germany before I was born.'

'Was your father a policeman?'

'He was. How did you know?'

Hare smiled. He was already warming to the man
sitting opposite him and regretted his earlier hesitation.
'My dad was a detective too and my sergeant's the son of
a serving policeman. It's funny how often it runs in the
family. That's true of criminals too, incidentally.'

Pünd considered. 'Yes. That is very interesting and
true. It is something which I may consider in the book I
am writing – *The Landscape of Criminal Investigation*.'

'Interesting title.'

'A life's work. Your parents are still living?'

'They're both alive and well. They retired to Paignton. I have a son and a daughter and they both want to continue the tradition. We're recruiting more and more policewomen, I'm happy to say.'

'Perhaps one day it will be your daughter who is the chief constable.'

'That would be something. Do you have children?'

Pünd shook his head a little sadly. 'No. That was not to be my good fortune.'

Hare felt he had strayed into a difficult area and quickly changed the subject. 'Were you a private detective before you came to England?'

'No. I arrived after the war and had to find a means to earn a living.'

'Well, you've done very well for yourself. I envy you. You must have come across some fascinating criminals.'

'Criminals rarely fascinate me, my friend.'

'Is that so?'

Pünd thought for a minute. 'They think, always, that they are cleverer than they really are, that they have the ability to defeat the police, the rule of law, the very essence of society in order to achieve their ends.'

'It makes them dangerous.'

'It makes them predictable. What makes them dangerous is their belief that they should not be stopped, that they are justified in what they do. I will not speak of my experiences in the war, but I will say this. The greatest evil occurs when people, no matter what their aims or their motives, become utterly convinced that they are right.'

The first course came and with it the wine. Pünd did the tasting and nodded his satisfaction.

'I don't want to spoil the evening by talking shop,' Hare said. 'But I've got to ask. Do you have any thoughts after today?'

'I have many thoughts and I must tell you that the witness statements with which you provided me were excellent. Your interviews could not have been clearer or more efficient.'

Hare was pleased. 'I still don't know who did it,' he said.

'But you have your suspicions.'

'I have.' Hare was aware that Pünd had turned his own question on him but he went on anyway. 'There were quite a few people who would have liked to have seen Miss James out of the way, starting with the proprietors of this very establishment. You saw that she had been in contact with an accountancy firm in London?'

'You did well to discover it.'

'Well, I checked every telephone number she'd called

in the last few weeks. She was about to engage a company from London to carry out a complete audit. The Gardners may not have been too happy about that, even if killing her to prevent it might have been a bit extreme.

'And then there's that butler of hers. I didn't believe a word his mother told us when we spoke to them in the kitchen, and looking at him sitting at that table, well … frankly … there's something about him that gives me the creeps. That producer, Cox, heard them arguing on the night of the crime and loudly enough for the sound to carry onto the front lawn. I'll bet you anything you like that he's up to no good.'

'What of Mr Cox himself?'

'Sīmanis Čaks, you mean! He could certainly have been the stranger at the door, the one who set the dog barking. He told me a string of lies and if Melissa James had pulled out of his film, more or less ruining him in the process, he could well have decided he wanted revenge.'

'Revenge … the oldest of motives. One finds it in the dramas of ancient Greece.'

'But if I was going to put my money on one person, it would still be the husband.'

'Ah yes! Francis Pendleton.'

'Thwarted love can be as destructive as revenge. From what I understand, he was besotted with her. Suppose he'd discovered that she was having an affair! You talk about classical drama, but that's William Shakespeare all over again. I'm sure you've read *Othello*. Desdemona gets strangled too.'

'That is interesting. It was also my impression that he was the most likely suspect.'

'He was certainly the last person to see her alive and we only have his word for it that he left when he said he did.'

'The car had gone.'

'He could have driven away and come back again. Let's not forget that the Chandlers heard someone come through the door.'

'But if it had been Francis Pendleton, would the dog have barked?'

'That's a good point.'

'There is also the matter of the murder weapon.'

'The telephone cord.'

'I have to say that it puzzled me.'

'You mean, why not just use his hands?'

Pünd shook his head. 'No. That is not what I mean. I will tell you this. For me, the telephone makes it less likely that Francis Pendleton killed his wife. Less likely, but not impossible. Were you able to confirm that he did indeed attend the performance of *The Marriage of Figaro* that night?'

'We've asked at the theatre. But there were four hundred people in the audience. We have no way of knowing who they were.'

'You might ask if anyone arrived late. Or if there was anyone in the audience who seemed distracted.'

'That's a good idea. I'll do that.' Hare drank some wine. At home, he might occasionally have a glass of beer with his evening meal and this was a rare treat. 'You may have noticed that he told me how much he enjoyed the performance.'

'I did indeed read that in your excellent notes.'

'He could have been lying, of course. But it's not the behaviour of someone who has just strangled his wife.'

Pünd raised his own glass and drank with half-closed eyes. 'It is true what Miss Cain observed, is it not,' he said. 'How sad it is that even in a place as quiet and as charming as Tawleigh-on-the-Water, there are still so many people who might be capable of murder.'

Outside, the waves broke, black against the pebbled shore.

II

Inside the lighthouse, the two children – Mark and Agnes Collins – had not yet gone to sleep. They were much too excited, lying in twin bunks in a room that was completely circular, halfway up the tower. Every time the beam swung round, it flashed past the two small windows, making the shadows leap. It was like being inside an adventure story.

In fact, the room had once been an office. Brenda Mitchell, Nancy's mother, had put the bunks in so that any children who came to stay could have the magical experience of sleeping inside a real lighthouse. She herself, her husband and Nancy had their beds on the ground floor in a much less interesting building that had been tacked on to the side. This was where the kitchen, living room and small bathroom were also located; the mother, father and daughter were confined in a space that could quite accurately be called too close for comfort.

Nancy Mitchell had read a few pages of the Narnia book that Mark had brought with him and now she smoothed the covers of the two bunks and turned out the lights, leaving a single lamp glowing on the floor. In just six months' time this room might be needed for a quite different reason. There would be a third child, and this one would be her own. A boy or a girl? She hadn't dared ask Dr Collins and anyway, she doubted that he would be able to tell.

She made her way down the winding stairway and through the door that led into the kitchen. Her father was sitting at the table, her mother stirring something at the stove. It was stew again. Brenda would have got the scrag-ends from the butcher, who always threw in a few bones at no extra cost so that they could make stock. All three of them had jobs but somehow they never seemed to have enough money to go round. Both women were forced to give their earnings to Bill Mitchell and he parcelled them out to them for housekeeping and all the other expenses. The trouble was that what he returned to them was always substantially less than what they had given.

Nancy thought of the sixty pounds she had received and which she had hidden inside the cover of her pillow. She had almost no private space in the lighthouse and she was too worried that her mother, who did all the washing, might come upon it accidentally if she left it with her clothes.

'How are the children, Nancy?' Brenda asked.

'They're still not asleep, Mum. I read to them and tucked them in, but they just wanted to look out of the window.'

'You should charge.' Bill Mitchell was a man of few words. He very seldom used more than three or four of them at the same time.

'What do you mean?' Brenda asked.

'Dr Collins and his missus.'

'Mrs Collins has always been very good to me. And they do pay me extra for babysitting.'

'They can afford it.'

Brenda Mitchell transferred the stew to the table and reached for three plates. 'Come and sit down, Nancy.' She stopped, examining her daughter. 'Are you all right?' she asked.

'Yes, Mum. I'm fine.'

'You look tired. And there's something else . . . '

Her mother knew. Or if she didn't know, she was suspicious and she would work it out soon enough. And of course she would tell her father. Brenda would be too afraid to keep that sort of thing from him, and even if Nancy begged her to stay silent it would be obvious soon anyway. When that happened, all hell would break loose. When you crossed Bill Mitchell, you soon knew about it. Nancy had lost count of the number of times she had seen her mother with dark bruises on her back or her arms – and she had felt the back of his hand occasionally too.

But she had made her plan. Everything was ready. As she lifted a plate to pass her father's dinner across, she realised she couldn't wait another day.

She would do it tomorrow.

III

In their London hotel, Leonard Collins and his wife were unable to eat a single mouthful. And it wasn't just because the food – rissoles, stewed carrots and mashed potatoes – was cold and unappetising.

They had taken a taxi directly from Paddington Station to the solicitor's office in Lincoln's Inn. There they had been greeted by the elderly Mr Parker, who shook their hands warmly and led them through the elegantly furnished chambers and into his private office. As they had followed him, Samantha had been aware of heads turning. The clerks and assistants were watching them and that gave her an inkling of what she was about to hear. It was like being famous. She had seen people behave the same way when Melissa James came into the room. *They know about us*, she thought. *And what they know is going to change our lives.*

She had been right. She wondered why they had even gone back to this room in Alleyn's, a tatty hotel in a Victorian terrace in Earls Court. It wasn't even a hotel really, just two houses knocked together, with cheap carpets and the smell of frying oil and old laundry. Their bedroom was small and they weren't going to get much sleep, not with the traffic thundering past outside. Shouldn't they have moved into the Ritz or the Dorchester?

Seven hundred thousand pounds.

It was like winning the pools – not that Samantha ever gambled. It was more money than she had ever dreamed of. More money than she could even understand.

The kindly Mr Parker had explained it all to them. First of all, there would have to be probate. They would appoint an agent to realise all Mrs Campion's assets, including the flat in Manhattan, the art collection, the stocks and shares. Although Samantha was the sole relative to benefit, Mrs Campion had left money to a library, a children's home and several charities. But at the end of the day, a sum approaching seven figures would be sent to the young woman she remembered so fondly and who was now Mrs Samantha Collins. It was beyond belief.

'I had no idea!' Leonard said. For once, even he seemed stunned into submission. 'I mean, when we got that letter I thought it might be a few grand. I know I joked with you. But I never thought, not really ... '

'What are we going to do?'

'I don't know, my dear. It's your money. You'll have to decide.'

The two of them stared at the food that was rapidly congealing on the plates.

'Maybe I can suggest one thing,' Leonard went on.

'What?'

'Well, we're behaving as if it's bad news. Look at the two of us, sitting here in silence, not even looking each other in the eye. Shouldn't we be celebrating?'

'I don't know. Money—'

'I hope you're not going to say it's the root of all evil.'

'No.'

'Or that it can't buy you happiness. Both those things might be true, my dear, but just think what it can do for us. Bedside Manor's falling to pieces. We've got that leak in the roof, and all the carpets upstairs need replacing. We always buy Mark and Agnes clothes that are two sizes too big so they can grow into them, and it's been ages since you treated yourself to a new dress.'

'You're right.' She reached out and took hold of his hand. 'I'm sorry, Leonard. Sometimes I think you must find it very difficult being married to me.'

'Not really. You were the only one who'd have me!'

She laughed. 'I'm going to use this money for both of us, for the whole family. And I'll give some to the church too.'

'The organ fund.'

'Yes.' Suddenly she was serious. 'I don't think the Lord would have sent us this money if he didn't want us to enjoy it.'

'For richer and for poorer. That's what we promised. And if we're richer now, it's hardly our fault!'

'We're going to start right now.' She let go of his hand, taking her knife and fork and laying them determinedly on her plate. 'I don't think we should change hotels. It's only one night and anyway, we're not going to splash out any money until I really know it's in the bank. But nor am

I going to sit here and eat this slop. I'm sure there must be a little trattoria or something in the neighbourhood.'

'I think I saw one near the station.'

'Then let's go out.'

'A night on the tiles!' Leonard Collins got up and kissed his wife.

It was only later, as they left the hotel arm in arm, that Samantha turned to him. 'What about Algernon?' she said.

'What about him?'

'We're going to have to tell him, Len. If it's as much money as Mr Parker said, he's going to find out anyway.' She sighed. 'And really, I think we ought to share some of it with him. After all, we grew up together. It doesn't seem fair.'

'Well, that's up to you, Sam. He's your brother. But if I may say so, it's not what your aunt wanted and you know he'll only blow it on – well, you know the sort of thing he gets up to.' She said nothing so he continued. 'If you want my advice, you won't say anything yet. If Algernon finds out before everything's been sorted out, he'll only make trouble. I say we wait until the dust has settled.'

There was a trattoria on the corner just ahead of them. It looked homely and welcoming, with yellow light spilling out of the windows onto the pavement. It still seemed to be open.

'Spaghetti and meatballs!' Leonard Collins exclaimed.

'And a glass of fizz!'

'Now you're talking!'

They hurried in.

IV

At that moment, Algernon Marsh was sitting in his bed-room – or rather, the bedroom he had been given all too temporarily – at Church Lodge. He had a large glass of whisky in one hand. In the other, he was holding the letter he had found in the bottom drawer of his brother-in-law's desk. He had read it several times. *'Joyce Campion, married to Harlan Goodis. A bequest . . . '*

He hadn't exactly been snooping. That would suggest an actual interest, a desire to find out more about Samantha and Leonard's private life. The truth was, apart from the occasional sanctuary they offered him, the free meals and the booze, he had no interest in them at all. A slightly bumptious country doctor in a dead-end town married to a religious maniac who probably made his life a misery – that was how Algernon saw them.

But he had known something was up. From the moment he had arrived at the house, Samantha and Leonard hadn't been behaving normally. There had been whispered conversations, exchanged glances, a sudden silence whenever he entered the room. And then, only that morning, he had come into the kitchen to find Samantha sitting at the table, reading a letter. She had folded it away the moment she'd seen him, but not before he had noticed the formal letterhead and the smart, white envelope it had come in. It was a solicitor's letter. He had recognised it at once.

'Bad news?' he had asked solicitously, pretending not to take too close an interest.

'No. It's not important.'

It was the way she had folded the letter away that had alerted him to the fact that she was lying: closing it up and sliding it underneath her cardigan, keeping it close to her heart in more ways than one. And then there was this trip to London, suddenly announced, as if the decision to travel five hours each way and stay overnight in some cheap hotel was completely normal behaviour.

The moment he had found himself alone, he had made a phone call. He had a friend in London who had spent three years working in the advertising industry in New York before a misunderstanding about his expenses allowance had resulted in his immediate firing. Somewhere in the back of his mind, Algernon was sure he had worked for Harlan Goodis.

'No. I never worked for him,' Terry had told him. 'But I met him a couple of times and everybody knew him.

He did campaigns for Minute Maid and Paper Mate and he helped launch Best Western Hotels. He started as a copywriter but by the end he had his own agency on Madison Avenue.'

'How rich was he?'

There'd been a snigger at the end of the line. 'Why are you interested, Algie? It's a bit late. He's been dead two years.'

'I know.'

'He was loaded. He had an apartment looking out over Central Park. Not just an apartment – a penthouse! He drove a Duesenberg convertible. Beautiful car. I wouldn't mind getting my hands on it, I can tell you. I don't know how much he sold the agency for, but I could probably find out.'

'Could you do some digging for me?'

'What's in it for me?'

'Come on, Terry. You owe me.' There was silence at the other end. 'I'll buy you lunch at the club. But we've got to move quickly on this. It could be important. He left all his money to his widow, a woman called Joyce Campion. Maybe there's a public record of the amount.'

'There are some people I can call. But they're in America. You'll have to pay me back.'

'Just do it,' Algernon had said and put down the receiver.

SOLE BENEFICIARY.

Those were the two words that leapt off the page. It wasn't fair. He and Samantha had grown up together. They had been ordinary, happy children and they had been close. And then a bomb had fallen out of the sky and had killed both their parents and taken away everything he had ever known and after that nothing had been the same. He still remembered the day their aunt had said she would be looking after them. He hadn't liked her from the start, with her hair dyed jet black, her withered cheeks, too much rouge. She behaved like a grande dame, but she still lived in a poky little house in West Kensington. What had Harlan Goodis ever seen in her?

She had always disapproved of him. She had wanted him to get a job like his sister, who'd been packed off to some hellhole in Slough. Accountancy, she had suggested, or maybe dentistry? She had a cousin who was a dentist and who might be able to help him. In his early twenties, Algernon had come to blame Aunt Joyce for the loss of his early life almost as much as he blamed the Germans – and his inevitable slide into the world of underhand dealing and crime had surely been her fault too.

Not that he had ever been a criminal. Not really. It had just been chance that had put him outside that club in Piccadilly even as a fight – an affray – broke out. If he hadn't been drinking, he would never have joined in.

He still remembered the trial, the way Aunt Joyce had looked at him as he was sent down for three months for disturbing the public order. She had looked even more disgusted than the judge! Before he had been taken down, he had turned round and stuck his tongue out at her and that was the last time he had seen her. He'd been glad when she'd packed her bags and gone off to America.

And now, all these years later, she had shown him what she thought of him. She hadn't just favoured Samantha over him. She had deliberately slapped him in the face. There was a tiny part of him that regretted that last gesture in the courtroom. It had cost him a half-share in what might be a fortune. But maybe he was kidding himself. She had always been a vindictive old bat. She would never have left him a cent.

There was one aspect of his character, however, that Aunt Joyce had underestimated and which Samantha, too, had ignored. Algernon Marsh never gave up. All his life (and unfortunately on that one occasion outside the Nut House) he had been a fighter. For example, he had launched Sun Trap on the back of a string of business failures and although things weren't looking too good for it right now, it had been remarkably successful, at least up to a point. Samantha might be rich. But Algernon knew things about life in Tawleigh-on-the-Water that she didn't. He was fairly sure he could use that knowledge to divert a good chunk of the fortune his way. Always assuming there was a fortune to be had.

The telephone rang. Algernon almost dropped his whisky in his haste to answer it.

'Algie?'

'Terry! Have you found out anything?'

'I've found out plenty. Hold on to your hat, mate. You're not going to believe this ... '

V

It was half past nine.

Phyllis and Eric Chandler were sitting in their private living room on the second floor of Clarence Keep. They had been listening to *Record Roundabout* on the wireless, but after a while Phyllis had grown tired of the comedy interludes and turned it off. Now the two of them were sitting in gloomy silence. Eric had offered her some hot cocoa – they always had cocoa before they went to bed – but she had refused.

'I'm going to turn in,' she announced suddenly.

'Ma ... ' There was a tremble in Eric's voice. 'I hate it when you're like this.'

'I don't know what you mean.'

'Yes, you do. You've always been like this, even when I

was a little boy and you were annoyed with me. You were disappointed with me the moment I was born, weren't you, because my foot was wrong. And when Dad went away, I know what he meant to you. I know you wish it was me, not him, that died in the war.'

Phyllis crossed her arms. 'That's a wicked thing to say, Eric. You should—'

'I'm not going to wash my mouth out with soap and water! I'm not ten years old!'

The two of them were used to speaking quietly. They knew their place in the house and it was their first duty never to be noticed unless they were needed, never to draw attention to themselves. But Eric had shouted at his mother and her first thought was to glance nervously at the door, making sure it was shut.

'You shouldn't have done what you did,' she hissed quietly. 'You should never have behaved that way.'

'You think I like being here? You think I've enjoyed working with you all these years?' His chest was heaving. He was on the edge of tears. 'You've never tried to see things my way. You don't have any understanding what it's like being me.'

There was something in his voice that moved her, briefly. But she didn't go over to him. She didn't get out of her seat. 'You shouldn't have lied to that policeman,' she said slowly.

'And you shouldn't have said what you said!'

'Maybe not. But I've already told you. They're going to find out anyway. And what do you think is going to happen then?' She folded her arms. 'I've made a decision, Eric. When this is over and the police leave us alone, I'm going to move in with my sister. I've worked long enough. And you're right, it's not healthy the two of us being here together.'

He stared at her. 'What about me?'

'You can stay here. I'm sure Mr Pendleton will look after you.' She glanced in the direction of the main house. 'Did he speak to you this evening?'

Eric had taken Francis Pendleton his supper at seven o'clock and had removed the tray an hour later. The master of the house had barely been out of the bedroom all day, sleeping for several hours after the medicine Dr Collins had given him, and then sitting, apparently doing nothing at all, on his own. He had hardly touched the food.

'He didn't say anything.'

'Well, you'll have to talk to him.'

'He won't keep me on. He won't even stay here. He'll sell Clarence Keep and go back to London.'

'Well, that's your lookout.'

Eric Chandler's voice quivered and, to his mother's disgust, he began to cry. 'Please, Ma,' he whimpered. 'Don't leave me.'

'I am leaving you, Eric. I should have done it years ago. After what you've been getting up to here, I never want to see you again.'

She got up and turned the wireless back on just as the presenter of *Record Roundabout* introduced 'The Blue Danube' by Johann Strauss. Mother and son sat listening, not looking at each other. Phyllis's face was stone. Eric was weeping silently. The orchestra struck up and the cheerful waltz began.

VI

Just down the corridor, Francis Pendleton was lying in the darkness, gathering his thoughts. He was neither asleep nor awake but somewhere in between, trying to separate the nightmare of everything that had happened from the reality of where he was now. He wanted to get up but he could barely move; the drug he had taken that morning was still paralysing his system. Above all else, there was the crushing weight of grief, the loss of Melissa, who had always been, right up until the end, his one true love. When he thought about her, he no longer wanted to live.

He rolled onto his side and very slowly, like an old man, got to his feet. He was still in the dressing gown and pyjamas that he'd been wearing when the detective chief inspector and that German man had come to see him in the morning. He had forgotten what he had told them and he couldn't remember their questions either. He hoped he hadn't given anything away.

He left the room, emerging into the corridor in his bare feet. The house was almost silent, the darkness almost tangible, as if he would have to brush it aside to continue on his way, but the velvet curtain was drawn back and he could hear, very faintly, the sound of waltz music coming from the servants' lounge. He wanted to tell them to turn it off but he didn't have the strength.

He had no idea where he was going but he wasn't surprised when he found himself there. He opened a second door and looked into the master bedroom, the room he had shared with Melissa for the four years of their marriage. No. That wasn't true. Towards the end, she had wanted more and more to sleep on her own. It had become her room, not theirs.

The moonlight was flooding in through the windows, illuminating the interior, and Francis cast his eye over the bed they had chosen together, the wardrobe that she had found in a little second-hand shop in Salisbury. He glanced at the two ormolu tables and felt a twist in his gut as he realised that the telephone was no longer there.

The police had taken it away, of course. Francis stood where he was, framed in the doorway as if pinned there, not daring to go any further in.

He would sell everything, he decided. He would sell the house and the furniture. He—

His eyes had travelled round the room and he had noticed something out of place. The chest of drawers between the windows. The top drawer was slightly open. Why should that be? He had been back into the room when the police were there and afterwards, when it had been cleaned. He had looked in only that morning. The drawer had been closed. He was sure of it.

He forced himself to enter through the doorway, breaking the invisible barrier. He reached down and opened the drawer. This was where Melissa kept some of her most intimate things – her stockings, her underclothes. He looked at the different items, remembering the shape of them and the warmth when she had worn them. And then somehow, in the fog of medication, he saw that one of them had been taken. A white silk negligée decorated with flowers that he had bought her in Paris. It had come from an expensive boutique on the Champs-Élysées. She had walked past and seen it in the window and said she liked it, so after they had returned to the hotel he had run all the way back to get it as a surprise. He reached down and fumbled through the other garments just in case he was wrong. But he knew that he wasn't. He had seen it, neatly folded, after the room had been restored. It had been on the top of the pile. It had been there.

Who had taken it? Who had committed this act of desecration?

Francis listened to the music wafting in through the darkness. He thought of Eric Chandler and the way he had always looked at Melissa. The two of them had laughed about it, but he had often thought there was something wrong. He wanted to go into the living room now. He wanted to confront both of them, the mother and the son. But he wasn't strong enough. He felt ill. It would have to wait until the morning.

Francis Pendleton groped his way out of the room and went back to bed.

VII

Atticus Pünd had returned to his room after an excellent dinner with Detective Chief Inspector Hare. There were various thoughts turning in his mind and he was not quite ready for bed so he lit a cigarette and stepped out onto the narrow balcony in front of his room. From here he had an uninterrupted view of the sea as it stretched all the way to the horizon, a single line, perfectly drawn by the moonlight. The moon itself was low in the sky and appeared almost as a single eye, watching him from the other side of the world. He listened to the rhythm of the waves and smoked his cigarette. The darkness was telling him something and he knew what it was.

He should not have taken the case.

Coming to Tawleigh-on-the-Water had been a mistake, and not just because he had been unable to meet the client who had sent him here. It would have been good to have come face to face with Mr Edgar Schultz and to have discovered his true motivation for hiring a private detective. '*We want to know what happened. We feel we owe it to her.*' That was what he had said on the telephone, but he had said other things too and they had not been true. There was also something in the letter he had received; a small point, but nonetheless one that had concerned him.

Had he been too hasty? Although he had not personally seen Melissa James's films, he knew she had given pleasure to many people in the world and for that she was to be admired. Perhaps that was why he had been so quick to volunteer his services. It was also true that, after a week, the police had made no arrest. Was that the job of the private detective, to bring justice where otherwise it might fail? He did not think so. He did not see himself as an avenger. He was more of an administrator. Here is the crime. Here is the solution. His job was to bring them together.

He had no solution yet. It occurred to him that most of the people he had so far met had a reasonable explanation for their whereabouts at the time of the crime. Francis Pendleton was on his way to the opera. Phyllis Chandler and her son had been with each other and it seemed unlikely (though not impossible) that one could have committed the murder without the knowledge of the other. Dr Collins had been in the surgery with his wife. The Gardners had been at the hotel. And so on.

Simon Cox? He had the opportunity but not, Pünd thought, the cold-bloodedness. Algernon Marsh? He claimed to have been asleep in his room after having had too much to drink. But his sister had said he'd arrived at the house forty-five minutes later than he claimed.

It was all wrong. Pünd had written about the shape of a crime, about how, in an investigation, events will arrange themselves until they become instantly identifiable. Such-and-such a person must have committed the murder because it is the only way that it makes sense of the overall design. The ten moments in time drawn up by Miss Cain should have illustrated exactly that. They should have presented themselves as the connecting points in one of those puzzles enjoyed by children: join the dots and a picture should appear. But it had not.

He exhaled smoke and watched it corkscrew in the air and then disappear into the darkness. At that moment he understood that there was an evil presence in Tawleigh-on-the-Water and that he had been aware of it since he had arrived. It was close to him. He could feel it now.

He went back into the room, closing the door behind him.

TWELVE
AN ARREST IS MADE

'Mrs Chandler, I wonder if I might have a word …'

Phyllis Chandler had just boiled the kettle when Francis Pendleton came into the kitchen. He was looking pale and very thin with hollows in his cheeks and dark shadows under his eyes, but there was a sense of determination about him that hadn't been there before.

'It's very good to see you up, sir,' she said. 'I was just going to bring you some tea and maybe a little toast for breakfast.'

'I don't want any breakfast, thank you. Where is Eric?'

'He's gone into Tawleigh. I asked him to pick up some more eggs.' She knew at once that trouble was coming. She could tell from his tone of voice and from the way he had enquired about Eric.

'There's something I have to ask you,' Francis went

on. 'Have either of you been into my wife's bedroom since ... ' He couldn't find a way to finish the sentence. 'Have either of you been in there?'

'I certainly haven't, sir ... '

'Because someone has taken something. I'm not imagining it because they left the drawer open and I know it was there.'

'What have they taken?' All the colour drained from Phyllis's face as she waited for the axe to fall.

'It's a very personal item. A silk negligée. I think you probably know the one I mean.'

'The pretty white one, with flowers?' She had ironed it often enough.

'Yes. You don't have it in the laundry room?'

'No, sir.' For half a second she had considered lying to him but what good would that do?

'Do you have any idea who might have taken it?'

Phyllis pulled a chair from the table and sat down heavily. Tears were welling up in her eyes.

'Mrs Chandler?'

'It was Eric.'

'I'm sorry?' She had whispered so quietly that he hadn't heard her.

'Eric!' She took out a handkerchief and wiped her eyes.

'But why would Eric ... ?'

'I can't answer that, Mr Pendleton. I don't know what to say to you. I'm so ashamed I could die.' Now that she had started, the words poured out of her. 'There's something wrong with him. He adored the mistress, but he let it go to his head and he couldn't stop himself. I've told him. I've already had words with him.'

'You knew about this?' Francis was shocked.

'Not about the negligée, sir. But I knew ... other things.'

'He took other things?'

'I don't know, sir. Maybe. He's not well—'

Francis held up a hand. This wasn't what he had expected and he didn't have the strength to deal with it. For a long moment neither of them spoke. Then he took a breath. 'I will be selling Clarence Keep quite soon anyway,' he said. 'I had already decided that. I can't live here any more, not on my own. But I think you and your son should leave at once, by the end of the day. My wife is dead and all he can do is—' He broke off. 'I should report him. Maybe I will report him.'

'I tried to stop him, sir.' Phyllis burst into tears.

'I'm sorry, Mrs Chandler. I know you're not to blame. But I want you both out of here. As for your son, when he gets back you can tell him that I don't want to see him again. He makes me sick.'

Francis turned round and left the room.

*

At the Moonflower Hotel, Atticus Pünd had just finished his breakfast when Maureen Gardner brought him
a note. It was from Detective Chief Inspector Hare, explaining that, as Pünd had suggested, he was going into
Barnstaple to ask further questions about *The Marriage
of Figaro,* and in particular if any audience members
had arrived late. The performance had begun at seven
o'clock. Even if Francis Pendleton had left the house at
6.15 p.m. as he claimed, he would only just have arrived
in time. Any later and it would have been difficult, if
not impossible. Certainly, he wouldn't have had time to
sneak back into the house, murder his wife, cover his
tracks, get back to his car, wherever he had left it, and
then drive into Barnstaple, park and make it into the
theatre in time for the overture.

Once again it all came down to the ten moments in
time that Miss Cain had drawn up – the picture that
refused to form. Pünd had been unable to get to sleep. It
had proved impossible to put the different permutations
out of his mind. They had tormented him for much of
the night.

Miss Cain joined him in the living room, but from the
moment she sat down she seemed out of sorts. She had

taken her breakfast in her room, as before, and began by handing him a sheaf of typewritten pages. 'These are my notes from yesterday,' she said. 'There was a lot to cover and I hope I haven't left anything out.'

'Thank you.' Pünd took the documents and quickly glanced through them. There was the interview with Simon Cox, the visit to Clarence Keep, Francis Pendleton, the Chandlers. 'This all seems to be in excellent order, Miss Cain,' he said. 'I did not see that you had packed a typewriter!' he added, with a twinkle.

'Mr and Mrs Gardner allowed me to use their office.' Miss Cain flinched, as if there was something she was holding back.

'There is something else?' Pünd asked gently.

'Well, yes. There is. I hope you won't think I've acted improperly, Mr Pünd, and I suppose it was kind of the Gardners to help me. But after ten minutes, they left me on my own and, remembering what the detective chief inspector said about the hotel's finances and what might be going on, I decided I might as well take the opportunity to have a look around.'

'My dear Miss Cain!' Pünd beamed at her. 'You are the true Sherlock Holmes. Or perhaps it is more Raffles, the gentleman thief, that you resemble. What did you find?'

'They were cheating her, Mr Pünd. There can be absolutely no doubt of it. Poor Miss James, putting her trust in two complete crooks!'

She produced three more documents, written and signed by Lance Gardner. They were addressed to different suppliers – food, furniture and laundry in Barnstaple, Taunton and Newquay. In each case, they apologised that, due to an error, an overpayment had been made and requested the company remit the difference by return of post.

'It's one of the oldest tricks in the book,' she said. 'I was the personal assistant to the manager of the Savoy in London for eighteen months and he explained the whole thing. You deliberately overpay suppliers, often by ten times the correct amount. It's easy enough to slip in an extra zero. You then write an apologetic letter, just like these ones, asking for a refund. But look where they're asking the money to be sent!'

Pünd examined the top letter.

'L. Gardner, Esq.' He read it out loud.

'Exactly. That's his private bank account. So he pockets the difference. There are three letters in your hand and they add up to almost two hundred pounds, and I found lots more tucked away in the files. I couldn't take any more or they'd have noticed they'd gone missing, but no wonder the hotel is in difficulties. Heaven knows how long this has been going on. They may have stolen thousands.'

'This is remarkable, Miss Cain.' Pünd checked the other letters. Sure enough, the amounts requested ranged from fifty pounds to over a hundred pounds. 'We must pass these to Detective Chief Inspector Hare as soon as he returns.'

'I would prefer it if you didn't mention how you got hold of them, if you don't mind, sir.'

'As you wish.'

'There is something else ... '

Miss Cain bowed her head and Pünd realised that it wasn't actually the theft of the incriminating letters that had been bothering her when she sat down. There was something else on her mind. 'I'm very sorry to have to tell you this, Mr Pünd, but I've decided to leave your employ. I will of course work out a month's notice, but I would like that notice period to start from today.'

Pünd looked up, genuinely surprised. 'May I ask why?'

'I have very much enjoyed working for you, sir, and I genuinely admire what you do. You are clearly a re-markable person. But as you saw, I became very upset yesterday when you were discussing the murder with the detective chief inspector. The descriptions of the killing I found – well, as I say, I was very upset.'

'You had every right to be, Miss Cain. It was wrong of us to speak so openly in front of you.'

'I don't blame you at all, Mr Pünd. Far from it. But I'm afraid it made me appreciate that I'm not entirely suited to your line of work. The hotel business, insurance, food manufacture – I've been comfortable and, I think, effective in all of them. But young women being strangled, and police officers, and all these people lying to you, that's quite another thing. I didn't get a wink of sleep thinking about it last night and by the time the sun came up this morning, I knew that as much as I hate letting you down, this isn't for me.'

'I quite understand.' Pünd smiled a little sadly. 'I accept your notice, Miss Cain. Although I must say you will be very difficult to replace.'

'Not at all. The agency has plenty of young women who will be just as good as me. I only hope you solve the case before I leave. I would like to see whoever did this brought to justice.'

'It is quite possible that you will have your wish. Here is the detective chief inspector and it looks as if he has news.'

It was true. Hare had come striding in with a sense of purpose and self-confidence they had not seen before. He came straight over to them. 'Good morning, Mr Pünd – Miss Cain. Have you both had breakfast?'

'Indeed so, Detective Chief Inspector. How was Barn-staple?'

'It was extremely revealing. I could kick myself for not having gone there before. My trouble was, I relied too much on local officers – although I'm not blaming them. I'm very grateful to you for suggesting I go round.'

'Are you going to tell us what you found?'

'Actually, if you don't mind, I'm going to ask you to trust me on this one. I'm going back to Clarence Keep. Would you like to come with me?'

'It would be my pleasure. Miss Cain?'

'Certainly, Mr Pünd. I'll just get my bag . . . '

*

There were two uniformed policemen waiting in a second car outside the hotel and on seeing them, Pünd turned to his companion. 'Do I take it, Detective Chief Inspector, that you are intending to make an arrest?'

'That's right, Mr Pünd.' Hare was a different man to the one who had greeted Pünd just one day before. 'I'm not expecting any trouble, but I thought it best to ask for two local men to come along.'

'You know who did it!' Miss Cain exclaimed.

'I think I do,' Hare replied. 'It follows on from what we were saying last night, Mr Pünd. Thank you for an excellent dinner, by the way. At any event, I think you're going to find the next encounter greatly to your interest.'

'Of that I am sure,' Pünd agreed.

They drove the short distance to Clarence Keep and once again Eric let them into the hall. He looked even clumsier and more dishevelled than usual and he was clearly alarmed by the sight of a police car and two men in uniform, almost trembling until Hare put him at his ease.

'We have business with Mr Pendleton,' Hare said. 'Is he up?'

Pünd noticed a look of relief pass across the butler's face. 'He finished his breakfast half an hour ago, sir.'

'And where is he now?'

'Upstairs.'

'Could you ask him to come down? And I would prefer it if you and Mrs Chandler remained in your rooms until I send for you. We need to speak privately with Mr Pendleton.'

That worried Eric again but all he could do was nod. 'I'll tell him you're here,' he said.

The detective chief inspector went into the living room with its sea views and French windows leading into the side garden and it was there that Francis Pendleton found him a few minutes later. He had managed to get dressed in a clean shirt and a suit without its jacket, but he was clearly knocked back by the sight of so many people waiting for him. Pünd was sitting on a sofa. Miss Cain was perched on a high-backed chair in one corner, as far out of the way as possible. Hare was standing in the centre of the room with one uniformed policeman by the door, the other at the French windows.

He quickly recovered. 'I'm very glad to see you,' he said. 'Do you have any news?'

'There has been a development, sir,' Hare said. 'It actually relates to what you told us about your movements on the day of your wife's death.'

Pendleton faltered. 'I'm sorry ... ?'

'Could I ask you to sit down, sir?'

'I'm perfectly all right standing up.'

'Even so ... ' Hare waited until Francis had sat down, then continued. 'When we were last here, and indeed in discussions you had with me before that, you said that you left at 6.15 p.m. to go to the opera and that your wife went to bed early as she had a headache. You briefly discussed the meeting she'd had at the Moonflower Hotel, but there was no disagreement between you. Is that correct?'

'Of course it's correct. It's what I told you.'

'You also told me how much you had enjoyed *The Marriage of Figaro*. You didn't mention anything unusual about the performance.'

'Because there was nothing unusual about it. It was a semi-professional company. They did it very well.'

'You were there from the very beginning?'

'Yes.'

'What about the singer playing Figaro?'

'I can't remember who played the part. But he was fine. Where exactly are you going with this, Detective Inspector?'

Hare paused before he answered. His voice was matter-of-fact but, at the same time, lethal. 'It was actually an unusual performance, sir. Had you been there at the beginning, you would have seen the director come onto the stage to announce that Mr Henry Dickson, who was playing Figaro, had been injured in a car accident. He liked to go for a walk before the performance and he was actually the victim of a hit-and-run. He was lucky not to be killed. So his part was played by a last-minute replacement, Mr Bentley, who unfortunately had to perform holding the libretto. The general consensus was that he really wasn't up to scratch and at the end of the evening quite a few members of the audience asked for their money back.'

Francis Pendleton had listened to all this in deathly silence.

'Did you attend the opera, Mr Pendleton?' the detective chief inspector asked.

There was another long pause. Then: 'No.'

'You didn't discuss the hotel finances with your wife. The two of you argued.'

Pendleton said nothing. He nodded.

'What time did you really leave the house?'

'I have no idea. Later than I said. But not very much later.'

'It was after you murdered your wife.'

Francis Pendleton buried his head in his hands. 'Thank God,' he whispered. 'You won't believe this, but it's all I've wanted – for this to be over. I'll make a full confession. I'll tell you everything. Am I under arrest?'

'If you'll come with us, sir, we'll formally charge you when we get to the station.'

'I'm sorry, Detective Chief Inspector. You have no idea how sorry I am. I don't know how I've managed to live with myself and I couldn't have gone on much longer.' He looked down at his feet. 'I need to put some shoes on. And can I fetch my jacket from upstairs?'

'Yes, sir. We'll wait for you here.'

'Thank you. I . . . ' Pendleton was about to say something more but then he dropped the idea and left the room, moving like a sleepwalker.

'Well, that was easier than I thought it would be,' Hare said. He turned to Pünd. 'We both agreed that he was the most likely suspect. And it turns out we were right.'

But Pünd looked uncertain. 'There is still the question of the telephone,' he muttered. 'And the ten moments drawn up by Miss Cain, the timings on which this entire case rests. I wonder, even now, if they will work.'

'It's a conversation we can have at the local police station, Mr Pünd. The important thing is that we've got the murderer. He's confessed. We'll have plenty of time to iron out all the details over the next couple of days.'

'There is something else I would like to ask you, Detective Chief Inspector. Have the police apprehended the driver who struck the unfortunate Mr Dickson with his car?'

'Not yet. They don't have very much to go on. Two people who went past at about that time think they saw a pale-coloured car parked on the side of the road, but they can't tell us what actual colour it was because of the rain and they didn't see the driver.'

'The pale colour, though. That is interesting . . . '

He might have continued, but at that moment Miss Cain suddenly cried out, pointing at the window. 'There!'

They all turned and saw the same thing. A figure had been looking into the room through the glass, spying on them.

'Who . . . ?' Hare began.

But the figure had already gone, darting away so quickly that it was impossible to know who it was. All they had seen was a head pressed against the glass with the eyes hooded by a hand. They couldn't even have said if it was a man or a woman.

Everyone acted at once. The uniformed policeman threw open the door and hurried into the front hall, followed by his colleague. Detective Chief Inspector Hare, realising that the French windows were the fastest way out, ran over to them and turned the key, which was still in the lock. With Pünd right behind him, he hurried outside.

They were at the side of the house. Francis Pendleton's bright green Austin-Healey was parked in its bay. The road was in front of them. As they stood there, the two uniformed policemen came bursting out of the front door. Hare quickly gave orders.

'One of you stay here. Make sure Pendleton doesn't leave. The other one, head off down to the main road and see if there's a car!'

One of the policemen positioned himself by the front door. The other hurried down the drive. Hare went over to Pünd. 'Did you see them?'

'I did see someone but I did not see who it was.'

'Eric Chandler?'

'He could not have moved so quickly. And his mother, also, is too old.'

Hare looked around the empty garden. 'Maybe it was

something completely innocent. A postman or a delivery boy.'

'They have taken great care to hide themselves.'

'That's true.'

Pünd and Hare continued round to the back of the house but there was no one there either. A back door led into an area behind the kitchen and when Hare tried it, he found that it was unlocked. Had the mysterious intruder come out that way? A low wall surrounded Clarence Keep, with shrubs on the other side. If they had climbed over, they would be invisible at once. Certainly, there was no one in sight. They had arrived too late.

And then the scream came, loud and high-pitched, from the hallway.

The policeman standing guard outside front the door was the first to go back in. Pünd and Detective Chief Inspector Hare arrived about ten seconds later. None of them would forget what they saw.

Miss Cain was standing at the bottom of the stairs with her back to the door. She was the one who had screamed and she was still almost hysterical.

Francis Pendleton was coming down the stairs. He had put on his jacket and his shoes. He seemed to be holding something in front of him. His face was completely white.

There was blood seeping through his fingers. Pünd remembered the film prop he had seen, the Turkish knife with its multicoloured handle that had been used in *Harem Nights*. He looked for it on the hall table, knowing it wouldn't be there. Francis Pendleton was holding it. The curved blade was buried deep in his chest.

He stumbled forward. Miss Cain reached out as if to embrace him and he fell into her arms. She screamed again.

Francis Pendleton collapsed on the ground and lay still.

THIRTEEN
POST-MORTEM

Detective Chief Inspector Hare took charge immediately. 'Look after her!' he shouted at Pünd as he sprang forward to examine the body. Pünd put his arm around his secretary, leading her into the kitchen. She was no longer screaming but seemed to be in shock. The front of her dress was covered in blood. The policeman was standing there staring, absolutely still. He was young, in his twenties, and had clearly never seen a dead man before, and certainly not one who had still been alive only moments before.

'Get upstairs!' Hare snapped at him. 'Search the house. It's quite likely that the killer's still here!' At the same time, he had gone down on one knee and taken hold of Pendleton's pulse.

The policeman raced up to the first-floor corridor

and disappeared round the corner. In the kitchen, Pünd found a chair and gently helped Miss Cain to sit down. She was trembling violently and there were tears streaming down her cheeks. Somewhere in the back of his mind it occurred to him that if she hadn't already resigned this would certainly have been the last straw. He didn't want to leave her alone and he was relieved when the second policeman, alerted by the screams, appeared at the door.

Pünd turned to him. 'Can you look after this lady?'

'Yes, sir.'

'Did you bring a radio transmitter with you?'

'I'm afraid not, sir. We had no idea ...'

'No matter. Detective Chief Inspector Hare will call for an ambulance and for further assistance. Please stay here.'

He was about to leave when a door at the back of the kitchen opened and Phyllis Chandler appeared. 'What's happening?' she demanded. 'I heard screaming. Why are the police here?'

'Mrs Chandler, I must ask you to stay here in the kitchen. On no account are you to enter the hall. If you would be so kind, could you make my assistant a strong cup of tea? She has had a great shock.' He leaned towards Miss Cain. 'I must leave you just for a few minutes. But I shall arrange for an ambulance to take you to hospital. You must try not to touch the clothes you are wearing because the police will need them for evidence. These people will look after you. I will be back soon.'

He nodded at Mrs Chandler, who was already reaching for the kettle, and went back into the hall just in time to see Hare standing back up.

'He's dead,' the detective chief inspector said.

'It is unbelievable. It happened right under our eyes.'

'And it was my fault!' Hare had never looked more defeated. 'I shouldn't have allowed him to leave the room.'

'I really do not believe you should feel any culpability,' Pünd assured him. 'It was a perfectly reasonable thing to do and this …' He glanced at the corpse lying at the foot of the stairs. 'None of us could have expected it.'

'I don't understand how it happened.'

'There are many questions that we will ask later. For now you must make a telephone call. We need two ambulances. One for Francis Pendleton, another for Miss Cain.'

'And I'll need to bring in backup.'

The policeman who had been sent upstairs came back down again. He was trying not to look at the body but he couldn't keep his eyes off it. 'There's nobody up there, sir,' he said. 'There was a man sitting in an upstairs kitchen but he says he works here.'

'Eric Chandler,' Hare said.

'Yes, sir. Nobody else. Would you like me to look outside?'

'That would be a good idea.'

The policeman edged past the dead man and went out.

'I'll start making some calls.' Hare went back into the living room.

Pünd was left on his own. A pool of dark red blood had spread over the wooden floor. Somehow it reminded him of the night before, the sea in the moonlight. He had believed then that there was an evil presence in Tawleigh-on-the-Water. He had not expected to be proved right so soon.

*

Three hours later, Detective Chief Inspector Hare and Atticus Pünd were in the living room of Clarence Keep, sitting opposite one other. For once they were ill at ease. Hare still blamed himself for what had happened and even Pünd was beginning to think that the killer had made a fool out of him. To be summoned to the scene of a murder a week after the event was one thing, but this time he had actually been present when it took place. It was something that had never happened before.

Events had moved swiftly since the crime had been

committed. Two ambulances and four police cars had arrived from Barnstaple and the ritual that follows any murder had begun. A police doctor had pronounced Francis Pendleton dead from a single stab wound to the heart. A police photographer had taken twenty different shots of the crime scene. Fingerprint experts had covered the entire area, having done the same thing upstairs only a week before. The body had been lifted onto a stretcher and carried out to the ambulance to be driven into Exeter for further examination. The second ambulance had already left with Miss Cain.

It had already been established that Dr Leonard Collins and his wife, Samantha, were still in London. Simon Cox, the producer, was at his home in Maida Vale. Lance Gardner had been at the hotel all morning and his wife, Maureen, had been working behind the reception desk as Nancy Mitchell had failed to turn up for work. She and Algernon Marsh were the only people associated with the investigation who were unaccounted for and the police were looking for them now.

The mysterious figure who had appeared at the window had vanished into thin air. Whoever it was, they had left no footprints or any other traces, and but for the fact that both Hare and Pünd had caught a glimpse of them, they could have been a figment of the imagination.

'It's my belief that Francis Pendleton committed suicide.' Hare broke the silence. 'Of course, there'll be a full inquest, but if you ask me that seems to be the only explanation. I mean, consider the evidence! The knife that he used – it was a prop out of one of Melissa James's films – was on a table right next to the stairs. He must have seen it as he went up to get his jacket and shoes. He'd just confessed to the murder of his wife and he knew it was all up for him. He grabbed it and took the easy way out. Maybe it's for the best at the end of the day. It saves the cost of a trial.'

'And what of the intruder?'

'I'm not convinced they could have killed him, Mr Pünd, even assuming that was what they came here to do. Pendleton was stabbed within about ninety seconds of your secretary seeing the figure at the window. To kill him, the intruder would have to continue all the way round the house and come in through the back entrance. That would have brought them into the kitchen. They'd have had to continue into the hall, take the knife and stab Pendleton before somehow disappearing into thin air. How would they have had time?'

'I assume nothing, Detective Chief Inspector. And I agree with you. It would have been very difficult – though not impossible – to manage the crime in the way you have just described.'

For once, Hare was agitated. He was on the defensive

and Pünd understood why. This was Hare's last case. He had hoped to retire at the end of a successful investigation with the thanks and congratulations of his superiors. He had not foreseen any further complications and he had been completely unprepared for them when they arrived.

'It all seems pretty straightforward to me,' he insisted. 'Francis Pendleton was a man who had just killed his wife and he'd been found out. You heard what he said. He actually wanted it all to be over.'

Pünd looked apologetic. 'It is perfectly possible that he strangled his wife. I have said as much all along and it is still the most likely scenario, particularly in light of the fact that he lied about the opera. But there is still the matter of the telephone to consider. You will recall that we discussed this at dinner last night.'

'Ah yes! The telephone. Why don't you explain yourself about that? You've obviously got a bee in your bonnet about it!'

'I'm sorry? A bee?'

'What's been worrying you about the phone?'

'Only this, Detective Chief Inspector, and it is something that struck me from the very beginning. You told me that you found no fingerprints on the telephone or the receiver.'

'That's right. It had been wiped clean.'

'But why would Francis Pendleton need to do that if he was the one who had used it as a murder weapon? He was not a stranger to the house. He would have used the phone many times. He had no need to cover his tracks.'

Hare considered. 'You're right. Although has it occurred to you that he could have deliberately wiped the phone clean to throw us off the scent?'

'That to me is unlikely.'

'What difference does it make, Mr Pünd? Francis Pendleton confessed to the killing! We were both in the room.'

'I did not hear him confess, Detective Chief Inspector. He said only that he intended to make a full confession.'

'Exactly!'

'But a confession to what?'

'I don't know.' Finally, Hare lost his patience. 'Perhaps he was going to confess to stealing sweets from the village shop or to parking on a yellow line. But since I had just arrested him for murder, I'd imagine that was uppermost in his mind.' He stopped himself. 'I'm very sorry, Mr Pünd,' he said. 'I really shouldn't talk to you that way.'

'Detective Chief Inspector,' Pünd began again, speaking slowly, 'you do not need to apologise, and please trust me when I say that it is not my desire to complicate the matter unnecessarily. But I do not believe it is the case that Francis Pendleton confessed to everything. And I can suggest to you three reasons why it is unlikely that he committed suicide.'

'Go on!'

'First of all, he left the room to put on his jacket and his shoes. You might think that if he intended to kill himself, he suggested that only as an excuse to be left on his own. But this is my point. He *did* put on his jacket and shoes. He was wearing them when he died. Why did he do that? If he was about to die, what would it matter to him what he was wearing?'

'If you'll forgive me for saying it, maybe you don't understand the way an English gentleman thinks, Mr Pünd. I investigated the case of a landowner over in Taunton who blew his brains out. He had money troubles and he left a letter explaining exactly what he was going to do and why. But he put on a dinner jacket before he did it. He wanted to look his best when he went.'

Pünd shrugged. 'Very well. Let us now consider the placing of the knife. It is on a table at the bottom of the stairs. But when Pendleton is seen by Miss Cain, he is several steps above. The knife is now in his chest. So what are you telling me has occurred? He has taken the knife with him to his room? He has then chosen to kill himself on his return as he comes down the stairs? It makes no sense.

'And there is also the method of his death,' Pünd continued quickly before Hare could interrupt again. 'Had Mr Pendleton been Japanese, then perhaps I might have accepted that he would perform on himself hara-kiri! But as you have rightly said, he was an English gentleman and have you ever heard of a person killing himself in this way? There were the razors in his bathroom. He could have hanged himself with a tie. But to take a knife and thrust it into his heart … ?'

'He was desperate.'

'But not desperate enough to die without his jacket and his shoes.'

'All right.' Hare nodded slowly, unable to escape the logic of what Pünd was saying. 'What do you think happened?'

'Until we have ascertained the identity of the person seen in the garden, I cannot answer that. But before we leave this house there is one question that must be resolved.'

'And what is that, Mr Pünd?'

'In Miss James's bedroom, why was the wallpaper torn?'

*

Phyllis Chandler had gone back upstairs after Madeline Cain had left. She was sitting in her small living room with Eric. They were surrounded by suitcases. Francis Pendleton had told them to leave by the end of the day and they had begun packing at once. Their departure had been interrupted by his death. They had barely spoken to each other since the morning and they weren't speaking now. Nor did either of them react when there was a knock at the door and Pünd came in with Hare.

'You are leaving?' Pünd asked, taking in the suitcases.

'Yes, sir. To be honest with you, I couldn't stay one more minute in this house. Not after everything that's happened.'

'You do realise you can't just disappear, Mrs Chandler,' Hare said. 'We may have to ask you further questions.'

'I'm not disappearing anywhere, Detective Chief Inspector. I'm going to my sister in Bude.'

'And your son?'

Phyllis glanced briefly at Eric, who shrugged. 'I don't know where I'll go,' he said. 'I don't have friends. I don't have anything. I don't care—'

Pünd took a step forward. He had seldom met two such unhappy people, trapped in a prison of their own making. But still there were matters to be resolved. 'Mrs

Chandler, there is something that I must discuss with you – and with your son.'

Hearing himself mentioned, Eric Chandler looked up guiltily.

'Let us start with this morning when Mr Pendleton was attacked. You were here in this room.'

'Yes, sir. We were packing.'

'So you had decided to leave before the terrible events that took place today?'

Phyllis swallowed, realising that she had given away more than she intended. 'As a matter of fact, Mr Pendleton had already given us our notice,' she said. 'He intended to sell the house and had no further need of our services.'

'It was still rather sudden,' Pünd suggested mildly.

'It was his decision, sir. I'm sure he knew what he was doing.'

Hare cut in. 'You must have heard Miss Cain cry out. Were you together at that time?'

Phyllis Chandler hesitated. She didn't want to tell the truth but she knew she had no choice. 'I was in here. Eric was in his bedroom.'

'I was packing,' Eric said. 'I didn't see anything.'

'Neither of us did.'

'You didn't look out the window? You didn't hear anyone go past?'

'Why do you keep asking me that?' Phyllis Chandler snapped. 'I've already told you that I'm hard of hearing. All we knew was that there were police in the house and we'd been told to stay in our rooms so that's what we did!'

'Why did Mr Pendleton want you to leave?'

'I've already told you—'

'You have told me a lie, Mrs Chandler.' Now it was Pünd's turn to become angry. 'And there can be no more lies. There have been two murders in this house and even though I understand completely your desire to protect your son, you can no longer deceive me!'

'I don't know what you're talking about, sir.'

'Then I will show you.'

Before anyone could stop him, Pünd walked determinedly out of the room. Hare went with him. Eric Chandler and his mother glanced at each other, then followed.

Pünd knew exactly what he was looking for. It was a strange coincidence that the wallpaper in Melissa James's bedroom had reminded him of the house in Knightsbridge where he had investigated the theft of the Ludendorff Diamond – but it had led his eye, at once, to an identical clue: a tear in the wallpaper. It still might have made no impression on him but he remembered what Simon Cox had overheard. '*She said something about the Moonflower being crooked.*' That made no sense. The Gardners might be crooked. There might be crooked activity taking place inside the hotel. But in what way could the hotel itself be crooked?

He did not go into the bedroom. Instead, he turned into the corridor that ran alongside it, still in the servants' wing of the house. Even as he went he was measuring distances and he came to a halt in front of the photographs that he had noticed before. They showed views of Tawleigh: the lighthouse, the beach and the hotel. With Eric and his mother watching him in silent horror, he lifted the picture of the Moonflower off its hook to reveal a hole that had been drilled through the brickwork behind.

'It is exactly as I expected,' he said.

Hare stepped up and put his eye to the hole. He found himself looking into Melissa James's bedroom. He remembered the patterned wallpaper on the other side, and knew that the hole would have been practically invisible. He looked back. Phyllis Chandler was on the edge of tears. Eric Chandler was fighting for breath, his face completely white.

'What's the meaning of this?' Hare demanded.

'It is what I believe is called a peephole,' Pünd said.

Hare looked at Eric with distaste. 'You're a peeping Tom!' Eric was unable to talk. Hare turned back to Pünd. 'How did you know about this?' he asked.

'You will recall the argument that the film producer, Simon Cox, overheard. Mrs Chandler said that she knew what her son had been up to. She had noticed that the Moonflower was crooked and she added that she had seen through it. She was referring, of course, to the hole drilled in the wall. Mr Cox did not hear everything that was said, but this much, you will agree, makes complete sense.'

Hare gazed at Phyllis with disgust. 'Did you know about this?'

The older woman nodded, her face utterly grim. 'I lifted the picture off the wall. That was the same day that it happened – the death of Miss James. I went down to look out of the window and I noticed it wasn't hung properly. That's why we were in the kitchen and didn't leave until later. How do you think I felt? I was shocked. My own son!'

'Did you also say that you would kill Melissa James if she found out?'

'No, sir!' Phyllis Chandler was horrified. Then she remembered. 'I said it would kill her if she found out the truth. That's what I said! And it would have. She trusted Eric. She had no idea he'd been spying on her.'

'I didn't . . . ' Eric tried to say something but the words wouldn't come out.

But now Phyllis was merciless. She continued: 'Then, just this morning, Mr Pendleton told me that someone had been into his wife's bedroom and taken some of her things.'

'What things?' Hare demanded.

'Personal things. Underclothes. From the drawer near the bed ... '

'That wasn't me!' Eric cried.

'Of course it was you!' His mother turned on him, furious. 'Why are you still lying? You're fat and you're lazy and you're sick in the head and I wish you'd never been born. God knows, your father would have been ashamed!'

'Mum ... '

It was a horrible sight. Eric was wailing, tears coursing down his cheeks. He had staggered backwards, his shoulders hitting the wall as he slumped down. Pünd and the detective chief inspector hurried over to help him, and together they managed to get him back into the sitting room. They sat him down on a sofa and Hare got him a glass of water. But he was unable to drink. He was sobbing helplessly. His mother was standing by the door, watching him with no pity in her eyes, and Pünd could not help feeling how much better their lives would have been if she had loved her husband a little less and her son a little more.

'What will happen?' Mrs Chandler asked. 'Are you going to arrest him?'

'It's clear that you have broken the law.' Hare sounded uncomfortable. 'You could be placed under arrest ... '

'I just liked to look at her!' Eric sobbed, the words almost incomprehensible. 'She was so beautiful. I would never have hurt her. I never took anything!'

Hare glanced at Pünd, who nodded. 'But as the two of you are leaving and as both Mr Pendleton and Miss James aren't around to bring charges, it's probably best that you continue on your way. Just make sure we know where we can find you. And Eric ... I think you should talk to Dr Collins and find someone who can give you some help. What you've done is very wrong.'

'I didn't—'

'I've got nothing more to say.'

Hare and Pünd left. Mrs Chandler stepped aside to allow them to pass. Neither of them looked back.

'I hope I'm doing the right thing,' Hare muttered as they went back downstairs. 'If Francis Pendleton was murdered, Eric Chandler may well be the most likely suspect. In fact, he's the only suspect. He was in the house – and you heard what his mother said. He was in one room. She was in another. Which means that, actually, she had no idea where he was. If he thought Pendleton was going to shop him for stealing his wife's knickers or whatever, that would have given him a motive.'

'What you say is true,' Pünd agreed. 'He is damaged.

His life has, I think, been unfortunate in many ways. And yet he does not strike me as a violent man. In his own, twisted way, he adored Melissa James. Would he kill the man to whom she was married?'

They had reached the hallway and a uniformed police officer approached them, coming out of the living room. He had been looking for Hare. He was holding a handwritten letter that had been placed in a transparent evidence bag. 'Excuse me, sir,' he said. 'I thought you ought to see this. We found it in the living room, tucked away in the bottom of a bureau. It was hidden among a whole load of old papers, obviously somewhere it wasn't meant to be found.'

He handed the letter to Hare, who read it carefully. 'Well, this might change your mind about things,' he muttered. 'Maybe I was right after all.' He showed the letter to Pünd. The paper was crumpled. The letter had been thrown away before it was finished.

13th February
My darling darling,
I can't go on living this lie any more. I simply can't.
We have to be brave and tell the world our destiny ...

'Melissa James was having an affair and she wanted Francis Pendleton out of her life. He couldn't bear the thought of losing her so he killed her and when he got found out he killed himself.' Hare took the letter back. 'Can you really think of another explanation?'

'I agree with you that it does seem, on the face of it, unarguable,' Pünd agreed. 'But even so, Detective Chief Inspector, there is one piece of information that we require before we can consider the investigation to be complete.'

'And that is?'

'Melissa James was having an affair. That much is evident. But with whom?'

FOURTEEN
HIT-AND-RUN

'What are you doing here?' Dr Collins asked.

'Actually, I was waiting to see you,' Algernon replied.

The doctor had come into the kitchen of Church Lodge to find his brother-in-law sitting at the table, smoking a cigarette. Samantha was helping the vicar with preparations for the next service and had taken the children with her. She liked them to spend time with her at the church. Mrs Mitchell wasn't due in to clean until later in the afternoon. Dr Collins had thought he was alone.

He was not fond of Algernon Marsh. He knew too much about his activities both past and present and resented having him stay in the house. But in this, as in so many other things, he had allowed himself to be overruled by Samantha, who had, he knew, a much more forgiving nature. He couldn't make her see that Algernon was trouble and had been since the day he was born. His parents might have been prescient. They had christened him with the name of a villain straight out of melodrama and he had certainly grown into it.

Seeing him now, Dr Collins felt a stab of annoyance. In a way, the two of them were complete opposites. He had been a doctor for fifteen years, first in Slough, then in Tawleigh, working for his patients around the clock for a salary that barely allowed him to support a wife and two children. He had never complained. Medicine had been his calling: even during the war years he had served with the Royal Army Medical Corps. Algernon, of course, had kept well clear of the action, with a desk job in Whitehall. With his expensive suits, his French car, his devious business schemes that were surely designed to benefit only himself, he epitomised the new generation that was dragging the country into an era of selfishness and hedonism.

Even the way Algernon was sitting at the table – *his* table – filling the room with his cigarette smoke came across as deliberately offensive. Dr Collins hadn't invited him here. He had simply arrived and now he was behaving as if he owned the place.

'I'm sorry. Are you waiting for me?' Dr Collins asked. For Samantha's sake, he was trying to be polite.

'Yes. I thought we might have a little chat.'

'I can't imagine what you think we might have to chat about, but anyway, I'm going to have to disappoint you. I have my case notes to study.'

'I'm sure they can wait.'

'I'm afraid they can't.'

'Sit down, Leonard. We need to talk.' It wasn't an invitation. It was a threat. There was something in his voice and the silken smile on his face that warned Dr Collins not to leave. Against all his better instincts, he took his place at the table.

'Thank you.' Again, Algernon managed to say the words in a way that utterly distorted their meaning. His eyes were pitiless as they took in the man sitting opposite him.

'What is this about, Algernon? I really don't—'

'It's about this.'

Algernon took a sheet of paper out of his pocket and unfolded it. With a start, Dr Collins recognised the letter addressed to Samantha from Parker & Bentley in London. Algernon placed it flat on the table between them.

'Where did you get that?' Dr Collins demanded furiously. 'You've been in my desk. How dare you? That's private!'

'You weren't going to tell me about it? Dear Aunt Joyce popping her clogs in New York and leaving Samantha – how much, exactly? I take it that's why you were in London yesterday.'

'It's none of your business.'

'It's very much my business, Leonard. I'm Samantha's brother, in case you've forgotten. I had to live with the old bag too.'

'She left you nothing, Algernon. She disapproved of your lifestyle – as, for that matter, do I. The amount of money is neither here nor there as you're not going to receive a penny of it.'

'Is that what Samantha says?'

'Yes.'

'Or is it what you persuaded her to say? From my memory, Sam always had a soft spot for me – at least until she married you. I bet you anything you like that she'd want to share her good fortune with me. How much did you say it was?'

'I didn't.'

'Well, I've done a bit of research on my own and from what I've heard, Harlan Goodis made a mint out of advertising. My friends tell me that we could be talking about a million quid.'

'What do you want, Algernon?' Dr Collins looked at his brother-in-law with undisguised contempt.

'I was thinking half would be fair.'

Dr Collins stared at him, then let out a bark of laughter. 'Are you mad?'

'You don't agree?'

'I've already told you my thoughts. The money was not left to you. It was left to my wife. It was the specific wish of your aunt that none of it should come your way and if Samantha will take my advice, once she has inherited the money she will have nothing more to do with you.'

'She listens to you, does she?'

'Yes.'

'Good. Then you'll be able to persuade her to think otherwise.'

'And why should I do that?'

'Because I know a thing or two about you, Leonard, which you might not want me to mention to Samantha – or to anyone else.'

It was as if Dr Collins had been punched in the face. 'What are you talking about?'

'Do you really want me to spell it out?'

'You're trying to blackmail me!'

'Trying and succeeding, I'd say.' Algernon leaned forward. 'Let's just call it a lack of professionalism in your dealings with certain patients.'

'I categorically deny whatever it is you're hinting at. There has never been any wrongdoing on my part and your pathetic attempts to discredit me will only land you in jail, which is what you richly deserve.'

'Samantha may not agree.'

'Leave my wife out of this!'

Dr Collins might have leapt out of his chair and thrown himself at the other man, but the conversation was interrupted by not one but two cars pulling up in the driveway outside. Atticus Pünd and Detective Chief Inspector Hare were in the first. Uniformed police officers followed behind.

Algernon got up and glanced out of the window. 'It looks as if we're going to have to continue this pleasant conversation later,' he drawled. He reached for the letter but Dr Collins snatched it away. 'We both know what we're talking about,' Algernon continued. 'Fifty-fifty. I'll keep quiet for the time being. But you're going to have to use all your charm and powers of persuasion on Sam. I won't give you long.'

The doorbell rang.

Dr Collins was staring at Algernon Marsh. He tore himself away and went to answer it.

*

Detective Chief Inspector Hare was standing on the doorstep and knew at once that something was wrong.

The usually calm and easy-mannered doctor was clearly upset, and not just because there were so many representatives of the law invading his home.

'Yes?'

'I'm very sorry to interrupt you, Dr Collins, but I wonder if your brother-in-law is in?'

There was something about the question that seemed to amuse the doctor. The shadow of a smile passed across his face. 'Algernon? Yes. I was just talking to him.'

'We'd like to do the same, if you don't mind.'

'You're not arresting him by any chance?'

'You'll forgive me if I don't share that information with you, sir.'

'Of course. Come in. He's in the kitchen … '

The two uniformed men stood outside the entrance. After what had happened at Clarence Keep, Hare was taking no chances. He and Pünd followed Dr Collins into the hallway. As they arrived, Algernon March strolled nonchalantly out of the kitchen.

'Detective Inspector! Mr Pünd! What a pleasure to see you. Are you here to speak to me or to my brother-in-law? I'm sure Leonard has got quite a few things to tell you.'

'Actually, Mr Marsh, it's you I've come to see.'

Algernon's face fell, although the smile was still pinned in place. 'This is all becoming a bit tedious, Detective Inspector.'

'That may be the case but I have to do my job.' Hare turned to the doctor. 'Is there somewhere private we can go, sir?'

'You can use my study if you like.'

Pünd had said nothing throughout all this but he had heard the jibe that Algernon Marsh had thrown in the direction of his brother-in-law. Dr Collins had a story to tell and Algernon knew what it was. Did it relate to Melissa James? Almost certainly.

'I'll see you later, Leonard,' Algernon said. 'You can have a think about what we were talking about.'

Pünd's suspicions were confirmed. There was definitely bad blood between the two men.

Dr Collins showed them into the study, which he also used as a surgery, with an examination couch in one corner and a curtain hanging from a rail. Pünd sat down to one side. Hare and Algernon Marsh faced each other across the desk.

'I'd like to talk to you about a company that you own,' Hare began. 'Sun Trap Holdings.'

'What's that got to do with anything?' Algernon half laughed. 'Do you want to invest, Detective Inspector?'

'It's Detective *Chief* Inspector, and I think I should warn you, Mr Marsh, that this is no laughing matter.' Hare paused. 'A great many people seem to have invested in this company. Would you like to explain to me what it actually does?'

'Certainly. It develops property in the South of France: hotels, villas, that sort of thing. It's like the gold rush over there. Cannes, Nice, St-Tropez – you may not have heard of them now but quite soon these are places the whole world is going to want to visit.'

'I believe that Melissa James was one of your investors.'

Algernon's face darkened. 'Who told you that?' He collected himself. 'Melissa had invested a small amount. Yes.'

'Ninety-six thousand pounds is hardly a small amount, Mr Marsh.'

'This is my private business. Who exactly have you been talking to?'

'Her bank manager. We have traced three separate cheques made out to Sun Trap Holdings by Miss James.'

'It's a small amount in comparison to the returns she would have made once the developments were complete.'

'And how many hotels and villas have you actually completed?'

'You're out of your depth, Detective *Chief* Inspector. It's more complicated than that.'

'It is actually very simple,' Pünd cut in. 'The system

was invented thirty years ago by an Italian gentleman by the name of Charles Ponzi. He induced investors to put their savings into a scheme that would never in fact pay them anything. But he used the money of later investors to pay dividends to the earlier ones, making them believe that all was well. Meanwhile, he took everything for himself.'

'I've done nothing illegal!'

'That may not be the case, sir,' Hare said. 'The Larceny Act of 1916, Section 32, explicitly prohibits the obtaining of money by false pretences with the intent to defraud. It carries with it a prison sentence of five years.'

'I wasn't defrauding anyone!' Algernon had shrunk into his seat, his early bluster replaced by a whining defensiveness. 'Melissa knew exactly what she was doing. I kept her fully informed.'

'And what exactly was your relationship with Miss James?'

'We were friends.'

'Close friends?'

'Yes!'

'Were you and Miss James sleeping together?'

Algernon gaped at the detective. 'I have to say, you're very direct, Chief Inspector. And I don't see why I should answer your question. It's none of your damn business.'

Hare was unabashed. He produced the letter that had

been found at Clarence Keep and showed it to Algernon. 'Was this addressed to you?'

Algernon took the letter and stared at it for some time. Pünd watched him carefully. Algernon Marsh was a calculated liar in the true sense that he calculated everything he said and only spoke the truth when it suited him. Even now he was weighing up the different possibilities. At last, he came to a decision.

'All right,' he said. His shoulders had slumped. He tossed the letter back on the table. 'Yes. "Darling darling". That's how she always wrote to me. And that stuff about running away together. We talked about it all the time.'

'So the two of you were in a relationship.'

'Yes. The fact is she was crazy about me. She knew that Francis was a mistake. He couldn't give her what she wanted.'

'And what was that?'

'Excitement. Challenge. Sex. What every woman wants. It began in London and I used to look in on her whenever I came to Tawleigh. Actually, it was the main reason I ever came to this dreary little place.' He glanced at the letter. 'Where did you get that?'

'We believe Francis Pendleton may have found it . . .'

'And killed her? Is that what you're saying? That's a nasty thought, but then he was entirely inadequate both as a husband and as a lover. It's hardly surprising she turned to me – and for what it's worth, I never did her any harm.'

'Apart, that is, from stealing from her.'

'Steady on, Detective Chief Inspector. That's a bit strong.'

'It's my impression, Mr Marsh, that you ran your business with the mentality of a hit-and-run driver. You had no sense of shame, no morality. You just did what you did and moved on.'

Again, Pünd saw it: the fear creeping back into Algernon's eyes as he played back what Hare had just said.

'I've done nothing wrong,' Algernon muttered.

'Mr Henry Dickson would disagree.'

'Henry Dickson? I've never heard of him.'

'He's an opera singer, currently in hospital in Barnstaple in a serious but stable condition. He was struck by a car on the Braunton Road earlier this week. The driver did not stop.'

'I hope you're not suggesting . . . ' Algernon's voice gave him away. The knowledge of his guilt was there in every word.

'Can you explain how the front of your Peugeot was damaged, Mr Marsh?'

'I can't. I didn't . . . '

'Your car was noticed by another driver who went past

the scene of the accident. We have this . . . ' Hare produced a second evidence bag with a half-smoked cigarette, the paper brown, damaged by the rain. 'We also know how much alcohol you had consumed at the Saunton Golf Club and have good reason to believe you were driving under the influence of drink.'

Hare waited for him to speak. But Algernon didn't need to say anything more. He knew he was finished.

'Algernon Marsh, I am arresting you on various offences under the 1930 Road Traffic Act and the Larceny Act of 1916. You do not have to say anything but I must warn you that anything you do say may be taken down and used in evidence against you. Is there anything you wish to say?'

'Actually, there is one thing.'

'And what is that?'

Algernon wasn't afraid. He had already worked it all out. 'I was in love with Melissa James and she was in love with me. That's all that matters to me right now, Detective Chief Inspector. You can arrest me if you really want to, but you'll never take that away from me.'

He was still smiling as they led him out of the house.

FIFTEEN
THE GIRL ON
THE BRIDGE

They had intended to escort Algernon Marsh to the police station in Barnstaple but when they reached Bideford Long Bridge they were stopped by an unexpected traffic jam. Detective Chief Inspector Hare knew at once that something unusual must have happened. It was the middle of the afternoon and there could be no obvious reason for ten or twenty cars to come to a standstill on each side of the river. Many of the drivers had got out and were looking at something in the very centre of the bridge. Leaving Algernon with the two policemen in the car behind, Hare and Pünd went to investigate. As they made their way forward, they heard some of the comments being made by the crowd.

'Poor girl!'

'Someone should do something.'

'Has anyone called the police?'

They continued to the front and saw at once what was happening.

A young woman had climbed over the stone balustrade that ran the full length of the bridge and was standing on the narrow ledge on the other side. She was perched forward, leaning over the river, clinging on with her hands behind her. The bridge was not more than twenty feet high but the water was fast-flowing and murky with swirling currents. If she let go, the fall might not kill her but she would almost certainly drown.

Hare had a grown-up daughter and felt a surge of pity for the young woman who had been driven to such an act. He guessed that she was in her twenties but it was only as he got nearer and saw her more closely that he recognised her brown hair, her slightly uneven features.

'It's the girl from the Moonflower!' he exclaimed.

'Nancy Mitchell.' Pünd had also recognised her.

'I have to stop her.' Hare pushed his way between two men who had been standing helplessly at the entrance to the bridge. At least none of the drivers had moved too close, understanding that if the girl felt threatened, she would jump.

Pünd reached out and took hold of the detective's arm. 'With respect, my friend, it might be better if I attempted to speak to her. She knows that you are a senior police officer and she may also know that to commit suicide is an offence against the law. If she sees you approach, it may alarm her ... '

'You're right.' There was no time for argument. Hare had positioned himself in front of the crowd and he turned round to face them. 'I'm a police officer,' he announced quietly. 'Could I ask you all to move back?'

The spectators did as they were told. At the same time, Pünd continued forward, finding himself alone on the now empty bridge. Nancy saw him coming and stared at him with eyes that were wide with fear.

'Don't come any closer!' she shouted.

Pünd stopped about ten paces away. 'Miss Mitchell! Do you remember me? I am a guest at the hotel.'

'I know who you are. But I don't want to talk to you.'

'You do not have to. There is no need to say anything. But please let me speak to you.'

Pünd took two steps forward and the girl tensed herself. He stopped and looked down at the churning brown water as it raced past. The crowd on the other side of the river stirred uneasily, but fortunately another policeman had arrived and was making sure they stayed back.

'I do not know what has brought you here or how you have been driven to an action as extreme as the one you are now contemplating,' he said. 'You must be very unhappy. Of that I am sure. Will you believe me if I say that no matter how bad things may appear, they will be better tomorrow if you allow tomorrow to do its work? That is the way of things, Miss Mitchell, and I am the living proof of it.'

She said nothing. He took two more steps. The closer he was to her, the less he would have to raise his voice.

'Stay where you are!' Nancy cried out.

Pünd showed the palms of his hands. 'I am not going to touch you. I wish only to talk.'

'You can't know what I'm thinking!'

'What you are thinking, no. What you are feeling, perhaps.' He took another step. 'I too have suffered, Miss Mitchell. I have endured terrible violence – in prison in Germany, in the war. My wife was killed. My parents were killed. I found myself in an abyss, alone, surrounded by cruelty and inhumanity which I cannot describe. Like you, I wished for death.

'And yet I did not die. I made the most stupid, the most irrational decision of my life. Against all the odds, I chose to survive! Am I glad I did so? Yes. Because here I am now and it is my hope that I can persuade you to do the same.'

'I've got no hope.'

'There is always hope.' Pünd took another two steps towards her. He was now so close that if they had both stretched out their hands, they would have touched. 'Let me look after you, Miss Mitchell. Let me help make the bad things that have happened go away.' She was still unsure. He could see her struggling to decide. He knew what he had to do. 'Think also of the child that you carry!' he said. 'Will you not give it a chance?'

She had been looking at the water but now her head snapped round. 'Who told you that?'

In fact it was Detective Chief Inspector Hare who had guessed. 'The miracle of life is written all over you,' Pünd said. 'And life is what you must embrace.'

Nancy Mitchell had begun to cry. She nodded weakly, then twisted round, still grabbing hold of the balustrade with both hands. Pünd sprang forward and put his arms around her, holding her close to him, lifting her to safety. A few seconds later, Hare arrived as Nancy sank unconscious to the ground.

*

Two hours later, Atticus Pünd and Detective Chief Inspector Hare were sitting on uncomfortable wooden chairs outside a private room on the first floor of North Devon Infirmary in Barnstaple, the same hospital where Henry Dickson was slowly recovering. And, Pünd realised, Madeline Cain must be somewhere there too. He had not seen her since the death of Francis Pendleton, although he had made sure she was well looked after.

The door opened and a young doctor came out.

'How is she?' Hare asked.

'I've given her a mild sedative and she's a little drowsy, but she wants to see you. I advise against it. After what she's been through, she needs to rest.'

'We'll try not to tire her,' Hare said.

'Good. She is pregnant, by the way. You were right about that. About three months. Fortunately, no harm will have come to the unborn child.'

The doctor walked away. Pünd and Hare exchanged a glance and went in.

Nancy Mitchell was lying in bed with her hair spread out on the pillow behind her. She looked rested and strangely serene. 'Mr Pünd,' she said as the two men sat down. 'I want to thank you. What I did ... what I was thinking of doing ... was very stupid. I feel embarrassed that I made such a fool of myself.'

'I am just glad that you are here and you are feeling better, Miss Mitchell.'

'Are you going to arrest me, Chief Inspector?'

'That's the last thing on my mind,' Hare replied.

'Good. I want to see both of you because I need to get this off my chest. Certainly before my parents get here. The doctor said they're on their way.'

Hare was surprised how assured Nancy Mitchell had become. It was as if her experience on Bideford Long Bridge had provided some sort of epiphany.

'I suppose I ought to start at the beginning. You were right, Mr Pünd. I'm sure the doctor will have told you that I'm expecting a child. I haven't told my parents yet but I've decided I want to keep it. Why should I have to put it up for adoption just because the local people of Tawleigh might not approve? My dad won't agree, but I've been afraid of him since I was a child and I'm tired of it. Maybe it's like what you said, Mr Pünd, and this is a chance for me to take control of my life.

'Before you ask, I'm going to tell you the name of the father even though I haven't told anyone else and I wasn't going to. But I suppose you have to know and so I'm going to tell you now. It was Melissa's husband, Francis Pendleton. Does that surprise you? That's what this is all about, isn't it, and it's the reason why I have to talk to you. I was not in love with him and, in case you're wondering, I didn't kill him, although I suppose I would say that, wouldn't I?' She paused. 'I'll tell you how it happened.

'I knew him quite well, of course. Miss James might have owned the Moonflower but he was in and out all the time. He helped her run it. I won't say we became friends but he seemed to enjoy talking to me. He also

wanted me to help him. He had this idea that the Gardners were cheating his wife in some way and he asked
me to keep an eye on them for him. I wasn't too keen
about that. I didn't want to be a spy. But at the same
time I was flattered that he'd asked me and I liked him.
He was always kind to me.

'And then one day, about three months ago, he came
to the hotel in a dreadful state. He didn't say anything
to me but he went straight to the bar and began drinking, on his own. It was my luck – my bad luck – to be
on night duty. This was the end of January and the hotel
was almost empty. Anyway, I left him on his own for a
couple of hours and then I went into the bar because I
was worried about him and I wanted to know everything
was all right.

'It wasn't. He'd had quite a lot to drink and he just
sort of blurted out that he'd discovered his wife was having an affair. I didn't believe it at first. I mean, she was
Melissa James! She was a big star. Then I thought maybe
he was mistaken but he said he'd found a page from a
letter she'd written – a love letter. He didn't know who
it was addressed to, though. There was no name on the
letter and he hadn't told her he'd found it. But he said it
was destroying him. He worshipped her. He really did.
He said he couldn't live without her. He was so intense it
was actually quite frightening.

'It was quite late by now and there were just the two of us and I tried to be nice to him – you know, to look after him. I said to him that he probably shouldn't go home, not in the state he was in, and I suggested he go to bed in one of the rooms upstairs. We had half a dozen to choose from. Well, he thought that was a good idea and I offered to take him up and that was my mistake. One thing led to another, as my mum would say, and that's what happened.'

Nancy fell silent.

'He didn't love me,' she continued, eventually. 'He just felt bad about himself. Melissa was the love of his life and she'd been unfaithful to him, so if he did the same to her, maybe it would make him feel better about himself. More of a man. As for me, I don't know what was going on in my head. Perhaps I was flattered that someone like Francis Pendleton should be interested in the likes of me, but actually I wasn't thinking at all and certainly not about the consequences.'

She sighed.

'I must be stupid. It's not as if I don't know about the birds and the bees and all the rest of it. I nearly died when Dr Collins told me. Of course, he immediately assumed that I'd have the baby adopted. I didn't tell him who the father was. Actually, I lied. I told him it was someone I'd met in Bideford. I didn't want anyone to know. I couldn't see that any good would come of it. Not for Mr Pendleton, not for Melissa, not for me.

'In the end, I did tell Francis. We'd hardly seen each other at all since that one night and I got the feeling he was deliberately avoiding me so I wrote him a letter. He had to know! After all, it was his child and anyway, I needed help. I thought he might look after me. I didn't expect him to leave his wife or anything like that, but he had plenty of money and I thought that maybe he would help me set up somewhere and I'd have the baby and start a new life.

'Do you know what he did? The very next day after he got my letter, he sent me an envelope with sixty quid and the address of a doctor in London. He wanted me to have an abortion. That was all! He didn't want to talk to me. He didn't want to have anything to do with it. How could anyone be so cruel?'

'It was you who came to Clarence Keep just before Francis Pendleton was killed,' Pünd said.

'I didn't do it, Mr Pünd. I swear to you.' She drew a breath. 'You've got to understand how I was feeling. I'd been humiliated. I was ashamed ... and angry. Of course, everything was complicated after what had happened to Melissa, but I'd written to him *before* all that, so he didn't have any excuse for not talking to me. He'd dismissed me because it suited him to and because he looked down on me. I didn't mean anything to him. At the same time, I knew I had to do something – and soon. My mum was already looking at me peculiarly and it wouldn't be long before my dad noticed too.

'I went round to the house to have it out with him. If you want the truth, I was going to threaten him. Either you look after me properly or I'll tell the whole world what sort of man you are. It wasn't as if he had anything to lose. Melissa wasn't around any more. He had her house, her hotel, her fortune. He could look after me. I was going to tell him that he had to live up to his responsibilities – or else!

'When I got to Clarence Keep, I saw cars parked outside and I wondered what was going on. I didn't ring the doorbell. Instead, I went round to the living room and peeked in through the window. That was when I saw you and the chief inspector – and there were two policemen in uniform and all! I knew at once that this was the last place I wanted to be so I ducked and ran – round the back of the house and over the wall, through the trees and down to the main road.

'It was only afterwards, when I heard about Mr Pendleton, that I got scared. Everyone was talking about it in the village. He had been killed too! It didn't take me long to work out that I'd been at the house at exactly the same time it had happened and that if the truth about us ever came out, everyone would think that it was me. I certainly had a good reason to stick a knife in him, the way he'd treated me. You probably think that too.

'Everything seemed completely hopeless. I was going to get blamed and on top of that, with him gone there'd be nobody to look after me. There's no way I can even prove the baby's his. My mum wouldn't be able to do anything for me. And my dad would kill me.'

She choked up and Pünd handed her a glass of water. She took a few sips, then handed it back.

'I know what I did on the bridge was stupid and wrong, but I couldn't see any way out,' she said. 'I just thought it would be easier for everyone, including me and the baby, if I wasn't there any more. I thought about walking into the sea. I never learned to swim. But then I decided the bridge would be easier. So I went there and made a complete fool of myself and now I'm here and heaven knows what's going to happen next, because I've certainly got no idea.'

She had reached the end of her story. She fell silent.

Detective Chief Inspector Hare had listened to all this without commenting but now he was the first to speak. 'It's just as well you told us all this, Miss Mitchell,' he said. 'We're now investigating not one but two murders and your testimony may help us make sense of it all. I'm sure you need to get some rest, but there is one thing I must ask you. Did you see anyone come out of the house when you were at Clarence Keep? I'm not questioning what you told us, but you're correct in thinking you were at the scene of the crime when Mr Pendleton was killed. You say you saw Mr Pünd and myself through the window. Did you see anyone else?'

Nancy shook her head. 'I'm sorry, sir. I just wanted to get away. I didn't see anything.'

It was the answer Hare had been expecting but it was disappointing all the same. 'Very well,' he said. 'We'll say no more about what happened this morning. The important thing is to look after yourself. You should talk to your mother and I'm sure Dr Collins can help you. There are organisations that can counsel young women in your position. The Mission of Hope is one ... and there's Skene Moral Welfare. You don't need to feel you're on your own.'

'I also will try to help you,' Pünd said. 'The words that I spoke to you on the bridge, they were true.' He smiled at her. 'You must look after yourself and your child, but you can reach me at any time.' He took out a business card and placed it carefully on the table beside the bed. 'Everything will work itself out for the best,' he assured her. 'You must think of me always as a friend.'

He and Detective Chief Inspector Hare got up and left the room. They walked back down the corridor, heading towards the main stairs. Hare looked exhausted by what he had just heard. He shook his head ruefully. 'Who'd have thought it.' He sighed. 'And where do we go next? This whole business with Tawleigh-on-the-Water turns out to be like the first labour of Hercules.'

'To what do you refer, Chief Inspector?'

'The cleaning of the Augean stables. We've got Melissa James having an affair with Algernon Marsh at the same time as he's cheating her with his fake business schemes. Then there's Francis Pendleton taking advantage of Nancy Mitchell. Eric Chandler is a pervert. The Gardners are thieves. Is there any end to it?'

'It is, I think, the fifth labour of Hercules, the stables. But do not despair, my friend.' There was a twinkle in Pünd's eye. 'The end is very much in sight!'

'If only I could believe that!'

They had reached the ground floor and Pünd was about to reply when he stopped and exclaimed with surprise: 'Miss Cain!'

It was true. His assistant was standing at the front door, fully dressed, holding a suitcase. 'Mr Pünd!' She was equally surprised to see him.

'How are you feeling, Miss Cain?'

'I'm much better, thank you, sir. Are you going back to the hotel?'

'That is our intention.'

'Then I'll come with you if I may.' She hesitated. 'Are we going to be staying here very much longer?' she asked. 'I must be honest with you. What I saw in that house – I'm never going to get it out of my head! The sooner I'm back in London, the happier I'll be.'

'I completely understand your desire to leave this place. I am aware that this has been a terrible experience for you and again I must apologise. But it may please you to know that I will be returning to London tomorrow, Miss Cain. By then the entire mystery will have been solved.'

'You know who did it!' Hare exclaimed.

'I know who killed Melissa James and Francis Pendleton, but I take no credit, Detective Chief Inspector. This was your investigation and it was you who gave me the clue that revealed everything.'

'And what was that?'

'It was when you spoke of the plays of William Shakespeare and in particular the death of Desdemona in *Othello.*'

'That's very kind of you, Mr Pünd. But I'm afraid I don't have the faintest idea what you're talking about.'

'All will be revealed. There is just one more piece of

information that is required and our work will be con-
cluded.'

'And what is that?'

Pünd smiled. 'For what reason did Melissa James go
to church?'

SIXTEEN
PÜND SEES THE LIGHT

Atticus Pünd had no time for religion. During the war, he had been persecuted not for what he believed but for what he was, a Greek Jew whose great-grandfather had emigrated to Germany sixty years before he was born, unaware that although he was bettering his own life, his decision would lead to the extinction of almost his entire bloodline. When Pünd had found himself in Belsen, he had seen Jews praying together, begging their God to deliver them from evil. He had also seen them taken away and murdered. He had known then, not that he had ever doubted it, that even if God existed He preferred not to listen, and all the stars, crosses and crescent moons in the world would not make an iota of difference.

That was what he still believed but at the same time he understood the need for religion and respected it.

As he walked into the churchyard of St Daniel's, he reflected that Tawleigh-on-the-Water would be a much poorer place without it. Here was a little world of its own, a green haven closed in by beech trees, the fishermen and -women who had created this community over the years still part of it, lying in their graves. The church itself dated back to the fifteenth century: a neat, handsome structure made from the Cornish granite known as moorstone, with a truncated tower to the west in need of some repair. Pünd felt a great sense of calm. He could imagine an English village without religion but he could not imagine it without a church.

Melissa James had come here an hour before her death. Why?

Samantha Collins, the doctor's wife, had seen her from a bedroom window but there was no evidence that Melissa had any religious beliefs or any time for the church, even though she had elected to be buried here. Pünd could see the freshly dug grave, waiting patiently for the police to release the body. Had she met someone here? It was, after all, a good place for an assignation. It was private, set apart from the centre of the village. It was never locked.

Pünd turned the heavy iron ring and the door creaked open. The inside of the church was a surprise. It was somehow larger than the exterior had suggested, bright and very neat, with a blue carpet running between the pews to the altar at the far end. Above the altar, three stained-glass windows told the story of the life of St Daniel, and as Pünd moved closer he found himself bathed in light from the late-afternoon sun that slanted down, immersing him in different colours. To one side of him was a stone font. On the other, a monumental brass with an engraving of the lord of the manor who lay below. It was the whole span of life in a single glance.

He realised he was not alone. A woman had appeared, walking from behind the pulpit, carrying a vase of flowers. It was Samantha Collins. Pünd was not surprised to find her here. He had read in the notes that Hare had given him that she was devoted to the church.

'Oh … good afternoon, Mr Pünd.' She seemed momentarily startled. 'What are you doing here?'

'I came here for a moment of contemplation,' Pünd said, with a smile.

'Well, you're very welcome. I won't be very long. I'm just freshening up the flowers. And I've got to put up the hymn numbers. The organ is terribly old and wheezy, but it might just have enough strength to get through another blast of "Onward, Christian Soldiers".'

'Please do not let me interfere with your work. I will return, very soon, to the hotel.'

But Samantha had put down the flowers and with

sudden determination she came over to him. 'I understand you've arrested Algie,' she said.

'I have arrested nobody, Mrs Collins. It is Detective
Chief Inspector Hare who has taken your brother into
custody and who is speaking to him now.'

'I suppose you can't tell me what he's done.'

Pünd shrugged his shoulders. 'I'm sorry.'

'No, no. It's all right. I completely understand.' She
sighed. 'Algie's always been in trouble for one thing or
another for as long as I can remember. I sometimes wonder how we can possibly be related when we're so different.' She hesitated, then plunged in. 'Just tell me this. He
hasn't been arrested for the murder of Melissa James,
has he?'

'You suspect him of the crime, Mrs Collins?'

'No! Not at all! That's not what I meant.' She was
clearly horrified. 'Algie's capable of a lot of things but he
would never deliberately set out to hurt someone.'

And yet he had hurt someone, Pünd reflected. He
had left them lying on the side of the road.

'But it's just that I know he and Melissa were close,'
she went on. 'As I told you, he was her financial adviser.'

'Is that how he described the relationship to you?'

'Yes. It probably meant he was after her money, but
there was no crime in that. She had plenty to spare.'

There was something in her tone of voice that alerted

Pünd. He remembered what she had said when he had
met her at Church Lodge. The two women had not been
close. 'Would it be correct to say, Mrs Collins, that you
were not very fond of Miss James?'

'I disliked her, actually, Mr Pünd.' The words had
spilled out before she could stop them. 'I know it's wrong
of me. One should find it in one's heart to be kind. But I
disliked her a great deal.'

'May I ask why?'

'Because I think she was spoiling Tawleigh-on-the-
Water with her expensive hotel and her expensive car
and all the people who came down here – the fans – just
to catch sight of her. It wasn't even as if she had acted in
anything for years and years. I thought her a very super-
ficial woman.'

'Were you aware that she and your brother were having an affair?'

That threw her. 'Did he tell you that?'

'He confessed to an adulterous relationship. Yes.'

'Well, that's typical of Algie.' She was furious. 'I don't
care what happens to him. If he goes back into prison,
that's his affair. Adultery is a sin and I'm not having him
in the house any more. I should have listened to Leonard
from the start.' She went on, barely pausing to catch her
breath. 'As for her, that's exactly the sort of behaviour I'd
have expected from a Hollywood actress. I'm not excus-

ing Algie, not for a minute, but if you ask me there wasn't a man in the village who was safe from her. She even latched on to Leonard, always on at him to treat her for illnesses that only existed in her head. That was Melissa James. She got what she wanted and heaven help you if you stood in her way.'

Perhaps it was the mention of heaven that had done it. Samantha stopped herself and looked around her, as if she had reminded herself where she was. 'Of course it's wrong of me to say bad things about a dead woman and I hope God has mercy on her. But I didn't like her and I really think she could have done more for the church, especially as she's being buried here. I mean, I mentioned the organ just now. She knew about all the problems we were having and she never gave a penny to the restoration fund. As it happens, I'm in a position to take care of it myself now. But you'd have thought she could have put her hand in her pocket. She didn't have to be so selfish.'

'You said none of this when we first met, Mrs Collins.'

'Well, at the time it didn't feel appropriate.'

Pünd had picked up on what she had said. 'I understand that you have come into some money of your own,' he said, adding, 'It is very kind of you to wish to give it to the church.'

'I wouldn't dream of keeping it all to myself. Anyway,

it's a very large amount. It was left to me by an aunt who recently passed away.'

'And the organ? I would imagine that will be an expensive purchase.'

'Oh yes, Mr Pünd. An organ is the most expensive item in a church after the building itself, and this one is going to be specially built for us by Hele & Co in Plymouth. We may be talking about more than a thousand pounds but Leonard agrees with me, the church plays a vital role in the community and really it's the very least we can do.' She paused. 'The church roof also needs renovating so we may do that too.'

'It is more than generous of you, Mrs Collins.' Pünd was smiling but suddenly he looked puzzled. 'This aunt of yours. May I ask if she also left money to your brother in her will?'

Samantha's cheeks coloured. 'No,' she said. 'Algernon received nothing in the will. I'm afraid he disappointed her very badly when he was young and so she chose to cut him out. I was considering sharing some of the money with him, but – particularly in the light of what you've told me today – I don't feel that's a good idea. Curiously, my husband has been trying to persuade me otherwise. He's come to the conclusion that it's unfair to keep it all for ourselves. I can't think why as when we first heard the news, he didn't even want Algernon to know. But I don't care what he says. I've made up my mind. Do you think that's wrong of me?'

'I think it would be impertinent of me to offer you any advice, Mrs Collins. But I will say that I completely understand your way of thinking.'

'Thank you, Mr Pünd.' She turned and looked wistfully at the cross standing on the altar. 'I'd like to have a little time on my own, if you don't mind. It's so easy, isn't it, to give way to hatred and unchristian thoughts. I feel, perhaps, I should pray for Melissa James and also for my brother. We're all sinners in God's eyes.'

Pünd bowed discreetly and left her to her ministrations, reflecting that she might also have considered praying for herself. He left the church and stood outside in the bright sunlight, surrounded by the graves. From here he could see Church Lodge and the window from which Samantha Collins had noticed Melissa James. He smiled to himself. He should perhaps believe in the power of the church more. The chance encounter had told him everything he needed to know.

SEVENTEEN
AT THE MOONFLOWER HOTEL

The main lounge at the Moonflower Hotel had been closed for the morning. A sign on the door apologised to guests that owing to a private function, it would not be available until midday, but free biscuits and coffee were being served in the bar. In fact, there were thirteen people who had gathered together before ten o'clock, including himself and Detective Chief Inspector Hare, and although Pünd was not at all superstitious, he had to concede that the gathering was certainly going to be unlucky for one of them.

He was standing in the centre of the room, wearing a neat, old-fashioned suit, his rosewood walking stick drawing a diagonal line from his hand to the side of his right foot. With his wire-frame spectacles and his quiet, studious demeanour, he could easily have been mistaken for a local schoolteacher, brought in to give a lecture on the history of Tawleigh or the local wildlife perhaps; the sort of event that often took place at the Moonflower.

His audience consisted of all the different people – suspects or otherwise – who had been involved in the deaths of Melissa James and Francis Pendleton. It had been Detective Chief Inspector Hare who had decided to bring them together. The effect was a touch theatrical, he knew, but this was his last case and why should he not enjoy a dramatic conclusion, even if he wasn't the one who was going to be placed centre stage? That role was to be taken by Pünd.

Lance and Maureen Gardner, the general managers of the Moonflower, were perched on one sofa, already looking indignant, as if they had nothing to answer for, while Dr Collins and Samantha were on another, holding hands. Algernon Marsh had taken an armchair and was sitting with one leg over his knee, his hands folded in front of him. It was hard to believe that he was still under arrest and had only been brought here because Hare had arranged it. Simon Cox had also been summoned from London and was sitting in an identical armchair on the other side of the fireplace.

Eric Chandler and his mother had chosen two wooden chairs in front of a bookshelf. They were sitting next to each other but there was a wide space between them and they were avoiding each other's eyes. Nancy Mitchell, who had been released from hospital, had also come with her mother and it was obvious from the way the older woman held on to her daughter that she now knew the truth about her pregnancy. Miss Cain was next to them, poised with her notebook and pen. She did not look happy and Hare remembered that she would much rather have returned to London. After everything that had happened, she almost certainly wished she had never come at all.

'I am very glad to see everyone here today,' Pünd began. 'This has been a most unusual investigation – for two reasons. The first is that there were several people who had a motive to kill Melissa James. There were also a few people with a motive to kill Francis Pendleton. But to find the person with a motive to kill first one and then the other, from the very start that has been a challenge to me.

'The second peculiarity of this case was drawn to my attention by my assistant, Miss Cain.' He turned to her. 'I am aware that this has been a terrible experience for you but even so I am indebted to you for providing me with what I have called the ten moments in time. I have asked my good friend Detective Chief Inspector Hare to reproduce them so that we can all examine the events between five forty and six fifty-six on the day that Miss James was killed.'

Hare had copied what Miss Cain had written onto a larger sheet of paper so that everyone in the room could see what had been written. Using two drawing pins, he attached it to the wall between the windows, much to the annoyance of Maureen Gardner. 'We don't need holes in the wallpaper, thank you,' she muttered. He ignored her.

5.40 p.m.: Miss James leaves the Moonflower.
6.05 p.m.: Miss James arrives home.
6.15 p.m.: Francis Pendleton leaves Clarence Keep for the opera.
6.18 p.m.: Dog heard barking. Stranger arrives at Clarence Keep?
6.20 p.m.: Front door heard opening and closing at Clarence Keep.
6.25 p.m.: The Chandlers leave. The Austin has gone.
6.28 p.m.: Melissa James calls Dr Collins.
6.35 p.m.: Dr Collins leaves his home.
6.45 p.m.: Dr Collins arrives at Clarence Keep. Melissa James dead.
6.56 p.m.: Dr Collins calls police & ambulance.

'As you can see, there are just seventeen minutes in which Melissa James could have been killed,' Pünd went on. 'It is very unusual to have such a narrow window of opportunity and this has also very much influenced my investigation. For example, it is impossible for Dr Collins or his wife to have committed the crime as they were at home at 6.28 p.m. when the telephone call took place. We know that a call was made at that time by Miss James as it was logged by the local exchange and, indeed, Mrs Collins overheard it. We also know that she was distressed by something and in need of a doctor or a close friend – and Dr Collins was both. Something had made her cry. There were tissues with her tears both in the bedroom where she was eventually found and in the living room downstairs.

'Why, I wonder, in two places? This has always puzzled me. Where did her last, unhappy experience begin? If it was in the bedroom, why did she not pick up the telephone and call Dr Collins from there? If it was in the living room, what made her go back upstairs? The evidence would suggest that when she became upset, she spent more time in the bedroom ...'

'How do you know that?' Dr Collins asked.

'There were two discarded tissues in the bedroom but only one in the living room. And there is another mystery. What actually happened to upset her? We still have no idea. Was the killer actually in the house when she made the call? Melissa James certainly believed so. *"He's here. I don't know what he wants. I'm frightened."*

These are the words reported to us by Dr Collins, which he heard on the phone.'

Pünd turned back to the sheet of paper he had pinned to the wall.

'We can add certain other details to this period of time. We know now, for example, that Miss James had argued with her film producer, Simon Cox, before she left the hotel. The two of them had a parting of the ways. Did she return to Clarence Keep after this? No. For reasons that are unclear, she drove to the church of St Daniel's, where she was seen by Mrs Collins. Meanwhile, Mr Cox followed her home but in fact arrived ahead of her. Approaching the house, he heard an argument between Mrs Chandler and her son.'

'It was a private matter!' Phyllis half rose from her chair.

'We do not need to go into the details here, Mrs Chandler. Do not upset yourself, please.' He waited until she had sat down again. 'As a result of this disagreement, you and your son did not leave the house to visit your sister until 6.25 p.m. and it is your testimony that is of great value now. You heard the dog barking at 6.18 p.m. and two minutes later the front door opened and closed. As the dog was known to bark when strangers came to the house, you assumed that this was the moment when the man who would terrorise Melissa James entered the property and, ten minutes later, caused her to call Dr Collins.

'And where was Francis Pendleton during all this? We know that he did not attend the performance of *The Marriage of Figaro* as he pretended to do. It is quite possible that he did indeed leave the house at 6.15 p.m., using the French windows from the living room. He would not have been seen or heard. Or he could have remained and killed his wife. But if that were the case, why did she not say as much to Dr Collins on that last telephone call? If she knew the name of the man who was about to kill her, surely she would have wanted him to know!'

Pünd stood examining the chart.

'It does not work,' he admitted. 'I cannot make it work. It is something that I have written about in my book, *The Landscape of Criminal Investigation*. Sometimes the facts will be presented to the detective in a way that seems to make sense but which makes no sense at all, and if that occurs you must accept that they may not be facts at all, that hidden amongst them are misconceptions that are blinding you to the truth.' He paused. 'That is what I have done. Almost from the very start, I have attempted to find an alternative sequence of events that would explain how Melissa James died and I will confess to you that I would have failed completely but for the brilliance of the detective chief inspector. He compared the crime to the death of Desdemona in Shakespeare's *Othello* and at that moment he unlocked for me what must have taken place.'

'And I suppose one of us is Iago,' Algernon sneered. He seemed amused by the whole thing.

Pünd ignored him. 'Let us go back to my first question,' he went on. 'What was the motive for the murder of Melissa James and why did Francis Pendleton also have to die?' He turned to Lance Gardner. 'You, Mr Gardner, had a good reason to kill her. She had warned you that she was intending to investigate the management of the hotel.'

'I had nothing to hide,' Gardner replied.

'On the contrary. Thanks to the good offices of my assistant, Miss Cain, we know that you have a great deal to hide. I know about the overpayment of suppliers and the way in which you have diverted the refunds into your own account. I have given the evidence to the detective chief inspector.'

'I'll be wanting to talk to you and your wife as soon as this is over,' Hare said, grimly.

'If Melissa James were to die, there would be no examination and the money that you have stolen would remain undetected. You had a motive to kill not just Miss James but her husband too, as Francis Pendleton also suspected you of financial malfeasance and would have continued to pursue you.'

'We didn't kill anyone!' Maureen Gardner exclaimed.

'And what of Phyllis and Eric Chandler? They too might have had good reason to kill first Melissa and then Francis. They had a secret. Eric had been involved in a particularly unpleasant activity at Clarence Keep—'

'She didn't know anything about it!' Eric said. His voice was high-pitched and petulant.

'So you say. But how do we know that she had not discovered your secret and threatened you? Then, when her husband stumbled onto the truth, you killed him as well. It could have been either of you: Eric because he was afraid or his mother because she was ashamed. It could even have been both of you, working together. It seems to me quite feasible that the differences between you could have been exaggerated, and let me remind you that you, and only you, were in the house on both occasions at almost exactly the time the murders were committed.'

'It's a wicked lie!' Phyllis spat out the words.

But Pünd had already moved on to Nancy Mitchell. He was a little gentler now, but her part in all this still had to be explained. 'And then we come to you, Miss Mitchell.'

'My Nancy did nothing!' Brenda Mitchell clutched her daughter tighter.

'That is, of course, what you would believe, Mrs Mitchell. It is what I also, with all my heart, wish to believe. But although it is true that your daughter was working at the hotel at the time of the first murder, she was most certainly present on the occasion of the second.' Pünd sounded almost regretful as he turned to Nancy. 'You have admitted as much. You tell us a story about looking in through the window and running away but it would have been perfectly simple for you to slip in through the back door and kill Francis Pendleton with the Turkish knife before making your escape. He had treated you badly. You were angry. We have already discussed the reasons and there is no need to air them again in public. But I will ask this. Is there anyone else in the room who would have been more motivated to act in so reckless and perilous a fashion?'

Nancy fell silent, casting her eyes down. Her mother comforted her. Neither of them spoke.

'What about me?' Algernon asked. 'Aren't you going to accuse me of doing Melissa in?'

'You find this amusing, Mr Marsh?'

'Well, it's more entertaining than being stuck in jail.'

'I think you'd better get used to jail time,' Hare muttered. 'I have a feeling you're going to be doing a lot of it.'

'Of course you had a motive to kill Miss James,' Pünd

continued. 'She had invested a great deal of money in a business of yours but this was actually money that you were stealing from her. We know that she was having financial difficulties. What would you do if she asked for the money back? Your entire scheme would collapse.'

'But she didn't ask for it back. She and I were planning to get married. Everything she had would have been mine anyway, so I'm afraid that's where your little theory rather falls to the ground.'

'Ah yes. The letter that she sent to you. "*My darling darling . . .*" as she called you.'

'That's right.'

'No, Mr Marsh. It is not right. I do not believe that Miss James was involved in a relationship with you – at least certainly not of a romantic nature. I believe that you fabricated the entire story because you realised that you could use it to achieve your ends.'

Now Pünd turned to Samantha Collins.

'When we met in the church, you told me that you had recently inherited a very large sum of money but that your brother had not.'

'Yes.' Samantha was clearly uncomfortable at finding herself the centre of attention.

'You did not want your brother to know.'

'Well . . .'

'Dr Collins asked me not to mention that you were

going to London on the day we visited you at Church Lodge,' Pünd reminded her. He turned to the doctor. 'I take it that the reason for your journey was connected with the bequest?'

'Yes,' Dr Collins admitted. 'It was.'

'Later, when the detective chief inspector arrested him, your brother-in-law said something that interested me. "*I'm sure Leonard has got quite a few things to tell you.*" It struck me at once that in reality he was not speaking to me. He was sending a warning to you.'

The doctor smiled weakly. 'I'm not sure about that.'

'And then, in the church, Mrs Collins told me that you had, inexplicably, changed your mind and that you were attempting to persuade her to share the bequest with him.'

'Well, I was just playing devil's advocate.'

'And who is the devil in this instance?' Pünd smiled briefly. 'Was Algernon Marsh blackmailing you?' Dr Collins said nothing, so he went on. 'Let us imagine that it was not he who was having the affair with Melissa James, but you. He somehow discovered the truth – it is possible indeed that Miss James informed him. He knew what it would mean to your wife if she found out. This I have witnessed for myself. In the church, Mrs Collins spoke of the sin of adultery and said that she would never see her brother again. To discover that her husband, the father of her two children, was engaged in an immoral relationship with a married woman – one can see easily the consequences.'

'It's not true,' Dr Collins insisted.

'But it is true, Dr Collins. It is the reason why you murdered her. It is the only reason that makes any sense.'

'You're wrong, Mr Pünd!' Samantha Collins was staring at Pünd with a mixture of horror and disbelief. She had let go of her husband's hand. 'Leonard only went to the house because she wanted his help.'

'You did not hear what she said, Mrs Collins.'

'I didn't hear everything she said. No. But I did hear someone asking for help and I recognised her voice.'

'And what is it that had upset her?' Pünd had turned back to Dr Collins.

'I told you—'

'You lied to me!' Pünd strode back to the chart on the wall. 'And the ten moments of time. They also lied. Let us examine them again in the light of what we know.

'At 5.40 p.m., Melissa James leaves the hotel. She is upset after her altercation with Simon Cox and she goes to the church of St Daniel's because it is opposite the house of the man she loves. She wishes to see Dr Collins and to tell him that she will be alone that night. Francis Pendleton is at the opera. They can meet. But before she can speak to him, she must check that he is on his own.

She looks at the house and sees Mrs Collins watching her from an upstairs window. What is she to do? She turns and enters the church as if that was the reason for her being there.

'At 6.05 p.m. she returns home, where Francis Pendleton is waiting for her. He knows that she is being unfaithful to him. He loves her more than anything in the world and the thought of losing her drives him to insanity. The two of them argue. Mrs Chandler does not hear this. She is a little deaf and anyway, she and her son are one floor down, in the kitchen, which has been built with thick walls. We will never know what is said between the husband and the wife. Perhaps he accuses her and she admits the truth and tells him that their marriage is over. That is what she had threatened to do in the letter she wrote but never sent. And so, in a fit of rage, Francis takes hold of the telephone cord and strangles her. It is 6.18 p.m. and the little dog is outside the room. He does not bark because a stranger has arrived at the front door. He barks because he has the instincts of many animals and knows that great violence is being done to his mistress.

'Francis Pendleton is in a rage. He is exactly as the detective chief inspector described. He has become Othello, strangling the one true love of his life. And then, when he sees what he has done, he turns and runs from the house. That is the sound of the door opening and closing which Mrs Chandler hears at 6.20 p.m. Of course, he does not go to the opera. He drives away. He sits and considers what he has done. He is full of remorse and fear and despair. When I saw him, even a week later, I knew that this was a man who had lost everything that mattered to him.'

'So he did kill her!' Miss Cain exclaimed.

'He did not kill her,' Pünd replied. 'This is where we made the mistake. What happens in the play of *Othello*? Othello wrongly believes that Desdemona is having an affair and strangles her. Iago's wife, Emilia, enters the room and Othello confesses what he has done. "*She's dead*," he says. "*Still as the grave ... I have no wife.*"

'But he is wrong! A few moments later, Emilia hears something and calls out: "*What cry is that? ... that was my lady's voice.*" It turns out that Desdemona has not yet been killed but is only unconscious. She recovers long enough to claim that Othello is innocent of the crime. And then she dies.

'This is what occurred with Melissa James. Strangulation can kill in many ways. Preventing blood flow and oxygen from reaching the brain is the most common. It can cause a heart attack. An artery may be torn. But what is perhaps less well known is that with strangulation, although unconsciousness will occur in seconds, death may take several minutes.

'So let us imagine what Francis Pendleton perceives. He strangles his wife. He believes she is dead. She falls and knocks her head against the bedside table. There is blood. She is not moving. Thinking that he has killed her, he runs out of the house. From this moment on, he believes himself guilty of murder.

'But a few minutes later, Melissa James recovers. She is alone in the house for the Chandlers have now left. She finds herself in the bedroom and she is distraught, with tears pouring down her cheeks. She has almost been killed! She uses not one but two paper tissues, dropping them to the floor. What will she do? She must call the man she loves and who, she believes, is in love with her. But she cannot call him from the bedroom as the telephone has been torn from the wall. So she must go downstairs to the living room to call him from there. Taking another tissue, she makes her way down.

'She calls Dr Collins at 6.28 and tells him that Francis Pendleton has tried to kill her. Dr Collins immediately leaves his home and arrives at Clarence Keep at 6.45 p.m. The time is in fact immaterial. When he gets there, Melissa is lying on her bed. She can barely speak.

'And what happens next?

'Dr Collins has been having an affair with Melissa James. One can understand the attraction. She is a glamorous Hollywood star. She owns a beautiful house, a hotel. She is about to appear in a new film. He has been thinking, perhaps, of leaving his ordinary wife and his boring life in a small seaside village. But everything has changed with the death of a relative who has left Samantha Collins an enormous amount of money. And Melissa has debts. Her business is failing. Suddenly, life with her seems less attractive.

'But at the same time, Melissa is demanding that they reveal their affair. What is it that she wrote in her letter? *'We have to be brave and tell the world our destiny.'* If Melissa speaks out as she threatens, he will lose not just his wife but her inheritance. For him it is an impossible situation.

'And suddenly he sees his opportunity. Everything has been prepared for him. Melissa James has been attacked. He was at home with his wife when she called him. The call will have been registered. Quickly, he takes hold of the telephone cord and continues the work that Francis Pendleton began, only, being a doctor, he knows how long he must apply pressure and he can also recognise the moment when life has been extinguished. The only evidence? There are two sets of ligature marks.

These, Detective Chief Inspector Hare notices, but he assumes, not unreasonably, that they were made during the struggle.

'Dr Collins kills Melissa James and calls the police. His story will be that he came to the house and found her dead. He does not tell them that she had named her husband as the attacker. It might have been tempting to do this, to say that Melissa had identified him – but he cannot be sure at what time Francis left the house and whether Melissa was seen still living after he had gone. Anyway, it does not matter to him. He knows that Francis Pendleton will be the most obvious suspect whatever he says. He makes, however, a second mistake which is of greater importance. He has handled the telephone and wipes it clean to remove his fingerprints. As I remarked to you, Detective Chief Inspector, this is something that Francis would not have needed to do.'

There was a stunned silence in the room. Everyone was staring at Leonard Collins. His wife was physically recoiling from him in shock. Algernon was half smiling, amazed that his brother-in-law should have been capable of such a thing – and yet the smile faded as he realised that any chance of his getting a share of the inheritance had just evaporated. Phyllis Chandler was horrified. Madeline Cain looked shocked.

Dr Collins got to his feet. He stood there like a man facing an execution squad. 'I really did think I would get away with it,' he said.

'Leonard ... ' Samantha began.

'I'm sorry, Sam. But he's right. Everything he said. A boring life, a boring wife ... I dreamed of bigger things. Say goodbye to the children for me.' He walked to the door and jerked it open. There was a uniformed police-man waiting on the other side. 'You'll forgive me if I don't listen to the rest of it,' he said. 'I think I'd prefer to be on my own.'

He went through the door, closing it behind him. There was a long silence. Samantha buried her face in her hands. Miss Cain wrote something in her pad and underlined it.

'So he killed her!' Hare couldn't believe what he had just heard. 'It all makes complete sense, Mr Pünd. It's ex-traordinary. But there's one thing you haven't explained. Why did he kill Francis Pendleton?'

'He did not kill Francis Pendleton,' Pünd replied. 'I'm afraid to say, Detective Chief Inspector, that I know, perfectly well, the person responsible for the death of Mr Pendleton.'

'And who was that?'

'It was me.'

EIGHTEEN
SITUATION VACANT

'I have a confession to make,' Pünd continued. 'I was at Clarence Keep when Francis Pendleton was killed and I see now that I was in some ways responsible for his death.'

'You killed him?' Algernon asked, incredulously.

'No, Mr Marsh. I was not the one who stabbed him with the knife, but if I had been more observant or if I had proceeded more rapidly with my deductions, it is a death that might have been avoided.'

'Nobody could have done more than you, Mr Pünd,' Miss Cain muttered. She was looking at him disapprovingly.

'It is kind of you to say so, Miss Cain. But I have learned a lesson in Tawleigh-on-the-Water and it is one that I will discuss one day in my book.'

'I think you'd better make a clean breast of it, Mr Pünd,' the detective chief inspector suggested.

Pünd nodded.

'It is strange,' he said, 'but standing on the balcony of my room on the night that you and I had dinner together, I had a strange presentiment that I should not have taken this case and events have proved me right. With your assistance I have solved the murder of Melissa James, but Francis Pendleton is another matter altogether.

'Once again I must ask, why was he killed? Who in this room would have had a motive to silence him? I have suggested already that Nancy Mitchell had the greatest animosity towards him and with good reason. The Gardners, perhaps, had reason to fear him. Mrs Chandler and her son, without doubt, felt threatened by him.'

'I never touched him!' Eric wailed.

'Oh stop snivelling, you big baby,' Phyllis hissed under her breath.

'Algernon Marsh is a ruthless operator who would do anything to protect his business enterprise. And we have yet to consider Samantha Collins.'

Samantha had been sitting as if in a trance from the moment her husband had confessed to the first murder. One of the policemen had brought in a cup of strong tea but she hadn't touched it. She was clearly in shock. Now she roused herself and looked up. 'What do you mean?'

'In the church you told me of your dislike of Melissa James. I wondered briefly if it might have driven you to kill her. You strike me, if I may say, as the sort of woman who would do anything to protect her good reputation, her family, her children. What if Francis Pendleton knew of the relationship between his wife and your husband? What might you do to prevent him from making it public?'

'That's ridiculous!'

'It was a thought only.' Pünd dismissed it. 'All these ideas came into my head, but I have dismissed each and every one of them. The Gardners may be petty criminals but they are not killers. Mr Marsh could have killed a man behind the wheel of his car, but he does not have the courage to do such an act deliberately. You, Miss Mitchell, are a good person and I wish you only happiness in your later life. Mrs Chandler, you could be more forgiving of your son, who needs, I would have said, your help rather than your anger. He, too, could not have committed this act of violence, and if he had, he would not have had the ability to disappear with the speed that was required.'

'So who was it?'

He looked around him.

'I will tell you why I should not be here,' he went on. 'I was approached by an American agent, a man named Edgar Schultz, who described himself as a senior partner at the agency of William Morris in New York. It was the first time I had been employed by a client I had never met and this made me uneasy from the start. I did make a brief investigation and can tell you that there is indeed such a man and he did represent Melissa James.

'In my dealings with Mr Schultz, however, I noticed at once certain peculiarities. The letter that he sent me, for example, was addressed to "Mr Pünd", but it is the practice in America to add a full stop after "Mr". The full stop in this case was absent. And then there was the subsequent telephone call in which the sound quality was remarkably good. During the brief conversation, the man to whom I was speaking mentioned "*some bright spark in the office*" who had suggested contacting me. This struck me as a particularly English turn of phrase and it seemed strange coming out of the mouth of an American. As I say, I noticed these two anomalies but I set them aside. The letter could have been typed in haste. Mr Schultz could have English ancestry.

'Last night, which was much too late, I telephoned Mr Schultz myself and knew at once that it was not the same man I had spoken to in my apartment in London. He confirmed that he had never written to me and did not know of my involvement. I have no right to be here in Tawleigh-on-the-Water. I was never, in truth, employed.'

'That's impossible!' Miss Cain exclaimed. 'I called

William Morris myself. The assistant put me through to Mr Schultz's office.'

'It is a mystery, is it not, how this trick was performed, Miss Cain. Is it possible that you could have asked the operator for the wrong number?'

'I hardly think so.'

'You were, I recall, very keen that I should involve myself in this matter.'

'I thought you'd find it interesting. There wasn't very much else on your desk.'

'That was the only reason?'

'What other reason could there possibly be?'

'Let us consider your behaviour since you arrived in Tawleigh-on-the-Water. When we first drove to Clarence Keep, you were, I would have said, quite awestruck by the sight of the house. You described it as "lovely" and then "gorgeous". I did not know you well but it struck me as out of character as you did not often venture an opinion. I also observed that you had considerable knowledge of the work of Miss James. At the house, you were puzzled that there should be a poster of *The Wizard of Oz* as she had not appeared in that film. Later, when we were speaking with Mrs Collins, you recognised an allusion to another of her films, *Pastures Green*.'

'Of course I knew her work, Mr Pünd. Doesn't everyone?'

'You would describe yourself as a fan?'

'Well . . . '

'It is an interesting word, that. There are some who believe it is a shortened version of "fanatic".'

'I really don't know what you're getting at.'

'Then I will enlighten you. I will begin first with a letter from one of Melissa James's most devoted fans.' Pünd produced a letter written on lilac paper in large, neat handwriting. Lance Gardner recognised it. The letter had been sent to the hotel. He had given it to Melissa himself. '"*The screen is diminished without you*,"' Pünd read. '"*A light has gone out of our lives*."' He lowered the page. 'Do you recognise those words?'

Miss Cain took a deep breath. 'I wrote them,' she admitted.

'You did not wish me to know that,' Pünd continued. 'Which is why you seemed to faint when we were in Miss James's bedroom. You knocked a pile of letters to the floor. You had seen your own letter on the top and knew that I would recognise your handwriting. Then, when you handed the pile back to me, you turned it upside down. It was a clever trick, that . . . '

'Well, it was a personal matter,' Miss Cain protested.

'As personal as the theft of an intimate item of clothing from Miss James's bedroom drawer?' Pünd looked at her angrily. 'For reasons we do not need to discuss at this present time, his mother was convinced that Eric had taken it.'

'I didn't!' Eric was quick to defend himself.

'I believe you. A man who has been found guilty of breaking into a bank will not deny stealing the money! You had already admitted to one misdemeanour. You had no reason to deny a second. But if it was not you, who was it?' He turned back to his assistant. 'You were left alone in the house, Miss Cain. This was after you had pretended to become faint. You had ample opportunity to enter the bedroom.'

Madeline Cain twisted in her seat. 'I've had enough of this!' she exclaimed. 'First you accuse me of lying to you. And now you say I'm a thief.'

'I am saying that you are a fanatic,' Pünd said. 'Melissa James attracted many people who wrote to her and who adored her and who came to Tawleigh only to see her. You were one of them. You had a fanatical admiration for her.'

'There's no crime in that.'

'But murder is a crime. Just now, when Dr Collins was exposed as Melissa James's killer, you appeared shocked. Why was that?'

'I'm not answering any more of your questions, Mr Pünd.'

'Then I will tell you. You were shocked because when

you murdered Francis Pendleton you did so in error. You killed the wrong man!'

The silence in the room was extraordinary. Now all the attention was on Miss Cain.

'You were in the room when the detective chief inspector accused Francis Pendleton of the murder, and of course Francis believed that he was guilty and confessed. He had no way of knowing that his wife had in fact recovered and had subsequently been strangled by someone else. He said he was glad that it was all over and that he would make a full confession.

'At this point, he went upstairs to collect his jacket and his shoes and all would have been well except that we were then distracted by the arrival of Miss Mitchell at the window. The detective chief inspector and I left the house immediately. The uniformed officers, also, were occupied with searching for the intruder. Eric Chandler and his mother were upstairs. That left you alone on the ground floor of the house, and you were there, moments later, when Francis Pendleton returned. You acted without thinking. I believe that you were motivated by an uncontrollable sense of anger and outrage. You picked up the Turkish dagger, climbed the stairs towards him and stabbed him in the chest.

'Moments later, the detective chief inspector and I arrived through the front door. You had your back to us so we were unable to see that you must have had a great deal of blood on you. And that is why you embraced Francis Pendleton as he fell – to conceal the blood that was already there. I do not think that it was an act of murder for you, Miss Cain, at least not in your mind. It was an act of retribution.'

Madeline Cain did not attempt to deny it. Her face was filled with a dreadful indifference, a sense that she had been right to do what she had done. She was on the edge of madness. 'I thought he had killed her,' she said, simply. She glanced accusingly at Hare. 'That's what you said. It was your fault.' She turned back to Pünd. 'And he confessed. I heard him.'

'There was no need to kill him!' Hare exclaimed. 'If he had been found guilty, the law would have taken its due course.'

Pünd shook his head sadly. 'But there, again, I am to blame. Just before I left London, I wrote a speech. In it, I suggested that capital punishment in this country might soon be abolished, and that in the last fifty years, almost half the death sentences handed down by the courts were commuted. Miss Cain typed it for me and we even discussed it.'

'If it was Francis Pendleton who killed her, he should have been hanged.' Madeline Cain was refusing to confront the fact that she had made a terrible mistake. Her eyes were out of focus. There was a strange half-smile on her lips. 'Melissa James was a force of nature. She was one of the greatest actresses this country has ever produced and it was just as I wrote in my letter. Now that she has gone, a light has been extinguished for ever.' She stood up. 'I'd like to go now.'

'I have just one question for you, Miss Cain,' Pünd said. 'Who was it on the telephone who called me, playing the part of Edgar Schultz?'

'It was a friend of mine, an actor. But he wasn't part of it. I just asked him to do it as a joke.'

'I see. Thank you.'

Hare went over to her. 'I'll drive you to the police station, Miss Cain.'

'That's very kind of you, Detective Chief Inspector.' She looked at him beseechingly. 'Do you think, just one last time, we could go past Clarence Keep?'

*

'Well, Mr Pünd, I suppose this is where we say goodbye.'

It was later that afternoon and Detective Chief Inspector Hare and Atticus Pünd were standing on the platform at Barnstaple station.

All the other witnesses had left the Moonflower Hotel. Algernon Marsh was on his way back to his cell in the police station in Barnstaple. He would be joined there by Lance and Maureen Gardner, who also had questions to answer. Pünd had been sorry to see Eric Chandler and his mother leave separately, still not speaking to each other. Was Phyllis Chandler really so disgusted by her son's behaviour, he wondered, or had she realised that she was in part responsible for the mess that his life had become?

At least Nancy Mitchell had departed on a more positive note. After Miss Cain had gone, she had approached Pünd with her mother and it had seemed evident to him that the two women shared a strength that had not been there before.

'I want to thank you, Mr Pünd,' she said. 'For what you did on the bridge.'

'I am glad that I was able to help you, Miss Mitchell. This has been a painful experience for everyone, but I hope you will soon be able to recover from what has happened.'

'I'm going to look after her,' Brenda Mitchell said, taking her daughter's hand. 'And we're going to keep the baby if that's what Nancy wants. I don't care what my husband says. I'm tired of being bullied by him.'

'I wish you both great happiness,' Pünd said, thinking that at least some good had come out of the events at the Moonflower Hotel.

Simon Cox had driven back to London. He had offered Pünd a lift, which the detective had declined. 'You're remarkable, Mr Pünd,' the businessman had said. 'Someone should make a film about you.' His eyes had brightened. 'Perhaps we could talk about that!'

'I think not, Mr Cox.'

Pünd had looked for Samantha Collins but she had left on her own. Hare had assured him that a policewoman would look in on Church Lodge to make sure that she and the children were all right.

The train, pulled by an old LMR 57 steam engine, puffed into the station with a great clanking of wheels and an exploding cloud of white vapour. Porters hurried forward as the doors opened and the first passengers got out.

'What will you do when you get back to London?' Hare asked.

'The first thing will be to find a new assistant,' Pünd replied. 'It seems that there is now a situation vacant.'

'Yes. It's too bad about that. I thought she was actually very helpful – when she was being helpful, I mean.'

'It is true. And what of you, my friend? You now begin your retirement!'

'That's right,' Hare replied. 'And thanks to you, I bow out on a high note. Not that I deserve any credit.'

'On the contrary, it was entirely down to you that the mystery was solved.'

The two men shook hands and then, carrying his case, Pünd climbed onto the train. Doors were being slammed shut all around him and a few seconds later the driver blew the whistle and released the brakes and with another burst of hissing and grinding, the train pulled out.

Hare watched it as it left the station and stood there until it had disappeared far down the track, then turned round and walked back to his car.

Moonflower Murders

The Book

It was a strange experience returning to *Atticus Pünd Takes the Case* after so many years. By and large, I don't reread books that I have edited, just as many of the authors I know seldom return to their earlier works. The act of editing, like the act of writing, is so intensive and occasionally so fraught with problems that no matter how pleased I may be with the finished product, I'm always happy to put it behind me. I don't need to go back.

And how did I feel as Detective Chief Inspector Hare walked back to his car and I turned the last page? It had taken me an entire afternoon and part of the evening to finish the book and I was afraid it had all been a complete waste of time.

On the face of it, *Atticus Pünd Takes the Case* had

almost no connection with the events that took place at Branlow Hall in June 2008. There is no wedding, no visiting advertising executive, no Romanian maintenance man, no sex in the wood. The story is set in Devon, not Suffolk. Nobody is beaten to death with a hammer. In fact, many of the incidents in the book are quite fantastical: a famous actress being strangled – twice! – the clue from *Othello*, the crazed fan writing on lilac paper, an aunt dying and leaving an inheritance of seven hundred thousand pounds. Alan clearly made these up and had no need to travel to Branlow Hall for inspiration.

And yet, unless I'd got everything wrong from the start, Cecily Treherne had read the book and had come away convinced that Stefan Codrescu was innocent. She had rung her parents in the South of France and told them: '*It was right there – staring me in the face.*' That was what she had said, according to her father. I had just read the book from cover to cover. I thought I knew all the facts about the real murder. And yet I still had no idea what Cecily had actually seen.

Somewhat to my own surprise, I had enjoyed the book, even though I was aware of the identity of the two killers from the start. As much as Alan Conway disliked writing murder mysteries and even looked down on the genre, he was undoubtedly good at what he did. There's something very satisfying about a complicated whodunnit that actually makes sense, and some of the pleasure I'd had reading the manuscript for the first time all those years ago came back to me now. Alan never cheated the reader. I think that was part of his success.

Not that it had been a lot of fun dealing with him. I must have spent hours working on the details, going over those ten moments in time, for example, making sure that they actually stitched together and that everything made sense. Most of the editing work was done over the Internet – Alan and I had always had a fractious relationship – but we did sit down together once in my London office and as I reread the book in the garden of Branlow Hall, I was reminded of the arguments we'd had on that long autumn afternoon. Why did he have to be so unpleasant? It's one thing for writers to defend their work. But he would raise his voice and jab his finger and make me feel that I was somehow trespassing in the sacred fields of his imagination rather than trying to help him sell the bloody thing.

For example, I would have liked him to have opened with Atticus Pünd. It was his story after all, and I wondered if readers would put up with four whole chapters before they met him. Nor was I happy with the chapter entitled 'The Ludendorff Diamond', which really sits as a short story outside the main investigation and has nothing to do with what happens in Tawleigh-on-the-Water. I wanted to drop it but he wouldn't listen. I might have rubbed a nerve because we both knew that, at seventy-two thousand words, the book had come in under length. This didn't matter terribly: quite a few Agatha Christie novels are short. *By the Pricking of My Thumbs* and *Death on the Nile* (a masterpiece) both sit in the high sixties. Taking out the theft of the diamond would reduce the book almost to the length of a novella and might damage its commercial chances, but the simple truth was that Alan wasn't prepared to do the necessary work to bulk out the rest of it so I was stuck with what he'd given me. I do like the chapter, by the way. It was my idea to put the tear in the wallpaper in Melissa James's bedroom so that at least there would be some excuse for including it.

Our most serious disagreement concerned the character of Eric Chandler. Eric had struck me as a fairly unsympathetic creation, and this was some years before modern sensibilities would make any author think twice before introducing a disabled character. Giving a man a club foot is one thing. Making him an overgrown child with a sexual perversion seemed almost deliberately offensive, somehow equating disability with inadequacy. Of course, at the time I had no idea that he was based on Derek Endicott, the night manager at Branlow Hall. It was, as Lawrence Treherne had said, a particularly cruel caricature and if I'd known about him I'd have fought all the harder.

I also came to blows with Alan over a moment in the denouement. When Atticus Pünd visits Nancy Mitchell in hospital – after saving her life on the bridge – he tells her that he will always be her friend and wants to help her. And yet, a couple of chapters later, he accuses her of murdering Francis Pendleton. 'He's hardly very kind!'

'He does it for effect!' I still remember Alan sneering at me in that slightly superior way of his.

'But it's not in character.'

'It's a convention. The detective gathers all the suspects and he picks them off one by one.'

'I know that, Alan. But does he have to pick on her?'

'Well, what do you suggest, Susan?'

'Does she even need to be in the scene?'

'Of course she has to be in the scene! The scene won't work without her!'

In the end, he softened it slightly – though with plenty of ill grace. I still didn't like it.

And so it went on. As I've mentioned, Alan liked to hide things in his books and it occurred to me now that he might have fought against some of the edits I wanted to make because I was unknowingly removing some of the secret messages that were so precious to him: Easter eggs, I suppose you might call them now. I've already mentioned that I disliked the name Algernon because I thought it was a bit pantomime. I thought it was unlikely that Algernon would have been driving a French-manufactured Peugeot in 1953. I didn't like the Latin numerals in the chapter called 'Darkness Falls'. They seemed to me to be stylistically out of keeping with the rest of the book. And, for the same reason, I was unhappy with the real people who cropped up throughout the text: Bert Lahr, Alfred Hitchcock, Roy Boulting, and so on.

He refused to change any of these.

I also had problems with 'Darkness Falls' as a chapter title – and this was definitely one of his Easter eggs. Despite everything, Conway revered Agatha Christie and often stole ideas from her. 'Darkness Falls' and the descriptions of Tawleigh at night are an obvious riff on her novel *Endless Night*, just as another chapter, 'Taken by the Tide', pays homage to *Taken at the Flood*. Using *Othello* to plant a clue is very much in her style; after all, she named four of her novels after Shakespeare's plays. She even makes a guest appearance in the text. On the train down to Devon, Miss Cain is reading the new Mary Westmacott, which was, in fact, Christie's nom de plume.

It wasn't just me. The copy editor got slapped down too. She had various issues, but one that I do remember was the LMR 57 steam engine that arrives to carry Pünd back to London in the final chapter. It was actually withdrawn a hundred years before the story takes place. It operated on the Liverpool and Manchester Railway rather than in Devon and it was mainly used for freight. Alan didn't care. 'Nobody will notice,' he said and it stayed in. But why? Surely it wouldn't have been so difficult to make the change. She also agreed with me that it would have been very hard to find a right-hand-drive Peugeot in 1953.

None of these discussions seemed to have any relevance to the question of who had actually killed Frank Parris, though. But the fact was, Alan knew the truth. He'd told his partner James Taylor when he got back from Branlow Hall, '*They've got the wrong man.*' So why did he hide it? Why hadn't he told the police? It was a question I had asked myself before, but after reading *Atticus Pünd Takes the Case* I was none the wiser, even if it now seemed that it contained not one but two sets of solutions between its covers. How could I get the book to unlock its secrets?

I began with the names.

Alan always played games with the names of his characters. In *Night Comes Calling*, the fourth Pünd novel, they were all English rivers. In *Atticus Pünd Abroad*, they were manufacturers of fountain pens. It didn't take me very long to work out what he had done in *Atticus Pünd Takes the Case*. Although some of them are quite obscure, the names all belong to famous crime writers. Eric and Phyllis Chandler give it away. Obviously, that's Raymond Chandler, who created Philip Marlowe, perhaps the most iconic of private detectives. Algernon Marsh comes from Ngaio Marsh, Madeline Cain from James M. Cain, who wrote *The Postman Always Rings Twice* and the wonderful *Double Indemnity*, Nancy Mitchell from Gladys Mitchell, who wrote over sixty crime novels – Philip Larkin was a fan.

But Alan had been cleverer than that. He had also linked each one of the main characters to the people he had met and interviewed at Branlow Hall, giving many of them the same initials and all of them similar-sounding first names. One example is Lance Gardner (from Erle Stanley Gardner), who had so offended Lawrence Treherne. Another is Dr Leonard Collins, who clearly has a connection with Lionel Corby (LC). By the same token, the Latvian producer Sīmanis Čaks must relate to Stefan Codrescu, although it's interesting that he has almost no role in the book. He isn't even really a suspect.

I realised that if I was going to work out what was going on in Alan Conway's mind, I had to draw some sort of map between the worlds of Branlow Hall in Suffolk and Tawleigh-on-the-Water in Devon, and the most obvious landmarks were all these characters and their relationships both to each other and to their real-life counterparts. I had finished the book sitting at one of the tables outside the hotel, but now the sun had gone in so I returned to my room, grabbed a notepad and sketched out the following.

MELISSA JAMES

Name taken from: P. D. James, author of *Innocent Blood* and *A Taste for Death*. Or possibly Peter James (he provided a quote for the book!).

Character based on: Lisa Treherne, Cecily's sister.

Notes: The characters have very little in common except for their first name: Lisa/Melissa. There is also one mention of the actress having a scar on her face (page 7). Lisa Treherne was possibly having sex with Stefan Codrescu, as seen by Lionel Corby. But in *APTTC*, Melissa is having an affair with Dr Leonard Collins.

Alan Conway's wife was also called Melissa and she seems to have had a close relationship with the gym instructor, Lionel Corby (LC). Is Alan suggesting the two of them were having an affair?

FRANCIS PENDLETON

Name taken from: American crime writer Don Pendleton, author of *The Executioner.*
Character based on: Frank Parris.
Notes: As well as the shared initials (FP), Conway clearly connects Pendleton with Parris. They both have curly hair and dark skin and on page 14 of *APTTC*, Francis is said to own a sailing boat called *Sundowner*, which is also the name of Frank's advertising agency in Australia.

Both men are murdered, one with a knife, the other with a hammer. Another connection. But there is nothing in the book that comes anywhere near Madeline's motive for killing Francis.

NANCY MITCHELL

Name taken from: Gladys Mitchell, author of the Mrs Bradley mysteries.

Character based on: Natasha Mälk. (Aiden told me the full name of the maid who found the body and the initials match.)

Notes: Not much to go on here as although Conway would have met Natasha, I never did. Nancy's affair with Francis doesn't seem to have any echoes in real life. Frank, after all, was gay!

MADELINE CAIN

Name taken from: James M. Cain.
Character based on: Melissa Conway?
Notes: There are no obvious similarities beyond the MC initials, but it might have amused Alan to turn his ex-wife into a crazed film fan and a killer. Alan had decided to get rid of Madeline anyway – he wanted James Fraser to appear in book 4.

DR LEONARD COLLINS

Name taken from: hard to be sure. It could be Michael Collins, pseudonym of American author Dennis Lynds, who wrote detective short stories. Or possibly Wilkie Collins, author of *The Woman in White* and *The Moonstone?*

Character based on: Lionel Corby (LC)

Notes: This is puzzling. Dr Leonard Collins is a murderer and a major character in *APTTC*. But he kills Melissa James, not Francis Pendleton. So is Alan deliberately saying that Lionel Corby did not kill Frank?

Also, there's one killer involved in the murder at Branlow Hall, but two killers at the Moonflower. I can't quite make sense of this.

SAMANTHA COLLINS

Name taken from: same as Leonard Collins.

Character based on: Cecily Treherne?

Notes: It's quite difficult to see where Samantha has come from and although she is briefly suspected, she only plays a small part in *APTTC*. The names Cecily and Samantha begin with the same homophone and on page 43 her face is described as 'square and serious', which would fit both women.

SIMON COX (SĪMANIS ČAKS)

Name taken from: Anthony Berkeley Cox, who wrote *The Poisoned Chocolates Case* in 1929. A second link with *APTTC* – another of his books was adapted by Alfred Hitchcock into the 1941 film *Suspicion*.

Character based on: Stefan Codrescu.

Notes: It's interesting that Simon Cox has only a relatively small part to play in *APTTC*, even though Stefan Codrescu is the central figure in the murder of Frank Parris. He isn't even a suspect really.

At the same time, Alan Conway takes a mean delight in characterising him not just as an Eastern European (Stefan from Romania, Simon from Latvia) but also as 'a small-time gangster who had just been released from jail', which is how Melissa describes him on page 51.

Did Alan believe Stefan was guilty of the crime? Or did he know he was innocent and just take pleasure in taunting him?

LANCE GARDNER/MAUREEN GARDNER

Name taken from: Erle Stanley Gardner – creator of *Perry Mason*.

Characters based on: Lawrence and Maureen Treherne.

Notes: Lance and Maureen depicted as petty crooks... probably for Alan Conway's personal amusement. They have no involvement in either murder. Lawrence would have been right to sue!

ERIC CHANDLER/PHYLLIS CHANDLER

Name taken from: Raymond Chandler

Characters based on: Derek Endicott – and presumably his mother.

Notes: As with the Gardners, Alan Conway doesn't seem to connect Derek Endicott to the murder of Frank Parris, although there's something he may have missed. Suppose Parris wasn't the intended target ... ?

The 'Peeping Tom' subplot plus poking fun at people with disabilities is vintage Conway. Did he meet Derek's mother? Maybe I should!

ALGERNON MARSH

Name taken from: Dame Ngaio Marsh, New Zealand's greatest crime writer, creator of the Roderick Alleyn detective stories.

Character based on: Aiden MacNeil, obviously ... as he had noticed (AM).

Notes: Aiden refused to talk to Alan. 'I met him ... for about five minutes. I didn't terribly like him.' In return, Alan turns him into a minor crook, close to a caricature. Alan's revenge? No suggestion, though, that he is a killer.

So much for the names. If Alan Conway had wanted to make it easy for me, then Francis Pendleton would have been killed by a character with the same initials as someone at Branlow Hall and that would have told me who had killed Frank Parris.

And now that I thought about it, that was exactly what had happened. Madeline Cain had killed Francis. So did Melissa Conway kill Frank? They were both 'MC'.

Even so, I just couldn't believe that Alan was deliberately pointing the finger at his ex-wife. First of all, by the time of the murder she had changed her name back to Johnson. Secondly, what motive would she possibly have had to kill Frank Parris? Anyway, there's another Melissa in the book – Melissa James, strangled in Chapter 4. She, too, could have been inspired by Melissa Conway. Alan seems to be thinking of his ex-wife as both a murder victim and a murderess.

Why did it all have to be so complicated?

There were two other clues that appeared in *Atticus Pünd Takes the Case* that had been deliberately drawn from the real-life events at Branlow Hall. I wrote them down on my notepad.

THE MARRIAGE OF FIGARO.

THE DOG THAT BARKED IN THE NIGHT.

It can't have been a coincidence that in *Atticus Pünd Takes the Case*, Francis Pendleton lies about going to a performance of the same Mozart opera mentioned by Frank Parris when he talked to Cecily Treherne. This time, even the initials match. It was still a mystery why Frank made up that story. Where had he really gone – and why bother making up a story at all? As for the dog, both Kimba at Clarence Keep and Bear, the golden retriever at Branlow Hall, had barked at around the time of the murders. Again, I was sure Alan was trying to tell me something and I made a note to ask Derek when I saw him again more about what had happened that night.

*

The next time I looked out of the window, it was completely dark and I was suddenly hungry. I closed my notebook and laid it next to my paperback copy of *Atticus Pünd Takes the Case*.

I was about to go down to dinner when I remembered something. I flicked back to the first page of Alan's novel and sure enough there it was. I was annoyed with myself. It was staring me in the face but I had almost managed to miss it altogether.

The dedication.

For Frank and Leo: in remembrance.

Frank was obviously Frank Parris. Leo had to be the rent boy that James Taylor had mentioned when I met him in London. Frank and Leo and Alan and James had all had dinner together. Frank Parris had helped Alan explore his sexuality. He had also enjoyed kinky sex with Leo.

In remembrance.

The words leapt off the page at me. Frank had been killed at Branlow Hall. Had Leo also died?

On an impulse, I took out my phone and fired off a text.

James – did I ever thank you for lovely dinner at Le Caprice? Great catching up with you again. One quick follow-up question. You mentioned a friend of Frank Parris's called Leo. Do you know anything more about him? Is it possible he died? Notice Alan's book was dedicated to his memory. Thanks. Susan. X

I didn't have to wait long. About a minute later, my phone pinged and there was the answer on my screen.

Hey Susan. Not much I can tell you about Leo. He worked out of a swish flat in Mayfair (God knows how he afforded it) but I heard he'd left London and no idea if he's alive or dead. He was quite a regular with Frank but I'm surprised the book was dedicated to him. Alan never mentioned him to me. Can't tell you very much more as only met him once. He was blond (dyed?) and pretty. Short. I never saw him undressed so I can't tell you how well endowed he was ... cut or uncut – I'm sure you're dying to know!!! He worked out a lot. In good shape. BTW, Leo may not have been his real name. A lot of us used false ones (better safe than sorry). Stud and Nando were always popular. Also pet names. When Alan first met me, I was Jimmy ... sweet and boyish. Have you got anywhere yet? Frank Parris was quite creepy, a real perve now I think about it. He probably got what he deserved. Call me if you come down again. Jimmy XXX

James had no idea if Leo was alive or dead. I wondered how I could find out.

Two More Days

As soon as I woke up, I tried FaceTiming Andreas. It would be half past ten in Crete and he would have finished his breakfast and gone for a swim. Then, assuming that there was nothing serious demanding his attention, he would have retreated to our terrace with a little cup of thick, black coffee (Greek, not Turkish) and a book. Andreas had been reading Nikos Kazantzakis when I left and he'd recommended him to me – as if I ever had any time to read.

There was no answer so I rang him on the mobile, which went straight to voicemail. I thought of calling Nell or Panos or anyone else who worked at the Polydorus, but that smacked of desperation. Anyway, I didn't want to get them involved in our personal affairs. That's the trouble with living in Crete. Everyone has a village mentality, even if they live in the towns.

I was still puzzled and, to be honest, a little annoyed that he hadn't replied. It wasn't as if I had pushed him into a corner. All I'd done was set out some of my feelings and suggest that we should talk them through. Was that really so extreme? It was true that Andreas was often slow opening his emails, but he must have seen the heading and known it was from me. There was a side to his character, I knew, that made him reticent about discussing issues, relationships, 'us'. Maybe it was something to do with the long-drawn-out days in the Mediterranean sunshine that somehow made them feel disconnected, even lazy, but a lot of the Greek men I had met were the same.

In the end, I gave up. I would only be in England for another few days. Cecily Treherne was still missing and I was running out of people to talk to, questions I could ask. Reading *Atticus Pünd Takes the Case* had provided me with almost no revelations at all. As to my own future, Michael Bealey had more or less told me that there was no chance of my picking up any publishing work, freelance or otherwise. So what options did that leave me? I could only go back to the Polydorus, sit down with Andreas and work out together what we were going to do.

I showered, got dressed and went downstairs. Breakfast was served in the same room where I'd had dinner with Lawrence, the waiters dressed in black trousers and white shirts, all of them bussed in from Woodbridge. There was a traditional buffet with fried eggs, bacon and beans all glistening in a slightly unappealing way under old-fashioned heat lamps. I had a sudden yearning for Greek yoghurt and fresh watermelon, but ordered from the menu and sat on my own with my notebook and a percolator of good coffee until the food arrived.

I had just started eating when I looked up and realised I was no longer alone. Lisa Treherne was standing over me, smiling – but it was the sort of smile that would put anyone off their Weetabix. I could imagine her looking at Stefan Codrescu in exactly the same way before she fired him.

'Good morning, Susan,' she said. 'Do you mind if I join you?'

'Be my guest.' I gestured at the empty chair on the other side of the table.

'Actually, I'd say it was the other way round.' She sat down primly. A waiter came across to offer her coffee but she waved him away. 'We're the ones looking after you.'

'And very well, thank you.'

'You like the hotel?'

'It's lovely.' I could see trouble coming. It wouldn't hurt to be nice. 'I can see why you're so popular.'

'Yes. And this is the high season, of course. In fact, that's what I want to talk to you about. How's your investigation coming on?'

'I wouldn't really call it an investigation.'

'Is there anything you can tell me about Cecily?'

'I reread the book yesterday. *Atticus Pünd Takes the Case*. I have a few thoughts about what may have happened.' I closed my notebook as if guarding its secrets.

'A few thoughts?' She glanced down at my plate. I hadn't ordered very much – a poached egg on toast – but from the look on her face you'd have thought I had emptied the buffet. 'The thing is, Susan, I don't want to be rude but you're staying in a room that we could be renting out for two hundred and fifty pounds a night. You're eating our food and probably dipping into our minibar too. You've managed to persuade my parents to pay you a quite extortionate sum of money and the only communication they've had from you so far is a demand for the first instalment. As far as we can see, you've done nothing.'

If this was her trying not to be rude I wondered what she was like when she was really determined to be offensive. I was reminded of Lionel Corby's description of her – '*a real piece of work*'. Perhaps I had been too hard on him when we met in London.

'Do your parents know you're talking to me?' I asked.

'Actually, my father has asked me to have this conversation. We want to bring an end to this arrangement and we think you should leave.'

'When?'

'Today.'

I put down my knife and fork, laying them neatly on the plate. Then I looked her in the eye and asked, as sweetly as I could: 'Did you tell your father you were having sex with Stefan Codrescu before you fired him?'

Her face flushed with anger when she heard that and the strange thing was that it made the scar on the side of her mouth stand out as if the injury had happened just a minute ago. 'How dare you!' she muttered in a low voice.

'You were asking me about my investigation,' I reminded her. 'I would have said that was quite a useful piece of information and that it casts a different light on things. Wouldn't you?'

It was interesting. I hadn't been a hundred per cent confident when I had made the accusation, but she hadn't denied it. Then again, all the evidence was there. At that first dinner, Lawrence Treherne had said how much Lisa had liked Stefan and that the two of them had spent lots of time together. Then she had fired him on what Corby had insisted were trumped-up charges. There were also sexual issues between her and her sister. '*They were always jealous of each other's boyfriends,*' Lawrence had said and it struck me that a large part of her dislike of Aiden MacNeil could have been down to old-fashioned envy.

'Who told you that?' she demanded. I was quite surprised she hadn't stormed out of the room. I probably would have.

'You fired him because he wouldn't sleep with you any more.'

'He was a thief.'

'No. That was Natasha Mälk, the maid who discovered the body. Everyone knew that.'

I was only repeating what Lionel Corby had told me but it seemed that once again he had been spot on. Lisa's face fell. 'He's wrong,' she muttered in a low voice.

'Lisa,' I said, 'I've arranged to see Stefan at HMP Wayland, in Norfolk. There's no point lying to me.' Actually, I was the one lying to her as I hadn't yet heard from Stefan – but she wasn't to know that.

She scowled in a way that would have congealed my poached egg if the heat lamps hadn't already done the work for her. 'Why would you believe anything he has to say? He's a convicted murderer.'

'I'm not so sure that he killed Frank Parris.'

It was funny but even as I spoke the words I knew with absolute certainty that they had to be true. Stefan had been arrested by a police officer who would quite cheerfully have locked him away for life simply because he was Romanian. The case against him was ridiculously slight. A hundred and fifty pounds hidden under his mattress? Nobody hides money under their mattress unless they're old ladies in a bad TV comedy and anyway, would he really have risked years in jail for such a tiny amount?

There were too many unexplained circumstances: the barking dog, the 'Do Not Disturb' sign that had been hung on the door and then mysteriously removed, Frank Parris lying about the opera. And, for me, there was still the biggest question of all. If Alan Conway had known the true identity of the killer (which had to be the reason why Cecily Treherne had disappeared), why had he chosen not to reveal it?

'If Stefan didn't kill him, who did?' Lisa demanded.

'Give me a week here and I'll tell you.'

She stared at me. 'I'll give you two more days.'

'All right.' I wanted to bargain with her but it would

only have made me look weak. At least I wasn't going to be thrown out before lunch.

She started to rise but I hadn't finished with her. 'Tell me about you and Cecily,' I said.

She sat down again. 'What do you want to know?'

'Did you get on?'

'We got on well enough.'

'Why won't you tell me the truth, Lisa? Don't you want me to find out what's happened to her?' She glared at me so I asked her: 'How did you get that mark on the side of your mouth?'

'That was her.' Lisa brought a protective hand up, briefly hiding the scar. 'But she didn't mean it. She was only ten years old. She didn't know what she was doing.'

'What were you arguing about?'

'It's irrelevant!'

'It might not be.'

'It was a boy. Not a boy ... a man. You know how little girls are. His name was Kevin and he worked in the kitchen. He must have been about twenty and we both had crushes on him. And he kissed me. That's all. One day, I was talking to him and I was giggling with him and he gave me a kiss on the cheek. When I told Cess about it, she got furious. She said I'd stolen him from her and there was a knife, a kitchen knife, and she threw it at me. She wasn't even aiming at me. But the blade caught me on the side of my face. It was very sharp and it cut me.' She dropped her hand. 'There was a lot of blood.'

'Do you still blame her for it?'

'I never blamed her. She didn't know what she was doing.'

'What about her and Aiden?'

'What about them?'

'When we last talked, I got the sense that you didn't like him very much.'

'I've got nothing against him personally. I just don't think he pulls his weight, that's all.'

'Do you think your sister loved him?'

'I suppose so. I don't know. We never talked about things like that.'

I had deliberately used the past tense and Lisa hadn't contradicted me. She too had decided that Cecily was no longer alive.

'What about you and Stefan?' I asked.

'What about us?'

'Tell me why you really fired him.'

It took her a few moments to make up her mind. Then she came out with it. 'I had sex with him a few times because – why not? He was good-looking and he was single and he didn't hold back, let me tell you! He was also a criminal with absolutely nothing going for him and if it hadn't been for me, he'd have been out on the street. So maybe you could say he was just returning a favour.

'But I never coerced him and if you're suggesting that I fired him because he wouldn't come into my bed any more, then you can get the hell out of the hotel and I don't care if you know who killed Frank Parris or not. Stefan Codrescu did what I told him to. That was part of the fun of it. I only had to snap my fingers and he'd come running. But unfortunately, whatever you may say, he was the one stealing money – not Natasha – and that was why I couldn't keep him here. The hotel mattered more to me.'

She stood up, the chair legs scraping against the floor.

'You've got today and tomorrow morning, Susan. Then I don't want to see you again.' She couldn't resist one last parting shot. 'Checkout is at twelve.'

Eloise Radmani

I wasn't sorry that Lisa Treherne had more or less fired me. I wanted to get back to Andreas and if I did have to leave England without solving anything, she had given me an excuse. I needed to talk to him. Were we still together? That was the question that most troubled me – certainly more than the small matter of who had killed Frank Parris eight years before.

I had less than forty-eight hours before my forced exodus from Branlow Hall. How was I to use them?

Before Lisa had arrived at my table along with her anger and her evident sexual frustration, I had been writing a list of leads I might follow and once I was on my own I took out my notebook and looked at them again. I had a lot to do and very little time.

My first priority was to visit Stefan Codrescu at

HMP Wayland. There was obviously a great deal he could tell me, starting with his memories of the night of the murder, his real relationship with Lisa, everything he had seen and heard, who had access to his room and, crucially, why he had confessed. But it might be weeks or even months before he replied to my letter and I simply couldn't wait that long.

Then there was Leo, the rent boy who had 'known' both Frank Parris and Alan Conway – I use that word in the biblical sense. If he was dead, as Alan's dedication suggested, then how had he died? And why had the book been dedicated to him in the first place? It was clear that he hadn't been Frank's life partner, just one of many, available at a price.

I needed to go back to Martin and Joanne Williams, who remained the only couple with a straightforward motive for the murder. I had thought them both remarkably creepy when I met them, but I now realised that they had told me an obvious lie. I should have spotted it when I spoke to them. It was Aiden who had actually given me the information that incriminated them and Lawrence had repeated it in his long email. Martin had come to Branlow Hall on the day of Frank's death. He had told me that without knowing he had done so.

I still hadn't spoken to George Saunders, the head teacher who had originally been allocated room 12 in the Moonflower Wing, nor to Eloise Radmani, Roxana's nanny and, perhaps, Aiden's acolyte. I also wanted to track down Alan's wife, Melissa. She had been living right next to the hotel when the murder took place. She could have strolled in at any time of the night without being seen.

And finally there was Wilcox, the name that Sajid Khan had accidentally mentioned to me when I saw him in Framlingham. I had managed to track him down and although he had nothing to do with the case, he was still a priority. I intended to deal with him that same afternoon.

I finished my breakfast and headed back to my room. But as I came out of the entrance hall, I noticed Eloise Radmani walking through the reception area with a basket of linen. Evidently, she was using the hotel laundry as an annex to Branlow Cottage. She saw me and turned away in the hope of getting out before I could stop her, but I wasn't going to let her escape. I hurried after her and caught her at the back door.

I quickly reminded myself of what I knew. Eloise came from Marseille. She had arrived at Branlow Hall in 2009, a couple of months after Roxana was born and a full nine months after the death of Frank Parris. Before that, she had been a student in London where she had met her husband, who had subsequently died of

AIDS. The first time we met, she had looked at me as if I were the devil. She was still far from welcoming, dressed in a muddy blue T-shirt under a loose-fitting jacket, adding a vague splash of colour to her palette of black and grey.

'Good morning,' I said, trying to be friendly.

'Hello.' She scowled.

'I'm Susan. We met briefly outside the cottage. I wasn't able to explain to you why I'm here.'

'Mr MacNeil has told me.' She said 'mister' and not 'monsieur' but her French accent was still on the edge of parody. 'You are trying to help find Cecily.'

'That's right. Is there any news? I was in London yesterday...'

She shook her head. 'There is still nothing.'

'It must be awful for you.'

She relaxed a little but her eyes were still wary. 'It is very difficult. Cecily was kind to me. She made me part of the family. And it is particularly hard for Roxana. All the time she is sad. She doesn't understand what is happening.'

'You've been with the family for a while.'

'Yes.'

'When did you last see Cecily?'

'Why are you asking me these questions?'

'Lawrence and Pauline have asked me to find out

what happened. I've talked to everyone. You don't mind, do you?' I was challenging her deliberately, wondering what it was she had to hide.

She understood. Briefly, she shook her head. 'Of course I don't mind answering your questions but there is nothing I can tell you ... '

'So when did you last see Cecily?'

'It was on the day that she died. Just after lunchtime. I had to take Roxana to the doctor in Woodbridge. She was not well. She had ... you know ... something with the stomach. Cecily told me she was going to take the dog for a walk. We spoke briefly in the kitchen of the house and that was the last time I saw her.'

'You took the evening off.'

'Yes. Inga from the hotel looked after Roxana.'

'Where did you go?'

There was that flash of anger which I recognised from our first meeting. 'What business is it for you?'

'I'm just trying to piece things together.'

'I went to the cinema in Aldeburgh.'

'What did you see?'

'What does it matter? A French film! How dare you ask these questions? Who do you think you are?'

I waited for her to calm down. She wanted to continue on her way but I stood my ground. 'What are you afraid of, Eloise?' I asked.

She blinked at me and I was astonished to see that suddenly she was close to tears. 'I am afraid that Cecily is dead. I am afraid that the little girl has lost her mother. I am afraid Mr MacNeil will be left on his own. And you! You come here and you pretend that this is all a *policier* – a detective novel. You know nothing of this family and you know nothing of me and of my struggles.'

'You lost your husband.'

If she hadn't been holding the laundry basket, she might have hit me. I saw her fists tighten on the plastic handles. 'Lucien was studying to be an architect,' she said. Her voice was husky now. 'He would have been a great architect. He had ideas – you would not believe! And do you know how hard I worked to support him? I washed dishes. I cleaned offices. I was the receptionist for an advertising agency and then I went to Harrods and I sold men's clothes. I did it all for him and then he was killed by your precious NHS who gave him the wrong blood and when he died they gave me no compensation. Nothing. He was everything to me and they killed him.'

'I'm sorry.'

I noticed two guests coming down the stairs on their way out for the day. I wondered what they would have thought if they had overheard our conversation. It wasn't the sort of thing you would have expected in a country hotel.

'Why does nobody leave me alone?' Eloise went on. 'First the police, then you! Aiden had nothing to do with the death of his wife. I tell you that from my heart. He is a good man and Roxana adores him.'

'What do you think happened to Cecily?'

'I don't know! I think maybe nothing happened to her. I think maybe she had an accident and now she is dead and you should go away and leave us alone.'

She swung the basket round and hurried out through the door. This time I didn't try to stop her. In her anger and her sense of martyrdom she had told me something which perhaps she hadn't intended. I decided to check it out.

I went straight back up to my room and found the number of Knightsbridge Knannies, the agency that Aiden had mentioned. He had used it to find Eloise in the first place. I rang it, pretending to be a mother who was considering her for a job. The woman at the other end of the line was surprised.

'I didn't realise that Ms Radmani had left her current employ,' she told me.

Does anyone still use the word 'employ' as a noun? But I suppose it was that sort of agency.

'She's still with the MacNeils,' I assured her. 'But

I'm afraid she's been having difficulties which have made her reconsider her position. You may have heard that Mrs MacNeil disappeared … '

'Oh yes. Of course.' That mollified her.

'I've interviewed her and I think she's wonderful but I just wanted to check one small detail on her resumé. Miss Radmani told me she had worked in an advertising agency and as it happens my husband works in advertising so I was just wondering which one it was.'

There was a pause and I heard the click of a computer keyboard as she found the information. 'It was McCann Erickson,' she said.

'Thank you very much.'

'If you speak to Ms Radmani again you might ask her to contact us. And if it doesn't work out with her I'm sure we can help you find a suitable candidate.'

'Thank you. I'll be in touch.'

I hung up and went over to my desk to open my computer, searching for the newspaper cuttings that I had looked at in London. The screen seemed to take an age to boot up but finally there it was in front of me, just as I had thought. It was from *Campaign*, the advertising magazine.

Sundowner, the Sydney-based advertising agency set up by former McCann Erickson supremo Frank

Parris, has gone out of business. The Australian Securities and Investments Commission – the country's official financial watchdog – confirmed that after just three years the agency has ceased to trade.

Frank Parris had worked at McCann Erickson. Eloise Radmani had been a receptionist there. The two of them must have known each other. And now she was here. Atticus Pünd had often said that there were no coincidences when you were investigating a crime. *'Everything in life has a pattern and a coincidence is simply the moment when that pattern becomes briefly visible.'*

I wondered if he was right.

Back to Westleton

I left the hotel and drove back to Heath House, the
family home that had been left to Frank Parris and
his sister, Joanne Williams. This time there was nobody working outside so I rang the front doorbell and
waited until it was opened. Martin Williams stood facing me, dressed in the same blue overalls as last time.
He was holding a hammer, which was an unpleasant
reminder of why I was here and indeed why I had come
to Suffolk in the first place – but then he was obviously
the sort of man who enjoyed doing odd jobs around the
house when he wasn't on the phone selling art insurance.

'Susan!' He seemed neither pleased nor displeased
to see me. Or perhaps, in a strange way, he was both. 'I
didn't expect to see you again.'

I wondered if he knew what his wife had said to me when I left.

'I'm very sorry to have to trouble you again, Martin. But I'm leaving England soon and a couple of things have turned up. If I could talk to you, it won't take more than five or ten minutes.'

'Do come in,' he said, adding cheerfully, 'I don't think Joanne will be too happy to see you, though.'

'Yes. She made that very clear.'

'It's nothing personal, Susan. It's just that she and Frank weren't particularly close and she'd much rather forget the whole thing.'

'Wouldn't we all?' I muttered but I don't think he heard.

He led me into the kitchen where Joanne was working, mixing something in a bowl. She turned and the half-smile on her face instantly faded when she saw who it was. 'What are you doing here?' she demanded. This time there wasn't even a pretence of politeness – and certainly no offer of tea, peppermint or otherwise.

'It's very simple.' I sat down as if to claim my place in the house. I also hoped it would make it a little more difficult for them to throw me out. 'The last time I was here, you told me two things that weren't true.' I had plunged straight into it. The way Joanne was looking at me, I knew I had to get this over with as quickly as possible. 'First of all, you said that Frank Parris wanted you to invest in a new agency, but since then I've learned that actually he had come to claim his half of the house – your house. He was going to force you to sell.'

'That's none of your business!' Joanne was brandishing the wooden spoon like a weapon and I was glad I hadn't arrived when she was cutting meat. 'You have absolutely no right to be here and we don't need to talk to you. If you don't leave my house, I'll call the police.'

'I'm working with the police now,' I said. 'Do you want me to tell them what I know?'

'I don't care who you're working with. Get out of here.'

'Hold on a minute, Jo.' Martin was equable in a way that was almost sinister. 'Who gave you that information?' he asked me. 'I think we have a right to know.'

Obviously, I couldn't tell them the truth. I had no particular fondness for Sajid Khan but nor did I want to get him into trouble. 'I've been talking to one of the estate agents in Framlingham,' I explained. 'Frank wanted to know the likely value of the house and he told them he had a property that was coming onto the market. He also told them why.'

Even as I was making all this up, I thought it sounded

unlikely. But Martin chose to believe me and didn't seem at all put out. 'I wonder what it is, exactly, you're suggesting, Susan?'

I wasn't sure how to answer that. 'Why did you lie to me?' I asked.

'Well, first of all because it was none of your business. Joanne's right about that. And although I'd say it's quite rude of you to suggest otherwise, what we told you wasn't actually so very far away from the truth. Frank wanted the money to start a new company and he looked on us as investors. Neither of us was particularly happy about it. We both love Heath House. Joanne's lived here all her life. But we spoke to our solicitor and there was nothing we could do so we resigned ourselves.' He shrugged. 'And then, of course, Frank died.'

'We had nothing to do with it,' Joanne added, unnecessarily. Her words only made it more likely that they had.

'You said there were two things,' Martin said.

'Why are you doing this?' Joanne stared at her husband with exasperation.

'We have nothing to hide. If Susan has questions she wants to put to us, I think it's only right and proper that we should answer them.' He smiled at me. 'So?'

'You told me that Frank Parris had complained

about the wedding at Branlow Hall. His view had been obstructed by a marquee.'

'I think I remember that.'

'Well, that doesn't quite work. He came to see you early on Friday morning. The marquee wasn't delivered until Friday lunchtime.' This was the information that both Aiden MacNeil and Lawrence Treherne had given me. Somehow it had lingered in my consciousness, almost like a flaw in an early first draft. Now I waited for a reply. 'I wonder how you explain that,' I said.

Martin Williams was unfazed. 'I'm not sure that I do.' He thought for a moment. 'Frank must have made a mistake.'

'He couldn't have had his view obstructed by something that wasn't there.'

'Then maybe he lied to us.'

'Or maybe you went to the hotel later that evening and saw the marquee yourself,' I suggested.

'But why would I have gone to the hotel, Susan? And why wouldn't I have told you if I had?'

'This is ridiculous!' Joanne insisted. 'We shouldn't be talking to this woman ... '

'Unless, of course, you're suggesting that I killed my brother-in-law because I didn't want to have to sell the house,' Martin continued. He looked at me and there was something in his eyes that I had never seen before. It was a sort of menace that quite unnerved me. What made it all the more shocking was that we were sitting in this pleasant country kitchen with its Aga and its hanging pots and pans and vases of dried flowers. It was all so ordinary and Martin was completely relaxed in his shabby work clothes. And yet he was staring me out, challenging me. I glanced at Joanne and I knew that she had seen it too. She was afraid for me.

'Of course I don't think that,' I said.

'Then if you've got nothing else to ask me, I think Joanne's right and you should leave.'

Neither of them moved. I stood up, feeling quite breathless. 'I'll show myself out,' I said.

'Yes. And please don't come back.'

'This isn't over, Martin.' I wasn't going to let him intimidate me. 'The truth will come out.'

'Goodbye, Susan.'

I went. To be honest, I couldn't wait to get away.

*

Had Martin just confessed to the murder of Frank Parris? '*I killed my brother-in-law because I didn't want to have to sell the house.*' He had spelled it out for me and in truth it was exactly what I had been thinking.

From what I had discovered so far, and working on the assumption that Stefan Codrescu was innocent, nobody else had any motive to kill Frank Parris. No one at the hotel had even known who he was. But Martin and Joanne had a bona fide reason that they had done their best to keep hidden from me. What was more, Martin *had* lied about the marquee and when I had challenged him just now he hadn't even tried to think up a reasonable explanation. He and his wife had both threatened me in different ways. It was almost as if they wanted me to know what they had done.

I got into my car and drove slowly out of Westleton until I found the house I was looking for – about a mile down the road. It was called The Brambles, a tiny, pink Suffolk cottage that looked as if it had been there for ever, standing on its own next to a farm, separated from it by a low wooden fence.

It was exactly the sort of house I would have expected Derek Endicott, the night manager, to live in. He had told me he lived close to Westleton and I had got the address from Inga before I left the hotel. It had probably belonged to the same family for generations. The clues were there in the old-fashioned television aerial on the roof, the outside toilet that hadn't been torn down or converted, the glass in the windows that had trapped the dust of centuries. The doorbell might have been added in the sixties. When I rang, it chimed out a tune.

After what seemed like an eternity, the door was opened by a very old woman wearing a loose-fitting floral dress – it was actually more of a smock – and supporting herself on a walking frame. Her hair was grey and tangled and she had hearing aids behind both ears. Lawrence had told me that Derek's mother was ill but I must say that on first appearance she looked quite sprightly and alert.

'Yes?' she asked. She had a strained, high-pitched voice that reminded me a little of her son.

'Are you Mrs Endicott?'

'Yes. Who are you?'

'My name is Susan Ryeland. I'm from Branlow Hall.'

'Are you here for Derek? He's still in bed.'

'I can come back later.'

'No. Come in. Come in. The doorbell will have woken him up. It was almost time for his lunch anyway.'

She turned her back on me and, leaning on the walking frame, edged herself into the single room that made up much of the ground floor. It was both a kitchen and a living room, the two jumbled together haphazardly. All the furniture was antique but not in a good way. The sofa sagged, the oak table was scarred, the kitchen equipment was out of date. The only nod to the twenty-first century was a widescreen TV, which perched uncomfortably on an ugly, fake wooden stand in the corner.

And yet, for all that, it was a cosy place. I couldn't help but notice that there were two of everything: two cushions on the sofa, two armchairs, two wooden chairs at the table, two rings on the hob.

Mrs Endicott lowered herself heavily onto one of the armchairs. 'Who did you say you were?'

'Susan Ryeland. Mrs Endicott ... '

'Call me Gwyneth.'

She had become Phyllis in Alan Conway's book but I could already see that the two women had almost nothing in common. I wondered if Alan had come here. I doubted it.

'I don't want to be in your way if you're about to have lunch.'

'You're not in the way, dear. It's only soup and shepherd's pie. You can join us if you like.' She paused to catch her breath and I heard a painful wheezing as the air entered her throat. At the same time, she reached down and for the first time I saw the oxygen cylinder that had been concealed beside the chair. She held a plastic suction cap to her mouth and breathed several times. 'I've got the emphysema,' she explained, when she had finished. 'It's my own silly fault. Thirty cigarettes a day all my life and it's finally caught up with me. Do you smoke, dear?'

'Yes,' I admitted.

'You shouldn't.'

'Who is it, Ma?'

I heard Derek's voice before I saw him. A door opened and he came in, wearing tracksuit bottoms and a jersey that was a little too small for him. He was obviously surprised to see me sitting there, but unlike Joanne Williams he didn't seem put out.

'Mrs Ryeland!'

I was quite impressed that he remembered my name. 'Hello, Derek,' I said.

'Have you got news?'

'About Cecily? I'm afraid not.'

'Mrs Ryeland is helping the police find Cecily,' he told his mother.

'That's a terrible business,' Gwyneth said. 'She's a very nice young woman. And a mother too! I hope they find her.'

'She's the reason why I'm here, Derek. Would you mind if I asked you a couple more questions?'

He sat down at the table. There was only just enough room for his stomach. 'I'd be happy to help.'

'It's just that there was something you said when we met at the hotel.' I continued carefully, making it easier for him. 'Cecily had read a book that had upset her. And about two weeks ago – it was a Tuesday, about the same sort of time as now – she rang her parents in the South of France to talk about it. She said there was something in the book that suggested Stefan Codrescu might not have killed Frank Parris after all.'

'I liked Stefan,' Derek said.

'Did I meet him?' Gwyneth asked.

'No, Ma. He never came here.'

'When I was talking to you about Cecily, you said something to me. '*I knew something was wrong when she made that phone call.*' Were you talking about the same phone call, Derek? The one she made to her parents?'

He had to think about that, untangling his memories of what had happened and also their possible implications for him. 'She did phone her parents,' he said, finally. 'I was at the reception desk and she was in the office. I didn't listen to what she said, though. I mean ... I didn't mean to.'

'But you knew she was upset.'

'She said he didn't do it. She said they'd got it all wrong. The door doesn't shut properly so I could hear some of it through the crack.'

'Why were you at the hotel, Derek? It was midday. I thought you only worked nights.'

'Sometimes, if Mum's had a bad week, I switch over with Lars. Mr Treherne is very kind like that. I can't leave her alone all night.'

'It's the emphysema,' Gwyneth reminded me. She smiled at her son. 'He looks after me.'

'So you were there during the day. Was anyone else nearby when Cecily made the call?'

He pursed his lips. 'Well, there were guests. The hotel was quite busy.'

'Was Aiden MacNeil there? Or Lisa?'

'No.' He shook his head. Then his eyes brightened. 'I saw the nanny!'

'Eloise?'

'She was looking for Cecily and I told her she was in the office.'

'Did she go in?'

'No. She could hear Cecily talking on the phone and she didn't want me to disturb her so she asked me to say she'd been looking for her and went off.'

'Did you talk to Cecily?'

'No. After she finished the phone call, she came out of the office and I don't know where she went. You're right that she was upset. I think she'd been crying.' His face fell as he said that, as if it was somehow his fault.

'Did you tell the police all this?' Gwyneth asked.

'No, Ma. The police didn't ask.'

I was beginning to feel uncomfortable, trapped in this small room between the invalid mother and her son. I felt a spurt of anger towards Alan Conway for manipulating them, turning them into caricatures in his book – but at the same time I knew that I had been complicit. I could have been more critical of Derek Chandler with his club foot and his schoolboy perversion, but I had gone ahead and published. And I hadn't complained when the book became a bestseller.

There was something else I had to ask. I didn't particularly want to do this either. 'Derek,' I began. 'Why were you upset on the day before the wedding?'

'I wasn't upset. There was a party for the staff. I didn't go but everyone looked as if they were having fun and that made me happy too.'

That wasn't what Lawrence Treherne had told me. In the lengthy statement he had written, he had mentioned that Derek had been in a strange mood, 'as if he'd seen a ghost'.

'Was there someone who'd come to the hotel who you recognised?'

'No.' He was scared. He knew that I knew.

'Are you sure?'

'I don't remember ... '

I tried to be as gentle as possible. 'You may have forgotten. But you knew George Saunders, didn't you?

The man who asked to change rooms and went into room sixteen. He was your headmaster when you were at school at Bromeswell Grove.'

It had taken me an hour on the Internet to get the information that I needed. There are dozens of websites that help old school friends reconnect: Classmates.com, SchoolMates, and so on. Bromeswell Grove also ran its own very active message board. I had been interested that a retired headmaster had been booked into the room where Frank Parris was killed and, almost on a whim, I had decided to check out if he had any connection with any of the staff or guests who had been at Branlow Hall at the time of the wedding. Derek's name had very quickly leapt onto my screen.

Reading the posts – and then cross-referencing them with Facebook – it was obvious to me that Derek had been viciously bullied at school ('fat', 'retard', 'wanker') and that decades later he was still being trolled online. Saunders didn't get off lightly either. He was a bully, a bastard, a paedophile, a pedant. As far as his ex-students were concerned, he couldn't drop dead soon enough.

Alan Conway used to say that the Internet was the worst thing that ever happened to detective fiction – which was one of the reasons why he set his own stories back in the fifties. He had a point. It's hard to make your detective look clever when all the information in the world is instantly available to everyone in the world at a moment's notice. In my case, I wasn't trying to look clever. I was simply searching for the truth. But I'm sure Atticus Pünd wouldn't have approved of my methods.

'Why are you talking about George Saunders?' Gwyneth asked. 'He was a horrible man.'

'He was at the hotel,' I said. I was still talking to Derek. 'You saw him.'

Derek nodded miserably.

'Did he see you?'

'Yes.'

'Did he say anything.'

'He didn't recognise me.'

'But you recognised him.'

'Of course I did.'

'He was a horrible man,' Gwyneth repeated. 'Derek never did anything wrong, but the other boys ganged up on him and Saunders never did anything about it.' She would have gone on but she had run out of breath and had to reach for the oxygen cylinder again.

'He always picked on me.' Derek continued where his mother had left off. There were tears in his eyes. 'He used to make jokes about me in front of all the others. He said I was useless, that I would never have any future. It's true. I was never good at that stuff – school and everything. But he said I'd never be a success at anything.' He cast his eyes down. 'Maybe he was right.'

I stood up. I was feeling ashamed, as if I had joined the trolls and the bullies by coming here. 'It's not true at all, Derek,' I said. 'The Trehernes think the world of you. You're part of their family. And I think it's wonderful the way you look after your mother.'

God! How much more patronising could I sound? I made my excuses and left as quickly as I could.

As I got back into my car, I reflected on what I had learned. I kept going over and over one thought in my mind. Just about every student who had been at Bromeswell Grove had disliked George Saunders. They'd all wanted him to drop dead. Just the sight of him had been enough to reduce Derek Endicott to a jabbering wreck.

But it had been Frank Parris who had died.

Katie

I'd phoned ahead and told Katie I was coming but for once I wasn't looking forward to seeing her.

She was in the garden when I pulled into Three Chimneys, pottering about with gardening gloves and a pair of secateurs, deadheading the roses or pruning the marigolds or whatever else it was that would make her perfect house just that little bit more perfect. I love Katie. I really do. She's the only line of continuity running through the haphazardness of my life, even though there are times when I'm not even sure if I really know her.

'Hello!' she greeted me brightly. 'I hope you don't mind a scrap lunch. I've bought it in, I'm afraid. Quiche from Honey + Harvey in Melton and a salad I've thrown together.'

'That's fine . . . '

She led me into the kitchen, where the lunch had already been laid out, and took a jug of home-made lemonade out of the fridge. She has a recipe where you mush up whole lemons with sugar and water and of course it tastes a whole lot better than anything you'll get out of a can or a bottle. The quiche had been warmed in the oven. There were even proper cloth serviettes in metal rings. Who does that anymore? What's wrong with a square of kitchen roll?

'So how's it all going?' she asked. 'I take it the police haven't found Cecily Treherne.'

'I'm not sure they ever will.'

'You think she's been killed?'

I nodded.

'That's not what you said the last time you were here. You thought it might just have been an accident, that she could have fallen into a river or something.' She considered what I'd just said. 'If she was killed, then you think that she was right and Stefan Whatever-his-name-was was innocent after all?'

'That about sums it up.'

'So what's changed your mind?'

It was a good question. At that moment I didn't have a clue – and I mean that in every sense. I'd talked to people, I'd made pages of notes, but nobody had slipped up; nobody had said anything or done anything that obviously pointed the finger at them. All I had, really, were vague feelings. If you'd asked me to draw up a list of suspects in order of likelihood, it would have looked something like this:

1. Eloise Radmani

2. Lisa Treherne

3. Derek Endicott

4. Aiden MacNeil

5. Lionel Corby

Eloise and Derek had both overheard the fatal telephone call. Lisa Treherne had serious jealousy issues with Cecily and had been jilted by Stefan. Aiden was married to Cecily and despite all appearances to the contrary, he still remained the most obvious suspect. Lionel was the least likely – but I hadn't liked him when I first met him and I thought there was something about him that just smelled wrong.

So where was I exactly?

In *Atticus Pünd Takes the Case*, the two deaths happen for very different reasons and, of course, it turns out that there are two killers. I was almost certain that what I was dealing with was simpler, that Cecily had been silenced for exactly the reason that her parents had suggested to me. She knew too much. She had rung them from a public place and she had been overheard.

She knew who killed Frank Parris because she'd read the book. I'd read it too, and even though I must have seen what she'd seen, for some reason it had completely passed me by. I was beginning to realise that I should have asked more questions about Cecily, her likes and dislikes, her preoccupations; I'd have had a better idea of what might have registered with her.

'It's just a feeling,' I said in answer to Katie's question. 'Anyway, I've only got today and tomorrow. Lisa Treherne has asked me to leave.'

'Why?'

'She thinks I'm wasting her time.'

'Or maybe she thinks you know too much.'

'That thought had occurred to me too.'

'You can move in here if you like.'

I would have liked that. I wanted to be close to Katie. But in view of the conversation we were about to have, I knew it wouldn't be possible.

'Katie,' I said. 'You know how fond I am of you. I'd like to think we're close.'

'We are close.' She smiled at me but I could see the fear in her smile. She knew what was coming.

'Why didn't you tell me about Gordon?' I asked.

She tried to brazen it out. 'What about Gordon?'

'I know about Adam Wilcox,' I said.

Five simple words and I saw her crumple. There was nothing dramatic: no tears, no anger, no exclamations. It was simply that in that one second all the pretence with which she'd surrounded herself – the flowers, the exotic salad, the home-made lemonade, the quiche from some fancy deli in Melton – was revealed to be exactly that, not real, and as it evaporated the desperate sadness that had been lurking behind it all along came bursting through. I would have seen it earlier if I hadn't been so obsessed with a crowd of people who had absolutely nothing to do with me. Oh yes, I'd picked up on the dead bush, the typos in her email to me, Jack's smoking, his motorbike, but I hadn't allowed them to make any emotional connection. I'd treated them like clues in a secondary crime story, something to be solved rather than taken to heart.

And then Sajid Khan had made his slip-up. At the end of our meeting, he mentioned that Katie had approached him and that he'd recommended someone called Wilcox. He'd quickly realised his mistake and he'd tried to cover it up but I'd known something was wrong. Why would Katie have been consulting a solicitor? Once again, the Internet had helped me. I'd started by typing '*Wilcox London Lawyers*'. I suppose I was lucky that it was a relatively uncommon name. My first search only brought up a dozen possible candidates. It was easy enough to dismiss Jerome Wilcox (trading standards), Paul Wilcox (intellectual property) and so on. Then I had a brainwave and tried '*Wilcox Ipswich Lawyers*'. I found Adam Wilcox on the first page. He specialised in divorce.

'Did Gordon tell you?' Katie asked.

'I haven't spoken to Gordon in a long time,' I said.

'Nor have I.' She tried to smile but that wouldn't work any more. 'I didn't want to tell you because it's so boring,' she said. 'After everything I've said to you over the years, I thought you'd sit there and think I was pompous and stupid and that it served me right.'

I reached out and took hold of her hand. 'I'd never think that,' I said. 'Not in a hundred years.'

'I'm sorry.' And now the tears came. She picked up her napkin and wiped her eyes. 'I didn't mean that. That wasn't fair.'

'Just tell me what's happened.'

She sighed. 'Gordon is having an affair with his secretary. Her name is Naomi. She's twenty years younger than him. Isn't that just the worst thing you ever heard?'

'It makes him sound ridiculous,' I said.

'He is ridiculous.' She wasn't crying any more. Katie had become upset because she thought she'd been unkind to me. Talking about Gordon just made her angry. 'I've had all the usual crap about how he loves me and he loves the children and he doesn't want to hurt the family but how he was secretly unhappy and she makes him feel young again and we all need a fresh start and blah blah blah blah. He's pathetic – but half of me blames myself. I should never have agreed to this "week in London, weekends in Woodbridge" arrangement. I should have known it would end in tears.'

'When did this all happen?' I asked.

'It started a couple of years ago, just after you went to Crete. Gordon said he was getting worn out with all the commuting and wanted to rent a one-bedroom flat near the bank and like a fool, I agreed. At first it was just one or two nights a week. But suddenly he was only home at weekends and he even managed to miss a few of those. Conferences. Foreign trips. Golf with his boss. God knows, I should have seen it. The writing wasn't just on the wall. It was in capital letters!'

'How did you find out?'

'A text. His phone pinged late at night and I saw it for a few seconds before it got covered over by his screen saver. I have a feeling sweet little Naomi probably did it on purpose. She wanted me to know. Of course she did.'

'Why didn't you tell me?'

'Send you an email to Crete? What good would that do?'

'I was here a few days ago ... '

'I'm sorry, Sue. I should have. I wanted to. But part of me was ashamed and I know that's ridiculous because I've got nothing to be ashamed about, but at the same time I've always gone on at you about you and Andreas and how you should get your life together and maybe I just wasn't brave enough to admit that my own life was falling apart.'

'You know I'd have been there for you.'

'I know. And don't have a go at me or I'll start crying again. I knew you'd find out sooner or later and I was dreading it.'

I had to ask. 'I suppose Jack and Daisy know.'

She nodded. 'I had to tell them. I'm afraid they've both taken it very badly. Daisy won't even speak to him. She's just disgusted by the whole thing. And as for Jack ... You've seen him. I'm trying to put on a brave face. "You've still got a father", "midlife crisis" – and all the rest of it. But if you want the truth, Sue, part of me is quite pleased that they've taken against him.

He's a selfish bastard and he's made a complete mess of everything.'

There was more coming. I could tell.

'He's spent a lot of money on Naomi. At the same time, his work at the bank has gone downhill and he's lost his job. Not that he cares at the moment. He's in his love nest in Willesden and all's right with the world. But we're going to have to sell this house. I could buy him out but I haven't got the money and basically it's fifty-fifty. I'm not going to give you all the financial details. It's a mess.'

'Where will you live?'

'I haven't even thought that through yet. Some-where smaller. Three Chimneys goes on the market next week.'

She got up from the table and put on the kettle. She needed to have a moment with her back to me. 'I'm glad you know,' she said, still not looking at me.

'I'm so sorry for you, Katie. But I'm glad I know too. There shouldn't be any secrets between us.'

'Twenty-five years! It's amazing how quickly it can all fall apart.'

She stood there waiting for the kettle to boil. Nei-ther of us said anything. Finally, she came back to the table carrying two mugs of coffee. We sat facing each other for a few moments more.

'Will you stay in Woodbridge?' I asked.

'If I can. All my friends are here and they've said I can work full-time at Greenways if I want to. Here I am, heading towards fifty and starting full-time work again!' She looked into the black pool of her coffee. 'It's not fair, Sue. It really isn't.'

'I wish I could help you.'

'Just knowing you're there helps me. And I'll be fine. This house has got to be worth quite a bit. I've got savings. The children are almost old enough to look after themselves ... '

We talked some more and I promised I'd see her again before I left Suffolk and that I was always at the end of a phone if she needed me. And I know it was wrong of me, but all the time I was thinking of Andreas and wishing that we'd never had that argument in Crete, that I hadn't written him that email, that I had never come to Branlow Hall.

Later that afternoon, I tried ringing him again. I still got no reply.

The Owl

I t was three o'clock when I got back to the hotel and
all I wanted to do was go up to my room, lie on the
bed with a damp cloth over my eyes and put the whole
business of Frank Parris and Cecily Treherne out of my
head. Lisa Treherne had given me until twelve o'clock
the next day to come to some sort of resolution but I
wasn't even close. I felt strung out after my meeting
with Katie. I was worried about her. And talking about
my so-called investigation had only shown me how
very little I had managed to find out.

But as I entered the reception area to pick up my key
I heard my name called out and, turning round, I found
myself face-to-face with the last person I'd expected
to see. Alan Conway's ex-wife, Melissa, was standing
there with a thin smile that said she knew I was sur-

prised to see her rather than that she was surprised or even pleased to see me. It had been two years since we had met briefly, in her home in Bradford-on-Avon, and she hadn't changed: short, chestnut hair, high cheekbones, an elegance that bordered on the austere.

'You don't remember me,' she said.

I realised I had been staring at her. 'Of course I remember you, Melissa,' I said. 'I just didn't expect to see you here. What are you doing in Woodbridge?'

'I lived here. After Orford, I rented a cottage in the grounds of Branlow Hall.'

'Yes. I heard.'

'I made a lot of friends here. Aiden MacNeil helped me at what was obviously a very difficult time for me just after my divorce. When I read about Cecily's disappearance, I thought I ought to come up and lend my support. You know, you've quite upset him.'

'I didn't mean to do that.'

'He seems to think you've got it in for him.' I didn't respond so she went on. 'I'm going back to B-on-A this evening, but I was hoping I'd see you. Would you have time for a cup of tea?'

'Of course, Melissa. I'd like that.'

I didn't want tea. And I certainly didn't want to sit there being accused by Melissa. But at the same time, I needed to speak to her. She had been at the hotel on the

Thursday before the wedding – in a bad mood, according to Lionel Corby, who had seen her at the spa. And although she had been separated from Alan Conway by the time *Atticus Pünd Takes the Case was published,* she had known him better than anyone. She had been married to him for eight years and she had been the one who had suggested he write murder mysteries in the first place. It was interesting that she had become friendly with Aiden MacNeil. I had thought Alan's book had been the only link between the death of Frank Parris and the disappearance of Cecily Treherne. Now I realised that she was another.

We went into the lounge. I would have preferred to sit outside with a cigarette but she had led the way quite forcibly. We sat down.

'So when did you see Aiden?' I asked.

'We had lunch together at the cottage just now. I came over to the hotel hoping that I'd find you.' A waiter appeared and I ordered a mineral water. Melissa had coffee. 'You know that he is very much in love with his wife,' she continued once we were alone. 'I saw them together before they were married and I can tell you. He dotes on her.'

'Did they invite you to the wedding?'

'No.'

So they weren't that close then. She saw what I was

thinking. 'I was closer to Aiden than I was to Cecily. He was the one who showed me round Oaklands, and when I moved in he made sure everything was all right. I told him about me and Alan and he sort of took me under his wing. He arranged the free pass at the spa for me and I had dinner with him once or twice.'

'So how well did you get to know him?' I asked.

'Are you thinking what I think you're thinking? The thing about you, Susan, is that you always were very direct, never one to spare anyone's feelings.' She half smiled. 'Aiden and I weren't in a relationship. We didn't have sex. The first time I met him was a few weeks before he got married, for heaven's sake! Anyway, he wasn't like that. He never tried anything on.'

'That wasn't what I meant,' I said, although of course that had been exactly the thought in my mind.

'I saw him maybe half a dozen times. And for what it's worth, when I had dinner with him, Cecily was there too.'

'What did you think of her?'

'She seemed nice enough although she didn't talk very much. She was probably nervous about the wedding. She'd had an argument with her sister and perhaps that had thrown her.'

'Do you know what they had argued about?'

'I have no idea. I'm not sure there was very much

love lost between them.' She paused. 'Actually, I seem to remember that Stefan's name came up. He was the man who was accused of the murder, wasn't he? Cecily was annoyed that Lisa had fired him.'

'Did you see much of Stefan?'

'I saw him once. He came over to Oaklands to unblock a drain. I gave him five pounds as a tip.'

The waiter arrived with a tray. She waited until he had gone.

'I didn't really notice a lot of what was going on when I came here, Susan,' she continued. 'You've got to remember that I was in a difficult position. The man I was married to and who was the father of my child had just told me he was gay and that he wanted a divorce. We'd sold our house in Orford. Freddy and I had no idea where we were going to live.'

Freddy was her son. He had been twelve years old at the time. 'Did Freddy stay with you at the cottage?'

'Some of the time. It was one of the reasons why I rented it. He'd just started at Woodbridge School and I wanted to be close.'

'Where is he now?'

'He's at St Martin's School of Art.'

I remembered that he'd been applying when Melissa and I last met. 'I'm glad he got in,' I said.

'So am I. I think what Alan did to Freddy was quite cruel. I've got absolutely no problem with a gay man coming out and I didn't even mind that it ended our relationship. I mean, I wasn't happy about it but I tried not to blame him. If that was his sexual identity, there was no point trying to hide it. But it was different for Freddy. He was twelve years old, in a new school, and suddenly he was reading about his famous gay father in all the newspapers. I have to say that the staff and teachers at Woodbridge School were marvellous, but of course he was teased and bullied. You know what boys are like. Alan never offered him any support. By then, he'd met James and moved into Abbey Grange and all we ever got from him were the monthly cheques.'

'Did Freddy ever stay with him?'

'He didn't want to. I tried to build bridges. I thought that was the responsible thing to do. I was wasting my time. Freddy didn't want anything to do with him.'

I'd witnessed that for myself. Freddy Conway had come reluctantly to his father's funeral in Framlingham two years ago. He had shown no emotion apart from a desire to leave as soon as he could.

'It's extraordinary to think that you were actually here at the hotel the weekend that Frank Parris was killed,' I said.

'Who told you that?'

'Lionel Corby.' She had forgotten who he was so I reminded her. 'He ran the spa.'

'Oh. You mean the Australian. Leo. Yes, I used to train with him.'

'Leo?'

'That was what I always called him.'

It was a thought that had never occurred to me. 'Did anyone else call him that?' I asked.

She shrugged. 'I don't really know. Why? Is it important?'

I didn't answer. 'He said you were angry about something.'

'When?'

'On the Thursday.'

'I really can't remember, Susan. It was a long time ago. It was probably nothing. Leo could be quite annoying. He was very full of himself. Maybe he'd pissed me off.'

She was right about Lionel. I'd thought the same when I met him in London. Even so, I got the feeling there was something else on her mind. 'Did you know Frank Parris?' I asked.

'Yes.'

'You'd met him?'

'I'd seen pictures of him in *Campaign* and Alan had talked to me about him.'

'He arrived that same Thursday at the hotel.'

'Yes.' She sighed. 'All right. It was quite an unpleasant surprise. I saw him in reception on the way to the spa. Maybe that was why I was in a bad mood.'

She leaned towards me. There were a couple of other people in the lounge and she didn't want to be overheard. 'Look, I've been very straight with you about me and Alan,' she began. 'We were married. He was gay. We got divorced. I'm not saying that things could have turned out any differently, but Frank Parris was the gatekeeper, if you like. He was the one who took Alan in hand and introduced him to this whole new world – the gay scene in London. They slept together, although Frank wasn't Alan's type. Alan liked younger boys from the very start. But Frank also took him in hand there – so to speak. He took him to clubs and helped him to find paid sex with kids barely out of their teens. And some of the stuff he was getting up to! I mean, I'm liberal-minded enough, but really, I didn't want to know.'

'He told you about it?'

'He got drunk once. He told me enough.'

'So you blamed Frank Parris.'

'Not enough to hammer him to death, if that's what you're getting at, Susan. But let's just say I didn't shed too many tears when I heard the news.'

Despite myself, I was warming to Melissa. When she had accosted me in the hotel reception, she had seemed hostile and accusatory. It was also hard for me to forget that she had once had a relationship with Andreas – admittedly, before I met him. But the more she spoke, the more thoughtful and intelligent she seemed. She had been the creator of Atticus Pünd as much as Alan. In another life, we would have been friends.

'You know that Alan dedicated the book to Frank Parris,' I said.

'*Atticus Pünd Takes the Case*? Actually, I didn't. I never read it.'

'It's the reason I'm here, Melissa.'

'I know. Aiden told me. Alan came to the hotel six weeks after the murder. He asked lots of questions. And then he used it all for his new story.' She shook her head. 'That's so typical of him. He could be a complete bastard when he wanted to be – which was most of the time, now I come to think about it.'

'You didn't see him when he was here?'

'No. I was away, thank God. I wouldn't have wanted to run into him. Not then.'

'He put a lot of the people who worked here into

the book. Lawrence and Pauline Treherne. Derek Endicott. Aiden. The main character is called Melissa. Maybe he was thinking of you.'

'What happens to her?'

'She gets strangled.'

Melissa laughed at that. 'That doesn't surprise me. He was always playing games. He did the same thing in *Atticus Pünd Investigates* and *No Rest for the Wicked*. And *Magpie Murders*, of course.' She looked me straight in the eye. 'Did he make Aiden the killer?'

'No.'

'He's not, Susan. Believe me. That's what I wanted to tell you. Nobody was kinder to me than Aiden when I first came here, and I told you, I saw him with Cecily. She was quite childish. She reminded me a bit of Dora in *David Copperfield*. A bit soppy. She never had anything very interesting to say. But Aiden was all over her. I think I'm a good judge of character and I can tell you, he'd never do anything to hurt her. You turning up and accusing him—'

'I haven't accused him of anything, Melissa.'

'That's not how he sees it.'

We might have begun an argument but just then Lars appeared, coming over to the table. 'Miss Ryeland?' he asked.

'Yes?'

'Do you drive a red MGB?'

'Yes.' I was puzzled and concerned.

'Someone has just rung reception. They say you're blocking their way.'

I had parked half an hour ago and as far as I could remember, I hadn't been near another car. 'Are you sure?'

Lars shrugged.

I looked at Melissa. 'I'll be two minutes,' I said.

I got up and left the lounge where we had been sitting. I entered the circular entrance hall and walked out the front door. What happened next was a series of images that hit me one after another, forming a sequence that told a story but would only make sense later.

My car was there. And just as I thought, it wasn't blocking anyone. I should have turned back then but I was still walking towards it, wanting to see who had complained.

Across the drive, in front of the hotel, I saw Aiden MacNeil. He shouted at me. I thought he was angry about something. Then I realised he was warning me. He was staring at something above me, out of my line of vision.

I looked up in time to see the most extraordinary sight. There was an owl, its wings outstretched, seemingly in full flight. It took my brain a microsecond to work out that it wasn't a real owl at all. It was the stone sculpture from the middle of the parapet that spanned the front of the hotel and which I had seen when I had arrived. But it wasn't flying, it was plummeting.

Towards me.

I was right underneath it. There was nothing I could do. I didn't have time to get out of the way. But then there was a dark blur and someone crashed into me, a man who had been near the entrance. I felt his arms around me and his shoulder against my chest as he rugby tackled me out of harm's way. Almost at the same moment, the owl hit the ground and smashed into fifty pieces. I heard the impact and knew without any doubt at all that it could have killed me.

As we fell, the man had twisted so that I had landed on top of him. He had protected me from the gravel. Aiden was running towards us, horrified. I heard somebody shout. It was already clear to me that this had all happened deliberately. I had been tricked. The telephone call. My car blocking the way. All done to get me out of the hotel.

The man who had saved me let go of me and I turned to him. I hadn't seen him but I already knew who he was. And I was right.

It was Andreas.

The Moonflower Suite

He pulled me to my feet.

'Andreas ... ' I said. 'What are you ... ?' But I was too choked up to finish the question. I had never felt anything like it, the sheer relief overwhelming me, not just because I'd had such a narrow escape, but because, inexplicably, Andreas was here. I pulled him close to me.

'You know, you're becoming quite a liability,' he said.

'How did you get here?'

But before he could answer, Aiden MacNeil arrived, looking horrified. He could have had no idea that Andreas and I knew each other so as far as he was concerned, some random passer-by had just saved me. 'Are you all right?' he asked. He sounded genuinely concerned and I felt bad that he had been number four on my list of suspects. Maybe, after this, I would drop him to number five.

I nodded. My arm and shoulder had been grazed by the gravel and they were already stinging. I looked at the broken pieces of the stone owl. There was a large dent in the ground where it had landed.

'There was someone on the roof,' Aiden said. 'I saw them!'

'What are you saying?' Andreas was still holding me.

'I don't know. But there was definitely someone there. I'm going up to check.' He continued past us, into the hotel.

Andreas and I were left on our own.

'Who was that?' Andreas asked.

'Aiden MacNeil. He was married to Cecily Treherne. He's one of my main suspects.'

'I think he just managed to stop someone from killing you.'

'What are you talking about?'

'He shouted a warning.'

'Aiden didn't save me. That was you.' I grabbed hold of Andreas and kissed him on the lips. 'What are you doing here, Andreas? How did you get here? And why didn't you answer my email?'

Andreas smiled at me in the way I remembered best: slightly crooked, challenging me. He hadn't shaved or brushed his hair. He could have come here straight from the beach. 'Do you really want to talk about this now?' he said.

'No. I want a drink. I want to be alone with you. I want to get out of this bloody hotel. To be honest with you, I wish I'd never come.'

Andreas glanced up at the roof. 'It looks as if someone else wishes the same.'

There was so much I wanted to say to him but once again we were interrupted – this time by the arrival of Lisa Treherne who had come hurrying out of the hotel. She was pale and out of breath. 'I just met Aiden,' she exclaimed. 'What happened?'

'One of those sculptures fell off the roof,' I said.

'Or someone helped it on its way,' Andreas added. 'Susan was almost killed.'

Lisa looked at Andreas indignantly, as if he was accusing her. 'I'm sorry?' she said. 'Who are you?'

'This is my partner, Andreas,' I explained. 'He's just arrived from Crete.'

'Aiden has gone up to the roof now,' Lisa said. 'There's a service door on the top floor.'

'Presumably, it's kept locked,' Andreas said. It was funny. I hadn't told him that Lisa had forced me out of the hotel, but I could tell that he had taken an intuitive dislike to her.

'I don't know that it is. But I can't imagine why anyone would want to hurt Susan.'

'Well, she's here investigating a murder and a disappearance so maybe someone's decided that she knows too much.'

This was all getting out of hand.

'I've hurt my arm,' I said. I showed Lisa the grazes. 'If you don't mind, I'm going up to my room.'

'I'll let you know if Aiden finds anything.'

Andreas had been carrying a travel bag that he had dropped when coming to my rescue. He snatched it up, then took my arm and led me into the hotel. As we passed through the doorway it suddenly occurred to me that we might well run into Melissa Conway, who was presumably still waiting for me in the lounge. It was one embarrassment I was keen to avoid so I steered him quickly into the reception area and stopped briefly at the desk where Inga was working.

'Inga,' I said. 'I have a guest in the living room. Could you tell her I've had to go up to my room?'

I didn't wait for an answer. Still leaning on Andreas, I headed for the stairs.

'Who was your guest?' Andreas asked.

'No one,' I said. 'It's not important.'

I didn't breathe until the door had swung shut behind us and we were alone in what I had come to think of as the Moonflower Suite. Andreas glanced with approval at the bed (Egyptian-cotton sheets, five hundred thread count), the flat-screen TV, the en suite bathroom. 'Beats the Polydorus,' he said.

I disagreed. 'Our views are better.'

I sat on the bed. Andreas went straight to the minibar and took out a miniature whisky and added some water. He brought it over to the bed and sat down next to me. I took a sip and felt better already, although I didn't know if it was the drink or having him next to me. I hadn't realised how upset I was by what had happened outside.

'Answer my question,' I said. 'How did you get here?'

'EasyJet.'

'That's not what I mean and you know it! I haven't heard from you for days. I thought—' I broke off. I didn't want to tell him what I'd been thinking.

Once again he took my hand. '*Agapiti mou,*' he said, and it just made me happier, hearing him speak to me in Greek. 'I'm sorry. Forgive me. I never got your email. Not until last night. It's the stupid computer. Your email went to spam.'

I should have remembered. There was a problem

with his computer. Just before I'd left we'd lost two bookings exactly the same way.

'I found it last night,' he went on. 'I was going to call you but then I decided to get on the first flight this morning. I wanted to speak to you face-to-face.'

'Who's looking after the hotel?' I asked.

'Don't worry about the hotel.'

'I'm sorry I wrote the email, Andreas. I'm sorry I left Crete.'

'No. You were right.' Andreas sighed. 'It's my fault. I've been trying so hard to make the Polydorus work that I haven't been thinking about you. We should have talked a long time ago and if you weren't happy you should have told me or I should have seen it for myself. The Polydorus was always my dream, not yours, and maybe I was selfish ramming it down your throat. But I'm not going to lose you because of a building. I can sell it. My cousin can look after it. I want us to be together again like we were, and if that means moving back to London and starting again, then that's what we'll do. I can get another job in a school. You can go back to publishing.'

'No. That's not what I want.' I held his hand more tightly. 'I want to be with you. That's all.' Maybe I was thinking about Katie or maybe it was the shock of what had just happened but suddenly my mind was clear. 'I can't stay here, Andreas,' I went on. 'I've more or less burned my boats in London. I sold my flat and to be honest with you, the publishing industry isn't exactly waiting for me with open arms. You know, if I could just get some editing work, even on a freelance basis, that would be enough for me. It's just that books have always been such a big part of my life and not having *any* connection with them in Crete … it's been a bit too drastic.'

'Have you been looking for a job?'

'I had lunch with a friend but it didn't come to anything.' I didn't tell him about my dinner with Craig Andrews. Nothing had come of that either so there was absolutely no reason to feel guilty – or so I'd persuaded myself. 'Can you forgive me, flouncing out the way I did?'

'There's nothing to forgive.'

'I thought you were angry with me. I thought that was why you hadn't got back to me.'

'I could never be angry with you. I love you.'

I drank the whisky. It was the first time I'd attacked the minibar since my arrival, but right then I was tempted to go back and hit the champagne. That reminded me. 'Have you had any money from Lawrence Treherne?' I asked.

'Not yet.'

'I did ask him to pay you.'

'I don't want the money, Susan. Not if it's going to get you killed.'

'Well, my big investigation is probably already over,' I said. 'And I may end up not even getting anything. I got fired this morning. Lisa Treherne wants me to leave tomorrow.'

'That was the woman we met outside.' He smiled. 'I knew I didn't like her.'

'It's all been a complete waste of time – and we've spent a lot of money on flights and hotels.' I got up. 'Well, you can stay here tonight and we'll eat the most expensive meal we can manage in the hotel restaurant. At least that's free. Maybe you can bully a cheque out of Lawrence Treherne. And tomorrow we'll go back.'

'To Crete?'

'The Polydorus.'

'And what are we going to do until dinner?'

'I think I've got an answer to that.'

I walked across the room to draw the curtains.

Just in time to see Martin Williams getting into his car. He was acting furtively, clearly not wanting to be seen. Only that morning I'd more or less accused him of murdering his brother-in-law. I'd threatened to expose him and the lies he'd told. And now he was here.

I stood there watching as he drove away.

HMP Wayland

The next morning, everything changed. I was having breakfast with Andreas when Inga brought
over a letter addressed to me. There was something
about the address on the envelope – the handwriting
clumsy and heavy-handed – that told me at once who it
had come from and the single sheet of lined paper that
it contained quickly confirmed it. Stefan Codrescu had
written to me. He had arranged for me to visit him in
prison that very day. All I had to do was register on the
Internet. I did that and a few hours later we were away,
Andreas and me in my MGB Roadster with the roof
down, speeding up the A14 to Norfolk.

I had never visited a prison before and everything
about HMP Wayland surprised me, starting with its
location in a quiet community of what looked like re-

tirement homes and bungalows a few miles north of Thetford. A series of narrow, twisty lanes brought us to a single red-brick building that might have been a university but for the ominous triple-height door that would presumably ratchet open to allow the prison vans in, and the endless stretch of walls and fencing behind. Though surrounded by houses, it was actually in the middle of nowhere with no public buses, no railway station for twelve miles and a twenty-pound taxi ride (each way) the penalty for anyone wanting to make a visit. It was as if the authorities were determined to punish families as well as the men locked up inside.

I stopped in the prison car park and Andreas and I sat together for a few minutes. I was the only one who was authorised to go in and we hadn't seen much in the way of pubs or restaurants nearby so it looked as if Andreas was going to be stuck in the car.

'I feel bad about leaving you,' I said.

'Don't worry. I flew all the way from Greece in the hope of being abandoned in a car park outside a maximum-security jail.'

'If they don't let me out, dial 999.'

'I'm dialling 999 in the hope they'll keep you in. Anyway, don't worry about me. I've got something to read.' He took out a paperback copy of *Atticus Pünd*

Takes the Case and I wondered if it was possible to love a man more.

Then I went into the prison.

It was funny how HMP Wayland managed to be modern and old-fashioned at the same time. Maybe it's the whole idea of locking people up that has had its day: fine for the Victorians but somehow too simplistic and, for that matter, too expensive, given all the technology and the resources of the twenty-first century. I entered a small, brightly coloured reception area decorated with warning notices about drugs and mobile phones that might be concealed about – or even inside – my person. I had to bend low to speak through a hatch to a uniformed officer who inspected my ID and took my mobile phone for safe keeping. With another couple of visitors, I entered a cage. There was a loud buzz and the door I'd just come through slid shut. A moment later, a second door slid open in front of me. I was now in prison.

A guard took us across a courtyard – on the other side of the fence – and we entered the visitors' block. I found myself in what I can only describe as the worst cafeteria in the world, too brightly lit, with about thirty tables screwed to the floor and a small window open-ing into a kitchen where food and drink could be purchased. Not surprisingly – this was a male prison – I was surrounded mainly by women. I noticed one of them eyeing me sympathetically.

'First time, dear?' she asked.

I wondered how she knew but I imagined that in a prison there would be all sorts of indications that would give you away. She seemed friendly enough, though. 'Yes,' I admitted.

'You should go up and buy food now if you want anything. When they let the men in, there'll be a long line and you won't have time to talk.'

I took her advice and went over to the window. I wasn't sure what Stefan would like so I bought him a selection: a hamburger, crisps, three bars of chocolate, two cans of Coke. The hamburger reminded me of something you might buy outside a football match late at night, only without the cordon bleu cookery. I sandwiched it between two paper plates, hoping it wouldn't get cold before he arrived.

About ten minutes later, the men began to appear, streaming in through a side door and heading towards their wives, mothers and friends sitting at the tables. They were all wearing tracksuit bottoms, sweatshirts and really horrible trainers. A few guards stood around the sides but the atmosphere was quiet, relaxed. I had seen photographs of Stefan Codrescu and recognised him at once. He didn't know me, of course, so I raised a hand and waved. He came over and sat down.

It was an extraordinary moment, meeting him. It was like coming across the central character in a novel but only after two or three hundred pages and in the knowledge that there are very few more before the end. All sorts of things went through my head. The first was that I might actually be sitting opposite a killer – but almost immediately I dismissed it. Even after eight years in prison, he had a sort of innocence that made him peculiarly attractive. He was well built with broad shoulders but still quite slight, like a dancer. I could easily see why Lisa Treherne would have wanted to possess him. At the same time, there was an indignation, a sense of injustice still smouldering in his eyes, a flame that the passing years had failed to extinguish. He knew he shouldn't be here and I was immediately convinced of it too.

Right then, I found myself questioning my own involvement in all this and suddenly I felt uneasy. I had come to England because I had been paid. I had taken on the case with the enthusiasm of someone solving a crossword puzzle when from the very start I should have realised that I was actually dealing with a massive injustice. Eight years in prison! While I had been tootling between Woodbridge and London, asking questions, making notes, he had been stuck in here. I had been fighting for a man's life.

There was something else about Stefan. He reminded me of someone – but at that moment I wasn't sure who.

He was examining the food and drink spread out on the table. 'Is this for me?' he asked.

'Yes,' I said. 'I wasn't sure what to get you.'

'You didn't need to get me anything. I'm not hungry.' He pushed the hamburger to one side and cracked open the can of Coke. I watched him take a sip. 'In your letter, you said you were a publisher,' he went on.

'I was an editor once. I actually live in Crete but I met Lawrence and Pauline and they asked me to come back to the UK.'

'Are you going to write a book about me?' He was looking at me with quiet hostility.

'No,' I replied.

'But you paid Alan Conway.'

'It wasn't quite like that. Alan wrote a book which has some sort of connection with what happened at Branlow Hall, but at the time I didn't know anything about you or Frank Parris. I only heard about it when Lawrence told me.' I paused. 'Did you ever meet Alan?'

Stefan said nothing for a moment. It was obvious that

he didn't trust me. He considered every word before he spoke. 'He wrote to me when I was in remand but why would I have wanted to meet him? He wasn't offering to help me. Anyway, I had other things on my mind.'

'Did you ever read the book?'

He shook his head. 'I haven't seen it in the prison library. They do have quite a lot of murder stories. They're popular here.'

'But you knew about it?'

He ignored my question. 'Where is Cecily?' he asked. 'In your letter, you said she's disappeared.'

Stefan hadn't known about Cecily – not until I'd written to him. And why should he have? He probably had limited access to newspapers inside the prison and Cecily's disappearance wouldn't have made it onto national TV. Again, I was angry with myself. I had broken the news to him without any thought of the consequences. It had just been another piece of the puzzle.

Now I chose my words more carefully. 'We still don't know where she is. The police are looking for her. They have no reason to believe that she's in any danger.'

'Why are you saying that? Of course she's in danger. She was afraid.'

'How do you know that? Did she visit you?'

'No. But she wrote to me.'

'When?'

By way of an answer, he reached into his pocket and produced a single sheet of paper, which he held on to for a moment before handing it to me. The first thing I saw was the date at the top of the page – 10 June. So Cecily had written this the day before she had disappeared! The letter was short, typed. I felt a stirring of excitement. It was new evidence. Nobody else could have seen it.

'Can I read this?' I asked.

'Go ahead.' He sat back, watching me all the time.

I unfolded the letter and read:

10 June

Dear Stefan,

You may be surprised to hear from me after such a long silence but we had always agreed not to write to each other again, and after the verdict, when you pleaded guilty, I thought it was better that way.

I was wrong. I'm so sorry. I know now that you did not kill Frank Parris. I still don't understand why you took the blame and I want to come and see you and talk to you.

It's difficult to explain. A man called Alan Conway came to the hotel after it all happened and wrote a book called Atticus Pünd Takes the Case.

It's just a detective story but he seems to have used people and things from the hotel. Mum and Dad are in it and Derek and there's a hotel called the Moonflower. The story isn't the same but that's not the point. I knew from the very first page who killed Frank Parris. I'd known it all along, but reading the book made it clear to me.

I need to come and talk to you. I'm told you have to put me on a list or something. Can you do that? I'm also sending the book to Mum and Dad. They'll know what to do. But I have to be careful. I don't think I'm in any danger, but you know what the hotel is like. Everyone knows everything and I don't want anyone to find out.

I'm writing this quickly but I will write to you again next week, I promise. And when I see you, I'll explain everything.

With love,

Cecily

So it was true. All along, Cecily had known the identity of the killer. She had actually found it on the first page. I wished now that I had brought the paperback with me. The book opens with Eric and Phyllis Chandler in the kitchen at Clarence Keep. There's a mention of florentines and Mrs Tiggy-Winkle, neither of which could have had any relevance to Frank Parris's murder. Then I remembered that Andreas had a copy in the car. Once I was outside, I would read the whole chapter again.

'As soon as I got this, I put her on the list for a visit,' Stefan said. 'I was wondering why I hadn't heard from her. Then you wrote to me. That was why I agreed to see you.'

'Stefan—' I felt completely out of my depth. There were so many questions I wanted to ask him but at the same time I was afraid of offending him. Eight years in prison! How could he seem so calm, so unaffected? 'I really want to help you,' I said. 'But I have to know. What exactly was your relationship with Cecily Treherne?'

'She was the one who hired me after I came out of the Carlford Unit at Warren Hill. Her dad had this rehabilitation programme. She was kind to me when I was at the hotel. And when I was accused of murder, she was the only one who believed in me.'

'You realise this letter could change everything?'

'If anyone actually believes her.'

'Will you let me keep this, Stefan? I'm in touch with the police detective who's looking for Cecily. He also investigated Frank Parris's murder.'

'Locke?'

'Detective Chief Superintendent Locke. Yes.'

For the first time, Stefan was angry. 'I don't want you to show him this,' he said. He took the letter back and folded it away. 'That man is the reason why I'm here.'

'You confessed.'

'He made me confess!' I could see Stefan fighting with himself, trying to keep his emotions under control. He leaned towards me, speaking softly but with venom. 'That bastard persuaded me that things would go easier if I pleaded guilty. All the evidence was against me. I had a criminal record. They'd found the money and there were bloodstains in my room. He said that if I signed a confession, he would put in a word for me and like the fool I was, I believed him. So I did what he said and I got life with a minimum of twenty-five years. That means I'll be nearly fifty before I'm free again. You give him that letter and he'll tear it to pieces. He doesn't want anyone to believe me. If I was found not guilty, how do you think that would make him look? He wants me to stay here and rot.'

He slumped back in his chair but he hadn't finished yet.

'I was finished the moment I came to this country,' he said quietly. 'I was twelve years old and I didn't want to be here. Nobody wanted me to be here. I was trash – Romanian trash – and the first chance they got, they threw me in this place and forgot about me. You think anyone will read this letter? You think anyone will care? No! I could die in here. I could kill myself tomorrow and I would except for the one brightness in my life, the one dawn that gives me hope.' I was going to ask him what he meant but then he asked: 'Do you know who killed Frank Parris?'

'No,' I admitted. 'Not yet.'

'You're an editor. Books! Not a lawyer. Not a detective. You can't help me.'

'Maybe I can.' I reached out and rested my hand on his arm. It was the first contact between us. 'Tell me what happened that night,' I said. 'Friday the fifteenth of June 2008.'

'You know what happened. A man called Frank Parris was beaten to death with a hammer.'

'Yes. But what about you? Where were you that night?' He wasn't going to answer so I went on. 'What are you going to do, Stefan? Go back to your cell and sit on your own? How will that help you – or Cecily?'

He thought for a moment, then nodded.

'I went to a party. Cecily and Aiden had a party for all the staff, next to the swimming pool.'

'Did you have a lot to drink?'

'I had some wine. A couple of glasses. I was very

tired. After a bit I didn't want to be there and I walked back to my room with the spa guy … '

'Lionel Corby.'

'Yes. He had the room next to mine.'

'Did you ever call him Leo?'

'No. I called him Lionel. Why do you ask?'

'It doesn't matter. Go on.'

'I was asleep almost at once. That's all there is to tell you. I slept all night and I woke up quite late. Maybe half past eight the next day. I didn't go back into the hotel. I didn't go anywhere near room twelve.'

'But Derek Endicott saw you.'

'He saw someone. It wasn't me.'

'Do you think you were deliberately framed?'

'Of course I was framed. Haven't you listened to anything I've said? I was the obvious target.'

'Tell me about you and Lisa.'

That stopped him. 'She's a bitch,' he said, simply, swearing for the first time.

'You were in a relationship with her.'

'There was no relationship. There was sex.'

'She forced you … '

'You've met her?'

'Yes.'

'Then why else would you imagine someone like me would want to have sex with someone like her?'

'And when you refused to do what she wanted, she fired you.'

'No, of course not. She was much cleverer than that. After I stopped seeing her, she came up with these stories about me stealing money and things. It was all lies. She was threatening me. She made sure everyone knew she was suspicious about me and then she fired me.'

'But you were still seeing her.' I was remembering what Lionel Corby had told me, what he had seen in the wood. 'A couple of weeks before the wedding, you were seen together in the wood near Oaklands Cottage.'

Stefan hesitated. I saw something, a memory, flash across his eyes. 'That was the last time,' he said. 'I thought if I gave her what she wanted I would get her off my back. It didn't work. Two weeks later she fired me anyway.'

He was lying to me. I don't know how I knew it and I had no idea what he was hiding, but his demeanour had changed. Some of that innocence of his had become tarnished at the edges. I thought of challenging him but knew it would do no good. I watched him as he finished the Coke and put it down, his hands enclosing the can, almost crushing it.

'You can't help me,' he said.

'At least let me try,' I replied. 'Trust me, Stefan. I'm

on your side. I'm sorry we didn't meet sooner but now that we have, I'm not going to let you down.'

He levelled his eyes at me. They were very gentle, a soft shade of brown. 'Why should I trust you?' he asked.

'Who else is there?' I replied.

He nodded. Then, very slowly, he took out the letter and slid it across the table towards me. 'This is all I have,' he said. 'There is nothing else.'

He stood up. Before he walked away, he took all the food from the table: the crisps, the chocolate bars, even the cold hamburger. That told me as much about life in prison as anything that had happened since I had arrived. Then, without another word, he left.

*

I couldn't drive.

Andreas took over behind the wheel. He hadn't asked me what had happened inside the prison. He could see that I was too upset to talk about it. We drove a few miles through the Norfolk countryside, which became just a little softer and more welcoming when it became the Suffolk countryside, and then stopped for a late lunch at a pub, the Plough and Stars, just south of Thetford. Andreas ordered sandwiches but I wasn't hungry. The food made me think of the horrible, cold hamburger that Stefan had taken back to his cell. Eight years of his life!

'Susan, do you want to talk to me about it?' Andreas asked, eventually.

The pub might have been a cheerful place on a Friday night. It had flagstones and a wood-burning stove and old-fashioned wooden tables. But we were almost alone. The man behind the bar looked fed up.

'I'm sorry,' I said. 'I just feel so angry with myself about the way I went careering into all this. First of all, I abandoned you. But seeing that poor man just now, stuck in that place ... '

'You know he's innocent.'

'I've known that all along, Andreas. I just never thought about it from his point of view.'

'So what happens next?'

'I don't know. That's the worst of it. I just don't know what else I can do.'

I remember the moment exactly. We were sitting in a corner. The barman was wiping a glass. The only other customer – a man with a dog – got up and left. A wind had sprung up and I could see the pub sign swinging outside.

'I know who killed Frank Parris,' I said.

'I'm sorry?' Andreas stared at me. 'I thought you just said—'

'I know what I said. But I've worked it out!'

'Did Stefan tell you?'

'No. He told me more than he meant to. But it wasn't him. It all just came together.'

Andreas stared at me. 'Are you going to tell me?'

'Yes. Of course. But not yet. I need to think.'

'Really?'

'Give me a little time.'

He smiled at me. 'You're worse than Alan Conway!'

We didn't eat the sandwiches. We got back in the car and drove off.

The Killer

We didn't go back to Woodbridge. We drove straight on to Heath House in Westleton. We walked up to the front door together and I more or less leaned on the doorbell, daring the occupants not to answer. After about thirty seconds, Martin Williams opened the door. He looked at Andreas with suspicion and at me with a mixture of surprise and anger. It had, after all, only been one day since he had told me never to come back.

'You can't come in,' he said.

'Are you busy?'

'Joanne doesn't want to see you. Nor do I. We told you that the last time you were here.'

'I know who killed Frank Parris,' I said. 'My friend,

Andreas, also knows. You can hear it from me or from the police. It's your choice.'

He stared at me, making his calculations. He wasn't a big man but he had been leaning diagonally across the door frame, blocking my way. For once he wasn't wearing overalls. He was dressed in jeans, leather boots and a paisley shirt open at the neck, as if he was about to go out line dancing. He straightened up. 'You're talking rubbish,' he said. 'But I wouldn't want you to make a fool of yourself. You can have five minutes.'

Joanne Williams came down the stairs as we entered the kitchen. She was furious to see me and didn't pretend otherwise. She didn't even look at me. 'What's she doing here?' she asked Martin. 'You promised me she wouldn't come back!'

'Hello, Joanne,' I said.

'Susan claims she knows who killed Frank,' Martin told her. 'I thought it best to hear what she has to say.'

'I'm sorry. I'm not interested.'

'Are you sure about that?' I said. 'Maybe I should repeat what I just told your husband – if you won't talk to me, I'll go straight to the police. Which is it to be?'

I saw them exchange glances and knew that they needed no further convincing.

'Come in here,' Martin said.

We went back into the kitchen. It was a room I was

beginning to know too well. Andreas and I sat on one side of the table, Joanne and Martin on the other. We glared at each other across the pine surface. It was like a council of war.

'This won't take very long,' I said. 'This is the third time I've come to see you and you'll be glad to hear it's going to be the last. As I explained at the start, I was asked by Lawrence and Pauline Treherne to look into their daughter's disappearance and to find out if there was any connection with the murder of Frank Parris eight years ago. The first time I came here, I won't say you lied to me, but let's just say that you were rather flexible with the truth. It didn't take me very long to discover that the two of you – and only the two of you – had a good reason to kill Frank Parris. The collapse of his advertising business in Australia meant that he needed money and so he was going to force you to sell Heath House, which had been left to you, fifty-fifty, by your mother. It was your family home and if he died, assuming he hadn't left it to anyone else in his will, you'd get to keep it.'

'He left it to Joanne, actually,' Martin said.

'Did he really?' Andreas and I both looked amazed.

'That's what he always told us.'

I shook my head in disbelief. 'That's what I just don't understand, Martin,' I said. 'Why are you telling me that? I'd have thought that's the *last* thing you'd want me to know. It just makes you look more suspicious. If you were left the house in his will, then you *definitely* had a motive for the murder, but here you are, blurting it out without a second thought. It's like when I came here yesterday and instead of denying everything like any sane man would, you spelled out exactly the reason why you might have committed the murder. Why have you even allowed me in now when you told me you never wanted to see me again?'

'Because I want to put these ridiculous accusations to bed.'

'That's not what it sounds like to me. Is that what it sounds like to you, Andreas?'

'No,' Andreas agreed. 'I'd say he's stirring it up.'

Joanne was watching Martin so intently that she might not actually have been breathing. I waited for him to speak.

'I think you should leave,' he said.

'It's too late for that,' I replied. 'I know the truth.'

'You can make any accusations you like. But you can't prove anything.'

'As a matter of fact, I can, Martin,' I countered. 'I can prove one hundred per cent, without any doubt at all, that you did *not* kill Frank. How can I do that?

Because as I told you at the door, I know the identity of the real killer and it wasn't you.'

'Then what are you doing here?' Joanne demanded.

'Because I'm fed up with both of you and I want to put an end to your little charade once and for all. From the moment I first walked into this house you've been pissing me around, play-acting—'

'I don't know what you mean!' Martin interrupted.

'Don't you, Martin? Well, I'll tell you. Let's imagine, just for the sake of argument, that you found yourself trapped in a generally shit marriage with a wife who bullied you and who made you feel small about yourself—'

'How dare you!' Joanne sat bolt upright, her cheeks darkening.

'That's more or less what my sister, Katie, told me. She had dinner with you once and she described you, Joanne – I think the word "ball-breaker" was the one she used. She said you walked all over Martin like a doormat. She wondered how the two of you even managed to stay together.'

'Well, that's her view ... ' Martin muttered.

'It's certainly not true *now*, is it! Things seem to have changed. You're definitely the one in control, Martin. Why is that, I wonder? Maybe it's because

Joanne's come to the conclusion that it was you who killed Frank and that actually you're quite a dangerous character. And maybe, just maybe, you've encouraged her to believe it because it gives you a bit of power and freedom in this house.'

'That's ridiculous!'

'Is it? It would explain why you told me about the will just now – and why you gave me such a rubbish answer when I challenged you about Frank seeing the marquee. From the very moment you and I met, you've been wanting me to suspect you!'

Martin stood up. 'I'm not listening to any more of this,' he said.

'Yes, you are, Martin. Because you actually tried to kill me! I saw you yesterday, sneaking away from Branlow Hall. Maybe you wanted me to see you, but I know it was you who dropped the stone owl off the roof. The trouble for you is that I've also got proof.' That stopped him in his tracks. 'When you called the hotel to get me out of the door you were already up there, in position. You waited for me to come out and then you pushed it off the ledge.' I turned to Joanne. 'Did he tell you what had happened?'

'He said he'd heard about it ... ' Joanne was staring at her husband in a way that made this whole visit worthwhile.

'Did he also tell you that he was recorded going in on CCTV and that the hotel switchboard can trace the call he made, that the number was logged? And did he mention if he was wearing gloves or not? Because the police are examining the fire door on the roof and the fragments of stone.'

This wasn't true. The police weren't actually involved. But they could well have been.

The colour had drained out of Martin's face.

'Tell me this one thing, Martin. While I'm in a slightly forgiving mood. Just reassure me that you weren't really trying to kill me and that you actually intended for me to see you sneaking away from the hotel. All you wanted was to frighten me, to make me think you were a threat. Because that was part of the game you were playing with your wife. Martin the killer! Martin the real man! You didn't kill Frank and you didn't try to kill me. That was just an image you were trying to project.'

There was a long pause but then at last it came, exactly what I wanted, though only a whisper. 'Yes.'

'Was that a yes, Martin?'

'Yes!' Louder this time.

'Thank you. That's all I need to know.'

I got up and walked out of the house with Andreas at my side. We hadn't made it to the garden gate before

Martin Williams came up to us. He was looking contrite, pathetic. He shouldn't have followed us out.

'I didn't mean any harm,' he exclaimed. 'You're right – what you said about Frank. And what I did yesterday at the hotel. I swear to you, I didn't want to hurt you. You won't tell the police, will you?'

Before I could stop him, Andreas lashed out. He swung round and his fist crashed into Martin's face. If this had been one of Alan's books, Martin would have been knocked off his feet and thrown, unconscious, to the ground. In fact, it was a lot less dramatic than that. There was a soft *thwack* and Martin was left standing, dazed, with blood streaming over his lip. It was possible Andreas had broken his nose.

The two of us walked away.

'You said you weren't going to hurt him,' I said, as we walked back to the car.

'I know,' Andreas replied. 'I'm sorry.'

I opened the car door. 'Apology accepted.'

Checkout

When I was editing *Atticus Pünd Takes the Case*, I had one other argument with Alan Conway. It concerned the last two chapters, in which Atticus gets all the characters together at the Moonflower Hotel.

I know scenes like this work well on television. I've seen David Suchet as Poirot, John Nettles as Barnaby, Angela Lansbury as Jessica Fletcher, and between them they must have done it a hundred times, closing in on one suspect after another until finally they reveal the real culprit. But that was exactly my point. I was worried that even in what was intended to be a homage to the Golden Age of detective fiction, the climax was a little overdone. I wondered if Alan could find another way of presenting the information.

Well, you've read the book. You know how much faith Alan had in my editorial judgement.

So he would probably have been amused to see me in the lounge of Branlow Hall, surrounded by no fewer than seven people and a dog. The dog was Bear, Cecily's golden retriever, and he at least was asleep in a corner. But the rest of them had come to hear me explain myself. I could almost feel the invisible TV cameras pointing in my direction.

This was my last day at the hotel. In fact, it was already past my checkout time. Lisa Treherne had asked me to leave, she had said, with the full support of her father, but I had rung Lawrence and told him that I knew who had killed Frank Parris and also what had happened to his daughter. I had reminded him that so far he hadn't paid me a penny of the money he had promised me, egged on, I'm sure, by Lisa. He had agreed to meet me in the afternoon.

'Come to the lounge at three o'clock and I'll explain the whole thing,' I said. 'And bring a cheque for what you owe me. Ten thousand pounds made out to Andreas Patakis.' Of course it should have had my name on it but Andreas had flown about two thousand miles in time to save me from a falling missile. I wanted him to be the one to have the pleasure of cashing it.

I had hoped that Lawrence would come alone, but

Pauline was with him when he arrived and Aiden MacNeil had joined them too. I suppose that was fair enough: he had the greatest stake in what had happened. He was still waiting for news of Cecily. I did think it a little odd, though, that he had brought Eloise Radmani along for support. The two of them were sitting next to each other on a sofa and it struck me that they seemed to have a nanny/employer relationship that was strange and rather sinister. At least they had left Roxana with Inga. Worst of all, as far as I was concerned, Lisa Treherne had also invited herself to the party. I had Andreas with me and she nodded briefly at him but ignored me, throwing herself into an armchair as if she'd already decided the whole thing was going to be a waste of time.

Finally, Detective Chief Superintendent Locke was sitting in a chair next to the door. It had been Andreas who had persuaded me to invite him, but it hadn't been an easy decision. I had no wish to see him again after our last meeting at Martlesham Heath. He was a bully and a racist and he was largely responsible for the injustice that had been done to Stefan Codrescu. But Andreas had insisted that someone from the police should be present. We had to make this official.

I was actually quite surprised he had agreed to come. Andreas and I had driven over to his office and it struck me that a pair of local sex offenders would have been given a warmer welcome. He had dismissed the idea that I knew who had killed Frank and became angry when I refused to tell him there and then. It was only the letter that Stefan had given me that changed his mind. It proved that Cecily had been convinced of his innocence and it made it clear that her disappearance was connected to what had happened all those years ago. Locke should have known about the letter. Its very existence made him look weak. That, I think, was the reason he was here.

It wasn't quite the assembly that Atticus Pünd would have addressed – no butlers, vicars or chambermaids – but even so I got a strange sense of his presence in the room. I could almost see him perching on one of the empty seats, his walking stick beside him, waiting for me to begin. I'd often thought that my whole approach to crime – the way I talked to people or examined the evidence – was somehow influenced by him and his ridiculous book, *The Landscape of Criminal Investigation*, and I suppose, all in all, I had warm feelings towards him. I thought of him as a mentor. This was strange, firstly because he was a fictitious character but mainly because I couldn't stand the man who had created him.

'We're waiting, Susan,' Lisa said.

'I'm sorry. I was just collecting my thoughts.' I smiled. Maybe I could enjoy this after all. I was certainly never going to do it again. 'Perhaps I should start by saying that I don't know where Cecily is but I do know what happened to her. I also know exactly what she discovered in *Atticus Pünd Takes the Case*.' There was a copy on the table in front of me. 'I'm afraid Alan Conway left her a message – several messages, actually – and in doing so he put her in danger.'

I glanced at Andreas. He nodded at me. He was watching my back.

'The thing about Frank Parris was that nobody at Branlow Hall had any reason to kill him,' I went on. 'He was passing through ... on his way to visit his sister and his brother-in-law in Westleton. He'd just come back from Australia. Apart from his half-share in a house here, he had no links with Suffolk. My first thought was that he had been killed by Derek Endicott. It could all have happened by mistake because Frank hadn't liked the room he'd been given and had been changed to room twelve, which was where a retired headmaster called George Saunders was meant to be staying. As it happened, Derek had gone to Bromeswell Grove, which was where Saunders taught, and he had a very rough time there. He was certainly very put out when he saw Saunders again.

'I could imagine a scenario in which Derek took a hammer and went upstairs in the middle of the night. It's dark in those corridors and he could have killed Frank without realising he'd got the wrong man. As it happens, we only have Derek's word for it that Stefan ever went into the room. Nobody else saw him.'

'That's a ridiculous story,' Aiden said. 'Derek wouldn't hurt anyone.'

'I agree. Which is why I've ruled him out. Anyway, Derek could never have arranged all the other clues that pointed to Stefan; in particular, the money under the mattress and the blood splatter. I just don't think he's clever enough.

'Now we're left with just the four of you,' I said. 'But there are two people missing from the room and I want to deal with them first. Let's start with Melissa Conway. She was staying in Oaklands Cottage on the edge of the estate and she was in and out of the hotel around the time of the wedding. She saw Frank and she wasn't happy about it. Part of her blamed him for leading her husband down the garden path; the path in this instance taking him to gay bars and bathhouses. Suppose she'd decided to get her own back on him for stealing her husband? Though it often surprises me, she did actually love Alan.

'What would have happened if Alan had discovered

the truth – that his own ex-wife was guilty of the crime? Wouldn't that have been a perfect motive for not revealing it in his book? He would have to keep quiet to protect her and, by extension, himself. The moment I heard she'd been here, I thought she was a likely suspect. But there was just one problem. She couldn't possibly have overheard Cecily make the phone call to her parents. She was probably at her home in Bradford-on-Avon when Cecily disappeared.

'However, Melissa said something to me that really got me thinking. She mentioned how she'd used the spa a lot when she was living in Oaklands Cottage and that she used to train with Lionel Corby. Only she didn't call him Lionel. She knew him as Leo.

'Now, as it happens, Frank Parris knew someone called Leo, a rent boy working in London. I found that out when I was there. The two of them slept together. Alan Conway even dedicated his book to Frank and Leo. I'm sorry if this is all a bit sordid by the way, Lawrence. And I'm afraid it gets worse. Frank wasn't just gay. He had quite curious sexual tastes, including bondage, S&M, that sort of thing. Suppose Lionel was Leo and Frank recognised him when he booked into the hotel? When I met Lionel, he mentioned that he'd had a lot of private clients in London. '*You have no idea of the sort of stuff I got up to!*' Those were his exact

words. I assumed he was talking about personal training but who knows?

'The trouble is, I've got the same problem as I had
with Melissa. Lionel could have been Leo and he could
have killed Frank but he wasn't here when Cecily made
the telephone call. I don't see how he could have attacked or hurt her. How would he even know she'd
read the book?

'But Eloise was here and she did know.'

The moment I spoke the words, Eloise Radmani lost
her temper in the way that Mediterranean people do so
well. 'How can you drag me into this!' she cried out. 'I
have nothing to do with it.'

'You were here when Cecily disappeared and you
even overheard the telephone call she made to her parents about the book. You were outside the office.'

'I had nothing to do with Frank Parris!'

'That's not true. You worked at the same advertising agency as him: McCann Erickson. You were the
receptionist.'

That took her by surprise, the fact that I knew. She
faltered. 'I was there only for a few months.'

'But you met him.'

'I saw him. We never spoke.'

'You were with your husband then, weren't you? His
name was Lucien.'

She looked away. 'I'm not going to talk about him.'

'I have just one question, Eloise. Did he have a nickname? Did you ever call him Leo?'

It was the one thing I needed to know, to be absolutely sure. I wasn't going to say this to her, and certainly not in front of the others, but it had occurred to me that the AIDS that had killed him might not have been the result of a faulty blood transfusion. Was it possible that he had found other ways to support himself while he was training to be an architect? Had Lucien worked under the name of Leo? Had he contracted AIDS as a result of having unsafe sex? That was what I was really asking.

'I never called him that. No one did.'

I believed her. Aiden and Cecily had hired her months after their wedding. I couldn't see how she might have been at the hotel on the night of Frank's death unless she had come under another name. And anyway, Derek had been sure he had seen a *man* stealing along the corridor towards room 12. Even as I confronted Eloise, I knew it couldn't have been her.

Andreas had opened a bottle of mineral water. He handed me a glass and I drank. Over by the door, Locke was sitting ramrod straight, trying to pretend he wasn't here. I was aware of the others watching me and dreaded what was coming next. But it wasn't my fault.

I had wanted to see Lawrence Treherne on his own. He was the one who had invited the entire family.

'There is another possibility,' I continued, choosing my words carefully. 'It did occur to me that Frank Parris might not have been the target at all. Suppose the whole point of the murder was not to kill him but to frame Stefan Codrescu?'

This was greeted with a less than enthusiastic silence. Eventually, Lawrence spoke. 'Who would want to do that?' he asked.

I turned to Lisa. 'I'm afraid we have to talk about you and Stefan,' I said.

'You want to trash us all? Is that your aim?' She shifted in her seat, crossing her legs.

'My aim is to tell the truth, Lisa, and like it or not you were very much part of what happened. You were "in a relationship" with Stefan.' I drew the inverted commas with my fingers.

'Yes.' She had already admitted it to me. She couldn't deny it now.

Her parents looked at us in dismay.

'He refused to continue that relationship.'

She hesitated. 'Yes.'

'Were you aware that Stefan was also having sex with Cecily?'

Now it was Aiden who was angry. 'That's a lie!'

'I'm afraid it's not.' I paused deliberately for effect. 'I saw Stefan this morning.'

'You saw him?' Pauline was astonished.

'I visited him in prison.'

'And he told you that about Cecily?' Aiden sneered at me. 'And you believed him?'

'He didn't tell me. In fact, he did the best he could to cover it up. But all the evidence was there. I just had to put it together.

'Lionel Corby told me that he had seen two people having sex in the wood near Oaklands Cottage a couple of weeks before the wedding. At first, he thought one of them was you, Aiden. But then he saw that the man didn't have a tattoo on his shoulder and realised it was Stefan. He couldn't see the woman from where he was standing. She was underneath. But he knew that Stefan had been seeing Lisa – against his will – and assumed it was her.

'He was wrong.' Again I addressed Lisa. 'How do I know? Actually, it's very simple. There was something that you said to me over breakfast, just before you asked me to leave. You denied that you had fired him "*because he wouldn't come into my bed any more*" and it was that turn of phrase that told me everything I needed to know.

'Why would you take the risk – and the discomfort –

of meeting him in the middle of a wood when you could quite easily have sex in your own home? You live alone in Woodbridge. You had no reason to hide. But of course, for Cecily it was different. She was sharing a house with Aiden. The two of them were engaged. She couldn't even use a room in the hotel. She might be seen. Sex in the wood was the answer.'

'Cecily would never have cheated on me!' Aiden was furious. 'We were happy together.'

'I'm sorry—'

'Lionel didn't see her! You just said that.'

'That's true.'

'Then you're lying!'

'I'm afraid not, Aiden. I've seen a letter that Cecily wrote to Stefan after he was sent to prison. It was very short and she hadn't written to him for many years. But the tone of it was still intimate. It was signed "*with love*".

'And it wasn't just that. When I asked Stefan if he had been with Lisa in the wood, he hesitated and then he told me that it *was* her, even though it directly contradicted what he'd said just a minute before. I knew immediately that he was lying and that he was protecting someone.'

I took another sip of water. Over the edge of the glass, Andreas caught my eye. He gave me a nod of encouragement. I had told him all of this on the way down from Norfolk and he knew what was coming next.

'There was something else that Stefan said,' I continued. 'It made no sense at the time but I looked it up afterwards and it confirmed what I had suspected all along. Once again it relates to you, Aiden, and you're not going to like it, but I wonder if you know anyway?'

'What are you talking about?' Aiden looked at me with poison in his eyes.

'Stefan was saying how much he hated England, but then he added: "*I could kill myself tomorrow and I would except for the one brightness in my life, the one dawn that gives me hope.*" I wondered what he meant. At the same time, talking to him face-to-face, I knew he reminded me of someone.' I couldn't dress it up any more. I had to come out with it. 'He's Roxana's father.'

'No!' A tortured cry from Aiden. He half rose from his chair and Andreas also got up, ready to protect me if he had to. On the other side of the room, Locke didn't even move.

'It's a wicked lie. There's no truth in it.' Eloise took his hand.

'How dare you—!' Lawrence was spluttering, wanting to throw me out. But he didn't because he knew I was right.

'Aiden is fair-haired. Cecily was blonde. Roxana has

black hair and she's the spitting image of her father. Aiden told me that Cecily chose the name and I think she did so quite deliberately. She knew who the father was. Roxana is a very popular name in Romania. It means "brightness" or "dawn".' I went on quickly, wanting to get this part of it over with. 'This is what happened. Lisa fired Stefan when he refused to have sex with her. And then she discovered that he was having sex with her sister, the same sister, incidentally, who had scarred her as a child. How did she feel about that? Wouldn't it be a great revenge on both of them to kill a complete stranger and frame Stefan so that he went to prison for life? If Lisa had been in her office, she could easily have heard the phone call that Cecily made to the South of France. That's what I've been thinking for a long time now. I was convinced that Lisa was behind both the crimes.'

'Then you don't know anything!' Lisa snarled. 'I didn't kill anyone.'

'I think we've all had quite enough,' Lawrence said. 'Detective Superintendent Locke, are you going to let her go on like this?'

Andreas cut in before he could reply. 'Susan knows who killed Frank Parris,' he said. He could have been a teacher once again, talking to a classroom full of boys. 'If you sit down and let her finish, she's going to tell you.'

The five of them – Lawrence and Pauline, Lisa, Aiden and Eloise, looked to each other. It was Aiden who made the decision for them. He sat down again. 'Go on, then,' he said. 'But maybe you can get to the point. I think we've all had enough of this ... speculation.'

For someone who had just been told that his daughter had been fathered by another man, he was surprisingly calm. But then I was sure he had always known.

'It all begins with the book,' I said. '*Atticus Pünd Takes the Case.* That's what this has all been about. Cecily saw something in it and that's why she had to disappear. The letter to Stefan that I mentioned just now – she wrote it after she had read the book.'

'Did she tell him what she'd seen?' Pauline asked.

'Unfortunately not. She did say that she had always suspected who had killed Frank Parris, but it had been proved to her on *the very first page*. The question is, what page was she referring to? I assumed she meant the first page of Chapter One, but there's nothing there. So maybe it was the author biography or the reviews or the chapter headings. I looked at them all. But actually, it was much simpler than that. It was the dedication. *"For Frank and Leo: in remembrance".*

'Why did Alan write that? Was it because they were

both dead? Or could it actually mean something quite different? Frank, of course, was dead. But maybe Leo wasn't and Alan was telling him that he remembered, that he knew who he was. Maybe it wasn't a dedication at all. Maybe it was actually a warning.'

I let this sink in. Then I continued.

'I never met Cecily and I wish I'd known her better because I've come to realise that her character is the key to everything that happened. When was she born, by the way? I'd imagine that it was sometime in November or December.'

'It was November the twenty-fifth,' Lawrence said. Then he added: 'How did you know?'

'That would make her a Sagittarius,' I said. 'And of course, astrology was very important to her. That was something that was impressed on me from the very start. Aiden told me that she started every day by reading her horoscope, but it was more than that. On the day of her wedding it told her to prepare for ups and downs and instead of just dismissing it with a smile or pretending she hadn't read it, she became very upset. When she went down the aisle, she was wearing an astrological necklace. I've seen the photograph: three stars and an arrow. Sagittarius. We stopped in a pub on the way down from Norfolk – the Plough and Stars – and it was the name that made me realise what had been staring me in the face all along. Astrology pretty much defined Cecily's life. Even her dog, Bear, was named after a constellation.'

Hearing its name mentioned, the dog thumped its tail once, lazily, against the floor.

'But it goes further than that,' I went on. 'In his long email to me, Lawrence mentioned that Cecily was first drawn to Aiden because they were "compatible". That's a word you often find in astrological charts. He actually met Cecily on his birthday, when he was showing her round a flat, and we know that was the start of August 2005, which would make Aiden ... '

' ... a Leo.' Andreas completed the sentence.

'Cecily would have known that Leo and Sagittarius go together very well. They're both fire signs: they share the same values, the same emotions; they come together in security and trust. At least, that was what she believed. And of course, she would have been assured by the tattoo that Aiden has on his shoulder. Lionel told me that it is a cosmic snake, a big circle with a tail. But actually what she saw is a symbol – some people call it the glyph – that is used to represent Leo.'

'I'm Leo,' Aiden said. 'She was Sagittarius. We suited each other. What's the big deal?'

'You knew Frank Parris.'

'I'd never met him before in my life.'

'That's not true. You claimed you were working as an estate agent in London, but even Lawrence was surprised how well you'd managed to do for yourself. You were in your twenties so how could you possibly have made enough money to get yourself a place on the Edgware Road? You had to be making money some other way. And here's another thing. When I asked a friend of mine who knows about these things, he was surprised that a twenty-something rent boy was able to work out of an expensive flat in Mayfair. He couldn't possibly afford it. But suppose he had the keys to an unoccupied flat as part of his job? Suppose he worked as—'

'You're wrong,' Aiden cut in before I could finish.

I ignored him. 'Let's go back to Frank's arrival at Branlow Hall. He doesn't like his room and you get sent in to sort it out. You meet and suddenly he's your best friend. I've listened to the recording of Cecily's interview and even she thought he was being too friendly. She said he was "all over" Aiden. Of course he was! He'd slept with you – quite a few times! And when he said goodbye, he folded his hands around yours. I remember that detail. It struck me as very strange.'

'He was a creep.'

'Cecily thought he was playing with you in some way. That he was sneering at you. And then there was that business with *The Marriage of Figaro*. He said it was his favourite opera, that it had a great story and that he was looking forward to seeing it at Snape Maltings. Except it was all lies. It wasn't actually on. What was that all about?'

'I've got no idea.'

'That doesn't matter, Aiden, because I think I have. What is the story of *The Marriage of Figaro*? It's about a pervy nobleman, the Count Almaviva. He's in love with Susanna, his wife's maid, but she's about to marry Figaro. So on the actual night of the wedding, the Count tries to use his "droit de seigneur", which gives him the right to take Susanna to bed with him.

'I learned a bit about Frank Parris when I was in London. He enjoyed sex games that included submission and humiliation. In a way, he saw himself as a bit of a Count Almaviva. Let's imagine that he came to Branlow Hall and bumped into a rent boy he knew from years back. He'd often paid Leo for sex. But now Leo's come up in the world. He's about to get married into a nice family with a nice job waiting for him on a plate. What will Lawrence and Pauline say if they discover the truth about their new son-in-law? Frank has got Leo exactly where he wants him and a delicious idea comes into his mind. He will exercise his droit de seigneur. He will fuck the groom on his wedding night.

'I think that when he put his hands round Aiden's, he was passing him a duplicate of his room key. By then the two of them had come to an agreement. It probably gave him a real kick giving Aiden his room key right in front of the woman he was about to marry.'

'You're making this all up,' Aiden said. 'This is all lies.'

'Well, let's see what happens next. Let's imagine that you've decided that you're not going to play along with what Frank has demanded. Instead, you're going to get rid of this sick pervert once and for all. And you've got the perfect fall guy to take the blame.

'You go to the party which Lawrence and Pauline have thrown for the staff. Cecily was taking sleeping pills – diazepam – and it would have been easy for you to steal a few of them and spike Stefan's drink. When he went to bed that night, he was drugged, not drunk. The following morning he was bleary-eyed. He would have slept through anything.

'Cecily had also taken a pill and she was asleep when you crept out for your midnight assignation. It was important to you that Stefan should be seen entering room twelve, but you had it all arranged. You collected the toolbox from the maintenance shed and put on a beanie just like his. You went in through the front door and took the lift up to the second floor. Derek Endicott was sitting in the reception area down below. How were you going to get him upstairs to see you?

'The answer was Bear, the dog. My guess is that you used the Irish brooch that sits on the table beside the basket.' I had it in my handbag and took it out, then unclasped the needle, which was about two inches long. I placed it on the table in front of Locke. 'When this is all over, maybe you should have it analysed, Detective Chief Superintendent. There should still be traces of Bear's blood. I think Aiden jabbed it into him and that's why he barked.'

I turned back to Aiden.

'So, Derek comes up to see what's wrong. He's kneeling to examine the dog and you flit past, going along the corridor towards room twelve. It's dark up there. He barely has time to see anything: just the beanie and the workbox. Of course, he assumes it's Stefan. Even so, he goes across to the corridor to see but by the time he gets there – only a few seconds – the man has disappeared. What does that tell us? Derek doesn't hear anybody knock. He doesn't hear voices. No explanations or greetings or anything like that. Frank might have propped the door open using a waste-paper basket or something, but I think that's unlikely. Part of the fun was Leo letting himself in and of course he has a key.

'You're in room twelve. Frank is waiting for you. You wait until Derek has gone back downstairs. And then you take out the hammer and beat Frank to death so violently that come the next day, he will be unrecognisable. There was a lot of anger in this murder. I knew that from the start. And you had every reason to be angry.

'But the night wasn't over yet. You took money from Frank Parris's wallet and you also needed some of his blood to sprinkle onto the bedclothes and the shower in Stefan's room. I think that's why you stole Lawrence's fountain pen, which had never been used and which wouldn't contaminate the blood sample. You used the reservoir to suck some of Frank's blood into the pen and then you took it, along with the money, to the stable block. There was a duplicate key in Lisa's office and it would have been simple for you to get hold of it too. Stefan wouldn't wake up. He was still drugged, sound asleep. He didn't hear the door open. He didn't see you hide the money and spray a few drops of Frank's blood. After that, you got rid of the pen and went back to bed.

'Let's not forget the "Do Not Disturb" sign. You had killed Frank because he threatened your marriage to Cecily. It was essential to you that the marriage went ahead. That's why you put the sign on the door after the murder. Presumably, you got Stefan's fingerprints onto it while he was asleep. And then sometime after the service and before the big party, you must have taken it down again. Why did you do that, Aiden?'

'I'm not answering any of your questions.'

'Well maybe it was because you didn't want to go on the honeymoon. After all, you didn't love Cecily. I don't think you even liked her. My guess is that you married her for the money and the security and the life of a country squire. Maybe it even gave you a kick, ruining her big day.

'And you almost got away with it. Except that a few weeks after the murder a writer turned up at the hotel looking for a story and it was your bad luck that he found you.

'Alan Conway recognised you too, didn't he? That's why you were reluctant to talk to him. I've listened to the tape he made when he was talking to Pauline and what's the first thing he says when he sees you? *"We've already met."* At that moment, everything makes sense for Alan. He knows who the killer is and in his own way he's taunting you just like Frank did a few weeks before. Of course, you have to try to cover yourself. *"Yes. I was in reception when you arrived,"* you explain, for the benefit of Pauline. But then what does he say a few moments later? *"Please, call me Alan."* And you reply: *"I'm not playing this game."* Because that's what it is, isn't it? An unpleasant game. You both knew the truth. You'd met over dinner in London ... and Frank Parris was at the table too!

'Nothing happens now for eight years. Alan has disappeared and you probably heave a sigh of relief when you hear he's dead. Maybe you've glanced at what he's written, but on the face of it *Atticus Pünd Takes the Case* has got nothing to do with Branlow Hall. You think you've got away with it.'

I took another sip of water. Everyone in the room was silent, watching me, waiting for me to continue. Only one of them – Locke – was sitting there with his eyes fixed on Aiden, realising what he had done and perhaps even what it might mean for his future career.

I put down the water. Out of the corner of my eye, I saw Andreas give me a smile of encouragement. I went on.

'Then Cecily reads the book.

'Let me go back to what I know of her character. Lawrence told me that she was too good-natured, too trusting, the sort who believes the best in everyone. He was talking about her relationship with Stefan but he could just as well have been referring to her relationship with you. Melissa Conway even compared her to Dora in *David Copperfield*. I think Cecily went into her marriage with the same innocence. She had no idea what she was getting into.

'But she found out soon enough. I don't know what it must have been like living with you, Aiden, but she must have known you weren't quite the Prince Charming of her dreams. Even in the early days when you were engaged, you obviously weren't up to much in the bed department because she was having to satisfy her needs with Stefan. And later on? Women are intuitive. We sort of get the idea when we're married to a homicidal maniac.

'But even if she suspected that you killed Frank Parris she still had no evidence – mainly because you had no reason to. You'd never even met him. So what happens when she opens the book and she sees the dedication – "*For Frank and Leo*"? If Aiden is Leo than suddenly everything that happened during Frank's visit – his strange behaviour, his lies – makes some sort of sense. And let's not forget that's exactly what you were to her. The beloved Leo to her Sagittarius.'

'Aren't you forgetting something?' Aiden looked at me defiantly. 'I was the one who gave her the book. I read it before she did. I told you that.'

'That's what you said to me, Aiden. That's what you wanted me to think because it made you look innocent. The book identified the true killer of Frank Parris, so whoever the killer was, he'd be the last person to let Cecily see the book.

'But the truth is, by the time I arrived at the hotel, you hadn't even read it; at least not all of it. Of course, you wanted to. You had to know what was in it – what Cecily had seen. But you had difficulty getting hold of a copy because, as it happened, there had been a major glitch at the distribution centre in Didcot. I actually met the publisher and he told me that nobody had been able to get hold of *Atticus Pünd Takes the Case* for about two months. The copy that you showed me was brand new and my guess was that it had only arrived a day or so before I did and you'd only just started it. When I asked you if you'd enjoyed it, you described it as twisty and said the ending had a sucker punch. But those weren't your words.' I picked up the paperback and handed it to Lawrence. 'If you look at the reviews that are printed at the beginning, you'll see that the *Observer* described it as twisty and the author Peter James said it had a sucker punch. I used to meet a lot of people in publishing who did the same. They pretended they'd read the book when in fact all they'd done was glance at the crits.' I glared at Aiden. 'You'd got as far as page 30. That's where Algernon turns up. You didn't have a clue what happened next.'

'Where is Cecily?' Locke hadn't spoken until now.

Finally, he got to his feet, choosing this moment to take charge.

Aiden didn't reply, so I did. 'I think he killed her.' I glanced at Lawrence and Pauline. 'I'm sorry. You have to ask yourself why Cecily made the call from her office in the hotel rather than from home – but of course she didn't want to be anywhere near Aiden. Unfortunately, Eloise overheard her and I suppose she told him.' I glanced at her. 'Did you?'

Eloise was staring at Aiden as if seeing him for the first time. 'Yes. I did.' I noticed she was no longer holding his hand.

'He knew that Cecily had worked out at least some of the truth and that he was no longer safe. So when she went for a walk, he went after her. He knew what route she was taking and it would have been easy enough to wait for her on the other side of the woods at Martlesham. I don't know how he killed her and I don't know how he had time to get rid of the body, but I think that to start with he put her in the trunk of his car. That's why he went to the charity shop in Framlingham with a completely random collection of her clothes, including a dress she'd just bought and which she'd never worn. He just needed to be sure that there would be a reason for her DNA to be in the back of the car if the police ever looked.'

Locke took a step towards Aiden. 'I think you had better come with me,' he said.

Aiden looked around him and at that moment there was something about him that reminded me of a trapped lion. Andreas stood up and put an arm around my shoulders. I was glad to have him near.

'Mr MacNeil . . . ' Locke continued. He reached out as if to take hold of him.

And that was when it happened. Aiden's face didn't change but something that I can only describe as nightmarish glimmered in his eyes and I knew that Frank Parris must have seen exactly the same thing in his last moments in the room at the hotel and that Cecily Treherne, too, would have recognised it in the wood near Martlesham: the look of someone about to kill you.

Aiden lashed out with his fist and at first I thought he had punched the detective under the chin. Locke was much bigger than him and powerfully built, but he seemed completely stunned by the blow, as if he didn't know how to react. For a moment everything was still, but then, to my horror, I saw blood cascading down the side of his neck, soaking into his shirt, and realised that as he stood up, Aiden must have grabbed hold of the antique brooch. He had driven the point deep into the detective's throat.

Locke let out something between a sob and a cry of pain. He fell to his knees, one hand gripping the wound. More blood gushed between his fingers. Nobody moved. Aiden stood there, blank-faced, still holding the brooch with the pin jutting out. I was terrified that Andreas would try something. But even he was stunned. The dog had got to its feet and was barking furiously. Locke was still on his knees, groaning. I saw Pauline turning away in shock. Aiden ran towards me and I flinched, expecting the worst. But then he had passed me and I heard a great crash of breaking glass and splintering wood and realised that he had kicked in the French window at the back of the lounge. I caught just one last glimpse of him disappearing into the garden.

Eloise had run over to Locke and was kneeling down, cradling him. Lawrence was caring for Pauline. Lisa had taken out her phone and was dialling for an ambulance.

Andreas took me in his arms. 'Are you all right?' he asked.

I was stunned. I was swaying on my feet. I could hear Lisa being connected to the emergency services. 'Just get me out of here,' I whispered.

We left the room together. Neither of us looked back.

Last Words

We weren't allowed to go back to Crete for a few days. Although I'd had nothing to do with the death of Frank Parris or the disappearance of Cecily Treherne, I still had to give a full statement, more or less repeating what I had said in the lounge of Branlow Hall. I got the feeling that I was being held personally responsible for what had happened to Detective Chief Superintendent Locke. He was lucky to be alive. The tip of the needle had punctured his carotid artery, which explained the massive blood flow, and but for the fast arrival of the paramedics he wouldn't have made it. The policemen who questioned me were unfriendly to say the least.

I couldn't possibly stay at Branlow Hall. The truth was, I didn't want to see any of them again: not the

Trehernes, not Eloise, not Derek, not even Bear the dog. Nor would I have felt comfortable moving in with Katie. In the end, Andreas and I took a room at the Crown Hotel in Framlingham, which was where I had stayed at the time of Alan's funeral. I liked it there. It was a comfortable distance from Woodbridge.

We knew very little of what was going on. We deliberately kept away from the newspapers and the police didn't tell us anything. But on the third day of our enforced stay, I received an envelope at the breakfast table. I knew where it had come from even before I opened it. The silhouette of an owl was printed on the envelope.

There were two letters inside. The first was from Lawrence Treherne. I was glad, finally, to see a cheque for the money he owed me.

Dear Susan,

I feel uncomfortable writing this letter to you, but first of all I am enclosing a cheque as agreed and apologise for the long delay. I hope you will not mind me saying that, in a way, you have done more damage to our lives than even Alan Conway managed, although at the same time I suppose I must thank you. We asked you to do a job and you did it very effectively, although none of us could possi-

bly have known how devastating the consequences would be.

I want to bring you up to speed on other developments which I am sure will be of interest to you.

The first is that Aiden MacNeil is dead. After that dreadful business at the hotel, he drove himself to Manningtree station, where he threw himself under a train. I'm surprised the police weren't able to stop him, but I'm afraid DS Locke had come to the hotel on his own – a grave error – and everything happened too quickly after that. Pauline and I both feel the same about his death. We bitterly regret that our poor, dear daughter ever met him and we are glad that we will never see him again. She was too kind-hearted and trusting. You were absolutely right.

Before he killed himself, Aiden wrote a letter addressed to me and the police have allowed me to retain a copy. I, in turn, have made a copy for you and I am enclosing it as it shows you what sort of man he was and what you were up against. It also answers a few more questions which I think will interest you, even though some of what he has to say is manifestly untrue. The cold-blooded manner in which he planned Cecily's death is almost be-

*yond belief. I should warn you that it is very hard
to read.*

    *There is one last thing that I wanted you to
know. Pauline and I feel very bad about the way
that we treated Stefan Codrescu, even though, of
course, we weren't in possession of the facts. We
understand that the police have already begun proceedings to allow him to be released from jail and
to rebuild his life and he should be free in a matter
of weeks. I have written to him to offer all the support that he might need. He is welcome to return
to Branlow Hall and it goes without saying Pauline and I recognise him as the true father of our
only granddaughter and will do our best to make
amends for what has passed.*

    *I hope that you and Andreas will be able to re-
turn to Crete soon, and once again, thank you for
what you have done.*

    Sincerely,

    Lawrence Treherne

That was the first letter. The second was written on
three pages torn out of a cheap exercise book that Aiden
must have bought on the way to Manningtree. His
handwriting was surprisingly childish with big loops

and i's topped with circles rather than dots. I didn't read it until much later that day, when Andreas and I were together in our room, armed with large whiskies. We needed them.

Dear Lawrence,

It feels strange to be writing to you, knowing that in about twenty minutes I'm going to be dead. I bet you won't be sorry to hear that! But prison isn't really an option for someone like me. I wouldn't last five minutes surrounded by all those pervs so I'm waiting for the next London train. One that doesn't stop.

Why am I writing this? I don't know, really. I never liked you or Pauline very much, to be honest. The two of you always patronised me as if I had to be grateful to you all the time when I was actually working my guts out at the hotel. But I feel close to you right now because I killed your daughter. I'm sure you'd agree something like that does bring people together.

This isn't a confession. You've heard it all already. But there are one or two things I want you to know. Get it off my chest, if you like. All the time I've been with you at the hotel and the cottage and *on holidays in France, I've always had to pretend. But now I want you to understand the real me.*

I always knew I was different. I'm not going to tell you about my life. I haven't got time and why would you care? But you have no idea what it was like growing up in Haghill, which is one of the shittiest parts of Glasgow, living on a shitty estate, going to a shitty school, knowing that I was special but that I was never going to have a proper life.

I wanted to be rich. I wanted to be someone. You look at footballers and celebrities on TV and you think they've been given so much. They've only got one small talent and the whole world falls at their feet. Well, I had a talent. I could make people like me. I had good looks. I was charming. But all of that was useless in a place like Haghill, so as soon as I could, when I was seventeen, I left home and went to London. I thought that was where I'd make it big.

Of course it didn't happen that way. In London, everything is against you. Three quid an hour washing cars. Five quid an hour waiting tables. Sharing a room with someone who'll steal your socks before they have time to get dry, paying through the nose for the privilege. And all around you more money than you can possibly imagine. Shops dripping with nice things. Smart restaurants and penthouses. I wanted it so badly and there was only one way I was going to get it.

I became Leo.

You have no idea what it's like selling yourself. Having rich fat old men pawing at you and doing what they want to you just because they can afford it. In case you're wondering, Lawrence, I was never a homosexual and I want you to know that. I did what I had to because there was no other way and I hated it. It made me sick.

But I made money. I'd managed to get a job with an estate agent. You see? It was that charm again. But it was Leo who made the real money. Three hundred quid a night. Five hundred quid a night. Sometimes a thousand quid a night. They were all cowards. A lot of my clients were married. Bloody hypocrites. I smiled at them and did what they asked me, even though I wanted to smash their faces in. But I knew that one day I'd escape. That was the thought that kept me going. I'd make enough money to leave Leo behind and have the life that I wanted for myself.

And then I met Cecily, showing her a flat.

I think I knew almost at once that she was the

one. *She was so thick and so bloody susceptible. The moment I told her it was my birthday, she was all over me. Oh – you're a Leo, I'm a Sagittarius. We're made for each other. Oh, oh, oh. We went out for a drink that night and she told me all about you and the hotel and her horrible sister who she hated and all the rest of it and I knew right then that I could get everything I wanted out of her. Because I was her little Leo.*

So we started seeing each other and I came to Suffolk and I met you and Pauline and everyone else and of course you all liked me because that was my one talent, and then Cecily and I got engaged. I chose a day when her Universal Day number was the same as her Life Path number because I knew that would be lucky for her and she said yes. Of course she did.

That was it. No more fucking Haghill and no more being fucked in London. I thought I'd got it all. I'd work in the hotel and I'd look after the guests because that was what I was good at. And if it's any consolation, I always knew that I'd have to kill Cecily eventually. And probably Lisa too. I wanted it all, you see. The hotel, the land, the money. It was the future I'd always dreamed of for myself and there was never going to be room for her.

When Frank Parris turned up two days before the wedding, I couldn't believe it! It's just like Susan said. The miserable bastard recognised me. And just for the sheer fun of it, he blackmailed me and forced me to come to his room on my wedding night so that he could do what he wanted with me. It makes me sick to the stomach even to think of it. I knew I was going to kill him. I couldn't stop myself. I went to his room like he asked, but instead of giving him what he wanted, I smashed his head in and I enjoyed every minute of it.

I'm running out of time. Let me tell you how it ended.

I knew Alan Conway the same way I knew Frank Parris. Another middle-aged pervert who preyed off boys like me. I'd have liked to have killed him too but he knew who I was and there was nothing I could do. I was terrified he was going to give me away but of course he couldn't do that without landing himself in it. Even so, I was relieved when he left the hotel and even more relieved a few years later when I heard he was dead.

I didn't know he'd written that fucking book. I didn't know Cecily had read it and I still don't know how she got her hands on it. Eight years later! Stefan in jail. And everything between Cecily and me as sweet as apple pie. Well, not everything. Of course I knew that Roxana wasn't mine. I think it's fair to say that I didn't find your daughter attractive, Lawrence. No offence. I knew she was seeing Stefan. She couldn't keep that secret from me. That was why I set him up and I can't tell you how much it amused me to see him jailed for life.

Cecily did suspect that I'd killed Frank Parris, certainly in the days after it happened and before Stefan made his confession. I'd always tried to keep up the pretence when I was with her but she'd seen through me a couple of times. She was stupid but not completely stupid and she'd realised I wasn't quite the Mr Perfect she'd dreamed about. Still, I managed to persuade her that Frank and I had never met and why would I have wished a complete stranger any harm? That was my defence and she believed it.

But then she read that book and everything changed. Frank and Leo. I was always waiting for something to go wrong and I realised I was in trouble even before Eloise told me about the telephone call she'd overheard. That was on a Tuesday and I knew at once that it was all over and that Cecily had to go.

I went out and dug her grave that night. Be-

fore I killed her. The thing was, you see, I knew I wouldn't have much time on the Wednesday. Killing her was one thing but burying her was quite another and I'd have to account for every minute of that day. So on Tuesday evening I drove into Rendlesham Forest and dug a hole. If you want to find her, it's on the other side of Bromeswell. Follow the track marked Number 12 and it's behind the seventh tree on the left. I carved an arrow into the bark and it'll point you the right way. Sagittarius. She'd have liked that.

I tried to pretend everything was normal on the Wednesday but I wonder if she knew? I've been faking it all my life. I'm good at it. But I could tell she wasn't herself. She took Bear for a walk around three o'clock and I followed her. I saw her park at Woodbridge station and I knew exactly where she was going so I drove round to Martlesham, parked the car and then came into the wood from the other side. There was no one around. There hardly ever is.

She knew exactly what I was going to do when she saw me and she didn't even try to put up a fight. 'I always knew.' That's all she said and when I put a stocking round her neck (it was one of her stockings) she just looked at me sadly and let me do it.

I'd brought some of her clothes and also a clean shirt for me. I dumped her in the back of the car and then drove hell for leather over to Rendlesham Forest to bury her. That was the riskiest part because I had to look out for dog walkers, but she was only above ground for about thirty seconds. It took me about twenty minutes to fill in the grave, whereas digging it had taken me bloody ages. Then I put on a clean shirt and drove over to Framlingham. I arrived at the charity shop a bit after four o'clock and it was like nothing had happened. I gave the woman there her clothes as well as some of my stuff and I included the shirt I'd been wearing when I'd been digging so that got rid of that.

And that was the end of it.

I really thought I'd got away with it and you know what makes me sad? It was the perfect murder. I didn't actually make any mistakes. Two perfect murders. I had you all fooled from day one and I only got caught because of things I couldn't control. It's Frank's fault that this has all happened. And Cecily's. And yours for bringing in that bloody woman from Crete.

Anyway, that's it. I've got to go. I've got a train to catch.

Aiden

Zeus's Cave

The night we finally arrived back at the Polydorus, Andreas and I threw a party for all our friends, partly to celebrate our return, partly to put the whole thing behind us. Panos, assisted by his eighty-six-year-old mother, cooked what looked like an entire sheep. We drank a crate of Argyros wine from the island of Santorini. Vangelis played his guitar and his bouzouki and we danced under an ink-black sky with the slenderest of crescent moons. A couple of the guests came down to complain but decided instead to join in. It was a wonderful night.

I slowly got back into the routine of life in Agios Nikolaos and two things happened that helped me on my way.

First of all, my sister Katie came out for a week, the

first time she had visited the hotel. She needed a break. She had begun the grisly process of divorce proceedings while Gordon had just moved in with his young love in some atrocious bedsit in London. We didn't talk too much about him. We didn't talk about Branlow Hall either. We walked together and visited some of the main tourist sites and enjoyed each other's company. The fact that she fell hopelessly in love with Crete only reminded me of what I'd been thinking of giving up.

Also – and this came right out of the blue – I was offered the job of associate editor at Penguin Random House. This was nothing to do with Michael Bealey, who had been less than helpful. It turned out that Craig Andrews had mentioned he'd met me to someone at the launch of *Time to Die*, the fourth book in his Christopher Shaw series. I must have told him I was looking for work because the next thing I knew, an email came from Penguin Random House and I was hired, admittedly on a freelance basis but with a four-hundred-page manuscript as my first assignment.

At the same time, Lawrence's cheque had taken care of most of our debts and to our surprise the second half of the season suddenly took off and we were completely full. With my new salary, we were able to bring in extra help, so although in the morning I was still rushing around looking after our guests and our staff (and trying to work out which of them caused me the more trouble), by lunchtime I was free to sit on the terrace doing the work I'd done all my life, completely at ease.

Even so, I couldn't stop thinking about everything that had happened – both at the time of Frank Parris's murder and immediately afterwards when Alan Conway had written his book. When I left London, I had brought with me all the notes that I had made during the investigation as well as the old manuscripts from my days at Cloverleaf. I'd also gone out and bought a complete set of the Atticus Pünd novels, even though it irked me having to fork out the money. As the summer wore on, I found myself poring over them, certain that there was something missing. I knew Alan too well. He was dangling something in front of my eyes but I just couldn't see it.

I understood why he had been unable to reveal the identity of the killer, why he had deliberately concealed it. Aiden had been right about that. Alan was riding the first wave of what would become international success with two bestsellers under his belt and a third on his way. His name was becoming known.

He had not yet come out as a gay man. Of course, it wouldn't matter. When he did finally announce that he had divorced Melissa and moved in with James, nobody cared. It's one of the better ways that the world has changed: nobody is afraid to express their sexuality, unless, perhaps, they're a hate preacher or a major Hollywood actor. At the same time, though, Alan must have been worried about the stories that 'Leo' might tell. Being gay is one thing but the sort of stuff he'd been getting up to with rent boys wouldn't have gone down so well. He was insecure. He preferred to keep these things quiet.

Exposing Aiden to the police would have put his own career in danger. At least, that was how he saw it. And, from a PR point of view, I have to admit that it might have been tricky. After all, Atticus Pünd is so wholesome. There's almost no sex in any of the books. Nobody even swears.

But surely he would have done something more than that dedication. Alan being the sort of man he was wouldn't have been able to sit on the secret. He would have to hint at it with his special brand of clues, his twists and turns, his little jokes. I reread *Atticus Pünd Takes the Case* half a dozen times and there were several passages I could have quoted almost off by heart. I made pencil markings on the pages. I sat there scowling in the sun.

Until finally I saw it.

With all the knowledge I had accumulated at Branlow Hall, I saw what he had done. It was the Red Lion pub in Tawleigh-on-the-Water that started me; such an ordinary name and yet chosen, I was sure, deliberately.

Everything hinged on Leo. And so Alan had mentioned him over and over again in the text, banging a subconscious drum that must have resounded in Cecily Treherne's mind.

But not quite Leo.

Instead, he put about a dozen lions into the book. They're everywhere.

It's not just the pub in Tawleigh-on-the-Water. The church is also dedicated to St Daniel who famously went into the lions' den. Atticus Pünd visits the church and sees the saint's ordeal depicted in the stained-glass windows.

Clarence Keep, the house where Melissa James lived, is named after *Clarence, the Cross-Eyed Lion,* a comedy film from the sixties, and William Railton who had supposedly owned it at one time was the architect who designed the four monumental lions in London's Trafalgar Square. Melissa's dog is a chow, a breed from China also known as 'puffy lion dog' and it's even called Kimba, a white lion in a television series from Japan. In the hallway, Madeline Cain notices a poster from *The Wizard of Oz* signed by the actor Bert Lahr. She remarks that Melissa never acted in that film. Lahr, of course, played the Cowardly Lion.

As the weeks passed, I became quite obsessive and I noticed Andreas becoming agitated as I found myself going back to the pages whenever I had the opportunity. Still they kept coming. Samantha has just started reading C. S. Lewis to her two children in Church Lodge so the book must be the first one: *The Lion, the Witch and the Wardrobe.* Melissa was meant to be starring in a film in which she would play Eleanor of Aquitaine. She would therefore be the mother of Richard the Lionheart. The silver cigarette box in Melissa's lounge is engraved with the MGM logo – a roaring lion. And on page 285 Detective Chief Inspector Hare makes a completely random remark about the first labour of Hercules, which he believes relates to the cleaning of the Augean stables. It isn't. It's the slaying of the Nemean lion.

Now I remembered some of the editorial disagreements that I'd had with Alan during the editing of the book. Of course he'd wanted Algernon's car to be a Peugeot. The silver badge that ends up smeared with the opera singer's blood is in the shape of a prancing lion. And a quick search of Wikipedia showed me that the LMR 57 steam engine that carried Pünd out of Bideford station, even though it was about a hundred years out of date, was also known as 'Lion'.

By the end of the month I was actually stealing out

of bed at night to continue my lion hunt. I hadn't even started the edit of my four-hundred-page manuscript and I noticed Andreas frequently looking askance at me.

And yet I still worried that I'd missed something in *Atticus Pünd Takes the Case.* I was sure that Cecily had seen something that I hadn't. I had the book. I had all my notes. There had to be something else. What was it?

I can remember exactly the epiphany, the moment when the novel revealed the last secret buried in its unpleasant heart. The awful truth is that it had been in front of my eyes all the time although I'm not quite sure why I saw it at that moment, sitting in my little office above the bar with the sun streaming in. I wish I could say that an owl flew past – we actually have quite a lot of them in Crete – but it didn't. For no reason at all, I was thinking how Cecily Treherne had liked anagrams. She had taken the name of the hotel and re-arranged the letters to make 'barn owl'. And that was when it hit me.

The first murder is committed by Leonard Collins. His name, obviously, conceals another lion. He is Leo.

But Madeline Cain is also a murderer and she kills Francis Pendleton – FP – the fictional equivalent of Frank Parris.

Madeline Cain is an anagram of Aiden MacNeil.

Andreas was in the room with me when I saw it. I remember howling with excitement, throwing paper into the air, rushing into his arms, almost crying with the stupid simplicity of it. He looked past me at the newspaper cuttings, the notepads, the letters – and the nine volumes that made up the adventures of Atticus Pünd.

He took my hands in his. 'Susan,' he said, 'will you be angry with me if I make a suggestion?'

'Of course I won't be angry with you.'

'We have each other. We have the hotel. You have your editing. Everything is going well for us.'

'So . . . ?'

'So maybe it's time to finish with all this.' He gestured at the scattered documents. 'You've found enough lions. And honestly, I think you've allowed Alan Conway to do enough damage to your life.'

I nodded slowly. 'You're right.'

'Here is what I would like to suggest. Why don't you take all this . . . all these papers and the books. Especially the books. Let's put them in the car and drive up to the Lasithi Plateau. It's beautiful at this time of the year with the olive trees and the windmills. I want to take you to the Psychro Cave, which is also known as the Cave of Zeus because they say that is where he was born. And I want you to put everything in a pile at the entrance and set fire to it as an offering to the gods, to thank them for bringing you back to me and to release you from all the dark shadows, the memories of what you've left behind. And after that I'll take you to a little hotel I know near Kaminaki and we'll have dinner together and we'll sit on the terrace drinking raki, surrounded by the mountains and looking at the stars, because, believe me, there is nowhere the stars look more magnificent.'

'Is Leo in the ascendant?'

'I hope not.'

'Then let's go.'

And that's exactly what we did.

About the Author

ANTHONY HOROWITZ is the author of *New York Times* bestsellers *Magpie Murders* and *The Sentence Is Death*, as well as the *New York Times* bestselling Alex Rider series for young adults. As a television screenwriter he created *Midsomer Murders* and the BAFTA-winning *Foyle's War* on PBS. He lives in London.